9/23/2008
For Leslie & Mark,
Your children & theirs—
Dave Spein

Deadly Freedom

A Novel

By David Spicer

CAMBRIDGE HOUSE PRESS
NEW YORK § TORONTO

Published by Cambridge House Press
New York, NY 10001
www.CamHousePress.com

Cover design by Nicola Lengua.
Composition/typography by Michael Axon and Rachel Trusheim.

Library of Congress Cataloging-in-Publication Data

Spicer, David, 1947-
  Deadly freedom : a novel / by David Spicer.
    p. cm.
  ISBN 978-0-9787213-6-7 (alk. paper)
  1. Renewable energy sources--Fiction. 2. Conspiracies--Fiction. I. Title.

PS3619.P536D43 2008
813'.6--dc22

2008003215

The events and characters in this book are fictitious. Certain real locations and public figures are mentioned, but all other characters and events described in the book are totally imaginary.

10 9 8 7 6 5 4 3 2 1

Printed in the United States of America.

For Mary, our children and theirs—and yours too.

Acknowledgments

To an engineer, perhaps the only thing more frustrating than an unsolvable problem is a solvable problem that's going unsolved. It was this frustration that led me to research what I consider to be the issue of our time—our continued dependence on oil for its energy content and the geopolitical problems that follow in its wake. Finding Professor Lee Stefanakos and his team of CERC researchers at the University of South Florida opened my eyes to what was possible. They became a real inspiration—and still are.

For a first-time novelist, finding a publisher can become more of a challenge than writing the book. I am indebted to Drew Nederpelt for his insights, guidance, and knowledge.

Rachel Trusheim is the Executive Editor at Sterling & Ross and now I know why. Rachel really understands the nuts and bolts of writing and, perhaps most importantly, how to convey that knowledge to a new writer. Thank you, Rachel.

Thanks to the talented graphic artist, Nicola Lengua, for all his hard work on the cover. Special thanks Anna Lacson, Michael Axon, Tim Woods, and everyone at Cambridge House Press.

"Make sure you're right, then go ahead."

– Davy Crockett

"If you hit something hard enough you can make a dent."

– Anonymous AT&T Bell Labs Director

For more information on DEADLY FREEDOM, the motivating factors and underlying technology, please visit: www.deadlyfreedom.com

Prologue

It finally happened:

Oil prices have gone over one hundred dollars per barrel causing gasoline prices to reach almost nine dollars per gallon on the west coast, and these prices are propagating east quickly. Even at those prices, gasoline is being rationed and long lines are forming at the pumps. The impact to our manufacturing capability is just now becoming apparent—and it's not good. Homeowners in the Midwest and Northeast who can't afford winter heating bills that have now tripled are migrating to the Sunbelt.

Atmospheric carbon dioxide is now approaching eight hundred parts per million and no one is arguing about whether this is the cause of global warming. Ironically, the homeowners migrating to the Sunbelt are now being confronted with more frequent and severe hurricanes in addition to the shrinking southeastern shoreline.

With the exception of Great Britain, which is teetering on the brink, Western Europe and the U.K. have succumbed to Islamic extremism allowing Muslims to gain control of these countries. It was carried like a plague on the silent wings of liberalism that swept Western Europe into believing they needed more leisure time, inexpensive immigrants to take care of their children, and better yet, fewer children to take care of. It was just a matter of demographics, just numbers; birth rates of the native citizens of these countries had fallen to 1.2 live births per female while Muslims had a birth rate of greater than 4.2. After just two generations, the native populations would decrease by a factor of four, while the Muslim population would *increase* by a factor of four. With that kind of population swing it didn't take long for Islam to gain legitimate control of host country governments. The most immediate visible result was a striking increase in the sale of burqas.

The endgame of terrorism had become obvious: it wasn't a threat to your life; it was a threat to your way of life.

With a birth rate of 2.1, the United States was the last remaining Western power with enough time to withstand the onslaught—if only it had the will.

But these were just some of the symptoms; the problem had been recognized many years before...

"This is an urgent warning to each and every one of you that there is a careful, deliberately planned campaign to swindle you out of your most important and valuable public utilities—your Electric Railway System...

...You will realize too late that the electric railway is unquestionably more comfortable, more reliable, safer and cheaper to use than the bus system. But what can you do about it once you have permitted the tracks to be torn up? Who do you think you can find to finance another deluxe transit system for your city...?"

– E. Jay Quinby, 1946 letter to the mayor of Los Angeles and mayors of other large cities on the buyout of the Pacific Electric Trolley Line by a subsidiary of General Motors and Standard Oil of California

Chapter 1.
Tampa, Florida

Rafi Haddad was going nowhere while listening to the Bose stereo he had retrofitted into his old Nissan Sentra. Tapping his left foot to Fleetwood Mac and with his right foot on the brake, he watched his gas gauge hover near empty. When the music stopped, the news on the radio wasn't good either. The never-ending Iraq War continued to escalate, pollution had reached the point where even the most skeptical global warming climatologists were worried, and OPEC had the country by the balls for the $8.79-per-gallon gasoline that he was waiting not-so-patiently for in a line wrapping two city blocks. Fortunately, he had allowed plenty of time to get to the professor's house for Thanksgiving dinner, and he'd already stopped to pick up the beer and wine that would be his contribution.

These Americans are amazing. They have so much technology and wealth to be thankful for yet continue to burn fossil fuel like there's no tomorrow. As frustrated as he was waiting in line, he couldn't help but smile to himself at the thought, glad no one in the cars around him knew what he was smiling about.

* * *

America was truly the "Land of Opportunity" for this graduate student from India—it also helped to be in the right place at the right time. At twenty-eight years of age and in the second year of an obscure solar energy PhD program, Rafi Haddad was picked up by Professor Will Elliot as the lead engineer on a newly formed University of South Florida (USF) research team.

America was also a "Land of National Holidays" with thirteen of them as compared to five in Rafi's native India. Such holidays meant intellectual downtime for someone without family in the country. Rafi had come to dislike the lapses in USF college activities that had become his life since arriving in the U.S. almost two years earlier. Fortunately his relationship with Elliot had led to his "adoption" by the professor and his wife, Ginny, who saw to it that he had a place to go on those long four-day weekends.

* * *

"Billy and Jeff, I could use some help down here," Ginny Elliot yelled up the stairway. Aged fifteen and thirteen, her two sons were like most teenagers, into their video games and downloading the latest version of "Doom" or swapping MP3s with their buddies. The last thing on their minds was helping Mom, but they knew they'd better respond before their dad got after them. *The "Prof" can manipulate them with Christmas just a month away,* she thought to herself. She knew Will would give his sons about fifteen minutes to get downstairs before interceding.

The Elliots lived the modest lifestyle afforded by a full professor of Electrical Engineering at the University of South Florida and a wife who had worked as a dental hygienist for the last twenty years. They still had a mortgage on their home, but their equity had increased nicely given escalating home values in the Tampa area. Will's dad was right, a home was one of the best investments a family could have. There was still the concern of financing their sons' educations and Billy was only three years away from making the leap to college. Like most families on modest incomes, the Elliots had talked of establishing college saving funds but had never made a serious effort to do so. They had savings accounts and some stocks and bonds that Will had inherited. But they were a long way from being able to afford two college educations. Hopefully both boys would go to USF and qualify for some level of scholarship money. The fallback was a second mortgage on their home, student loans, or some combination.

On the plus-side, six months ago, Will Elliot's work on solar energy had attracted attention from NASA who had asked him to submit a proposal for a near-earth orbit project. If his project was selected from the fifty competing proposals, he would be a mission specialist on an upcoming shuttle flight. Elliot proposed a project to measure the sun's intensity at varying altitudes as the basis for a pilot program to convert solar energy into electricity high above the earth's interfering atmosphere, beaming it to earth via microwaves. Three months later they informed him that he had been selected. During the last three months he had been in training in Houston and across the peninsula at Cape Canaveral. This project meant extra publicity, a financial kick-start for his research, and much-needed extra income for the family. He enjoyed the challenges and NASA camaraderie immensely. Ginny wasn't too enthused about sending her husband up in the Space Shuttle, although their sons beamed with the attention they were receiving at school.

"Hey, Dad, what time is Rafi coming?" Billy asked as he dutifully set the table, wanting to make sure his father saw him in order to register proper Christmas credit.

"He said he'd be here about five-thirty. We aren't eating until six-thirty and he wanted to get here to see the beginning of some of the football games. I'm just warming up the TV. The pre-game show for the Florida vs. Florida State game is just starting."

Ginny cringed, knowing they would be glued to the TV for hours.

"Good deal," Billy replied, "I hope he brings his iPod so we can swap some music. He has a great collection."

"Yeah," Will said, mostly to himself, "he must have, because he lives with that thing."

The Elliots had taken Rafi in as one of their own. He had become like an older son living outside the home and given the recognition of a full family member. He was too old to legally adopt, but if he wasn't, they would have.

The relationship began when Professor Elliot, then head of the Electrical Engineer Department, convinced the dean that the school should begin an active research program into renewable energy sources specifically focused on solar energy given their location in Florida's Sunbelt. In a short while, this program became formalized as the "Clean Energy Research Center" and began attracting research funding and specialists in solar energy from around the world. The school's initial investment paid off in both new student tuitions and national media attention.

Rafi Haddad was a student in one of Elliot's "Double-E" classes and had impressed his teacher intellectually with in-depth knowledge of his specialty: solar generation of electricity through a variety of technologies. Successful research programs are soon given acronyms by the people in the programs and those doing business with them. A measure of Elliot's success was the buzz around his new program which had become known in alternative-energy circles as simply "CERC."

As Elliot's team became a magnet for the entire school it was decided he should spend his full time running the program and was given funding for a student assistant to be lead engineer. Given the number and quality of students around the world who were migrating to USF and the CERC program, it was ironic that the best, brightest, and most qualified was someone already on campus, Rafi Haddad.

Rafi had graduated near the top of his class from the Indian Institute of Technology, one of the best Indian engineering schools, and had worked as an electrical engineer in India. But he realized his true calling was in solar energy and USF had the best program. In addition to his native Indian, he was fluent in English, Arabic, and German, the latter most important given the amount of solar research being carried out in Germany.

Shortly before six there was a knock at the door, and Ginny was the closest. "Hi, Rafi, happy Thanksgiving, come in."

"Hi, Ginny, sorry I'm late," Rafi said as he handed her the two bottles of wine he'd brought. "I had to stop for gas or I wouldn't have made it, and you know what the gas lines are like."

"Do I ever," Ginny smiled. "I wish you guys would hurry up with that solar thing you're working on so I wouldn't need to worry about gas lines any more. Thanks for bringing the wine, you really didn't need to—but we're glad you did." She gave him a quick hug. "Would you put that beer into the fridge for me?"

"Sounds good," Rafi said as he followed Ginny toward the back of the house, "Hey, Professor, happy Thanksgiving," he said after spying Elliot in the family room watching television.

"Hi, Rafi, after you put those beers away, bring a couple out here. The Florida vs. Florida State game is about to start."

"Not so fast, guys," Ginny said. "Dinner is just about ready and I need you to pour the drinks."

"I can handle that," Rafi volunteered quickly, "I assume it's wine all around except for Billy and Jeff?"

"Yes, please, Rafi. Let's go with the Merlot you brought, that looks like a good one." Ginny loved Merlot.

"Sure, will the professor be sitting at the head of the table as usual?" Rafi asked, wanting to make sure he understood the seating plan.

"Yes, thanks," she replied.

Elliot finally dragged himself away from the big-screen television in the family room, leaving the sound up loud enough for him to monitor the progress of the game. Ginny hated when he did that because the family wouldn't have his full attention. On the occasional big play, he had a history of jumping up from the table to see who had scored. But she knew this was a special day for football fans and her husband was one of the biggest.

Ginny Elliot had become a great cook. Being married for twenty-five years and raising two active boys on a tight budget meant lots of home cooking, and she'd become good at it. Tonight was a full turkey dinner with stuffing, mashed potatoes and gravy, green beans, and a multi-layered Jell-O salad, leaving the kitchen quite a mess. Will would tackle the dishes after dinner. He was always willing to "pay the price" for an outstanding meal.

Following an Elliot family tradition, they held hands around the table and Will said grace. Food was passed, plates were filled, and conversation quickly turned to football.

Halfway through the meal and in mid-conversation, Ginny noticed her husband sitting quietly, contemplating the plate of food in front of him, looking as if he had dropped out of more than just the conversation.

"Hey, Will," Ginny said, cutting across and through the football discussion going on between Rafi and the boys, "are you alright?"

"Actually, I'm not feeling well, a bit dizzy and my eyes don't seem to focus. If I didn't know better, I'd say something I ate didn't agree with me."

"Well, we've all eaten the same things, but you do look a bit gray," she began to worry. "Perhaps you should lie down."

All eyes turned to him.

"Hey, Dad, are you alright?" Billy asked.

Elliot took another drink of the wine in front of him, trying to gather himself. It seemed to make him dizzier, something unusual for a guy who often had wine with meals.

"I think I'm fine, Billy, but your mom may be right, I might just need to go upstairs and lie down for a while."

As he tried to push himself up from the table, he appeared glued to his seat, paralyzed. It seemed he could not overcome his own weight pressing him into the chair.

"I don't think I can get up," he announced with surprise and concern to the whole table.

"Will, you're scaring the hell out of me!" Ginny said, shocking her sons. They had never heard their mother use the "h" word. It was not so much what she said, but how she'd said it.

"Rafi and Billy, please help Dad upstairs while I call the doctor." Ginny tried desperately to regain her cool.

The meal was all but forgotten. Concern was apparent in everyone's eyes having never seen Elliot look so bad. A very noticeable gray pallor had enveloped his entire body: face, neck, forearms, and hands.

As Rafi stood to approach, Elliot's arms shot out to his sides and he began speaking in a voice they'd never heard. "Stay back, I can get up myself," he ordered. His hands went quickly to his head, pressing on both sides forming a vice as if he could squeeze out the pain. "Ginny," he yelled, "help me, my head…"

The entire room was frozen for what seemed like minutes. "Billy, quick, call 911!" Ginny screamed as she raced to the other end of the table and put her arms around her husband. He stared at her with glassy, hollow eyes. His attempt to speak came out as a loud growling moan. Visibly gasping for breath, he began to fade. His head slipped between his hands and landed with a sickening thud in the half-eaten plate of food in front of him.

"Will, *Will*!" Ginny shrieked through what had become hysterical crying.

Little Jeff had not moved from his chair, wide-eyed and frozen in place by the events unfolding in front of him. His screaming was triggered more by his mother's hysteria than his father's plight.

"Will, hold on honey, the ambulance will be here soon," she said with her mouth pressed close to his ear without knowing if what she said was true or if he could even hear her. "Rafi, help him *please*," she said with pleading eyes.

Rafi moved in quickly to raise Elliot's face from the table in an attempt to begin CPR. But the man, who a moment ago was not strong enough to raise himself up from the table, had suddenly become ferocious. He began vomiting and convulsing in a way that threw him violently backwards from his chair and onto the floor. There followed a horrible gagging, gurgling sound as every muscle in his body shuddered uncontrollably. Mercifully, the convulsions lasted only a minute before his body was released by the demons that had possessed it.

Throwing her body over him, Ginny screamed, "My God, my God, he's dead!"

Chapter 2.
Blue Marble

"*Atlantis*, T-minus-thirty-minutes and counting," rasped the anonymous voice from mission control.

"Roger," came the equally emotionless response from Kirk. Familiar words to anyone on the planet who'd been alive for the last twenty years, and very familiar to Jim Kirk, Shuttle Commander of the *Atlantis* mission code-named SOLAR.

Routine, thought Kirk. He had the identical information on the control panel in front of him. *Must be for the benefit of the media, but PR keeps these old tubs flying.*

Kirk was a seasoned veteran of three prior shuttle flights. He had received his pilot training in the Air Force, surviving twenty combat missions over Viet Nam. One such sortie resulted in his F-102 being shot out from under him followed by a scary— perhaps too scary—snatch-and-grab rescue to save his bacon. Compared to 'Nam, he considered flying the space shuttle *safe*. With his acceptance in the Astronaut Corps came the nickname, "Cap'n Kirk" after James T. Kirk of *Star Trek* fame. While Jim's middle initial wasn't "T," just having the same first and last name was enough to lock in the moniker. He'd endured it for many years, learning to enjoy the notoriety.

"Dan, you copy that?" squawked Kirk over the intercom.

"Roger."

Dan Johnson was the shuttle pilot on the mission. While Kirk could fly the shuttle as well or better than anyone, that job would formally fall to Johnson. NASA had long ago concluded that the shuttle commander should be a pilot, capable of taking the controls at any point. But in an age of specialization, flying the shuttle was the full-time responsibility of the shuttle pilot. The commander's job was defined as being the coordinator of the crew and its mission, the ultimate authority on-board. Someone once said NASA had modeled the roles of commander and pilot after the CEO and COO of a corporation.

With thirty minutes left in the countdown, everyone in the crew knew exactly what should be done. Checklists in hand—a formality since these were committed to memory—they proceeded with countdown activities.

"Davidson," Kirk called into the intercom.

"Sir," Davidson replied smartly.

"Give me the status of your systems in ten minutes so we can determine if this mission is a go."

* * *

Mission Specialist Jason "Doc" Davidson was the most nervous of the crew. Every other member had received extensive shuttle training for the last several years and some even had previous shuttle experience. In addition, this mission was focused on Davidson's experiments, and that pressure added to the beads of sweat gathering inside his helmet. Without a "go" from him, the SOLAR mission would never leave the pad. "Mission Specialist" was the NASA euphemism for "consultant." NASA had learned long ago they couldn't possibly provide all the technical talent for every mission from within their permanent ranks. The mission specialist role allowed them to go outside NASA, not unlike a corporation hiring consultants.

The problem with the Mission Specialist Program was training. While every astronaut in the corps accumulated years of shuttle training before their first flight, it was unrealistic to assume mission specialists would have anywhere near that amount. Their careers had been focused elsewhere, which is what made them valuable for missions requiring their unique expertise.

Lack of training in a space shuttle environment was a cause of concern for all mission specialists, but it was especially worrisome for Davidson. Originally, Professor Will Elliot had been tapped for SOLAR. A colleague of Davidson's from Colorado State University, Elliot was halfway through his six-month mission training when he died of a massive stroke at the too-early age of forty-six. Davidson had attended the funeral in Colorado when Elliot's wife, Ginny, mentioned Elliot had wanted Davidson to get the call when the opportunity for a solar mission first arose. Both Davidson and Elliot had applied for the position with fifty other candidates. If not for Elliot's untimely death, Davidson would never have known he'd been NASA's second choice.

Even before his friend was laid to rest, Davidson was contacted by the NASA program manager to see if he was available to fill the role, evoking a variety of emotions. The first was guilt, his opportunity coming at the cost of a close friend. Next came anxiety. With only three months of training left, would he be ready? And what would the stress do to him? The doctors had said stress was a major factor in Elliot's death. Davidson struggled with that diagnosis, having completed a nerve-racking project with Elliot in the recent past.

Then there was the difference in approach. Elliot was a "holistic scientist," convinced there was a strong relationship between religion and science. Jason, on the other hand, considered himself to be a pragmatic, "hardcore" scientist in the mainstream of scientific thought, believing in a clear separation of science from religion, evolution from creation.

NASA's program manager had given Jason twenty-four hours to make his decision before moving on to a third candidate. SOLAR was a mission that couldn't be postponed; another mission was right behind it, one with a military payload allowing no slippage. Either SOLAR would launch in three months or the opportunity to study solar radiation in space would be lost for the foreseeable future.

With only a few hours remaining to contemplate his decision, Jason secluded himself in his home office to weigh the alternatives. It seemed unfair he didn't have a partner, like Elliot had Ginny to help make a decision of this magnitude. After using as much time as he could afford, Jason decided to pick up the baton where his friend had left it, taking nine months out of his life to achieve the goals of SOLAR—a once in a lifetime opportunity. His response to NASA: "I'm in."

* * *

"Roger. Will do, Cap'n Kirk." Jason was still getting familiar with the intercom. The rest of the crew used it as a natural extension of their thought processes. He had, however, become comfortable using the Commander's nickname. Being considered "one of the guys" was important on a mission requiring tight coordination within a small team. He'd come to know Kirk as well as anyone could over the last three months as they had rehearsed everything about the mission.

Kirk knew little about SOLAR experimental technology details. His job was to ensure that *Atlantis*—as a platform for SOLAR—was positioned to maximize the probability for success. Jason's job was to perform the experimental tasks exactly as specified in the mission plan.

Although he had run his tests continuously for the last two hours, one more simulation wouldn't hurt. His recurring fear was that certain steps, endlessly simulated by the computers in front of him, had the finite possibility of going wrong. There were portions of reality that couldn't be simulated, and SOLAR had several of them. The shuttle's cargo doors, for example, might not operate as specified, resulting in a failed mission. He knew he shouldn't struggle with things beyond his control, but they bothered him anyway.

The SOLAR mission was designed by Elliot and NASA to study the effects of altitude on the strength and uniformity of the sun's radiation. One possible result of this study was Elliot's idea of putting massive solar arrays in orbit, converting the energy gathered into electrical power. Such energy could be beamed back to earth in the form of microwaves to a "farm" of antennas that would convert the resulting electricity to commercial grade and merge it onto the existing power grid.

Technically, the receiving antennas were called "rectennas" for *rectifying antennas*. They would convert the microwaves received to usable DC current, a technology originally developed in the '60s. This mission would provide the needed information on the best type of orbit, altitude, and other parameters. A lower orbit would result in less power needed to beam the microwaves to earth, but would require multiple ground stations. A higher *geo-*

stationary orbit would require more power to transmit, but the beam sent back would be stationary as well, needing only one very large ground station.

The experiment included one small satellite with a set of photovoltaic cells carried in the cargo bay of *Atlantis*. Since the shuttle was confined to low earth orbit, whenever a satellite needed to be sent into higher orbit, it was launched from the cargo bay. Although intricate, this method yielded a geostationary launch in two steps, which simplified many aspects of the mission. From a launch perspective, the SOLAR satellite was no different than many communications satellites that had used the shuttle as a platform in the past. From a functional perspective, it was very different.

The SOLAR satellite was designed to take precise measurements of the sun's ability to produce electricity via the photovoltaic effect, a physical phenomenon discovered back in 1839 by a French physicist. For the SOLAR mission, the satellite would be launched from *Atlantis* to an altitude of 22,300 miles into a geostationary, geosynchronous orbit. However, the satellite would make its assent in steps to allow solar intensity and uniformity information to be gathered along the way. While there had been numerous theoretical studies of solar intensity at various altitudes, this would be the first empirical data gathered. SOLAR was an important milestone in producing a practical solar energy collection system. It would also provide data for other scientific work in process.

Jason was responsible for all aspects of the satellite once it left the cargo bay. This meant he needed to push a button to initiate the launch that would trigger a series of automated steps, each of which would be monitored in sequence. While the first steps performed initialization, subsequent steps would cause SO-

LAR to gather critical readings at each altitude. If one step wasn't completed according to spec, moving to the next would eliminate the ability to go back to the previous one, resulting in the loss of vital information. Essentially, Jason embodied a miniature mission control for the small satellite held in the belly of the shuttle.

With the ten minutes allocated, Jason would have plenty of time to simulate each step, essentially a software test, since he couldn't actually open the doors and launch SOLAR while he was lying flat on his back on the launch pad. As with all good software tests, these included exercising the "failure legs" of the code, and if a failure did occur, the step could be restarted before going on to the next.

"Davidson to Kirk."

"Go, Doc."

"S...sir, all simulations have been successful," Jason said haltingly, his speech affected by nerves and the growing vibrations shaking the launch vehicle.

"Thanks, Doc," Kirk replied, "that was quick. I'll be running through my checklist with the rest of the crew until launch. Feel free to listen in or just relax until the final countdown in about twenty minutes. I know engineers like you feel luck has little to do with success, but good luck anyway."

"Roger that, Cap'n." Jason would take all the help he could get, including luck. After consuming the last ten minutes in what felt like seconds, twenty minutes of silence would seem an eternity. With nothing better to do, he closed his eyes and listened to some '70s rock he'd brought along. *Relax, Jason.*

* * *

"Kirk to pilot," the commander said with the "private" switch in the "on" position.

"Sir?"

"Do me a favor. While I run through the remainder of our pre-flight with the team, would you give our mission specialist a call to keep him occupied? He's pretty keyed-up and we need to keep him loose. This mission isn't going to be worth a damn if his experiments don't go off without a hitch."

"Understand, sir, I'll get him on the line. For the record, all my systems are *go.*"

"Roger that, and thanks, Dan."

* * *

"Pilot to Davidson," Johnson squawked.

"Sir?" Jason said, stirring from "Any Way You Want It," one of his favorite Journey tracks.

"I've finished my section of the pre-flight and understand you have too. Thought we could chat a bit while we wait for the countdown."

"Roger that." Davidson was getting more comfortable with the intercom lingo. "Where would you like to start?" *I'll bet Kirk put him up to this. I must sound nervous as hell.*

"Why don't you tell me about how you went from engineer to astronaut?"

"Sure," said Jason, taking a few moments to gather his thoughts. "This trip is the culmination of a recurring dream I've had since the inception of the space program. My first recollection goes back to our days trying to catch the Russians after their success with *Sputnik-I*. You're probably not old enough to remember that. I was standing out in the quiet of our backyard star-

17

ing at a very clear night sky in the direction of this new satellite guided by an article in the *Chicago Tribune* on what to look for and where to look. We saw nothing but stars. I'd never been into astronomy and it took fifteen minutes for my eyes to adjust to the vast array visible that night. We saw movement in various parts of the sky which turned out to be aircraft. Then, as we were about to give up, my brother saw something moving too fast to be a star and too slow to be an airplane. Its pace and brightness were steady and it moved in a way that made it unmistakably *Sputnik*. I was hooked.

"A steady diet of Superman, Buck Rodgers and Flash Gordon comics along with various TV series stimulated my imagination. At the ages of eight and five my brother and I would strap on capes made from dad's old raincoats. Leaping off the basement steps, we would measure the distance jumped and compare it to the distance without the capes. Naturally, we found we could 'fly' further with the capes than without, documenting our results on an old blackboard. We would march my mom and dad downstairs to present our findings, complete with demonstrations. I can almost see them winking at each other. But, back then, belief in The Scientific Method allowed no doubt in our minds."

As Kirk had predicted, Jason just kept discoursing on his engineering interests, education, and various jobs in the industry.

"As you know, Dan," Jason continued, "my job on this mission is to gather data to support NASA's interest in collecting solar energy in space and beaming it back to earth in the form of microwaves."

"Professor, what do you think about that possibility?" Johnson broke in.

"Interesting you ask. Honestly, I don't personally believe such a plan has even the *remotest* chance for practical application, a point on which Elliot and I obviously disagreed. While you can imagine building a solar cell array large enough to gather many megawatts of power, this energy would need to be transmitted to 'antenna farms' creating a high-powered microwave 'column' wreaking havoc on anyone or anything passing through it. Whether I believe in Elliot's vision or not is of no consequence, I'll get the accurate measurements NASA wants. They'll be immensely valuable for other studies too. I'm just thankful for the opportunity to conduct this mission and enjoy the billion dollar ride into space—I think."

* * *

In the pre-launch silence that preceded the final countdown, Jason grew restless. He was sitting atop a bomb loaded with tons of hydrogen and oxygen.

"Ten, nine, eight... three, two, one..." the almost-mechanical voice at mission control broke in again, words Jason had heard many times on television. They sounded different this time as he sat above the throbbing space shuttle poised to leap off the launch pad. Much more ominous when he realized it was *he* who was going to be hurtling upward at seventeen thousand miles per hour just eight and a half minutes after liftoff. Unable to resist the comparison, he remembered the muzzle velocity of an M-16 rifle was about two thousand miles per hour. In just eight and one half minutes he would be traveling eight and one half times the speed of that bullet. *Unbelievable*, he thought.

"We have ignition and liftoff!" the controller screamed over the roar of the engines.

Nothing in Jason's training could have prepared him for what he was experiencing. It began as a small vibration that grew quickly to a violent shudder. It was inconceivable that a seventy-ton space shuttle could shake so violently and still hold together, a testament to the physics of solid rocket boosters and the engineers who built them.

Then motion. Almost imperceptible at first, Jason sensed in the midst of violent shaking that he was actually moving—upward. Then, acceleration. He was slammed into his contoured seat at three times the force of gravity. While he'd been trained to experience this force in the centrifuge, combined with the violent shaking, he could feel his eyeballs vibrating against the back of their sockets. He tried to pick his head up from the seat cushion to lessen the effect, but g-forces glued him down better than any epoxy. The best he could do to minimize the feeling was to shut his eyes, tight.

Amidst the sounds of the commander and pilot radioing their progress to mission control, Jason's was one of several voices on the intercom yelling "Go, go!" While normally a sedate engineer, the exhilaration of liftoff was too much. The mission was at a critical point. No going back, no opportunity to hit the "undo" button. In a few minutes Jason was either going to be in safe orbit or he was going to be dead!

Silence. The solid rocket boosters and external fuel tank had been jettisoned and the main engines had been shut down. Until forty-five minutes into the flight to make a correction in the orbit, Jason and the shuttle would be traveling at 17,500 miles per hour in vibration-free *silence*. Reaching circular orbit four hundred miles above the earth, the deployment altitude for the collection experiments, Jason was beginning to get a sense of what the early astronauts described as a *religious experience*.

"Commander to Davidson."

Jason was startled to hear his name amid all the other radio traffic. "Sir?" *Shouldn't he have more important people to talk to right now?*

"How do you like your first ride in the 'Vomit Comet'?"

"I skipped breakfast," Jason said, "a good thing since I couldn't have reached for the bag if I needed to."

"Good man. We'll be making a couple of orbits and then you should prep to begin your experiments at 0800. By the way, as a new rookie in space, I'd be interested in your first impressions."

Jason took a moment to gather his thoughts. "Commander, I guess I'd summarize by saying that Dr. Elliot was right."

"How so? I didn't get to know him that well."

"Will was a 'tree-hugger' and conservationist. He believed the earth was constrained by finite resources, and that we needed to conserve and live within our constraints. I was the one, like many scientists, who believed mankind could keep expanding our frontiers to fully utilize all the resources earth has to offer and then move beyond to harvest the resources of our solar system.

"From our position in orbit I'm already in awe of how fragile and rare our earth is. First, there are the cities that are blotted by nitrous oxides and unburned hydrocarbons, and these are just the *visible* results of taking carbon from the earth and burning it. *Invisible* carbon dioxide, as a source of global warming, is probably even more dangerous to our world.

"Second, we need to reprioritize our space program to protect ourselves from asteroid and comet 'events' that could eliminate our species. These events have happened in the past and will happen again."

"So you think that a manned mission to Mars should be put on the back burner?" asked Kirk.

"Commander, it's just a matter of priorities. Proposing manned missions to other planets sets a dangerous expectation that we could actually colonize somewhere other than this 'Blue Marble' we call the Earth. We are most certainly alone and must protect this planet at all costs, taking advantage of the only source of infinite energy available, the sun. We can explore other planets when we have secured this one. If we screw this planet up we have nowhere else to go!"

Chapter 3.
Vienna, Austria

Obere Donaustrasse 93 might seem an odd address for the world's most powerful organization. A central member of "old Europe," Austria is clearly on the "consumer" side of the petroleum ledger, yet Vienna is the host city for the headquarters of the Organization of Petroleum Exporting Countries, OPEC, a cartel representing the majority of oil producing countries.

While some would say the United Nations is the most powerful organization, those would be people who put politics ahead of finance. But it's well known that finance controls politics and there is no organization on earth with more control over world finance than OPEC. As has been well-demonstrated, they control a large portion of the world's oil production and can wreak economic havoc on any number of countries simply by adjusting the flow of oil through their spigots. Located in a commercial area of the city, OPEC headquarters is in a non-descript building yet easily identified by the large baby-blue "OPEC" sign.

The OPEC cartel was created at a meeting in Baghdad in 1960 by five founding members: Iran, Iraq, Kuwait, Saudi Arabia, and Venezuela. The home of its first official headquarters was Geneva, Switzerland. The move to Vienna occurred five years later.

Switzerland and Austria have several common characteristics. Both are politically neutral, and both support anonymous numbered bank accounts. The secret Swiss bank account was abolished in 1991. Perhaps a good reason for the move to Austria.

* * *

It was a brisk fall Monday morning and Dr. Afsar Al-Shar left his home on Wasnergasse Street heading to his office at OPEC headquarters. As deputy secretary of OPEC, Dr. Al-Shar had a lofty position and a salary that justified a nicely furnished apartment within walking distance of his office, and with an expansive view of the Sportplatz athletic facilities across the street. He often walked home through the Sportplatz when he felt the need to get away from the din of incessant traffic. Normally Afsar had time for a coffee at a local café on Wasnergasse, but this morning he needed to be at the office earlier than usual to prepare for a meeting with two non-OPEC oil ministers from Russia and Gabon. He missed reading his morning *Tehran Times*, tucked faithfully under his arm.

Dr. Al-Shar was a mid-level Iranian bureaucrat and quite proud of his position as OPEC's deputy secretary. Born in Tehran, he received his Doctorate in Philosophy from London's Chelsea College. Living in England had afforded him the opportunity to perfect his language skills, so important in the world of business and international politics. Upon his return to Iran, Afsar's goal was to enter the diplomatic service with the dream of becoming his country's ambassador to a world power. Instead, his background was attractive to local Iranian OPEC officials where he ultimately accepted a job, working his way up from the local office to his present position. This background meant he would never become the secretary general, having had no field experience. His wife, Afareen, meaning "to create," and the daughter they "created," BahAr, became his primary motivation.

Afsar reported to Sheik Abdul Al-Farar, the current secretary general of OPEC and a Saudi. OPEC leadership rotated among member countries, but Saudi Arabia held the post most often given their dominant share of oil reserves among the membership.

Afsar had been working for the last three months to set up today's meetings. OPEC's ultimate goal was to control the world's oil through membership of all the countries producing oil for export. While this goal would never be entirely achieved, OPEC countries controlled about 40 percent of production and 77 percent of proven reserves. They wanted to control 80-90 percent of both. To achieve this, Afsar needed to behave like other businessmen, working hard to keep his current "customers" happy and just as hard to gain market share. He often had to placate his current member countries, some of which were run by prima-donnas. This was made more difficult by the dynamic politics between members. At times, Afsar joked with his staffers that their job was a lot like herding cats—although these cats were like lions, any one of which could take off his head.

Several months prior, at a non-OPEC oil conference that OPEC was attending as a "wolf in sheep's clothing," Afsar met the Russian oil minister, Sergei Abramova. Abramova was dropping hints that Russia "might entertain considering to think about" (Afsar was familiar with these subtleties) an association with OPEC. It was important to note that "join OPEC" wasn't mentioned although both men knew that's what it meant since there was no other type of association. That discussion led to to-day's meeting, which was the next step in the mating dance.

A Russian membership would be a real coup for OPEC—adding 14 percent to production and 7.5 percent to proven reserves—and a large feather in Afsar's cap. On the other hand, it wasn't clear how much influence Abramova really had, though he had the title that implied the clout. Russia was still Russia and Sergei may or may not have the green light from his higher-ups, most importantly the Russian president. Afsar had tried various ways to see if Sergei had "run this up the flagpole" with his superiors, but Sergei was on to that game. He wasn't about to expose his cards to OPEC. The more information he held, the better he'd appear to his president.

Gabon, a small African country, was in a very different situation. Compared to Russia it was a very small player. Its 0.3 percent production and 0.2 percent proven reserves was miniscule by any measure. Gabon's importance was political. It was one of only two countries that had ever "left the fold" of OPEC, Ecuador was the other.

Gabon originally joined OPEC in 1975 and left in 1994 when it decided OPEC's quotas were too restrictive, thinking it could profit better on its own. Gabon's oil minister, Mani Sidibe, was also at the non-OPEC conference and met briefly with Afsar to explore the possibilities of rejoining the cartel. Everyone must eat crow sometime and countries were no different. Since cutting ties to OPEC, Gabon's oil prices had fluctuated wildly causing revenue trauma for a country that imported almost everything it consumed. When oil prices were driven down, they could not purchase enough of the basics to feed a growing population. When oil prices were up, they would start new projects only to curtail them on the next downward swing. The material impact of adding Gabon was minor to OPEC, but it would teach some of the other member countries a lesson, certainly the smaller ones. That itself would be of considerable value. It would be a very interesting day for Afsar, hosting two countries with wildly different characteristics yet a shared goal.

"Good morning, Klera," Afsar said as he entered his suite of offices.

Klera Bieler had been Afsar's secretary for almost three years, joining him a few months after he started with OPEC. She was a local Austrian, the nationality of most of his staff. It made good business sense to hire "locals" wherever possible since they knew the languages and didn't require relocation. Her primary post was the reception desk at the entry to his office suite where she could intercept guests. She knew everyone in the building and how to get things done for her boss.

"Good morning, Doctor," she said. Klera always retained an air of formality in the office and only used his first name in social settings.

Afsar took a quick glance around, his eyes settling on the coffee machine. "Coffee! I need a cup. I didn't have time for my normal stop this morning."

"I thought that might be the case, so I took the liberty of getting in a bit early myself. I'll bring a cup into your office—cream and no sugar, right?"

Afsar made a mental note to himself to look up Klera's current salary. She had a six-month review coming and he wanted to start thinking about an increase. *A good secretary is worth her weight in gold.*

"Correct, and thank you, Klera."

"I also reserved the large presentation room on three last night and have prepared the projector and seating for your two guests at ten this morning. The PC connection to the projector is working fine. You can leave your presentation on the server and access it over the network when you're ready."

He had two hours to update his PowerPoint presentation prior to the meeting. There was always new information available he needed to incorporate. Thank Allah for computers. "Klera, this office could not function without you," Afsar said loudly from his office.

"I know," Klera said, just loud enough to be heard.

OPEC prided itself on operating with very little overhead. No excess staff, and the furnishings, though sufficient, were understated. If there was anything about the office that could be construed as extravagant, it was the meeting rooms on the third floor.

Since OPEC was an organization comprising many countries, communications between and among the members and itself were critical. While many meetings were held in the member countries, strategic and important tactical meetings were held at headquarters. All six formal meeting facilities were on the third floor, with small conference rooms scattered about on the first two floors for internal meetings.

* * *

Klera sat down at her desk as the phone rang.

"Deputy Al-Shar's office," she said.

"Hello, this is Sheik Abdul, is this Klera?"

"Yes, Sheik, it is."

"Hello, Klera, it's good to hear your voice. How have you been?"

"Thank you, sir, I'm well. What can I do for you this morning?"

"I'm in town this week for a series of meetings and understand the Russians will be meeting with Dr. Al-Shar this morning. I have some time and would like to attend."

She was taken aback, hoping her voice wouldn't betray her. "Really, that's wonderful. The presentations are scheduled to begin at ten and I'll tell Dr. Al-Shar. I'm sure he will be glad to see you."

"Thank you, Klera, I will be there just before ten."

"Thank you, sir."

Klera hung up the phone and thought for a moment. Sheik Abdul Al-Farar was the secretary general of OPEC. While her boss ran the operation on a daily basis, he reported to the sheik who lived in Saudi Arabia and normally only came to the Vienna office for prescheduled member meetings. Dropping in unannounced was highly irregular. Afshar had not invited the sheik, she would have known about it if he had.

Klera liked her job. She had a steady income with ample benefits, a short commute to the office, and prestige among her neighbors. She genuinely liked working for the doctor but knew his position was political in nature, making hers political as well. If a new deputy secretary were to appear on the scene he would want to bring in his own staff. That happened a lot with political positions. Both Klera and her boss understood how things worked yet never spoke of them. *Stop being paranoid.* She picked up her phone and again dialed her boss.

* * *

"Dr. Al-Shar."

"Yes, Klera."

"The sheik called from the airport. He's on his way in and asked me to inform you."

There was a long silence. Afsar was taken aback. Why hadn't the sheik asked Klera to connect him directly?

"Thank you, Klera," he finally said. "I thought he might make an appearance given the importance of the meeting with the Russians," he lied. That the sheik would attend the meeting uninvited and unannounced was a complete shock. He didn't want Klera to sense his concern.

"Should I be doing anything special to accommodate the sheik?" she asked.

After another delay, Afsar said, "I don't think so. If I have any ideas I'll ring you." They both hung up.

Afsar had reason to be concerned. In his recent interactions with his boss, the normally affable sheik seemed much more stressed than normal, raising a red flag with Afsar. Using his access to the entire OPEC database, his research showed that while there was still plenty of OPEC oil in the ground, a large percentage of that oil was not going to be retrievable—a situation one of the papers he found called "Peak Oil." Apparently, the energy cost of retrieving a barrel of oil was approaching the energy contained in a barrel of oil. Once that threshold was crossed, the remaining oil would be economically irretrievable. OPEC was running out of oil!

Prior to this discovery he considered his discussions with Sergei Abramova to be "informal," or "off the record." He had only mentioned in passing his discussions with Russia and Gabon in his monthly status call with the sheik. He was hoping to use this meeting to set the hook. Like all businessmen, Afsar knew his future was all about expectations—setting them, and then, more importantly, meeting them. Adding Russia to OPEC's membership would be a huge step in his career with the cartel. It would bring prestige to the sheik and recognition for himself among all the member countries, and after all, it was they whom he served. Adding Russia would be a real coup and would cement his position within OPEC for years to come, especially given the dire nature of current OPEC reserves. If, however, Afsar set the expectation that Russia was going to join, and then didn't for any reason, the complete reverse would happen, dishonor for the sheik and more than likely an opportunity for Afsar to look for a new job, at the very least.

Afsar now understood the importance behind the sheik's attendance. *How did he know of the meeting? I wanted to use today to cement the relationship and then discuss it with the sheik.* Afsar had a history of high blood pressure. His wife had given him a portable measuring kit to keep in his desk. He opened the drawer.

Chapter 4.
Beijing, China

China has one of the oldest continuously recorded histories, dating to 2500 BC. Since then, it took over 4,500 years for China to become the fastest growing economy in the world, most of the increase happening in the last sixty years. "Young" nations like the United States had an advantage when it came to economic power. They didn't need to overcome the inertial baggage of a lengthy political and economic history. Yet with 4,500 years of baggage, China has arrived at an economic status rivaling the United States, with India not far behind.

Beijing is not the largest city in China, but it is the most important. Within the city proper there are 7.5 million people, considerably smaller than Shanghai with about ten million. Unlike Shanghai and China's other largest cities that are dominated by commercial enterprise, Beijing is paced by its role as capital, giving it a governmental, bureaucratic ambiance.

* * *

Zeng Ju woke at 5:30 AM to allow for his usual ninety-minute morning routine. He began with forty minutes of Qigong exercises to prepare for a stressful day. He then bathed and had his breakfast of congee, a watery rice gruel that westerners might mistake as porridge—until they tasted it. During the end of his meal he was joined by his wife Xiumei and two sons, Liaoping and Guoping. The discussion around the table centered on articles in the *Beijing Morning Post*. Unlike western news media that focused on war, violence, crime and gossip, the *Morning Post* highlighted accomplishment, filled with superlatives: "fastest," "biggest," and "brightest." There was a story about the newest bullet train that would connect Shanghai with Beijing, including its cost and projected speed between the two cities—*largest, fastest*. There were stories about local sons and daughters who participated in this project and the importance of their roles—*quickest, brightest*. In China, good news did sell.

At seven o'clock Zeng pushed himself away from the breakfast table, bid good day to his family, and left his luxury apartment on Nanganzi Street in the affluent Chongwen District for the short ride to the Ministry. Unlike most commuters, he was provided with a car and driver for the day, which could end as late as two or three o'clock the next morning. As China's minister of foreign affairs, Zeng had come to expect such perks, as well as the occasional long day.

Zeng had spent much of the weekend preparing for a meeting with his boss, Wu Jianzhong, president of the Chinese Communist Party. Wu was concerned about his country's supply of oil and had asked Zeng for an update on current status and future prospects. In China, as with most developing countries, oil was the fuel—both literally and figuratively—for its economic and political well-being. China consumed much more oil than most countries given its booming economy and the number of people it took to keep it moving—and more importantly, keep it *accelerating*.

When Zeng took the job as minister of foreign affairs, he assumed most of his activities would revolve around the growth of China and how that growth would affect its relationships with neighbors and trading partners. More recently, his focus was on oil since China did not have a minister of energy to concentrate on oil-related issues. Zeng sometimes felt his country needed such an energy "czar," freeing him to spend time on other more important foreign affairs issues. But if oil became a major focus for his boss, he could raise his personal political capital by being the person to head energy initiatives, the "go-to" guy for oil. *Best to keep the responsibility*, he reasoned.

Zeng wasn't sure what direction his meeting with the president would take, making preparation difficult. On his ride into the office he flipped through the memos and presentations he'd been collecting for the past year, in hopes some of them would be useful. He felt confident he could speak to the issues without referring to his research. But it was always good to have backup.

The twenty-minute ride to the office was quiet with the exception of the rustling of papers in the back seat. Arriving at the Ministry, Zeng was met at the curb by his personal secretary, Chen Fai. Chen opened the rear door, took the large valise filled with Zeng's meeting materials, and escorted him through the building. The role of personal secretary was highly valued in China and came with considerable prestige, seen by many as a stepping stone to the position of minister, or other high-ranking official. Zeng had spent seven years as personal secretary to his predecessor and credited that experience for his present job. In China, the position of personal secretary was one to which many men aspired.

The Ministry was a work of art located on the southeast corner of Chao Yang Gate, East Second Ring Road, just east of the

Forbidden City. The building had a gray convex exterior with a footprint of over 650,000 square feet. Its interior floor space was over twice that.

The 8,600 square foot Olive Hall served as the main reception area with a stainless steel and glass ceiling allowing an abundance of natural light into the space. The front wall was a huge relief depicting "China Civilization." Beginning on the left with Han Dynasty stone carvings, to the image of the *Long March 2* rocket launch on the right, the relief encapsulated almost five thousand years of development.

There were sixteen rooms scattered throughout the building designed to support working meetings. There was also an International Conference Hall that seated 670 people and a dedicated Press Hall. Behind the building was the Ministry's courtyard with a huge central flowerbed decorated in horticultural splendor.

Entering through the large glass doors, Zeng strode with Chen to the elevator, his young assistant carrying the heavy valise. When the elevator stopped in the main lobby, people rushed to catch it. They made way for Zeng and Chen after recognizing their minister—and then crowded in. Chen pushed the button for the seventh floor. He and Zeng did not speak. It was clear Zeng had important matters on his mind. *Safer to save conversation for the privacy of the minister's office*, Chen thought.

The quiet ride up the glass-enclosed elevator seemed to refresh Zeng's mind. When they arrived in his office he finally said, "I'm expecting the president at about nine o'clock. Instead of using the conference room you reserved on Friday, I'd like to host him in my office."

"Certainly, sir, I assumed that might be a possibility and had your office swept by security on Friday. You will notice your conference table has been moved away from the windows. I will cancel the conference room and redirect the refreshments I ordered to your office."

"Thank you, Fai, I will use the remaining time to review emails from the weekend and continue my preparation."

Chen left the office abruptly to make the new arrangements.

* * *

Promptly at nine Zeng's phone rang. Chen announced the president had arrived with his security detail. Zeng had been surprised the president would want to meet at his Ministry office instead of the capitol building. But it was good for the president to get out and be seen in other government offices. *Ever the politician*, Zeng thought. It would also be good for Zeng to be seen hosting the president. *Ever the politician.*

Security was tight. On any given day, security at the Ministry building was thorough, but today the president was being escorted by his own staff, who had been coordinating with Ministry security for several days.

Nine o'clock was peak traffic time in the Ministry of Foreign Affairs. The president had visited several times before, and his arrival always caused a commotion. Flanked by his entourage, Wu made his way through crowds of people who could not help but mill around, point, and look in his direction. They had seen him many times on television—he seemed shorter in person. His guards forming a flying wedge, the ensemble parted the sea of people around the elevator with the president smiling and waving, seeming oblivious to the security. When the elevator arrived, the president and his party had a private ride to the seventh floor.

* * *

Zeng responded to the knock on his door. "Good morning, Mr. President."

"Minister Zeng, thank you for meeting with me. I have been anxious to discuss your work on oil policy," Wu said, extending his hand.

"It is my pleasure to host you, sir," and the two men retreated to the small conference table that had been moved into a well-lit but windowless corner of the office.

The Ministry security team returned to their normal duties while the president's people shut the office door. Four of them remained outside with backs against the wall, monitoring traffic in the hallway, talking into their sleeves and listening through nearly invisible earpieces connected by thin wires running up inside their suit jackets. They would remain in this position for the entire meeting. They could summon the assistance of Ministry security in seconds if necessary. Radio frequencies had been coordinated in advance.

Wu Jianzhong was a young boy in 1949 when China turned to communism. His father was active in the Communist Party, making politics the only life he had ever known. Wu was educated as an engineer, taking jobs in various Ministry positions. He entered politics at the provincial level where he learned the power of networking to get things done. He rose quickly through the ranks to national prominence, considered by both supporters and detractors to be a strong leader, and a fair one.

"Ju, I'm not sure how long this meeting will last. I need to get an overall grasp of our energy situation, specifically oil," Wu said.

"Mr. President, in that case I will have Chen clear my calendar for the day. I have scheduled lunch in the dining room and I will add an afternoon break. Would you like to begin with a cup of tea?"

"Thank you, my schedule earlier did not allow for that luxury," Wu said.

Zeng hit the speed-dial button marked "Chen" on his desk phone and asked him to serve the tea *immediately*.

"Ju," the president continued, "I need to understand our current oil consumption, production, and import levels. I have some thoughts on where we need to go with regard to oil, but we also need an overall energy strategy. I suspect you have some thoughts as well. After we have completed the status discussion and I understand the issues, we can use the afternoon for brainstorming."

"That would be fine, sir. Although my responsibilities are much more general than just energy, the topic has been my focus for some time. I have been reviewing my materials for the last several days," Zeng nodded toward his valise and stack of papers. He had exaggerated a bit on the energy focus, but was confident he knew more than his boss.

"Excellent," the president said. "Now, there is something I shouldn't need to say but I will anyway. This meeting is to be kept in the *strictest* confidence. You will see why shortly."

A knock at the door interrupted. Chen entered silently, placing a tray on a side table.

Zeng wanted to start by asking a question. The brief interruption by Chen gave him the opportunity. "Mr. President, may I ask what has transpired recently to bring this meeting about? The answer may help me organize my thoughts."

"Certainly. There have been recent inquiries to my office about our current position on energy, specifically oil. Our economy is growing at an unprecedented rate and our needs for energy will grow proportionally. I fear we have been taking oil for granted and need to prepare for the future. The future is something I need to understand."

Sitting back in his chair and taking his first sip of the hot brew, the president continued. "I should start with some background. This country has many centuries of documented history, rivaled only by Egypt and India. Our very earliest years were ones of creativity and invention. We invented silk and ink. We discovered the tea that you have so graciously provided. We invented paper and the idea of moveable type that made printing presses practical, so we could put something on the paper we had just invented," the president smiled.

"The vast 'middle' of our history, the 'dynastic period' was characterized by warring provinces and the subjugation of our own people. We built the Great Wall to separate our factions and keep them from killing each other. Then we invented gunpowder to help them kill each other. Like moveable type, this technology was quickly copied.

"Although we must never lose sight of our history and how it has shaped the present, it is our recent past that is most important. The majority of our citizens have no personal recollection of our history prior to the formation of our Communist Party in 1949. Unfortunately those who do will soon be gone, as will I. Our early experience with communism brought us a great leader in Mao, but also caused a civil war with our great leader, Chiang, who then retreated to Taiwan. It also created hardship and oppression for our people since we followed the principles of communism literally, without thought to moderation and practicality.

"Ironically, it was the oppression of our people, primarily in our agricultural and rural areas, that caused them to work around the system. This first glimmer of entrepreneurism led to the success we enjoy today. The economic stress experienced by these farmers forced them to work outside the collective we had created, a system that pooled their output to the state. By making a pact among themselves, they were able to produce more than what was required by the government, profiting from the unreported excess. Entirely illegal. Fortunately, we had a wise leader in Mao who knew when to look the other way. It is this pattern of the individual, working around the system to achieve financial freedom that has led to our current success.

"Our rural capitalism worked so well it moved to our cities where it was amplified by enormous resources of people and money. We now have the largest communist nation in the world fueled by capitalism. Capitalistic communism is an oxymoron to some, but an ideology that we have time-tested. It is working so well that our rural entrepreneurs are now migrating to the cities in great numbers. Families are investing the best of their youth to send profits back to the farms, as long as the farms exist. But that is another concern.

"Our country has become the manufacturing floor of the world. While the Americans used to outsource production to Japan and then Korea and Taiwan, these countries now come to us! And in many cases the Americans now outsource directly to us, bypassing their former partners. We have formed thousands of private companies in Shanghai, Beijing, and other large cities that can produce goods with the best quality and lowest cost. While we have become the highest quality provider for shoes, belts, clothing and other staples, we are beginning to achieve the same status for high-end electronics and other technologies.

"Which brings us to this meeting, Mr. Zeng. We have the second largest economy in the world and the fastest growing. Our economy is currently two-thirds the size of the United States', and twice that of Japan's. Our real competitor is India, which will surpass Japan in a few years, as we will surpass the United States. Our problem, and one India shares but to a lesser extent, is GDP per capita. Our GDP divided by our population is 92nd among the nations measured, which means we are achieving our success on the backs of our citizens. We cannot expect them to accept this position for long."

"How do you see us solving this problem?" Zeng asked.

"As you know, we are already doing everything we can to control our population, even limiting each family to one child. Yet our population continues to grow. To better compensate our workers we must dramatically improve GDP through higher productivity. Increasing productivity means increasing automation which requires a corresponding increase in energy. And our ranking of 92nd in GDP per capita is actually optimistic, since it is based on our official census of 1.3 billion people. Everyone in the government knows this figure is understated by about two hundred million unaccounted migrant workers, the equivalent of a 'migrant country' the size of Japan within our own."

The president paused to collect his thoughts, allowing Zeng to catch up on the notes he was taking. Wu caught a second wind, "Without the assured availability of energy to fuel our economic growth we will have a serious political situation. In effect, we would be 'surrounded by insurmountable opportunity,' a politically unstable situation, which could impact my job and yours, Mr. Zeng. I assume you like your job as well as I like mine?"

"I do, Mr. President. You've put it quite clearly, I am impressed by your thought processes," Zeng said with a smile quickly returned.

In fact, Zeng *was* truly impressed, not just brown-nosing his boss. Wu was not only an astute politician, but had a clear understanding of his country's history, psychology, technology, and economics. He had described a complex situation in terms anyone could understand. Zeng had the feeling Wu was rehearsing a speech the president would soon be delivering to a larger audience.

"Good, then let us turn our attention to the issues we have with oil."

"Mr. President, let me begin with some basic facts. I will round off these numbers so we can do some mental arithmetic. We currently consume over six million barrels of oil per day, and this number has been increasing as dramatically as is our GDP. This corresponds to the point you've made, the correlation between GDP and energy consumption. We use roughly one third the amount of oil as the United States on a daily basis. As a percentage of total world oil consumption, the United States uses about 25 percent and we consume one third of that, or approximately 8 percent. Our usage grew 11 percent over the previous year and we expect this annual increase to become the norm for the next several years."

"Let me stop you there, Mr. Zeng," Wu interrupted. "As long as we're talking about consumption, I'd like to understand your views on the pollution we generate from it. This is an issue affecting the workers we rely on today and more so in the future, one our citizens are discussing."

"Yes, sir, pollution is a problem we have not adequately addressed, nor has the world. I am not a climatologist, but I researched this issue for our meeting. The biggest area of concern is carbon dioxide levels in greenhouse gases. In 1997 the concentration of CO_2 in the atmosphere was 368 parts per million, or PPM as it's called. It was thought then the tolerable threshold for CO_2 was 550 PPM at which point we would see average temperatures rise three to nine degrees Fahrenheit causing seas to rise one to two-and-a-half feet by the year 2100 and twenty-two feet to forty-three feet in the next millennium. Our scientists say the absolute upper limit of concentration is 1100 PPM at which point the world may 'go dark' in their words. We are already past the 'tolerable' threshold with concentrations of 700 PPM, almost double the concentration since Kyoto. At this point, even the most skeptical of our climatologists believe global warming is real and the root cause of the weather changes and flooding we are seeing around the world. They also tell me that every gallon of gasoline we burn is adding another five pounds of carbon, which becomes 20 pounds of carbon dioxide, to the atmosphere."

"So what should our strategy be?" Wu asked.

"Unfortunately, we cannot solve this problem by ourselves, nor can any one nation. We need to continue growing our economy, which will demand more and more energy. The only way to break the cycle is to adopt clean alternative fuels and these are several years out, based on the Geneva energy conference I attended two years ago."

"Where is the progress being made?" Wu asked.

"The Germans and the Americans have university-level research programs in the solar and hydrogen areas."

"We should monitor their progress. In the meantime we have 1.5 billion citizens of our own to feed. What can you tell me about oil production in our country?"

"Yes, sir," Zeng said, shifting gears and shuffling papers. "We currently produce over three million barrels of oil per day domestically, which of course means we must import about half of our daily consumption."

"Interesting," the president jumped in. "I imagine the energy increases needed to fuel our growth will mean significantly more imports, which leads me to ask about our domestic reserves. What can we expect from our own wells?"

"Reserves are an interesting topic, not just for us, but for the world. All discussions of oil reserves should be met with skepticism. There is no standard way to measure reserves, although there seem to be standard *definitions* left to interpretation. Oil that has been discovered and remains in place is considered in 'reserve.' Then, based on complex calculations involving many variables, the probability for successful extraction is estimated. If there is a reasonable certainty that the oil can be recovered given current and projected future technology and operating conditions, the reserves are considered to be 'proven,' which is all we will consider today. The remaining reserves are assigned as 'probable,' meaning greater than 50 percent probability of being recovered, and 'possible,' meaning less than 50 percent probability. Using those definitions, and caveats, the best estimate of our *proven reserves* is twenty-three billion barrels, which is about 2 percent of the world's total."

"Ju, I understand. But this leads to questioning our refining capacity. It does no good to get oil out of the ground, or import it, if we cannot refine it into gasoline and the other fuels we use. Do you know where we stand with refining capacity?"

"Yes, sir, our current position is good. We are only using 70 percent of our capacity, which is enough to meet our current needs. But this will change quickly if our demand for fuels is to increase as dramatically as you predict."

There was a knock at the office door.

"Yes, Fai, come in," Zeng said to the closed door, anticipating Chen's arrival.

"Mr. Zeng, the dining room tells me your lunch is ready when you are."

"Mr. President, should we take a break for lunch?"

"Ju, we are making good progress," the president said. "I'd prefer we have our lunch brought to your office so we may continue. We would lose too much time if we move to the dining room and my presence will cause a disturbance for everyone in the building, a situation I try to avoid when possible."

"Certainly, sir."

"Fai, would you ask the dining room to deliver our meals?"

"At once, Mr. Zeng," Chen Fai said as he left to make the arrangements.

"This has been a good morning," Wu said, using the interruption to start a new discussion. "Let's begin to think about an energy strategy. My first concern is refining capacity. As you said, we currently have 30 percent unused capacity, but that will be utilized quickly as our economy grows, so I would like to get a program in place immediately to project our future needs and begin expanding refinery capacity. I am sure there will be relatively long lead times involved. We have both the technology and people who can do this effectively and probably more efficiently than any other country.

"Second, we will need to expand our imports. We need an assured supply of oil for at least the next fifteen years."

"Yes, sir, but should we also consider expanding the use of our own reserves?" questioned Zeng.

"Ju, we also use oil as a raw material in the production of many things, including varnishes, plastics, and lubricants. I am concerned about burning our own petroleum for energy when it could be used for making products we sell. I would rather be burning imported oil with the hope that in the future, alternative energies will be available for that purpose. But we will still need our oil as a raw material since plastic will still require petroleum, a role that, say, hydrogen cannot fill. We should consider our own reserves as a 'bank' for future product development and save our oil for the highest and best use."

"But," said Zeng, "won't we be competing with others, included America, for additional imported oil? All the oil consuming nations are getting their supplies from the same exporting countries."

"Indeed, but we can position our approach as 'joint-development' of new wells. We will invest with our partners for future rights to the oil found. This will be politically strategic since we will be helping our partners in the discovery process while guaranteeing our future supply from multiple sources. It will appear that we are not taking away reserves from their current customers, but finding new reserves. I suggest we approach Canada and Saudi Arabia as potential partners."

"But won't others, certainly the United States, be able to do the same thing? And OPEC countries like Saudi Arabia have limits on their production enforced by the organization."

"We need to be creative. We need to fund our partnerships with resources that make sense for each country. In the case of Canada, they are not an OPEC member and can certainly use the money, essentially an annuity for a long period of time in return for a guaranteed flow of oil. In the case of Saudi Arabia, money will be less persuasive. They may prefer access to our technology instead of cash."

"Sir, what technologies did you have in mind? And couldn't the Americans do the same?"

"I remind you, this meeting is being held in strict confidence... The technologies I am thinking about are weapons technologies. After all, we're already trading nuclear technology to Iran for their oil."

"Oh," said Zeng, noticeably caught off guard, followed by a palpable delay to grasp what was said. "Are you concerned how that would be received by the rest of the world?"

"Ju, the only 'rest of the world' we need to concern ourselves with is the United States. We are the next superpower and need to begin acting that way. Our economic expansion—and theirs— will be directly proportional to the availability of energy. At our current rate of growth, compared to the United States, we will surpass them in a matter of years. We need to be prepared. But to do that we need assured oil supply and delivery. With the possible exception of Russia, which we could connect to with a pipeline, our oil will need to be shipped to us on the high seas. As a superpower we need to be sure those ships can get here, which is why we are building our own 'Blue Water Navy.'

"The Americans have invested over six hundred billion dollars and thousands of lives in their Iraq War, something for which we and every other country should be thankful. We would all benefit from the future stability. But they have not done anything to secure energy resources for their future. Now they are in a difficult domestic political position.

"We, on the other hand, can probably invest one tenth of what they have spent and guarantee our oil requirements for the next fifteen years. Saudi Arabia has the largest reserves and wants to maximize the value of those reserves ever mindful that if or when viable energy alternatives are found the value of their reserves will decrease dramatically. We can help them achieve their goals."

"But," Zeng said, "Saudi Arabia will probably not be able to meet our sourcing objectives and those of the Americans at the same time, which could lead to conflict."

"Ju, the Americans have always been intrigued by Cervantes' *Don Quixote*, in search of the impossible dream, unreachable stars, and the like. They are idealists at the expense of practicality. Their recent behavior in Iraq continues this pattern, yet we have much to thank them for. Their defeat of the Japanese freed us from a long-term enemy in 1945. It was their President Nixon who came here extolling the virtues of capitalism, and we have progressed to the point of nearly surpassing the teacher. Now their war on terror, if successful, will rid the world of much instability that is injurious to conducting business. Ironically, after Japan invaded our country, it was America that cut off Japan's supply of oil leading to Japan's attack on Pearl Harbor. Our new navy needs to be able to protect our shipping lanes even from our 'friends.'

"The Americans have made several attempts to improve relations with us, yet each time they begin by criticizing our form of government and what they claim to be our 'human rights' violations. First they insult us and then they make rectifying the insults a condition of partnership. It seems they will only be content when the entire world embraces an ideology forged in their own image.

"Without the discovery of a practical alternative, oil will be the cause of our next conflict. We must be prepared. This means establishing an assured supply. On the other hand, if we are to believe the amount of oil the world has in reserves, it could be a long time before we run out of it, forestalling a potential conflict."

"Sir," Zeng offered, "I met briefly with the Saudi oil minister recently. I will begin a discussion to line them up as a secure provider. There is, however, something you should be aware of when thinking about how much time we and the rest of the world have before we run out of oil, something I learned from my trip to the Geneva energy conference. We will never completely run out of oil, instead, it will get prohibitively expensive to extract and that point will come much sooner than most people think, a phenomenon that is being discussed as 'Peak Oil.'"

"Ju, let's have lunch and then tell me what you know about this Peak Oil."

Chapter 5.
Peak Oil

Professor Jason Davidson's notoriety as a NASA mission specialist had provided the credentials to teach at a number of universities. After his flight and the completion of interminable reports documenting his results on "The Effects of Altitude on Solar Energy Density," he was recruited by five different schools to take visiting professorships focused on energy. The University of South Florida was an easy choice. He'd been a professor of electrical engineering there prior to his Atlantis mission. He'd be setting up the first "Energy Studies" curriculum in the state of Florida. He wouldn't have to move, and perhaps best of all, USF would provide him a rent-free apartment in the Magnolia complex on campus. He'd have a "walking commute" during the school week and could use his beach house in Sarasota as a weekend getaway.

Davidson had come quite a distance from his roots in Moline, Illinois. His father was a very successful nuclear engineer and plant manager of the Quad Cities nuclear power plant just north of Moline, a good-size city just across the river from the larger city of Davenport, Iowa. In Jason's case, the acorn didn't fall far from the tree. His father's engineering background and ham radio interests meant that Jason had access to a lot of technology at home. He had obtained his ham radio license at the age of thirteen and fixed televisions and radios as a hobby. Yet for some reason he gravitated toward appliances, dismantling and then reassembling them to see how they worked.

His favorite appliance was the microwave oven his father brought home one Christmas: an Amana "Radarange." Jason had been reading about radar systems and their inner workings. The arrival of the Radarange was timely. He was especially intrigued by the magnetron tube, the source of radiation for both a radar system and his mother's new oven. He snuck up late that evening, and with the help of his brother—the Radarange weighed over one hundred pounds—brought the device into his basement workshop. There he proceeded to dismantle the oven to gain access to the magnetron tube. By the next morning, when his father was going to demonstrate cooking eggs electronically, the Radarange had gone missing, and so had Jason. His dad knew where to start looking.

When his parents came down to the dimly lit basement, Jason was "conducting" a mythical orchestra, waving two long neon bulbs, glowing brightly in the presence of the unshielded radiation, free from electrical connections.

"Son, can I ask what in the *hell* you're doing?" he asked.

"There was an article in *Mechanics Illustrated* about how neon gas will fluoresce in the presence of electromagnetic radiation."

"Can you translate that into English?" his mom requested.

"Yeah, I can get these neon bulbs to glow by passing them in front of a radar set, and your new microwave oven has all the components I needed. Isn't this cool!"

His dad wasn't amused. "Is that what's left of our microwave oven on your bench over there? Why did you have to take it apart?" It was becoming clear that he didn't appreciate the scientific value of this experiment.

"Well, Dad," Jason explained, "for safety reasons, the oven's case shields us from the radiation, and I had to expose the magnetron tube to get these bulbs to glow."

"So you're telling me that this is dangerous!"

"Actually, only if we're exposed for a long time, and then they say it *could* cause sterilization. The studies haven't been conclusive."

"Jesus Christ! I'm getting the hell out of here, and so should you. Put that oven back together right now so I can get breakfast started," he said as he escorted Jason's mom upstairs. She tried to hide it, but Jason caught her chuckling to herself.

Jason's inquisitiveness led him to focus his high school years on the sciences, with emphasis on mathematics and physics. Excelling in these classes as a freshman allowed him to take the advanced versions in subsequent years.

Upon graduation, Jason had the urge to strike out on his own. His mom was apprehensive, his dad didn't object. Passing the local Air Force recruiting office one day, he was enticed by the opportunity to travel and by all the electronics he could get his hands on. He spent the first year of his enlistment learning airborne Electronic Counter Measures (ECM) technology and the next three applying that knowledge to B-52s on a SAC base. Upon discharge, he had saved a considerable amount of money, and with the GI bill, could afford to go to college.

His selection of a college was narrowed to those specializing in science and engineering, settling on the University of Illinois at Champaign-Urbana where he received his master's degree in Electrical Engineering and Computer Science. The U of I was a logical choice; the university was highly regarded among engineering schools and close enough to home for a weekend commute, yet far enough to allow the feeling of independence—something appreciated by both Jason and his father.

After graduation, Jason was recruited by Bell Laboratories, where he worked for almost twelve years, the first two spent at Stanford getting his PhD, courtesy of the company. Twelve years made for a long apprenticeship, but working at one of the world's premier research institutes gave him a computer engineering education unequaled anywhere in the world. The time also taught him something about business and risk versus reward. While Bell Labs gave him exposure to all the latest technology, it didn't afford him an opportunity to make a lot of money—a good living, but not a lot of money.

It took considerable mental and emotional effort to leave Bell Labs, but Silicon Valley was calling and Jason was bitten by the entrepreneurial bug. The go-go years in California presented him with opportunities that were unimaginable elsewhere. He had become a technology mercenary. When the money was in electronics, he started a small personal computer peripherals company that was acquired by IBM a few years later. When the Japanese and their Asian neighbors commoditized the hardware components business, the money shifted to software, and he shifted with it.

But the Internet, with its nearly unlimited cheap bandwidth, allowed China and India to commoditize software with developers who would work for less than a dollar an hour. They received requirements from the U.S. and shipped finished software back, all at the speed of light through an undersea fiber-optic cable. Commoditization meant Jason needed to find a new technology interest and he began to ponder, "What's next?"

His series of successful startup experiences, where stock options and equity were more important than salary, left Jason in a position of financial independence at an early age. A position that allowed him to do the kind of work he enjoyed without being overly concerned with income. It was time to give something back and Jason felt it should be through teaching, while researching his next business opportunity.

* * *

Jason was deep in thought at 10:00 AM as he left the USF Library for the short walk to the Engineering Teaching Auditorium.

"Professor Davidson," came a voice trailing from behind.

No response.

"Professor Davidson," more persistent this time, and louder.

"Yes," Jason said out loud, almost to himself, not conscious who was calling. After a few more steps that his inertia took him, he stopped and turned to look back.

"Professor Davidson, can I walk with you to your ten o'clock lecture?"

"Of course, Rebecca, I'm sorry," he said looking at his watch. "I was deep in thought and I'm...actually *we're* late for class, young lady."

Rebecca Stevens was one of the bright bulbs in Jason's Energy Studies course. A chemical engineering major, Rebecca—she liked to be called Becky, but Jason would never allow himself that level of familiarity—was one of those rare individuals who had defied the odds. In Jason's experience, at a certain level of engineering study only 10 percent of most classes were women. But those making it that far were usually near the top of their class. Rebecca was one of them.

She was also the class flirt. She sat in the front row and made sure she got his attention by participating in his class more than most students.

He was embarrassed that he'd been spotted running late to his own lecture. But he was easy to recognize: chino pants, a long-sleeve white shirt open at the collar, a comfortable pair of hushpuppies that felt more like slippers than shoes, and an old herringbone sport coat with leather patches on the elbows. He wore the jacket on cool mornings and would carry it the rest of the day. It had a *professorial* look to it.

Letting Rebecca catch up and end her cell phone call, Jason said, "Let's pick up the pace, I hope I haven't lost any people who might have given up on me today. I think they're supposed to allow ten minutes of leeway, I hope that applies to visiting professors as well."

Entering late was always easier when you had a student in tow. There was a chance the others might assume you'd been counseling and be more inclined to accept a late arrival. When Jason and Rebecca entered the hall through the large double doors in the back, he wasn't sure what he'd find. They hadn't passed anyone leaving, which was a good sign.

The room was packed. Looking a bit sheepish, he made his way to the podium on stage as Rebecca took her seat in the first row where she joined the entire standing-room audience on their feet to sing "Happy Birthday." Jason never liked such outbursts. It was apparent from Rebecca's smile that she'd been sent to find him when he hadn't appeared, explaining the cell call she had completed to alert the class.

"Thank you. And thank you for celebrating the fact that I have one less year left on earth," he said with a fake sneer. "But seriously, this is very nice. Where's my cake?" A laugh from the students broke the ice.

Jason loved this lecture hall. The podium was designed to allow presenters to connect their laptop to the AV system, projecting their small screens onto a twenty-foot theater screen. It also provided an Internet connection to reference information on the Web, a feature that could be dangerous as Jason had found out firsthand.

During one of his lectures, he had forgotten to disable his Instant Messenger software. As he was addressing the audience with his back to the screen, a wave of snickering swept through the crowd, building to full-scale laughter. His first thought was to check his fly as inconspicuously as possible. A dangling zipper wasn't outside the realm of possibility—it had happened once before. He then glanced back at the screen to see a *very* personal message from Jill Roberts, a professor of Journalism at USF and his girlfriend of three years. The message, detailing their sexual calisthenics the previous evening, hung in space for the class to study. From that day on, he made sure to disable automatic launching of Instant Messenger.

"Okay, let's get started," he said. "How many of you believe the earth is flat?" Jason often started his lecture with an attention-getter. The class went quiet followed by a wave of laughter that swept the room. There were no takers.

"I was hoping at least one of you was a member of the Flat Earth Society and could convince the rest of us the earth really is flat. Too bad. Only then would we have a mathematical argument for an infinite supply of oil. Because the earth isn't flat, today we'll be discussing something called 'Peak Oil,' a recent focus in the oil industry that's become a hot topic.

"This course is entitled Energy Studies and as the syllabus says we will discuss all forms of energy, from fossil fuels to renewables. We've been spending more time on oil than I anticipated at the beginning of the year, but with the cost of oil hovering above ninety dollars a barrel it's probably justified.

"Before we jump into Peak Oil, let's review where we stand. This country currently consumes twenty million barrels of oil per day, about 25 percent of the world's total consumption, far more than any other country. China is second, consuming over six million barrels per day and they're gaining rapidly. Keep in mind they have almost five times as many people as we have in the United States, so we can expect a large increase in their demand as they embrace capitalism.

"Our current domestic production of oil is about 7.4 million barrels per day, which says we import about 60 percent from other countries to make up the shortfall. More than half of that comes from the Middle East, and Central and South America.

"Something else we need to look at is refinery capacity. Our current capacity is about seventeen million barrels per day. Another constant to keep in mind is that a forty-two-gallon barrel of oil can only yield about twenty gallons of gasoline. Said another way, only 48 percent of a barrel of oil can be converted into gasoline."

"Professor," Rebecca's hand shot up in a way that couldn't be ignored. Her bare midriff rose dangerously high as she raised her hand. "We're using twenty million barrels of oil a day and can refine only seventeen million barrels a day into gasoline. How are we making up the difference?"

"Good question, Rebecca. We're importing over a million barrels of refined gasoline per day primarily from Europe where they have the technology to create the sophisticated, expensive blends we require. We haven't built an oil refinery since 1976, primarily because the price of gasoline has been artificially low for a long time. With higher prices here to stay, it will become viable for oil companies to think about adding refinery capacity. Unfortunately, there are long lead times involved.

"Now let's look at reserves. First, I'll tell you that any discussion of oil reserves and relative reserves is suspect. And the data that follows will illustrate why. Be that as it may, the U.S. is *believed* to have about thirty billion barrels of reserves which is only 2.5 percent of the world total. So here we are: 5 percent of the world's population using 25 percent of the world's energy with only 2.5 percent of the reserves. That in itself is a forecast for disaster. It appears we'll be importing oil for a long time, doesn't it?"

"Professor," a hand shot up in the back.

"Yes, Rafi." It was nice to have a "shill" in the crowd who would ask questions. Sometimes that was all the class needed to trigger a good discussion.

"What about new oil field discoveries? I've read about the Arctic National Wildlife Refuge in Alaska that's supposed to have billions of barrels of oil in reserve. Could finds like that have a significant impact on proven reserves?"

"The press calls it ANWR," Jason answered, "since we need an acronym for everything. ANWR is 1.5 million acres of unspoiled land on Alaska's North Slope. Obviously, any additional oil finds will delay our day of reckoning, but we need to look at that quantitatively. The studies I've seen by proponents of ANWR indicate it will take ten years to bring those fields on line. When they do, they will produce about one million barrels a day for twenty to thirty years—and this is from the *proponents* of the plan. Other estimates are as low a 600,000 barrels per day. Remember, we're already consuming twenty million barrels a day and that number is projected to reach thirty million in the ten years it would take to get ANWR into production. This means we would be destroying one of the last major wildlife refuges in the northern hemisphere to provide just 3 percent of our oil production. Does anyone in the room think that's a good idea?"

A buzz of discussion followed, but no one made an attempt to answer directly. Davidson waited a few moments to let the question sink in and then repeated the challenge. "Seriously— and don't be afraid to voice your opinion even if you don't think it's the popular one. Does anyone now think ANWR is a good idea?"

More silence and some whispering followed, "Okay, I rest my case," he said.

"Professor," Rafi said. "I've got one more question. I've been doing some quick calculations. If the world has 1,150 billion barrels of oil in reserve and we're using it at the rate of eighty million barrels per day, doesn't that mean we have almost forty years worth of oil remaining?"

"Good question, Rafi," Jason responded. "By the way, class, if you really want to scare yourself with that eighty million barrels per day number, just convert that to seconds and you will see the world is using almost one thousand barrels of oil *per second!*

"Rafi, I wish we had forty years of oil left. There are two things we have yet to consider, the quality of the reserve estimates and the concept of Peak Oil. Let's talk about the estimates first and look at some numbers," Jason said as he put up his first PowerPoint slide.

Year	Abu Dhabi	Dubai	Iran	Iraq	Kuwait	Saudi Arabia*	Venezuela	Spurious Amount
1980	28.00	1.40	58.00	31.00	65.40	163.35	17.87	0
1981	29.00	1.40	57.50	30.00	65.90	165.00	17.95	0
1982	30.60	1.27	57.00	29.70	64.48	164.60	20.30	0
1983	30.51	1.44	55.31	*41.00?*	64.23	162.40	21.50	*11.3*
1984	30.40	1.44	51.00	43.00	63.90	166.00	24.85	0
1985	30.50	1.44	48.50	44.50	*90.00?*	169.00	25.85	*26.1*
1986	31.00	1.40	47.88	44.11	89.77	168.80	25.59	0
1987	31.00	1.35	48.80	47.10	91.92	166.57	25.00	0
1988	*92.21?*	*4.00?*	*92.85?*	*100.00?*	91.92	166.98	*56.30?*	*192.11*
1989	92.21	4.00	92.85	100.00	91.92	169.97	58.08	0
1990	92.00	4.00	93.00	100.00	95.00	*258.00??*	59.00	*88.3*

TOTALS: Declared Reserves for above Nations (1990) = 701.00 Gb - Spurious Claims = 317.54 Gb

data from Dr. Colin Campbell, in SunWorld

In the above table, the bold italicized numbers are considered spurious reserve claims. Also curious are the instances of reserves remaining identical over a period of years, despite intensive production. It can be seen that fully 45% of all the above reserve claims are questionable - even neglecting repeatedly unchanged reserve data.

"What you'll find is that there are no standards for reporting reserves, it's left to each country to define their own. This slide shows the historically reported reserves of the major oil producers in the Middle East. Looking at this table, there are two reasons to suspect its accuracy. The first is that each country at some point has dramatically raised the amount of their reserves. In 1988 Iran doubled their reported reserves. In 1990 Saudi Arabia, already the country with the largest reserves of 170 billion barrels increased their report by 52 percent. The second issue is that for many reported years reserves have *never decreased* even though these countries have been pumping oil out of the ground like mad.

"It's believed that some of the uncertainty in OPEC country reserves stems from the fact that OPEC regulates production of its members based on their proven reserves. By inflating those reserves, countries would be allowed to produce more oil, and so they did.

"This leads to the only conclusion we can draw: No one *really* knows how much oil the world has in reserves, which is critically important to the topic of Peak Oil.

"The concept behind Peak Oil is that once you have depleted half the oil in a given oil field, the next barrel extracted will be more expensive than the previous barrel until you ultimately get to the point that the energy it takes to extract a barrel of oil from a field is equal to or greater than the energy in a barrel of oil. At that point there's a net energy loss. In practice, the point at which it becomes *economically* prohibitive comes well before that.

"This is probably worth a demonstration. First, I'll need an assistant from the audience."

Even in college, most people were afraid to be singled out, tending to look the other way, which made them all the more apparent. He was hoping someone else would come forward, but of course, Rebecca raised her hand.

"Yes, Rebecca Stevens—come on down!"

"Okay, Professor, what can I do?" she asked, bouncing down the stairs while looking directly into his eyes.

He hesitated for a moment. "I have here an accurate 100 ml graduated cylinder filled with water to the 50 ml line. This water will represent oil in our experiment. Over here I have a plain household sponge sitting in a shallow pan. The sponge is very dry would you say?"

"Yes, Professor."

"We're going to let the sponge represent an oil field. Now I'm going to pour all 50 ml of water into the sponge, and as you can see the vast majority of the water is being held by the sponge, the pan beneath is slightly damp underneath the sponge, but would you agree that our 'oil field' now holds essentially 50 ml of 'oil?'"

"I would."

"Okay, I'm going to take this funnel and place it inside the opening of the cylinder and ask Rebecca to pick up the sponge, being careful not to lose any 'oil.' Now, Rebecca, please apply the *minimum* pressure to the sponge that results in one half, or in this case 25 ml of water, to return to the cylinder."

Rebecca carefully held the sponge until she positioned it over the funnel, and then gently squeezed it until the water came to the 25 ml mark. "There, Professor."

"Thank you, Rebecca, please continue holding the sponge, and tell us, how much pressure, qualitatively speaking, did you apply to return the first 25 ml to the cylinder."

"Actually, very little."

"Good, let's return half of what remains in the sponge, or an additional 12.5 ml, to the cylinder."

Rebecca needed to fold the sponge in half to better squeeze the last 2 ml to get to the 37.5 ml mark on the cylinder. "Okay, Professor."

"And this time, how much pressure did you need to apply, Rebecca?"

"Quite a bit, especially to get the last 2 ml into the cylinder."

"So we should be left with the remaining 12.5 ml in our oil field. Let's see how much we can get back."

With this, Rebecca squeezed as hard as she could over the funnel without losing any water and got the level up to the 47 ml mark. "Now, how difficult was that?"

"Very difficult, Professor," she said.

"Thank you, Rebecca, you can take your seat."

She did, giving him a smile over her shoulder as her eyes caught his.

"So you see," he said after a quick recovery, "getting the first half of the oil out of this field was quite easy, getting the next half quite difficult, and getting all of it was impossible.

"The term Peak Oil was first introduced by M. King Hubbert, Chief Consultant with Shell Oil in a seminal paper entitled 'Nuclear Energies and the Fossil Fuels,' presented at a meeting of the American Petroleum Institute in 1956. Although the title is fairly generic, it was in that paper he invented what's become called the 'Hubbert Curve.' That curve describes the time-value production of a finite resource such as coal or oil from which he produced the following graph that I've taken directly from Mr. Hubbert's paper."

Jason went to the next slide in his presentation.

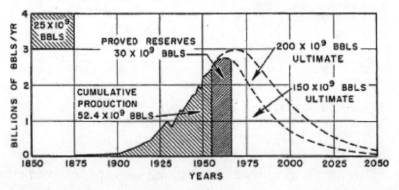

Figure 21 – Ultimate United States crude-oil production based on assumed initial reserves of 150 and 200 billion barrels.

"This figure shows U.S. production over time, with actual production up to the date of the presentation in 1956. From that point, Mr. Hubbert forecast the remaining curve for the proven reserves of thirty billion barrels and assumed 'ultimate' reserves as indicated by the dashed lines. The important part of this curve is the peak which occurs in the 1970 timeframe. At the time the paper was published, many people in the industry felt it was just a fringe theory; we would keep discovering oil in this country. These were probably the same people who believed the earth was flat. By 1990, the industry was no longer considering the Hubbert Curve a theory. Based on empirical data, the peak occurred right where Mr. Hubbert predicted.

"Now let's look at *world* oil reserves."

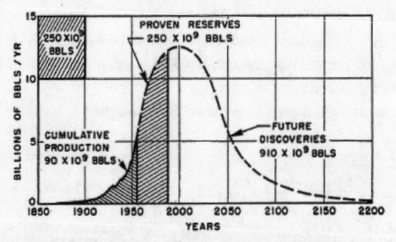

Figure 20 – Ultimate world crude-oil production based upon initial reserves of 1250 billion barrels.

"This figure, also directly out of the same paper, predicts oil production for the entire world based on individual country estimates. Mr. Hubbert's prediction was that Peak Oil for the world will occur in the year 2000 timeframe after which production would decline with a corresponding increase in cost for retrieving every additional barrel. Because we don't have enough history yet, we can't confirm his prediction. So the question is, can we tell when the peak has occurred without the benefit of hindsight, without waiting fourteen years as we did to confirm his Peak Oil curve for the U.S.?

"Since we can't accurately predict what the *ultimate* reserves are for the world, are there any metrics that we could be looking at to indicate when the peak occurs, any other observations that would help?"

Several hands shot up.

"Yes, John— John Byrnes, right up front."

"What about gas prices?" John asked.

"What about them? Where are you going with this?" Jason challenged.

"Gas prices are something we can monitor very easily. If we're not at the peak, I mean if we are *left* of the peak, then shouldn't gas prices come down because one of the gas companies will have more reserves and want to take market share from the others?"

"Excellent, that's the way it should work in a free market economy. The trouble with using gas prices is they're too far downstream and other factors could have an effect. For example, suppose we're refinery limited and not oil limited, and as we discussed, we *are* refinery limited since we already have to import refined gasoline products to meet present needs. In that case oil companies would be able to sell all the gasoline they had at the current price. Since none would have excess, there would be no incentive for one of them to lower the price since they couldn't supply more than they're currently providing. But you're on the right track.

"So let's focus on oil metrics. It used to be that OPEC would control prices by producing more oil when prices got too high. It was in their best long-term interests to do so since high oil prices would stimulate research into alternative fuels that would have the effect of sharply devaluing oil they hold in reserves. However, China and India are now consuming much of what used to be excess OPEC capacity. This means OPEC can't produce any faster, although they have much more they can produce in total. But their rate of production has maxed which would indicate they've reached Peak Oil. Of course, they'll never admit they can't step up production and will say consuming countries, especially the United States, don't have enough refining capacity and therefore producing more oil will not lower gasoline prices.

"So the question is, how accurate is Mr. Hubbert's second prediction? He appears to have been correct about the U.S. Peak Oil period hitting in the 1970s, we have history to prove it. Let's watch those oil metrics and see if we can spot the peak for global oil. It may be sooner than we think. The thing to remember about Peak Oil is that while we'll always have oil in the ground, there comes a point where the cost of retrieval is more than the benefit of retrieval, which is why there will always be oil in the ground!"

"And what do you think will happen to oil prices when the global Peak Oil point is reached?" asked John.

"Well, the good news is OPEC will no longer control oil or oil prices. The bad news is that no one else will either, which is the same as saying there will be no OPEC-like monopoly on oil production. The resulting competition and its affect on prices for the expensive oil that remains is anyone's guess. Remember, Japan attacked Pearl Harbor primarily because we had frozen their assets here and embargoed their supply of oil five months earlier in retribution for their occupation of China. So we have an historical precedent that countries will go to war over oil. And we now have many more industrialized nations in competition for oil than we had back in the 1940s. There may well be a high cost for a critical, dwindling economic resource, a cost substantially more than money."

"In that case, shouldn't the government be funding more research like the work your CERC team is doing here?" Rebecca asked.

"Good question. You'd think so, wouldn't you? If our usage of oil was relegated to that of a feedstock for such things as lubricants and plastics, our demand would fall to about one million barrels per day! That would eliminate imports entirely and dramatically reduce the likelihood of future wars. And our friends in the Middle East would need to develop real economies based on other goods and services to survive."

Byrnes, who was also class clown, couldn't help himself, yelling over the noontime bell, "Perhaps they should go into the integrated circuits business—they have plenty of silicon!"

Chapter 6.
Motivation

It was 5:00 PM Saturday when Jason decided to call Bob Daniels. Daniels was a professor of computer science at USF and longtime associate. They had met at Jason's last startup and then worked together at NASA when Jason was mission specialist for the SOLAR flight. Daniels was Jason's chief of operations for the CERC team, and over the years served as self-appointed CERC historian.

"Hey, Bob, yesterday you mentioned that you needed a sixth player for poker tonight. You still have an opening?"

"What happened, *lover boy*, did Jill throw you out?" Daniels mocked.

"Actually, she got sick this morning. I've been taking care of her all day and she thinks I should air myself out. So in a way, she *has* thrown me out!"

"Sorry, man, I was just kidding. I hope she's feeling better. Yeah, I could still use one more player. Be here at seven-thirty. And bring your money, buddy, you're going to need it."

Daniels held a weekly poker game at his house on the beach every Saturday in recent memory. Jason had been a frequent player until Jill came along and changed his priorities. He took a lot of ribbing from Daniels, but it was all in good fun. It would be good to play again, to take his mind off of the problems they were having at CERC, not the least of which was funding. The enjoyment was leaking from his project like air from a retread tire.

It was a short ride from his apartment to Daniels' beach house and Jason arrived right at seven-thirty. The real enjoyment of these games was that the other four players had nothing to do with work or the university. Two of the guys were Daniels' neighbors. Another was Bill, a roofing contractor who had re-roofed Daniels' house, and the other was John, a fishing buddy who kept his boat in Daniels' marina.

The evening progressed as Jason had remembered. Lots of beer, periodic dirty jokes, and enough cigar smoke to force opening the back window facing the beach and the front door to get a breeze through. From the outside, it probably looked like the place was on fire. All of this with the TV on in the background adding nothing more to the game than white noise.

By one-thirty in the morning, the game was over. One of the neighbors and the fisherman had left a half-hour earlier complaining of their losses. Then Bill, the roofer, had to leave when his wife called him on his cell. His four-year-old had the flu and was vomiting all over the place. Time for dad to pitch in and let mom get some sleep. Three players weren't enough to sustain a good poker game so they all cashed in their chips.

As usual, Daniels was the big winner. He had been playing poker since the eighth grade and was skilled at keeping up a good line of chatter while not giving a hint as to what he was thinking or holding. He had a phenomenal mind and Jason was sure he had memorized all the odds on the specific five- and seven-card games they played.

After the other two had left, Jason offered to stick around and help clean up. "Hey Bob, where do you keep the shovel?" Jason asked, only slightly kidding. "I just folded up the table and you should see what's underneath!"

"In the garage, and I don't want to see," came the answer from the kitchen. "Actually, the shovel may not be a bad idea. If you find anything on the floor that's moving, you'll want to kill it first!"

After cleaning, Daniels opened another two beers from a refrigerator that seemed to contain an infinite supply. "Here you go, buddy," he said. "You don't need to be home right away I assume."

"No, I think Jill was concerned I could catch what she's got. There might be something going around. Bill's daughter may have the same thing. I gave Jill a call around eleven-thirty and she said she was doing okay."

"Good," Daniels said, "let's sit down and shoot the shit for a while. I'm still too awake to sleep."

"Sounds good, what's the topic?" Jason asked knowing it was going to be either sports or women.

"Work."

That caught Jason off guard. Normally, they didn't talk about work on weekends because they talked about it all week. It had never been officially agreed to, but there was an unwritten rule between them that work discussions were only held at work. Weekends were for refreshing the mind. "Sure, what's up?" Jason asked, somewhat concerned.

"You."

Now Jason *was* concerned. He knew he'd better let Daniels get out whatever he needed to say. "Go ahead. What about me?"

"I'm glad you could make it tonight. Something's been eating at me. Remember, I've had a few beers, so don't take this too personal."

"I have too, buddy. Thanks for the warning."

Daniels couldn't hold back. "The guys in the lab are starting to talk. They've begun feeling that you've become less connected to the work. Like you're drifting. They come to me with this shit and I do my best to assure them it's not true. But I've got to tell you, even I've noticed lately that you don't have the same intensity you had when we started. I don't want to let the team know that, but I'm not sure how long I can hold them. Is there something going on with Jill? You seem distracted, or less enthusiastic. Whatever it is, if our lab rats sense you aren't in this all the way, they'll find something else to do."

Jason was taken aback. He sat next to Daniels on the couch for several minutes, taking long draws on his beer, finishing it before talking. "Can I have another one?" he asked, holding up the empty Corona.

"Sure," Daniels said, knowing it would loosen him up.

While Daniels went to his never-ending supply, Jason had time to absorb what he had just been told. It wasn't good. He took time to think before answering.

"Look, Bob," Jason said as Daniels returned with a fresh longneck, "I have my ups and downs like everyone else. I assure you it has nothing to do with Jill. She's one of the high points in my life that keep me going. You and I have been at this for three years and I'm sure I don't always have the intensity I had when we started."

"Yeah, man, but recently, you're down a lot more than up! It's concerning to me, both for the team, and personally. If you're not really into finishing the system, I've got to find something else to do. I'm not getting any younger. You've got to realize that the team feeds off of you—and not just for ideas, but for energy… the human kind."

Again there was a pause while Jason thought about a response. "Wow, this has caught me by surprise. I have to be honest with you, Bob, because you'd know if I wasn't. Now that you've made me think about it, I *have* been down. I try not to show it, but apparently I'm not doing a very good job at that either. Our investors have been all over me recently. I think it's natural when you add a new investor like we just did with National Oil. They start talking with our existing investors and stirring the pot. They ask why it's taking so long to get the results we've been talking about, which jolts our old investors even though they *know* why it's taking so long."

"Look, Jason, those fuckers don't have a clue." Daniels was now starting to show the effects of a dozen Coronas. But the anger was real. He always became brave in this condition and Jason appreciated the candor. "All they care about is the dollars. They don't have the foggiest fucking idea what our technology really does or how hard it is to solve the problems we've already solved. I'm surprised they don't show up for meetings wearing their green eyeshades."

"You're right, but we can't expect them to understand the technology. By rights, they *should* be concerned about the dollars and the future of their investments. I know it sucks, but that's their reality. Our new investor, this 'Nat from National,' has been talking to Brad from DOE and now they want more details on the schedule. We have to admit, we've had to slip our projections."

"But how the hell do you forecast breakthroughs?" Daniels asked rhetorically. "It's not like we're building something that's been built before."

"I know. It's discouraging, but that's *our* reality." Jason said, stopping to look at his watch. "Man, look at the time. Holy cow, it's two-thirty. I need to take a leak. You know why beer runs through you so fast?" He thought he would try to lighten up what had become a somber mood as he headed toward the bathroom.

"No, but I'm sure you're going to tell me," was Daniels response with attitude.

"Because after you drink it, it doesn't need to change color."

Daniels didn't respond. He had turned up the sound on the TV that had been running in the background all night.

"I said, it doesn't need to change color!" Jason repeated louder as he returned.

"Hey, boss, just because I didn't laugh, doesn't mean I didn't get it. Don't quit your day job."

That got them both laughing as they settled deeper into the couch. It was small relief. They had a problem at work, didn't have a solution, and the wind had come out of their sails. They didn't talk for a while, knowing what each was thinking wasn't good. They finished off their beers and got two fresh ones.

"Hey, look at that," Daniels said as he turned the volume up even louder. "That's the hurricane hitting Miami and working its way up the coast. Seems to be the east coast's turn this year. We're up to the letter 'Z,' they're calling this one Zelda. Those CNN guys are nuts to be out in it."

"Winds are now 140 miles per hour, which makes it a category four," Jason said as he watched the read-out that CNN posted in the lower right-hand corner. "Some day one of the guys they stick out there is going to get hit with a section of metal roof flying by, and *he* will become a bigger story than the hurricane."

"Yeah, or maybe a *shorter* story," Daniels said with a grisly smile. "How many times do they need to show these things? We now have four or five every year. In fact," Daniels joked, "they could just run a tape of one from last year, and we wouldn't know the difference."

"You're right," Jason laughed, "it's amazing they continue to risk their lives like this. Let's see what else is on, we've seen enough hurricanes."

Daniels switched to Fox News and they were showing a tape of a special that had aired earlier in the day. "This is their special on pollution. I saw it advertised," Daniels said. "Our atmospheric CO_2 is creeping above 700 parts per million. They say this is enough to warm the ocean currents near the equator that are causing the hurricanes. Think there's any truth to that?"

"You know," Jason said, needing to roust himself from dozing off, "I've heard lots of debate from a number of guys who specialize in climate, and they don't agree. Some believe it's what you just said, others think hurricanes are a response to some cyclical thirty-year pattern, not CO_2 levels. There is one thing that seems to be in agreement."

"What's that?"

"No one has found any good coming from increased CO_2. I just hope we have enough time to solve the problem before we kill ourselves—another reason we need to finish our work. Let's turn back to CNN, watching hurricanes is more interesting. You want another beer?" Jason asked, headed for the kitchen with a bit of a wobble. "I'm going to have one more and then I should go."

"Sure," said Daniels, flipping channels.

When Jason returned, the hurricane was gone; perhaps CNN had gotten the message. They were showing a special that had also aired earlier on the care wounded Iraq War veterans were receiving. The correspondent was talking with one of the doctors as they walked through a ward at Walter Reed filled with GIs suffering from a variety of injuries. Periodically they would stop and talk to a soldier who was burned or had lost a leg. These were brave young men who had been through hell and would have a lot more to go through before they could return to the civilian world. *At least we're giving them the best medical care*, thought Jason.

As the camera continued its course, something interrupted Jason's eye. He'd had too many beers and didn't quite catch it, but there was something different about one of the GIs. He sat up to stir himself and began watching more intently, maybe there were others. There it was again. In the foreground that passed by too quickly was the image of a young girl lying on one of the beds. He was sure it was a girl—she stood out in a sea of bandaged men needing shaves like a Statue of Liberty.

"Bob," Jason said, "did you see that? There was a wounded girl on one of those beds."

"Yeah, I know. I saw some of this earlier today. There are a lot of female GIs who've been injured over there. If we keep watching, they'll interview some of them in a minute."

"Jesus Christ," Jason swore. "I knew we had girls over there, but I thought they were in support roles."

"I'm sure many are, but there are also quite a few in the field."

"So when did we decide it was a good idea to put our women into combat? I didn't vote for that, did you?" Jason's voice was getting louder, unable to control his anger.

75

"Of course not, but they've wanted equal opportunity for a long time. Look, Jason, you've had a lot to drink…"

"There she is again. They're going to interview her."

Her name was Carol Hendrick, Sergeant Carol Hendrick of the 1st Cavalry Division out of Fort Hood, Texas. CNN flashed it on the screen as the talking head approached to ask for an interview.

Jason could see her more closely now. His eyes filled. Some of it was the beer. He had consumed too much. But mostly it was the sight of a beautiful twenty-year-old soldier named Carol Hendrick. The contrast of her clear porcelain unmarked face against missing left arm and right leg was too much. She had gotten too close to a roadside bomb that now had a name. They were now called IEDs for Improvised Explosive Device. The military needed official names for everything. "Roadside Bomb" was way too descriptive. After all, "RB" could be confused with a well-known sandwich.

"Jesus Christ, Bob. This is sick. She's beautiful. I'm old enough to be her father. She has a father somewhere who must be absolutely devastated." *But probably thanking God right now that she's alive,* he thought. "Look at her. She should be going out on dates. Going to college. Having a career, getting married, having babies, she's just a kid for Christ sake! What the hell is going on?"

Daniels had never seen Jason like this. He knew the beer had something to do with it, but he'd never seen the man cry, and now *his* eyes started to water. Jason got up and started pacing.

"That is fucking it. I've had enough. *We* can put an end to this shit." Jason was past the beer and well into his adrenalin. "You wanted to talk about work, let's fucking talk about work. You want inspiration? We just saw it. We have two hurdles facing us, the first is hydrogen storage. We need to research the metal hydride solutions you were talking about the other day. Then there's the efficiency of our solar conversion. The best we seem to be able to get is about 15 percent. There's some new research on optical antenna technology that says we can get 80 percent. That would put us over the top, well over the top."

"Wow, where the hell have *you* been?" Daniels asked.

"Sleeping at the fucking switch I guess. Do you realize that this country is spending an enormous amount of money and the lives of people like Carol Hendrick on unsolvable symptoms to a solvable problem? We live in constant fear of terrorists, global warming, pollution, and energy shortages. It's like waking up in a damn Stephen King novel! What a bunch of dumb fucks we are! We have spent billions, *billions* on symptoms that have no solution while ignoring the problem that can be solved. And CERC is damned close to solving it! If we eliminate our dependence on their oil, those camel jockeys can just continue to kill each other for another thousand years. We can get our kids the hell out of there."

"Do you think we should pull out right away?" Daniels asked.

"I wish there was an 'undo' button we could push. Unfortunately certain conditions need to be met before we can leave."

"You mean the Iraqis would need to demonstrate they can control the situation first..." Daniels assumed.

"Actually, no. I mean certain conditions *here* need to be met! Our invasion was based on the false pretenses that Iraq had Weapons of Mass Destruction and strong ties to al Qaeda. Now, Iraq has become a haven for al Qaeda and terrorists themselves have become the WMD, which means they now have both— that's the hornets' nest we've created. Before we can leave we need to protect our borders, which are incredibly vulnerable to hornets. If we've learned anything from Iraq, it's that we can't win militarily because terrorism is an ideological war. Ironically, we can defeat terrorism without firing a damn shot, and that was just as true *before* the invasion as it is now. Driving the value of their oil to zero will take away their oxygen—their money. They'll have to form a functioning economy based on real goods and services, becoming productive members of the global society. And if not, they can go pound…fucking sand!"

Daniels waited a minute to make sure his boss was finished. "So let's divide and conquer," he said, clearly the more sober of the two.

"What do you mean?"

"Look, I'll work on the storage solution. I've been tracking that stuff anyway. You're the fucking antenna specialist. Why don't you get hold of the optical guys you were talking about? Let's divide up the team on Monday and set sail."

"You and your God-damned boating analogies," Jason laughed wiping the tears from his cheeks. "By God we're going to do this, and it's going to be for Carol Hendrick, *Sergeant* Carol Hendrick."

"Welcome back, boss."

"Thanks, Bob, I've been an ass. I need to get home. Have you seen my keys?"

"Hold on, Jason, do you know what time it is? You can't drive like this. If you get stopped they'll put you away for a long time. Put your feet up on the couch and go to sleep. I need to get to bed myself. We can finish cleaning up in the morning."

Daniels retired to his bedroom, but returned shortly to put away the mayonnaise he had left out. Jason was asleep. Moving quietly, Daniels could hear him mumbling. If there were words, the only ones he recognized were "lithium polymer," some kind of battery technology. He covered Jason with the light blanket he kept draped over the back of the couch for just such occasions. *Thank God for Sergeant Carol Hendrick.*

Chapter 7.
Board Meeting

The CERC offices were located in the basement of the Engineering Building on the USF campus. Three years before it was a godsend to have any space at all, but now the team was outgrowing the basement and Jason had his eye out for better quarters. He knew it was a pipedream, especially when his next round of funding was uncertain. His investors would never approve of paying rent, but he enjoyed looking anyway. *They love the idea of free space, but they don't have to work here.* Investors reveled in bragging about their lean startups. Financials always trumped operational efficiency, especially in pre-revenue days.

CERC office space included one large bullpen with ten desks. No cubes or even partitions, just desks. Around the periphery were three offices and a large conference room that had come to be called the "War Room." Any time a major problem was identified, the entire team would assemble there to work out solutions. It was not uncommon for such sessions to last twenty-four hours or more.

Jason had one of the offices, Bob Daniels another. The third housed the group's computer systems, which included a number of servers, an Internet gateway and local-area-network equipment. It also had a large air conditioner to keep all that equipment happy. The team called it the "Meat Locker" since some-one had seriously over-engineered the cooling capacity.

Jason and Daniels spent many hours every week in one or the other's office, both lined with whiteboards on three of the four walls. Most of the time they kept their doors open for a feeling of accessibility with the team and to allow what little air was circulating in the basement to reach them. They had a plan to bleed some of the excess air conditioning from the Meat Locker into the bullpen and their offices, but that was an unfunded project. They would need to acquire the ductwork and install it themselves under the cover of darkness to avoid a run-in with the school's unionized HVAC contractor.

After Elliot's death, CERC had disbanded for several months before Jason, in addition to accepting Elliot's position on the NASA SOLAR mission, agreed to step in and restart the team. His entrepreneurial background proved invaluable in positioning CERC in the energy research field and raising a significant amount of funding. He was also able to attract Bob Daniels as his chief of operations and essentially, his right hand man. The two were in sync about nearly everything, with one exception: Rafi Haddad. Rafi was the lead engineer inherited from Elliot's original team. Both felt he was an outstanding technical contributor, but Daniels had misgivings that he would only admit were "gut feelings."

Every six weeks Jason held a review meeting with investors, essentially a board meeting that included the U.S. Department of Energy, DOE, and National Oil, the largest oil company in the country. DOE had been an initial investor and provided the bulk of CERC funding. National Oil was a new investor that Jason had added three months earlier. He found it interesting an oil company would want to fund alternative energy research. On the other hand, it made sense if the company really believed viable alternatives to oil existed and wanted to keep abreast of such developments.

After making his usual visit to the student union and library, Jason was in his office by ten o'clock. His board meeting started at two and if it went like most, it would last until six, by which time his audience would be ready to call it a day. Jason and Daniels had four hours to update their slide presentations. Thank God for PowerPoint. Every six weeks they would start with a copy of their last presentations and update each slide to keep it current. Investors wanted to see all the financials of the operation including expenditures, cash in the bank, headcount, and hiring plans. With operational issues covered, they wanted to see the technical progress, where Jason typically spent the bulk of his prep time leaving the financial and admin update to Daniels.

Today's meeting would be more stressful than most. It had become clear at the last meeting that the CERC team would need another round of funding before it could ever produce revenue. The existing investors weren't making noises like they were interested in participating in another round, which would mean finding a third investor, something extremely unlikely without the clear support from the existing two. Davidson and Daniels needed to hit a homerun today.

Brad Spencer would be representing DOE. Brad had been the DOE contact when Jason first pitched CERC for funding over three years ago. Brad understood many of the technical details, was excited by the prospects of alternative energy, and was well connected in DOE. He was also important for the future of CERC since there could be several more years of research before his investment saw any significant breakthroughs. He seemed outwardly satisfied with their progress. Besides, keeping tabs on the work in Tampa was enjoyable, especially in the winter.

Nathan "Nat" Wood was the National Oil representative. Nat was the guy whom Jason had pitched six months before. CERC and the university wanted both industry and government investors. Besides National's money, Jason knew it was critical to get different perspectives on the results of their work. DOE was important for gathering additional funding and had visibility to other related government-funded projects. In National Oil, CERC had an energy industry leader who could advise along business lines that would never come from a government agency. This would be Nat's second meeting. Jason hoped he'd be excited by the ideas and anxious to report up his chain.

Nat was bringing a guest to this meeting, a lawyer by the name of Sandra Bilson. She was a principal in the consulting firm of Braddock and Bilson, a Washington, D.C. practice providing strategic consulting and lobbying services to National on retainer.

Through her activities Bilson had become something of an energy industry "talking head." Jason had seen some of her "Future Energy" press releases and wondered why a naysayer like her would be coming, if not to denigrate their work. Her public statements downplayed alternative energy as some form of science fiction, implying abundant oil would be around for the foreseeable future. *Maybe she's a member of the Flat Earth Society.* But it was Nat's prerogative and Jason would be cordial. Such was the reality of keeping investors happy, and Jason had plenty of experience. He knew that Bilson was there to help National decide on whether to invest in an additional round—or not.

At promptly two o'clock Jason's phone rang. It was his assistant, Emma, to say that Brad Spencer had arrived. Emma would escort most guests to the lab, but Brad had been there often enough to know his way around.

Jason stuck his head into Daniels' office. "Okay, Bob, Brad's here, I'm done with my slides. I'll stall him for a few minutes, then come join us in the War Room. Just save a copy of your slides on the server. I created a folder in the normal spot for this session."

"Just about finished," Daniels said, "although I could use a few minutes for clean-up. I'll join you as soon as I get these saved."

Brad entered the lab without knocking. He walked in acting like he owned the place, and in some respects, he did, at least the CERC portion. Everyone in the bullpen was ready. As usual, Jason had sent out an email several days earlier alerting the team to the board meeting. Dress code was not a big thing in university research and CERC was no different. For important visitors—and investors fit that category—Jason insisted on long pants, shoes and socks, and clean shirts. Of course, there were days when surprise visitors had an opportunity to see the latest fashion in cut-offs and sandals.

As usual, Brad was overdressed with expensive gray slacks, white shirt, and dark blue blazer. At least he had learned not to wear a tie. Ties were no longer *de rigueur*. Jason had a closet full of the damn things gathering dust. But even without the tie, Brad stood out. The engineers were polite but aloof to such guests. They were still young enough to respect knowledge over money.

Jason was in the conference room setting up the projector when Brad walked in. He looked up from his laptop.

"Hey, Brad, how you doing this afternoon?" Jason asked.

"Just fine, Professor, can I get you a cup of coffee out of the machine?" As an engineer, Jason was enamored by machines, but he also understood their limitations. Making coffee was one of them.

"You must have a death wish, I'll pass. Emma will have some of the real stuff when she brings Nat and his guest. First one here gets the good chair, and that's you today." Jason couldn't resist playing up his lack of resources.

"Jason," Brad replied, "before the rest of the team gets here, I think we should talk about your plans for another round of funding. Based on your current burn rate it looks like you have about nine months of cash remaining. Nat and I have been talking this week about trying to bring in a third investor to lead the next round. How would you feel about that?"

Not a good sign, but Jason knew this was coming. His current investors were getting cold feet when it came to another round of funding and wanted to draw in fresh blood.

"You've been doing your homework," he said. "I'd like to have that discussion at the end of today's session."

"Sure."

"Hey, Brad, how are you today?" Bob Daniels asked as he joined the two in the conference room, which quickly stifled the funding discussion. Daniels was aware of the funding issues but neither Jason nor Brad wanted team members dwelling on them.

"How's the resident rocket scientist this afternoon?" Brad called Daniels a "rocket scientist" because he'd been one for part of his career at NASA. He had a lot of respect for Daniels, which was one of the reasons Jason was able to get his grant from DOE. Raising money took more than a good idea and one smart guy, it took a good team and Daniels was an essential member.

"Doing well, we should have an interesting meeting. By the way, have you had an opportunity to meet the consultant Nat's bringing? We were introduced briefly in D.C. a few months ago."

"I have, Bob. Her office isn't too far from mine. I had an opportunity to meet her over dinner last week. We first talked about traveling down here together, but she had to meet with Nat in Houston and will be coming with him."

"Is she as attractive as I remember?" asked Bob with a boyish look. He had never married and was known around campus as having an eye for the ladies.

"Bob, you have a one-track mind. The good news: she *is* attractive. The bad news—for you anyway—is that she's engaged to a CIA agent and will be married in two months. A *big* CIA agent I met at dinner."

"Thanks for the warning."

Emma entered the lab followed by Nathan Wood and his consultant. Emma was pushing a cart with a large urn of coffee along with donuts and cookies. She proceeded to wheel the cart into the conference room, plug in the coffee urn, and set out the refreshments.

"Emma, thank you very much. I think you're too good for Jason," Brad said with a wink. "And if *you* ever start believing that, we could use you in Washington."

"Thank you, Mr. Spencer, it's my pleasure. Professor Davidson lets me know I'm appreciated.

"Brad," offered Daniels as Emma turned to go, "she'd never make it out of the parking lot. The team would let the air out of her tires before she had a chance to leave."

"Gentlemen," Nat Wood began, "let me introduce my guest. This is Sandra Bilson, our consultant and a principal in the firm of Braddock and Bilson. Sandra, this is Brad Spencer whom I think you've met from DOE; Professor Jason Davidson, the head of CERC; and Professor Bob Daniels, his right hand."

"Yes, hi, Brad. Hello, gentlemen," said Bilson.

The group got settled and started the small talk that always precedes meetings. This gave Jason an opportunity to take Sandra Bilson in and at one point caught himself staring. The little thumbnail picture of her attached to the end of each of the articles she'd published hadn't done her justice. This was an attractive lady, not just a smart one.

"Okay," said Jason when it appeared the small talk was tapering off. "I'd like to present the normal operations update so we have enough time at the end to provide you with our development progress. Bob will walk us through changes on the financial and admin side over the last six weeks. My presentation will focus on our technology progress and use some of the materials I'll be presenting at the International Energy Conference in California next week."

. Daniels slid the laptop and mouse over in front of him and presented the details on their burn rate, staffing levels, and the other proforma administrative information the board had come to expect. His last slide made it very clear the team had nine months of cash remaining.

When Bob was finished, Jason said, "I know there's interest in our plans for another round of funding. I'd like to hold off until the end of the meeting for that discussion. Let's take a fifteen-minute break to allow our investors to make some phone calls. I can tell there's some pent-up demand based on the number of times you've been looking at your Blackberries."

There was something insidious about those little email machines. Ever-present and always functional, they invariably distracted their owners from whatever they were supposed to be doing. It's a wonder anybody got anything done in a world of Blackberries and the context switching they caused. Jason refused to carry one. He had disciplined himself to process email twice a day using his laptop.

The break gave Bilson an opportunity to introduce herself more thoroughly. "Professor Davidson, it's a pleasure to see you again. I've seen your presentations at several seminars and read most of your articles. You're becoming known as one of the most prescient alternative energy proponents in the field."

"Thank you, Sandra, it's a pleasure to see you as well. I found it interesting we were able to attract Nat and National Oil as investors since our goal is to eliminate the need for fossil fuels. Your involvement piques my interests even further."

"Yes, Professor, I've been asked to get involved in their strategic planning. National Oil is smart enough to know that at a minimum they need to stay abreast of alternative energy progress. Ultimately they may want to shift more investment to alternative energy programs, which is insightful on their part. My job is to help guide them as to what's real and what isn't, along with realistic timeframes."

Nice words, Jason thought, *National may have other investments in mind. She's looking for ways to give us the axe.* "Very good, I hope you're able to get what you came for. Feel free to interrupt during our presentations if you need more information." He was actually pessimistic about how open-minded National would be when it came to alternative energy, and suspected their real goal was to track progress to see how they could combat it. Having National Oil on the board of investors was a risk, but the project needed a devil's advocate in addition to a devil's funding.

The participants began drifting back into the conference room and took their places.

"I'd like to get started on our development progress," said Jason. "I have only one requirement before I do—that all Blackberries get turned off. We need your complete attention and experience shows when your Blackberry is vibrating in your pants it's hard to concentrate." That got a smile from the audience, with Bilson turning a slight shade of red. "We have some important results to share with you and I can't compete with those damn things!"

Brad and Nat glanced at each other indicating they couldn't imagine functioning without their toys, yet they did as Jason asked.

"Thank you. Now I'm going to put up a slide we'll use the rest of the afternoon."

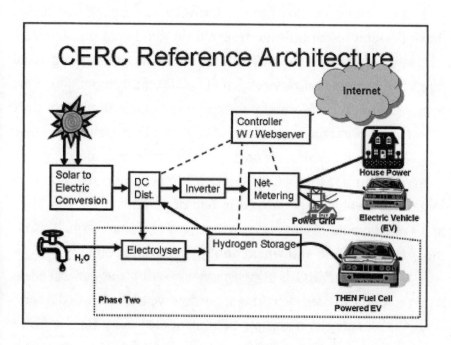

"This is what I'll be referring to as CERC's Reference Architecture, a concept taken from the software industry. Reference Architectures focus on the functional breakdown of a system and the interfaces between functional blocks. They include performance requirements of each component without going into implementation details. This provides isolation between each of the functional boxes in the picture, allowing different teams to focus on solving different problems. Since the interfaces between the boxes must remain the same, we can work on improving one component knowing the system as a whole still functions without requiring changes to the others. For the sake of Ms. Bilson, let me digress for just a moment. Brad and Nat, some of this will be a review." Glancing up, he received an acknowledging nod from both his sponsors.

"There are a number of universities and other research organizations involved in future energy studies, including the future use of oil and other fossil fuels. CERC and other organizations have decided to concentrate research on the use of non-fossil fuels, so-called renewable energy sources. Some of these organizations are focusing on bio-mass, wind, solar, and so on. There are many alternatives, too many for any one organization to explore effectively. If each organization were to explore each alternative, it's likely a practical solution to our future energy needs would never be found. Much of the work would be duplicated. So, most organizations have specialized in one or perhaps just a few alternatives. By pooling our information we can share which directions have promise and which don't. Divide and conquer.

"At USF, CERC is focused on exploring the general ideas laid out here. In overview, this slide says we are interested in pursuing solar energy for the production of electricity for the home and the generation of hydrogen as an energy storage medium for electric homes and electrically powered vehicles. Also important is what this slide says we are *not* doing. CERC is *not* exploring bio-mass, wind, or other potential forms of energy. Not that they don't show promise, but because others are exploring those approaches.

"So let's begin at the source of *all* our energy, the sun, and I mean that quite literally. It can be shown that all of the energy on and within the earth has been created directly or indirectly by the sun. During daylight hours, solar energy arrives at earth with a power density of 1.37 Kilowatts per Square Meter (KW/M^2). Of course this power is lessened by our atmosphere and has been measured between 0.8 and 1.1 KW/M^2 at the earth's surface. Since engineers like nice rules of thumb to remember such things, we'll use a convenient value for solar power density of 1 KW/M^2 in our calculations. What that says is when you consider the total surface area of the earth facing the sun at any point in time, we have an enormous amount of solar energy available to us. The problem, of course, is that this energy is diffuse, which drives to our conclusion that solar energy needs to be used or stored where it is gathered, or fed into the utility grid.

"Our first component here on the left," Jason said using his laser pointer, "is a device to convert the solar energy gathered into electricity. We're considering a number of alternatives that vary in cost, efficiency, and maintenance—which of course is another cost.

"Regardless of the conversion device chosen—and there could be multiple solutions here—the output is a direct current that is fed into a Direct Current (DC) Distribution device. This device gathers DC current from the solar panels, the Hydrogen Storage System, or both depending on how it's programmed, which I'll describe later. It then distributes that power to the Inverter, the Electrolyser, or both.

"Let's stay on the upper path to the Inverter. This device is used to convert direct current to 60 Hertz alternating current (AC), which is our standard in the U.S. That will allow us to use all of our existing electrical appliances and other devices in the home without modification. Other countries would need to convert to their local standard. For example, in the U.K. they run at 50 Hertz. These days you see inverters being used in cars all the time. They take 12 volts from the battery and convert that to 120V 60 Hertz power you can use to plug in a television or some other small appliance. These inverters typically have a maximum output of about 600 watts. The principle of our inverter is the same, it just handles 10 KW average and up to 60 KW peak, so it can be used to power the entire house."

"Professor," Bilson interrupted, "I thought we were here to discuss the creation and use of hydrogen as an alternative fuel? You seem to be taking us down a different path."

"Thank you, Sandra," Jason said, hoping no one saw his eyes roll. *She's starting already.* "We are indeed here to discuss hydrogen, but we need to take an indirect route for reasons which should become apparent. The path to a clean energy economy needs to be more than technical, it must be economical. Dealing with hydrogen has its challenges.

"The next functional component in our architecture is labeled 'net-metering.' This device will allow us to feed the power we generate to the home, to the power grid, or both. It also allows energy from the power grid to flow to the home when we've consumed all storage and are not generating solar electricity, for example, at night. Net-metering allows the homeowner to sell generated electricity to the local utility when excess solar power is available. It's called *net*-metering because at the end of the month, the customer's bill reflects the net amount of energy used. That could conceivably be a negative number meaning the utility would pay the customer for the excess—at lower rates, of course, than they charge. Approximately thirty states support some form of net-metering. Some require their power utilities to support it, and others just request that support. The fact that each state has its own program is something that probably needs to be addressed at the national level. Brad, perhaps that's something you could look into?"

"Sure, Jason, I wasn't aware of the diversity among states on this issue. I'll do some research," he volunteered.

"Jason, what about safety concerns?" Sandra asked. "If there was an outage on the grid, wouldn't it be dangerous for the crews to work on the lines when some homes would be generating potentially lethal current?"

"A good point," said Jason, worrying Bilson was going to try shooting down all their ideas. *Little Debbie Downer!* "I was going to defer the discussion about the control infrastructure, but your question raises a good issue. Let's address it now.

"The concern about homes generating lethal currents for maintenance crews has been considered. The box at the top of our drawing labeled 'Controller – With Webserver' is a dedicated computer that controls the entire system. It also contains a built-in *micro-webserver* allowing the system to be monitored and controlled remotely by both the homeowner and utility. There are two interfaces. One is a web browser interface providing a convenient user interface for control, and the other is a set of Web-Services for another computer to control certain aspects of the system programmatically. WebServices are a relatively new technology standard for machine-to-machine communications over the Internet with a security model allowing only authorized machines access. This technology enables the utility to isolate solar electricity generation with a computer cycling through all the homes in the affected area needing to be isolated. It then validates the connections have been broken. The electric utility industry calls this 'islanding.'"

"I think I've got it," said Sandra. "So basically what you're proposing is controlling a distributed power grid with an existing distributed information grid—the Internet."

"Correct. Sandra, I couldn't have said it better," smiled Jason, surprised at what appeared to be Bilson's now-genuine enthusiasm.

"So let's move to the next layer in the architecture," he continued. "The hydrogen layer. As you can see on the left, we begin with water. Our Reference Architecture stresses a renewable approach front to back. Most of earth's elements contain hydrogen and there are many ways to extract it. Some sources of hydrogen, like natural gas, involve the use of hydrocarbons that pollute the atmosphere, a perverse way to produce hydrogen that doesn't provide a renewable cycle. We won't go there. By starting with water we only have oxygen as a byproduct and that's not a bad thing. Remember, oxygen is what green plants generate. Good old H-2-O is fed into our Electrolyser where we provide a DC current derived from our solar panels. The Electrolyser separates the hydrogen and oxygen, routing the hydrogen to the storage system and letting the oxygen escape. Later, when the fuel cell combines hydrogen and oxygen to generate electricity, the byproduct is water, which completes the renewable cycle.

"The Hydrogen Storage system is monitored and controlled by the central controller. It has two outputs, one to the DC Distributor, and the other to a vehicle. The first connection is required when we have excess hydrogen stored and we choose to use some of it to power our house either during peak electrical usage, or at night, minimizing our reliance on the power grid. How much hydrogen we use for electricity generation is up to the homeowner and is regulated by parameters the user establishes with the controller. Of course the second output is used to fill the fuel cell of our car."

"But, Jason, don't hydrogen-powered cars have the 'chicken-and-egg' problem I read about?" asked Sandra. "Homeowners aren't willing to invest in expensive hydrogen generation until automakers produce fuel cell cars, and automakers aren't willing to invest in fuel cell cars until there are enough users who can afford them *and* have hydrogen fuel available."

"Exactly, Sandra. This is why we have an evolutionary approach for both the cars and the generation of hydrogen. The key to understanding this approach is to remember that there is no such thing as a fuel cell vehicle, or FCV. There are only electric vehicles and batteries. A fuel cell is just a form of battery.

"So as shown in Phase One, there is no hydrogen generation at all. The generated solar electricity powers the home and charges an electric vehicle that uses lithium-ion or lithium-polymer technology with a capacity of 100 KWH, enough to drive over four hundred miles on a charge. During peak production hours, excess electricity is transferred to the local utility via net-metering.

"In Phase Two, we introduce hydrogen generation via electrolysis with storage in fuel cells. These fuel cell batteries are used for both the home and vehicles, built from the same technology, which we'll discuss later."

"So we're talking about energy independence at the homeowner level," said Sandra. "Can we generate enough energy to support a home's electrical and transportation requirements?"

"Good timing, here's the next slide."

Home Energy Requirements

- Electrical
  - Average All-Electric Home Consumes 24,000 KWH per year or 2,000 KWH per month
- Vehicles
  - Assume 2 Cars Each Driven 14,000 miles/year
  - Average Electric Vehicle Gets 5 Miles/KWH
  - Total Miles/Month = 2,333
  - Energy Required = 2,333/5 = 466 KWH per month
- Total Requirement ~ 2,466 KWH per month

"Let's look at home energy requirements on a monthly basis. As you know, electrical energy is measured in kilowatt hours, or KWH—basically power consumed in kilowatts multiplied by the time you have consumed it measured in hours. If you look at your monthly electric bill you'll see you pay per KWH, and you can see exactly how much you used during the month. To put things in perspective, if you had a 100-Watt light bulb turned on for ten hours, you would have used 100 * 10 = 1,000 watt-hours, or said another way, 1 KWH. As we see on the slide, we assume the average all-electric home uses 24,000 KWH per year, or 2,000 KWH per month.

"Let's look at the energy required to power our vehicles for the month. We're assuming a family with two electric cars, each driven an average of fourteen thousand miles per year. The average electric vehicle can travel five miles per KWH of energy. The total miles driven in a month is 2,333. This means that we will need 466 KWH of energy every month to power our transportation.

"So if we total our electricity requirement and our vehicle fuel requirement this family needs about 2,500 KWH per month, rounding up to the nearest hundred. That naturally leads to the question: how much energy can this house generate? Let's look at the next slide."

Solar Energy Production

- Pure Solar Energy
  - Assume 1,000 SQ FT of Solar Cells
  - Assume Sun Collected 6 Hours per Day
  - 1,000 * 0.1 * 6 = 600 KWH per Day
  - 600 * 365 / 12 = 18,250 KWH per Month
- Factor in Efficiencies
  - 80% for Electrolyser
  - 10% for Affordable, High Volume PV
- Total = 18,250 * 0.8 * 0.1 ~ 1,500 KWH
  - Which means we would not even have enough energy to provide electricity to the home
  - Need to focus on Solar Conversion Efficiencies

"Let's start with pure solar energy collection, forgetting for a moment about energy conversion. We'll assume we have one thousand square feet of solar cells deployed on the roof of this house, a rather conservative size since on average more space would be available. It's a nice round number. Recall each square meter generates 1,000 watts, which works out to about 100 watts, or 0.1 KW of power for each square foot. We'll further assume we collect sun six hours per day, which means we collect 600 KWH of energy every day. Converting that to an average month, we multiply by 365 days and divide by twelve months to get 18,250 KWH per month.

"Good news! We only need 2,500 KWH and we're capturing 18,250—except we now need to take into account conversion efficiencies. Electrolysers can generate hydrogen from water at about 80 percent efficiency, but today's affordable mass-marketed Photo-Voltaic (PV) cells yield only about 10 percent. This is conservative, since many operate at 12 percent and *very* expensive 'Olympic silicon' can actually run at 25 to 30 percent. But we want to be conservative so we'll use the 10 percent number. This means our 18,250 KWH of pure solar energy ends up providing only about 1,500 KWH of usable energy every month, which is not even enough to provide electricity to the home, much less two vehicles."

"So, Jason, your architecture is off by a significant amount," Sandra injected—almost gleefully it seemed to Jason. "You would need solar panel efficiency of 20 to 30 percent."

"That's right, 'Houston, we have a problem'—pun intended for those from Houston," Jason said, smiling at Nat. "And the problem does lie in those conversion efficiencies. Electrolysers have been around for a long time and at 80 percent efficiency, there's not much left to be mined. That means we must turn our attention to solar conversion efficiency. Just 10 percent leaves a lot to be desired.

"Today Bob and I are prepared to discuss two major breakthroughs regarding hydrogen storage technology and solar conversion. We know we have enough solar energy striking the earth's surface to power our world. These two ideas are going to make that economically feasible."

Jason noticed that the room had suddenly become quiet. He wasn't sure whether they were on information overload or enthralled. In either case, they needed a break.

"I can see by the looks in your eyes you need to either get to your cell phones and Blackberries or you need a bathroom break. I need one too. I'll ask Emma to bring down a fresh pot of coffee. We'll reconvene in thirty minutes."

"Jason," Brad broke in, "this is exciting. I suspect we'll be going past our normal six o'clock time, and I'd like to spend some time with you afterwards. I need to make some calls and see if I can get a later flight."

"I'll be doing the same thing," said Sandra, "Brad and I are on the same flight back to D.C."

"I should do the same," offered Nat.

"Okay, Emma is on her way down and she can help get your tickets changed," Jason said, "I'll be back in thirty minutes."

Chapter 8.
Riyadh, Saudi Arabia

As the plane circled Riyadh's King Khaled International Airport, Zeng realized he would never get comfortable flying on government aircraft. He had not traveled outside his country in quite a while. Given China's rising status, most of the important people he met came to Beijing. Being on official government business usually meant having a security detail tagging along, but this time there were twice as many agents on board.

Zeng would be negotiating one of the most important relationships in which his country had ever been involved. To deflect suspicion, the meeting had been leaked to the press well in advance. It was touted as a routine high-level, minister-to-minister exchange in the ever-shrinking global society. Having the title of Foreign Minister allowed Zeng the cover of being able to discuss almost anything regarding foreign relations without putting a spotlight on oil. Avoiding the title of Oil Minister or Energy Minister was a stroke of genius—perhaps luck.

His plane touched down on a little-used high-security runway some distance from the others and a long way from any public access. At the far end of the runway he could see the line of Saudi security vehicles prepared to escort him. Zeng was concerned about what appeared to be more than normal security.

But in the capital of the largest petroleum producing country, what *was* normal?

When the wheels finally came to a complete stop, the doorway opened. The mechanical stairway was unhinged and lowered to the ground. Amenities, like jetways, didn't exist this far from the terminal. His entourage deplaned as they normally would: four of his security team went down first, followed by Zeng and then the last four. There to greet him on the tarmac was his host and friend, Sheik Abdul.

"Good morning, Mr. Minister," the sheik said as he extended his hand.

"Good morning, Sheik, and thank you for the fine reception."

"Not at all, a pleasant flight, I trust?"

"Just fine, Abdul, very pleasant."

As the two were talking, the sheik guided Zeng to his personal limo for what Zeng thought would be a long ride twenty miles south to the city. Instead, the car veered off to an even more secluded area of the airport grounds where a helicopter was waiting with rotors turning.

"I hope you don't mind riding in one of these," the sheik said, shouting over the turbines. "Some of our guests prefer to drive, but for security reasons we thought this would be both faster and safer. This helicopter shuttles back and forth between the airport and palace several times a day, enough to be practically invisible."

"Good idea," Zeng shouted back. Zeng was pleased with the setup for this trip. Publicly he was meeting with his host, the sheik, and it was billed as a generic get-acquainted session. In reality, these talks would include the sheik and Prince Faareh, brother of the king, one of forty brothers—and second in command. Everyone knew, with the king's approaching eighty-fifth birthday, the prince was being groomed to replace him and already had an enormous amount of power, certainly enough to do this deal.

What would have been a lengthy vehicle procession became a short flight. Looking down, Zeng was struck by the contrast. Most of the space between the airport and Riyadh was barren desert. Finally the city came into view. A true oasis, Riyadh erupted from the desert floor with tall buildings, wide streets, and six-lane freeways; home to over four million people. Zeng couldn't help think about what Riyadh would look like if it hadn't been for one simple fact: Saudi Arabia was literally floating on a sea of crude oil. Not just any crude, but some of the easiest to extract and cheapest to refine, which made it that much more valuable. It had been almost fifty years since oil was first pumped here and Zeng wondered if his hosts ever considered what life would be like without it. *Probably not, they have grown up in positions of privilege and wealth, knowing nothing else.*

The big Sikorsky arrived at the palace, stopping over the helipad closest to the building. It rotated 180 degrees and descended, first quickly, and then more slowly until the wheels touched down with a mild jolt. The engines had no sooner shut down than two palace security agents arrived at its side. They opened the door and escorted the sheik, Zeng, and his security team to the safety of the palace, all ducking under the still-thudding rotor.

In the lobby, Zeng's team was escorted to the security office where they would coordinate with palace guards. Zeng and the sheik went directly to the elevator, stopping at the second floor for their meeting in a relatively small, very well-appointed conference room directly across the hall from the elevator. Zeng thought the room could accommodate a dozen people, max.

After some small talk with Sheik Abdul, the prince finally entered the conference room in full robes and headdress. As Zeng stood, he realized the prince was a larger man than he'd expected and wondered if this might impact negotiations. Like most Chinese, Zeng was smaller in physical stature, but he'd never allowed that to get in his way.

"Prince Faareh," Abdul began, "this is Foreign Minister Zeng Ju of the People's Republic of China. Mr. Zeng, this is Prince Faareh." Apparently no additional title was necessary, none was offered. *"Prince" is probably enough*, Zeng thought.

"Mr. Zeng, it is a pleasure to meet you, I trust you have had a pleasant journey thus far," the prince said in near-perfect English.

"Your Highness, my trip has been very pleasant, thanks to the hospitality of the sheik. I bring you warm regards from President Wu."

"Thank you, Mr. Zeng. Convey my regards to your president on your return. Please be seated and we can get to the business at hand. The sheik has briefed me on your discussions," the prince said as he took his seat. "We are quite interested in hearing what you have to say."

"Thank you sir," Zeng responded. "It is important for me to mention at the outset that we believe our two countries will benefit from a strategic relationship, the nature of which needs to be kept in strictest confidence, of course. For appearances, this meeting is a general discussion with Sheik Abdul who has been instrumental in positioning these talks."

"Mr. Zeng, you will be glad to know the Saudi government, and myself specifically, keep all strategic discussions top secret."

"Thank you, sir, I was certain you would, but I wanted you to know that we understand the sensitivity of these discussions as well."

"Agreed."

"Your Highness," Zeng continued, "China has the second largest economy in the world, second only to the United States. Beyond that, we are the fastest growing major economy in the world. We grew at over 11 percent last year, over twice the rate of the United States and we estimate in ten to fifteen years we will overtake America and have the largest economy in the world. In a few short years we have already become recognized as a superpower, and in the next ten to fifteen years China will be *the* superpower."

"Mr. Zeng, I continuously monitor our place in the world along with the other countries we believe bear watching. China's economic performance has not escaped us. I concur with your assessment."

"Thank you, Prince. But as you know, to sustain such growth requires political stability, leadership, and natural resources. Chief among these resources is energy. Energy and political stability are not unrelated. A stable political environment is crucial to the motivation of my country's 1.5 billion citizens, and to maintain our growth will require a proportional increase in energy. We currently consume over six million barrels of oil per day, roughly one third the consumption of the United States. We are probably not as efficient in our use of that energy as we should be, and as our economy eventually levels off, we should become more efficient. However, at this point in our country's history, we need to focus on the growth our citizens have come to expect."

"An astute observation. Political stability relies heavily on setting and meeting the expectations of your people. Once they have experienced those expectations they will continue to set higher goals for you as well as themselves, a subject we understand fully. Although our population is a mere twenty-three million, what you say contains universal truth. Please continue."

"Thank you, Prince. We have been modeling our current oil usage and projecting future growth. We know we will need an assured supply of oil for at least the next fifteen years. My president has instructed me to find a source—or sources—who can guarantee a considerable volume of oil for that period of time. This has led to my discussions with the sheik, who graciously set up this meeting. We believe Saudi Arabia is the one country that can be a single source for our growing energy needs. If we are not able to strike a deal, we must seek similar talks with the other major producers."

"You have my attention, Mr. Zeng."

"Your Highness, my country would like to structure an arrangement to jointly develop new oil-producing projects in your country that would be used to meet our needs, and share in the proceeds of any excess. My goal for this visit is to either come away with an agreement in principle from which we can later develop an agreement in detail, or to come away with an understanding that no such agreement is possible while retaining friendly relations."

"Diplomatically stated. But to have even an agreement in principle would require some specificity. Developing new oil projects is costly and guaranteeing oil production could either be a good thing for our country or a bad thing depending on the price associated with that guarantee. Do you have any specifics you can provide within the context of an agreement in principle?"

"We have. I can present some basic parameters around which we can continue discussions."

"Basic parameters would be a start," said the prince glancing at his watch, "and I am glad you are prepared to present them. Unfortunately I have another commitment I must attend to and I would rather not go into your details until we have adequate time to do the discussion justice. I suggest the three of us continue this meeting over dinner at my residence. Would that work with your schedule, Mr. Zeng?"

Zeng was pleased he had the prince's attention, but had reservations about delaying the substance of the discussion to the evening since something of higher priority might supersede that meeting as well. "It would, sir," Zeng said with all the confidence he could gather, made easier since he had no alternative.

"Sheik Abdul, please escort Mr. Zeng and see that he has access to telephone, email, and anything else he needs prior to our dinner. Be at my residence at seven o'clock. And thank you for arranging this meeting."

"Very well, Your Highness," the sheik replied as the three men stood and shook hands.

Chapter 9.
Breakthrough

"**H**ow did we do on the flights?" Jason asked as his audience returned.

"Fine," Brad offered, "Sandra and I are on the ten o'clock; later than we would have liked, but certainly safe. We also had time to make some phone calls."

"I have a little less time," said Nat. "I'm at nine-thirty. Thank Emma for us, she's great."

"I'll do that," said Jason, "she knows the ropes." He reconnected his laptop to the projector and returned to the presentation in progress, taking a moment to gather himself.

"We should now have plenty of time to complete this review. Let's go back to our Reference Architecture, we were about to go into detail on two breakthroughs we've had in the last two months. The first has to do with the way we'll be storing the hydrogen we generate, the second is the way we see converting solar energy into electricity, a radically different approach for each. Bob Daniels has been focused on storage technologies so I'm going to turn this part of the presentation over to him."

"Thanks, Jason," Bob said as he again slid the laptop over to take the controls. "I'd like to start with a review of the various energy storage technologies we've been looking at, beginning with their energy densities as shown in this slide."

Energy Densities

Energy carrier	Density(KWH) by weight(lbs)	Density(KWH) by volume(gals)	Fuel tank size (gals)	Fuel tank weight (lbs)
H₂ Gas, 200 atmospheres	15.1	2.01	165	10
Liquid H₂, 20 degrees Kelvin	15.1	8.97	37	10
H₂ as metal hydride	0.26	12.1	28	1260
Natural gas, 20 MPa	6.3	9.80	34	52
Propane (liquid)	5.8	28.5	11.7	56
Methanol	2.5	16.8	20	130
Gasoline	5.8	33.3	10	58
Diesel fuel	5.3	36.9	9	63
Lead-acid battery	0.014	0.342	973	24255

"The first column shows the type of energy carrier, the second column the energy density in KWH by weight in pounds, the third shows energy density by volume in gallons, then the size of a fuel tank in gallons that would yield the same amount of energy as ten gallons of gasoline. The last column is the weight of the fuel tank in pounds required to hold an amount of fuel equal in energy to ten gallons of gasoline.

"Let's start with gasoline which is our reference fuel. As you can see, gasoline contains 5.8 KWH of energy per pound, 33.3 KWH of energy per gallon. Of course, the fuel tank size is ten gallons since this is what we're comparing against, and the weight of that tank is fifty-eight pounds.

"Now, let's look at hydrogen. Our first entry is for compressed hydrogen at 200 atmospheres of pressure. Note we don't even consider uncompressed hydrogen gas as the volume required would be outrageous. So our compressed hydrogen contains 15.1 KWH of energy per pound, and 2.01 KWH per gallon. To store as much energy as a ten-gallon tank of gasoline, we would need a 165-gallon tank and that tank would weigh ten pounds. Well, a 165-gallon tank to go just 250 miles is highly impractical, much better than uncompressed hydrogen, but still not viable.

"Now let's look at liquid hydrogen. Until recently, we and others have felt this would be the best way to store hydrogen, since the tank size would only need to be thirty-seven gallons."

"Bob," said Nat, "that sounds promising, but you've already said you've moved on to other choices, what were the shortcomings with liquid hydrogen?"

"Well, Mr. Wood," Bob said, not yet comfortable using Nat's first name, "it turns out there are a number of problems with hydrogen in a liquid state. The first is producing it. The boiling point of hydrogen is twenty degrees Kelvin, which is minus 423 degrees Fahrenheit—not many colder liquids exist. Then we have the problem of containing that liquid in very expensive dewars, not to mention existing piping becoming brittle, resulting in leaks. The problem is not just the flammability of the escaping hydrogen, but the fact it's escaping at a temperature of minus 423 degrees Fahrenheit. For comparison, the boiling point of liquid propane, which many people deal with today for their barbecue grills, is minus forty-two degrees Fahrenheit."

"So the problem is the infrastructure to support transporting hydrogen," Nat said.

"Exactly. Two months ago we came upon a material sciences group focusing their research on hydrogen storage within solid metal hydrides. These materials are like a sponge for hydrogen. The most promising is Lithium Metal Hydride, or LiMH for short. As you can see on the chart, the density by volume of 12.1 KWH per gallon is almost 35 percent better than that of liquid hydrogen, something that came as a complete surprise to us. The downside, of course, is the weight of that storage, which requires a 1260-pound tank to store the equivalent energy of ten gallons of gasoline. But mitigating the weight is the safety factor. Let's look at the next slide for a summary."

Hydrogen Storage: Metal Hydrides

- Hydrogen in gaseous form
  - requires too much space
- Hydrogen in liquid form
  - much more dense
  - must be kept at 20 Degrees K (-423 Degrees F)
  - Dangerous
- Stored within a Solid (e.g., Lithium Metal Hydride)
  - Safe – in fact safer than gasoline
  - Energy per unit volume is surprisingly 35% greater than liquid form
  - Tank is heavy

"This slide summarizes our evaluation of hydrogen in its various forms. As I said, hydrogen in gaseous form, even condensed gaseous form, requires too much space. Hydrogen in liquid form is much denser, but must be kept at minus 423 degrees Fahrenheit making it quite dangerous. Hydrogen stored in LiMH tanks is admittedly heavy, but its energy per gallon is 35 percent better than the liquid form. Filling a LiMH tank can be done under moderate pressure at room temperature; the gas is then re-leased by heating the tank.

Nat, now fully engaged, asked, "What about the safety issues with hydrogen?"

"There are safety concerns in crash situations—we assume that people driving hydrogen powered electric cars will still have accidents. But we find hydrogen stored in LiMH tanks is safer than gasoline. Where gasoline tanks rupture and then explode, you can saw a LiMH tank in half and the hydrogen will just leak out into the atmosphere; burning, possibly, but no explosion. If time permits, I have some video of an experiment we ran firing an incendiary bullet at a LiMH tank with the energy equivalent of a five-gallon tank of gasoline, and then at a five-gallon tank of gasoline. The results are—explosive."

"I'm sorry, Bob," injected Bilson, "but hydrogen has a serious PR problem. No one can talk about hydrogen without seeing that image of the Hindenburg."

"That's right, Ms. Bilson," Daniels responded, taking on a defensive tone he hadn't wanted to reveal. "However, what they need to realize is that although the hydrogen within the blimp burned, it was not the *cause* of the explosion. Recent research found that the skin of the Hindenburg was coated with a water-proofing material to avoid absorbing rain that would make it too heavy to fly. Unfortunately, that waterproofing material was highly combustible and caught fire in a static electric discharge as the ship was landing. The proof of that is in the footage they show on TV periodically. What you see is a large amount of violent flame. Hydrogen burns invisibly. So it was the skin of the ship that caused the disaster."

"Very interesting, Professor," said Bilson. "That's something more people will need to understand. Going back to your storage technology, I assume this is what you are proposing for cars, but what technology would be used for the home?"

"Actually, Sandra," Daniels replied, now more congenial, "we're going to recommend the same technology for both. Obviously the tank for the home would be larger than the tank for the car. One other thing we need to discuss is the ability to use this storage technology as a fuel cell, for both home and car storage.

"If you remember Jason's overview, he showed hydrogen storage technology would be used to fill the car. It would also convert hydrogen to electricity via a built-in fuel cell to power the home during usage peaks or in the evening when there's no sunshine. The control for this switchover is built into the tank by means of the central computer."

"Jesus," Brad came to life, "this is tremendous! I'm looking forward to that video of exploding fuel tanks," he said with a smile to the group. "Looks like you guys have nailed the storage problem. But Jason said there was another breakthrough."

"Yes, that has to do with how we convert solar energy to electricity. I'm going to turn this back over to Jason. That's his bag."

Daniels slid the laptop back across the table where Jason was ready to pick up the next slide. "Do this for Carol, boss," Daniels furtively said to Jason, hoping no one else would hear. Jason nodded his acknowledgement and noticed Bilson looking curious. She may have heard something but seemed to let it pass.

The image of a maimed Carol Hendrick flashed in Jason's mind, jarring him. He recovered quickly.

"Thanks, Bob. As you know, CERC and others have been investigating semiconductor Photo Voltaic, or PV, cell technology for some time. As I said earlier, we are assuming we can get PV solar panels with an efficiency of about 10 percent at reasonable cost. The maximum recorded efficiency is about 30 percent, but those cells are far from being economically manufactured. But as Ms. Bilson pointed out, that's the efficiency we want, 30 percent.

"This has led us to think out of the box, and I mean *way* out of the box. Current silicon PV cells are based on the particle nature of light. When sunlight strikes the semiconductor, photons elevate electrons to higher levels of energy—higher band gap. Our 'out of the box' approach is to consider the electromagnetic, or wave properties of light and receive those waves through an antenna. Such an antenna is not a new idea," said Jason as he put up the next slide.

Rectenna

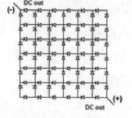

- Rectenna (<u>Rect</u>ifying An<u>tenna</u>) Invented by William Brown, Raytheon, 1961
- Designed for Power Transmission Using Microwaves

"In fact a gentleman by the name of William Brown who worked at Raytheon described such a device for transmitting power via microwaves in 1961, which is shown schematically in this slide. It's called a 'rectenna' because it rectifies the microwave energy into usable direct current. Recently several companies have begun to consider light's wave properties for energy conversion. Through nanotechnology they have built optical rectenna arrays that can receive electromagnetic radiation in the light spectrum, an approach that promises a paradigm shift of monumental importance. Let's look at the properties of such a device.

> # Optical Rectenna
>
> - Based on the Wave-Nature of Light
> - Dipole Antennas Operating in the 1,000 Terahertz (10^{12}) Region of Light
> - 'Receives' Light and Converts it Directly into Electricity
> - Embedded Diodes Convert to DC
> - Theoretically 90% Efficient
> - Current Examples: 70% Efficiency heading toward 80%

"Optical rectennas are based on transforming solar energy directly into electricity. Like their microwave ancestors, they are based on leveraging the wave-nature of electro-magnetic radiation. Unlike the microwave variety, they operate at *much* higher frequencies in the visible spectrum, about one thousand Terahertz, where a Terahertz is ten-to-the-twelfth Hertz. These are dipole antennas one half wavelength in size, and at these frequencies that means 0.15 microns. A micron is one millionth of a meter. To give you a relative sense of size, a human hair is about ten microns in diameter, so we're talking about dipole antennas that are slightly larger than one hundredth the thickness of a human hair! The only way such devices can be built is through the new *nanotechnology* you've been reading about.

"We know that sunlight is randomly polarized. In other words, all the various frequencies or colors of light travel in random orientations. The micro-dipoles are oriented in random directions and contain micro-diodes to rectify the AC 'light' current into usable DC power more efficiently. Optical rectennas are 90 percent efficient in theory, and the samples we have developed are 70 percent efficient. In manufactured quantities this probably drops to 30 percent. This single breakthrough can and will change the world." Jason paused to let the side conversations subside. "Any questions?"

"Holy Mother of Gawd!" exclaimed Nat, unable to mask his south Texas accent, "Why the hell haven't we heard about these ideas before?"

"Nat," replied Jason, "like many breakthroughs, this one needed several things to come together. The 'planets have aligned' for renewable energy production and storage in a way that will ultimately eliminate our dependence on fossil fuels."

"Jason, this is very significant," said Bilson, picking up on Nat's excitement. "Now that we've had a chance to see the entire architecture I'm wondering what the ramifications will be for traditional oil companies. We've been looking for ways to leverage National's existing assets in any new energy economy and hoping research such as yours will show us where those opportunities might be. What you've shown us today is revolutionary and could make a Hydrogen Economy a reality."

"Thank you, Sandra, the last two months have been quite exciting around here. I credit the work that Bob has done on developing our Reference Architecture. The challenge we have as a country—and perhaps as a global society—is introducing revolutionary technology in an evolutionary way. But I need tell you that we are NOT advocating a Hydrogen Economy."

"I thought that's what your work was all about. The Hydrogen Economy is at the center of the media buzz. It's what the oil and automotive companies are touting as the future."

"I know. But the Hydrogen Economy buzz is a real red herring being promoted by those industries—sorry, Nat. The infrastructure required to transport hydrogen is not even on the horizon. Our interest in hydrogen is strictly as a storage medium for electricity. Our architecture can better be explained as one that supports an Electric Economy."

"Then it looks like you have another PR problem," Bilson replied. "The media continually carries stories about the Hydrogen Economy and fuel cell vehicles; how it's going to take decades to get the infrastructure in place."

"Yes, and it's the auto and oil industries who promote those ideas. And they're right about the timeframe. On one hand, they get public credit for the forward-looking research they advertise. On the other hand, they know that as a country, we don't have the patience to wait decades, which means they are really promoting staying with fossil fuels. Very clever. They purposely do not talk about an Electric Economy because we have much of the basic infrastructure in place today."

"Okay, so can you explain what the impact of the Electric Economy might be on National Oil and the others?" Bilson asked with concern for her client.

"Sure," said Jason. "When we started this work almost three years ago, the mission we gave ourselves, and sold to our investors, was the establishment of an infrastructure that would support a renewable energy economy in a *clean* way. And the word *clean* is paramount here. We could always generate hydrogen from fossil fuels but doing so would be counter-productive. It would waste a tremendous amount of energy, and spew even more hydrocarbons into the atmosphere than we're doing today.

"Three years ago we didn't know where our goal would take us or how we would get there. The first year we basically thrashed our way through a variety of ideas. It wasn't until we put together our Reference Architecture that we had a roadmap."

"Jason," Bob Daniels jumped in, "I think it's important to say this 'thrashing,' as you put it, was actually a valuable step since it laid the groundwork for the architecture and helped eliminate alternatives that would have been dead ends."

"Good point. Our brainstorming may have saved us time in the long run, and since time is money, we may have saved our *investors* some of that too," Jason said with a smile he hoped would be appreciated by those in the room.

"In any event, our early evaluation of solar conversion technologies hammered home a couple of points. First, solar energy is very diffuse with only a few regions in the country where it can be gathered centrally. Second, since the sun only shines intermittently, we needed a way to store the electrical energy we gather.

"We had a number of problems to solve in the area of storage. First, there was the density problem Bob discussed. We needed to get hydrogen energy at least as dense as its liquid form. The problem then became one of distribution. Our existing oil and natural gas distribution infrastructure is not capable of handling liquid hydrogen. At minus 423 degrees Fahrenheit, the pipes currently carrying fossil fuels would become brittle and crack. Clearly that wouldn't work. In fact, hydrogen storage argues for creation and storage of hydrogen at the point of use, at the home or business. But then, we weren't content with home-owners dealing with cryogenic hydrogen, which is when Bob's work with metal hydride storage fell into place.

"So bottom line, in the immediate future, we see power utilities playing an important role in the establishment of a highly distributed and integrated power distribution grid. However, we don't see the relevance of the existing oil industry infrastructure given the properties of hydrogen and solar energy. Sorry about that, Nat."

"Hey," said Nat, "this is important to know sooner rather than later. It tells me my company needs to be involved in energy storage technologies in a big way. Unfortunately, the dinosaurs that run my company are not going to be happy with your breakthrough. They have a history of resisting change, and this portends change on a *massive* scale."

"Good point," Jason said, relieved. "Oil companies need to become *energy* companies. By analogy, if the railroad companies of the past had considered themselves *transportation* companies they would have become airlines. Instead, they're now stuck with an aging infrastructure."

"I like that analogy, can I use it at home?" asked Nat, smiling.

"Royalty free."

"You and Bob have presented some impressive technology today," Nat said. "I guess National Oil can take comfort in that it will take decades for enough homes to have this technology before it will make a dent in the oil market."

Jason could see that Nat was genuinely relieved, which reinforced his feeling that Nat and National were only participating to defend their current position. Visions of Carol Hendrick came to mind and it was time to play his next card.

"Before you get too comfortable, Mr. Wood," Jason said using Nat's last name for emphasis, "I should tell you that we're aware of the market penetration problem and have been working with another research team on a battery breakthrough."

Jason hesitated at this point, scanning his audience to make sure he had their attention. He did.

"Remember, a fuel cell is just a battery that's charged with hydrogen. We realize it will take time to get the distributed infrastructure we've talked about today in place. The other team we're working with has a lithium battery technology that will allow an electric vehicle to travel four hundred miles on a single charge, and that charge can be delivered over the existing electrical grid. Cars built with this technology could be delivered and in use in months, not years."

"Professor, this is intriguing," Bilson said after some deliberation. "Suppose every car in the country was now an electric vehicle. How much more electricity would we need to support that demand?"

"Good question. We've looked at that number. Given an efficiency of five miles per kilowatt hour, which is average for today's electric vehicle technology, it would take an additional 10 percent electricity generation."

"That's it?"

"That's it."

"But 10 percent of a very big number is still a big number," Bilson said as she tried to fathom the scale of the problem. "And how would we generate that much electricity?"

"You're right. In 2005, the last year we have data, this country consumed about four trillion kilowatt hours of electricity. But you need to realize that with just today's technology that would require about five thousand square miles of solar panels, and an additional five hundred miles to cover the electric vehicle usage. With the technology we've presented today, we would have a factor of three improvement in efficiency."

"So with less than two thousand square miles of real estate we could generate enough solar electricity to power the country and its electric vehicles," Sandra computed.

"Correct, but we need to keep in mind that solar will only be useful for peak daytime usage. Unless we go with thermal solar generation that includes storage, we will need conventional sources for off-peak production," Jason clarified, but could see his audience was struggling. "Let me put that into perspective. The state of Arizona is about 115,000 square miles. So we're talking about approximately 2 percent of that space to generate all the electricity we use, and if you've been to Arizona, you know they have plenty of uninhabitable space—perhaps one more slide will make the point."

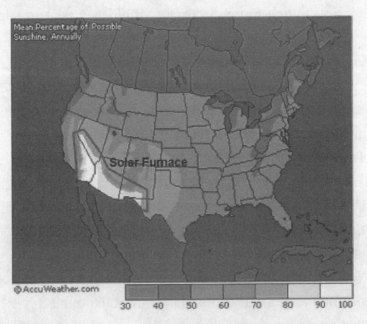

120

"This is a picture from AccuWeather.com showing the region in the southwest where we receive 80 to 100 percent of the total available sunshine year-round. I've drawn a border around this area that measures about 150,000 square miles, a 'solar furnace' capable of providing all of the energy our Electric Economy will need for many generations to come, and most of this land is already owned by the government."

"If electricity is going to be so plentiful," Nat Wood joined in, now visibly less confident, "why haven't the automobile manufacturers started to produce electric vehicles?"

"Nat, the automobile industry is made up of a lot more than just car manufacturers. There are whole supply chains of companies that produce radiators, carburetors, transmissions, exhaust systems, starter motors, solenoids to start the starter motors, and thousands of other parts. Electric vehicles need none of these components. Just take a look at an internal combustion engine. It has hundreds of moving parts. An electric motor has just one, the rotor connected to the driveshaft. Then there's the automotive services industry. Think of the billions of dollars spent on engine repair parts, service stations, and oil changes. None of this is required for an electric vehicle. The fundamental problem for the auto industry is that pure electric vehicles are much more the domain of Silicon Valley electrical engineers than Detroit mechanical engineers. In fact, there is a Silicon Valley company called Tesla Motors that is currently building high-performance pure electric roadsters that will outperform the fastest, most expensive Porsche or Ferrari at one third the cost."

"Interesting," said Nat, still looking for holes. "But how much would it cost a person to operate an electric car?"

"The average American drives about thirty miles each day. As I said, electric vehicles typically get about five miles per kilowatt hour, and in the evening off-peak times—when we would be charging our cars—electricity costs about ten cents per kilowatt hour. So we're talking about two cents per mile or sixty cents per day."

"Amazing," Brad jumped in. "So what are the next steps and what kind of timeframes are involved?"

"Does this mean you're interested in participating in our next funding round?" Jason asked, glancing at Daniels.

"Based on what we've heard today, I'm confident DOE will be interested in participating," Spencer said. Then looking at Nat Wood, "In fact, we may not want to include a third investor and keep this for DOE and National. Nat and I can have that discussion privately after he has time to come to grips with what we just heard."

Jason and Bob Daniels gave each other a look equivalent to a visual "high-five."

"In that case, there are a number of avenues to pursue," Jason said. "What we can demonstrate today uses essentially hand-built components, and I'm talking mainly about the optical rectenna technology. We need to move this into a form that can be mass produced. There is good progress on the Lithium Metal Hydride storage technology that Bob discussed, but we need more work on what we're calling the *switchable* storage that will either release hydrogen as a gas for your car, or run as a fuel cell to power your home or feed the electrical grid."

"But this is revolutionary," Sandra added. "How do you phase it in?"

"Exactly why we need an evolutionary approach to the revolution. We need to introduce the core of this technology in a way that makes economic sense to the homeowner, thus the need to support solar power generation and electric cars with lithium batteries first, fuel cell batteries second. Focusing on solar power generation can cost-justify much of the architecture and begin to eliminate pollution from power plants. Standardizing the net-metering laws would go a long way toward speeding this up. Then we can introduce hydrogen storage, and finally fuel cell batteries. And that last step will occur naturally when the auto manufacturers realize they have a market of homeowners capable of supplying hydrogen."

The audience grew quiet as they processed all they had heard. Brad was first to break the silence.

"Jason, this is taking our current fossil fuel economy and turning it on its *head!*"

"It is Brad, and it will have the same effect on the *world's* economies. Removing the world's energy dependency on unstable governments will free resources to focus on real economic progress."

It was time for the meeting to end. A number of side conversations had erupted around the table. Jason's day had begun early. He was tired and anxious to meet Jill for dinner. Daniels had been up most of the night working on his storage technology results and wasn't in much better shape.

"I think it's a wrap," said Jason. "I'm glad everyone had an opportunity to move their flights back or we wouldn't have made it."

Nat was the first to stand and walk over to Jason, his consultant close behind.

"Jason," he said, extending his hand, "impressive results. I have mixed emotions. On one hand, I'm excited about the future; on the other, I don't look forward to presenting your findings back in Houston."

"Nat, our results are what they are. As I said, we had no pre-conceived solution, we've only gone where technology has taken us."

"Jason," added Bilson, "I've been a critic of your work in the past, just not believing there was a viable renewable energy alternative."

"You're kidding," Jason said with mock sincerity.

"Now that I've met you and Bob, and seen your progress, I'm a believer. But, I also share Nat's concern over the reception this will get in Houston."

"Well, it won't be the first time I've had to look for a new investor," Jason smiled as Nat moved away.

"Jason," she said, moving him off to a quieter location and lowering her voice, "I'm actually concerned for more than just your funding."

There was a noticeable pause as he considered what she had said. "What do you mean?"

"My cell phone number is on the business card I gave you earlier. Call me at seven-thirty tonight. I'll be at the airport in one of the lounges." She paused to think for a moment. "Actually, we can't do this on the phone; meet me at the Tampa International U.S. Air Club Lounge at seven-thirty." It was clear she wasn't asking.

She shook Jason's hand and smiled, making sure Nat noticed she was ready to leave. Jason was bewildered.

Brad was the next to approach. "Jason, a very impressive presentation today, you've made incredible progress. Can we talk outside for a second?" Brad led Jason out of the conference room and then into Jason's office and shut the door.

"When you opened the meeting today you mentioned you were going to be giving part of this presentation at the International Energy Conference next week. I'm concerned about divulging too much information. You've made significant progress."

"I'm glad you're impressed, Brad, but I've been attending and speaking at these conferences for years."

"I understand, but think this through. We're talking a new paradigm. This will change the world. We need to maintain all the advantage possible for our country. We have to discuss just how much information should be exposed, and how to go about it. There are people in high places who are both impressed and concerned, which is all I can tell you at this point. We need more time to talk. You need to join me for dinner at the airport at eight o'clock. I'll be in the Delta Crown Room."

"Sure," Jason said, not mentioning he was going to be there anyway. He didn't know what was going on, but for the time being, he wanted to keep Sandra and Brad separate. "I don't have a membership there any more, but when I arrive I'll call your cell phone and you can come out and get me."

"Perfect!"

Chapter 10.
The Deal

The sheik dropped Zeng off at his hotel, the luxurious Al Faisaliah on King Fahad Road, a short distance from the palace. Zeng's security team had arrived in advance, occupying the rooms around his suite, and had swept all the rooms for bugs— Standard Operating Procedure. The Al Faisaliah was Riyadh's best hotel and the place to stay for the world's oil players.

Once Zeng had freshened up he used his secure cell phone to call President Wu. Zeng reported the initial meeting had gone well and that postponing the real meat of the discussion until dinner was a positive indication. President Wu agreed, and Zeng felt relief that he had both the attention of the prince and the approval of his boss. That night he would have to drive the point home and "close the deal."

* * *

The sheik's limo swung into the hotel's circular driveway at six-thirty to pick Zeng up for the short ride to the prince's residence. Zeng had been waiting with his guards underneath the three-story portico under three of the largest chandeliers he'd ever seen. There was a considerable amount of traffic on King Fahad

Road but the night was quiet, the air still, and the temperature warm from the heat radiating off the desert floor.

The doorman opened the rear passenger door and Zeng entered the plush black leather cavern taking a seat beside the sheik.

"Good evening, Ju."

"Abdul, thank you again for arranging an audience with the prince and your hospitality. You've made this visit quite pleasant."

"That is the responsibility of a host and my pleasure. We haven't a long way to his residence."

"Abdul, you know the prince well, how are we doing so far?" asked Zeng, careful to use "we."

"I'd say we are doing quite well, my friend. I have been to the prince's residence many times for meetings, but this is the first time I have been invited to dine. This is a good sign."

The remainder of the ride was taken in silence, Zeng impressed by the magnificence of the city skyline in the distance, the number of new American cars, and the flurry of people on the streets.

After a few turns toward the outlying area of the city, the limo pulled up to a large ornate gate supported by two massive pillars.

"We are here," said Abdul as he lowered his window to announce his presence and that of his guest.

The guard instantly recognized Abdul and motioned to the guardhouse. The gate was huge and seemed to take forever to swing open. As the car passed through, Zeng could see that it was so large that each half rested on a motorized trolley running on a semi-circular track allowing it to swing on its hinges.

This was more than a residence, it was a compound—a palatial compound. The driveway leading to the house in the distance was at least a half-mile long. On the way the limo passed a horse stable and several outbuildings that in themselves would be small estates in any other country.

"These are the guest houses, perhaps on your next visit we can arrange one of them for you," Abdul smiled. "The stable houses twenty of the finest Arabian stallions in the world."

"Impressive," said Zeng.

As the car swung under the home's portico, two doormen appeared from nowhere on either side of the car, opening both rear doors simultaneously. Prince Faareh was standing at the top of the stairway illuminated from behind by the bright interior lights passing through the open double-wide doorway with arms outstretched. He had two large dogs, one on either side that seemed to be standing at attention. Zeng guessed they were Salukis.

"Welcome, Mr. Zeng, I am glad that you could reschedule, please come in."

With the prince leading the way, the three of them walked down a long and wide hallway towards a large well-lit dining room with one immense table under another massive chandelier. There were three servants in the room, one standing behind each chair. Somehow the Salukis knew not to enter and waited outside.

"Mr. Zeng," the prince said, "Please be seated. I hope you enjoy what my chef has prepared this evening. I suggest in the interest of time, we continue our discussions while dinner is being served. I want to make sure we give your ideas the full consideration they deserve."

The prince was speaking English, and well. Zeng had hoped they wouldn't need an interpreter, his Arabic was a disgrace. Zeng's assigned servant pulled out his chair and held his napkin.

He had the distinct feeling this man was going to be standing over his shoulder for the entire meal.

"Thank you, Your Highness, I appreciate this opportunity. As I stated in my opening remarks in your office, my country is growing at a rate that will cause us to be the world's largest economic power in ten to fifteen years…"

The prince held up his hand to interrupt. "Mr. Zeng, if it is alright with you, we may want to keep this dinner rather informal and dispense with our servants for the evening."

Zeng was relieved by the way the prince wanted to handle the privacy of the meeting. "Of course."

With a wave of his hand, the prince dismissed the servants who would only reappear to serve, then quickly retreat.

Zeng continued, "We understand to achieve our goal we will need energy resources proportional to our tasks, an enormous amount of energy and significantly more than our internal resources can supply." *Besides, burning is not the best use of our oil, which we want to save for creating products*, he thought.

"I understand your position. Let's get to the specifics of your proposal."

"Your Highness," Abdul jumped in, glancing at Zeng who knew it was time for the sheik to participate. "In my negotiations with Mr. Zeng, we discussed a number of options that would meet China's needs. One of the options we intend to present today is to participate in a joint development program to open new fields dedicating enough new oil to meet China's needs."

"In what form would this joint venture take?" asked the prince.

"Mr. Zeng?" Abdul passed the ball back to Zeng who had worked out the details.

"Your Highness," Zeng said, "I am authorized to tell you we are considering investing thirty-five billion dollars in a joint venture that will assure China an adequate flow of oil for the next fifteen years."

"Thirty-five billion dollars is a lot of money, Mr. Zeng, but fifteen years is also a long period of time. How much oil do you think that money will buy?"

"Your Highness, let me be more specific. That money is what we are considering just the *development* investment. In addition, we would be paying you for each barrel of oil we consume at an agreed upon price—actually within a range of prices. This, of course, with the understanding we would have first access to this oil and would guarantee some minimum usage."

The prince's eyes widened.

"We would commit to buying three million barrels per day initially and believe our daily purchases would increase to twelve million barrels per day over the next fifteen years. Even if it did not, we would commit to the three million barrel rate over the fifteen year duration." Zeng knew this was a safe commitment since his country already used six million barrels per day. China had no long-term contracts like he was proposing with the Saudis, so some of their current suppliers could get squeezed. That was business.

"Yes, but what about price?" asked the prince.

"We would pay market prices bounded by a floor to protect you, and a ceiling to protect us. We propose that as a minimum we would pay no less than thirty-five dollars per barrel, when the market falls below that floor. As the ceiling, we would pay no more than 120 dollars per barrel. Otherwise we would pay market price. To put this into perspective—although there is no way to accurately predict our actual usage—if we assume China ramped up oil consumption from three million barrels per day to twelve million barrels per day, at the end of fifteen years, on average, we would be consuming seven-and-a-half million barrels per day. If we also assume that the market price stays at the average of the floor and ceiling, then we would be paying $77.50 per barrel. This amounts to 581 million dollars per day, 212 billion dollars per year, or approximately 3.2 trillion dollars over the life of the agreement. Of course, any excess oil produced as a result of our joint venture would be sold at market and we would expect to share in that revenue, fifty-fifty."

The prince had been listening all along, making notes on a piece of royal stationary using a plain yellow "number two" pencil, taking time to contemplate the offer.

"An impressive proposal. I appreciate the effort you and the sheik have put into it. But let's look at the risks from both sides. During the course of the next fifteen years, there is some likelihood that someone, probably the Americans, will develop a non-fossil fuel alternative, and this agreement would lock you in to minimum payments regardless."

"Correct," Zeng said. "We have considered such a scenario and based on our intelligence, there is no such solution in sight. The United States is one of a handful of countries with the expertise to develop such technology. But, regrettably for them, their politicians believe the answer to oil shortages is more drilling. They have devoted precious little resource toward alternatives, just small projects at the university level."

"Interesting," said the prince, "I understand we have recent intelligence indicating some of the university research you mention may be bearing fruit. Our teams should compare notes to make sure our information is consistent."

"Thank you, Your Highness, we would appreciate those insights," Zeng said.

"Let's consider the ceiling price," said the prince. "Conceivably, without some clean energy alternative, the market price of oil will exceed the 120 dollar per barrel ceiling that you propose, and may exceed it significantly. We could be leaving a lot of money on the table."

"Yes, Your Highness, but that ceiling would apply only to China, unless you made similar arrangements with other consumers. And it would apply only for the newly developed wells we jointly finance, and only up to a maximum of twelve million barrels per day. This arrangement does have some risk for each of us, but also great rewards. We believe the benefit of an assured supplier-consumer relationship benefits both countries in ways that exceed the risks."

"Mr. Zeng, I can assure you an agreement of this magnitude could only be made with one partner. However, we face another risk in regard to the ceiling. And that risk is specifying prices in U.S. dollars, a currency falling against the other major currencies, and specifically the euro. By pricing our product in dollars, as the value of the dollar falls, we receive less purchasing power for each barrel of oil sold and dollar received. This causes us to raise oil prices for everyone and could take us to the 120 dollar per barrel ceiling that you propose based only on a weakened dollar."

"Yes, Your Highness, we have made this initial proposal based on dollars since that is how you currently price your oil."

"Mr. Zeng, when we—actually, OPEC—first began pricing our oil in the 1960s, there was only one stable currency, the U.S. dollar. Today, there is only one other global currency in competition with the dollar that we could consider, the euro. As we have watched the dollar fall, and raised our prices accordingly, we have given some thought to pricing in euros. Your proposal gives further credence to that notion, especially with the concept of a ceiling that could be *artificially* reached if we remain in dollars."

"But, Your Highness," responded Zeng, "valuing oil in euros will cause the world's economies to divest themselves of dollars creating more erosion."

"Actually, it would be worse than that. As the price of oil rises, valuing oil in dollars will lead to higher U.S. trade deficits since oil is a major import component for them. This of course leads to a weaker dollar which causes us to raise oil prices, which completes the cycle. This is the problem I spoke of earlier, caused by the Americans' inability to control their trade deficits. They are great inventors, but promptly rely on others, including China, to manufacture everything. And their failure to conserve energy or develop a serious alternative energy program has put them in this position.

"Now," he continued, "consider oil no longer being valued in dollars, but euros. As you say, many of the countries paying for their oil in dollars would need to convert to euros. They would be forced to do so to avoid the slide in the dollar's value given everyone else would be doing the same. That sell-off would make dollars even less valuable, which would significantly raise the cost of oil to the U.S. and others still holding dollars. That would increase their trade deficits leading to an even weaker dollar—a death spiral for their economy!"

"Your Highness, wouldn't this eventually cause a threat to the entire *world's* economy?"

"It would indeed hurt *all* infidels, which leads me back to your proposal. You have suggested an initial investment of thirty-five billion dollars for our joint venture. What makes you think we want thirty-five billion dollars?"

"Actually, Your Highness, we would propose thirty-five billion in *value*. Perhaps in technology you might find useful."

"Mr. Zeng, we already have the world's most modern technologies. What would you propose?"

Zeng paused for a moment to contemplate how he should say what came next; the implications were immense. There was no other way to say it. "*Military* technologies," replied Zeng.

"Mr. Zeng, suppose you delivered thirty-five billion dollars of planes, missiles, and bombs tomorrow. We would not have the people or expertise to use them. The non-OPEC countries are close to their peak if not there already, which means their oil is about to become much more expensive. The world will be turning to OPEC to fill the void, and the country that will be the last to peak is Saudi Arabia. And we are closer to that point than we once thought. The United States has been our protector for many years, and in return, we have provided them with additional production whenever they thought it was needed. However, with the growth in demand from China and India, we also are reaching the point where our wells will peak. We require new drilling projects, like you are suggesting, to open new fields. But as you propose, new fields developed in this manner would be used to supply China first, which, coupled with valuing oil in euros, will make our American friends very unhappy."

"But then, what can we provide as an investment if not money, or military technology for your defense?"

"Mr. Zeng, I'm afraid what we may need is *protection* from our former protectors—quite literally thirty-five billion dollars of military defense to protect us from a desperate superpower on the verge of losing that status due to their own lack of political and fiscal controls."

There was silence as the ramifications of what had just been said settled in. The discussion had turned a dark corner. Zeng had more information than he wanted. He could hear the large ceiling fan turning slowly overhead. Moments—which felt like minutes—were passing by.

Zeng broke the silence, "Sir, couldn't the U.S. approach other OPEC countries with a joint development proposal to defuse the situation?"

"Mr. Zeng, in case you haven't noticed, Saudi Arabia *is* OPEC. We chair the organization, provide all the leadership, and control at least one third of the total reserves. Based on the inflated reporting by some of our members, we probably control more than that. As the industrialized nations of the world begin to run out of oil, as they surely must, they will be turning to Saudi Arabia, not OPEC."

"In that case," Zeng asked, "assuming we can come to terms on the specifics, how long would it take to get new jointly developed fields into production so we could begin drawing our initial three million barrels per day?"

"Ju, do you know how to tell the difference between oil drawn from the proposed wells and oil drawn from existing wells?"

"No, Your Highness, I have very little technical background in fossil fuels."

"You needn't worry. There is no way to tell the difference, which means that when we get the details of our agreement worked out we can begin providing China immediately. There is, however, one thing we should worry about."

"Yes, I see. The Americans could come to you with a similar proposal."

"Ju, the Americans have attacked a neighbor; they do not live in this neighborhood, but we do, which makes doing business with them very difficult."

"Then you must mean military action from America?"

"No, Ju, per our agreement you would be protecting us from that. The only thing that could get in the way is the Americans developing a fossil fuel alternative. With this agreement in place, neither of us would want to see that happen, would we?"

Zeng had the distinct feeling his deal was now completely out of control. It had gone from a relatively simple development project to a full scale military alliance! He wasn't sure how President Wu would react, perhaps favorably. It would mean no upfront costs since China would need to protect their oil suppliers against aggressors anyway.

Zeng said, thinking out loud, "But how would we prevent someone from developing an oil alternative?"

"We've done a good job so far. Every time the infidels need additional oil and prices start to rise, we open the tap to provide more. Our analysts tell us as long as the price remains under 110 dollars per barrel, the Americans are willing to pay for it. Above that mark they will be incented to develop alternatives. But even then, it will take years for them to do so."

"But the non-OPEC countries are at or close to their peak. Won't that and the arrangement we just discussed push oil prices and the Americans over the threshold?"

After what seemed like a long delay, the prince said almost to himself, as if no one else was listening, "In that case we might have to 'club' them."

136

They were both speaking English. Zeng thought he had misunderstood. Perhaps it was just a figure of speech, but the prince's tone was ominous. He wanted to look like he understood, but he didn't. He just nodded.

Chapter 11.
Tampa International Airport

As soon as his investors had left, Jason phoned Jill to explain the change in plans. She was disappointed they wouldn't be having dinner, but understood.

Jason hated airports. He'd spent too much time during his career waiting in line for rental cars, security checks, and cancelled or delayed flights. Since 9/11, security procedures had become outrageous and parking almost non-existent as much of the space was deemed dangerously close to the terminal. The general hassle factor of flying had increased by a factor of ten, forever changing the airline industry's business model. On top of that, Sandra and Brad had overlooked the fact that he would need to go through security to get to the lounges. He needed a valid ticket and boarding pass. Before leaving his office, he bought a ticket online; the cheapest same-day ticket to "Anywhere" was a round-trip on U.S. Air to Miami for 340 dollars. A flight to Miami was as good as any since he wouldn't be using the ticket. *I'll probably end up on some security watch list as a potential terrorist threat*, he thought.

It was 7:25 PM when he finally cleared security and could see Sandra waiting outside the entrance to the United Club.

"Hi, Jason," she said as he arrived out of breath. "Come on, I'll sign you in."

Sandra had commandeered a medium-sized table with her laptop open and papers scattered about. They sat down.

"Something to drink?" she asked, waving a hostess over.

"Sure, the run here has made me thirsty. I'd like a Sam Adams, please," he said.

"Thanks for joining me, I apologize for dragging you out, I know the hours you must be putting in. How did you get in here without a ticket?"

"I didn't," Jason replied, holding up his round-trip to Miami. "Sorry, I didn't feel comfortable talking on the phone."

"I have to admit, you raised my curiosity. I know Nat was looking for a solution that would be more amenable to National Oil."

"Jason, the discussion we're about to have is completely off the record. You need to be aware of some things."

"You have my attention," Jason said, unable to miss the intensity in her eyes.

"We don't have a lot of time. Let's cut to the chase. I don't think you fully understand the impact of your research. I've been thinking about your meeting for the last several hours. I've got a question: If the auto industry is playing the games you described, why wouldn't the federal government step in?"

"Actually," Jason said with renewed focus, "they *have* been involved. Back in the '90s, the state of California passed a Zero Emission Vehicle, or ZEV, mandate that would force automakers to produce 10 percent of their vehicles with zero emissions by 2003 in order to do business in California. The majors then set about to develop such vehicles. GM produced an all-electric car called the EV1, Ford released an all-electric version of their small

Ranger pickup, and Toyota produced an all-electric version of their RAV4 called the RAV4-EV. Their initial programs only allowed leases of these vehicles and there were long lines of takers. Ironically, while they were building the cars, they were lobbying behind the scenes to weaken the new mandate, which culminated in a lawsuit filed by GM and Chrysler against the state."

"So where do the feds come in?"

"Easy, they came in on the side of the automakers and forced the state to weaken the law! That's because our administration back then was from…"

"… the *oil* industry!" Sandra completed his sentence.

"Exactly. And the president's chief of staff had been a lobbyist for GM before joining the administration."

"Amazing. But you said that the Big Three were already building their electric cars."

"They were hedging their bets. They really didn't want to manufacture electric cars for the reasons we spoke of at the meeting. And to show you how much GM didn't want to be in that business, they refused to sell the electric cars they had leased at *any* price. Instead, they allowed the leases to expire, retrieved the cars and crushed them out in the desert."

"But now they're introducing hybrids that run on a combination of gasoline and electricity. Won't they solve the problem?"

"I wish they would, Sandra. Today's hybrids are a compromise, and a bad one; the auto industry's way of stalling; a way to avoid production of truly clean electric cars. They equip them with anemic batteries that can only take cars a mile or two on electricity and then need to be charged. And to charge them, they use the internal combustion engine, one of the least efficient sources of power to turn a generator. It's no wonder they get only marginally better fuel economy."

"But I've read that people would be reluctant to plug their cars in at night."

"What you've read has come from the auto industry. Let me ask you, do you have a cell phone?"

"Sure, I think everyone does now."

"And at night, what do you do with that phone before you go to sleep?"

"I plug it in to recharge the battery," Bilson answered, knowing where this was going.

"Of course. Millions of us now do the same thing, and we don't find that too onerous. Cars would be no different. The fact is, the auto industry doesn't want to introduce 'pluggable hybrids' because that step would take them dangerously close to the next step: pure electric vehicles."

"The auto industry lobby has tremendous leverage," Bilson said, shaking her head.

"As does the oil lobby, Ms. Bilson," Jason said with a smile, looking directly into her eyes.

"Exactly, which brings me back to my point. Do you realize the impact your research is going to have on National Oil, the people I represent?"

"I'm sure it's not what Nat would have wanted, but we need to be completely honest about our discoveries and the reasons we've taken the path we presented. I think Nat understands since he knew that up front. National Oil's funding of our research gives them an advanced look at one of the potential directions for renewable energy."

"It's not Nat I'm concerned about, he's really just a pawn. I hate to use that word, but it's the one that comes to mind. People like Nat are well-intended employees who feel they're making a contribution by monitoring funded research from startups and universities like yours. He's going to dutifully report back to his management about the progress you've made. And that's when the shit's going to hit the fan."

"I'm not completely clear on what you are saying," Jason said, taken aback by the sudden graphic language. "National is contractually committed to continue funding for the next nine months."

"It's not the funding I'm worried about, nor is their funding something you should be worried about. They'll continue participating just to have access to your research, especially after today."

"Then what *should* I be concerned about?"

"Your health.

"I don't think you understand the potential impact of your research. National Oil has assets of about 150 billion dollars, seventy-five billion in plant and equipment infrastructure. Based on what you told us today, your team is about to flush that down the toilet!"

"So you're saying that National Oil might harm me in some way?"

"Jason, this is not just about National Oil. I also consult for other companies in the industry. You think National lives in a vacuum? They're just one of the big five oil companies that control almost 60 percent of this country's refining capacity. You think these companies don't talk? The five CEOs meet monthly! You think gas prices go up in lockstep by accident? Wake up! National's assets are just one component of the oil industry. When you consider it's not just a U.S. industry but an international one, the total assets at risk may be one hundred times National's.

"And then there's OPEC! Their members have enormous wealth in their reserves, the value of which would go to zero if we have a viable renewable energy strategy. Together, we're talking many trillions of dollars here! And beyond the money, OPEC would completely lose their political influence in the world. You're going to make a lot of enemies, and for the kind of impact we're talking about, people disappear. People *die*."

Jason could see by her intensity that she was honestly concerned. A cold chill went down his back. "Look, I admit we've been so focused on solving the problem that we haven't spent enough time thinking about the roll-out. What would you suggest I do?"

"The first thing you need to do is take what I've told you seriously. The genie is out of the bottle and you can't put it back. After Nat turns in his report tomorrow, anything could happen."

The storm in her eyes had grown even stronger, her sincerity palpable. "Sandra, I appreciate your concern and the fact you've felt the need to confide in me."

"Look, I've been a vocal critic of your work for some time. That comes from living on one side of the equation for too long, and believing what I hear from the oil industry. I truly believed we had enough oil to last into the foreseeable future. The work of your team has made at least one alternative scenario a realistic possibility. Our discussion of Peak Oil today has helped me reframe the issues. This is…explosive!"

"I'm glad you now understand, and I appreciate your concern. I'll take everything you've told me into consideration, but CERC needs to keep going."

With that, Jason told Sandra he had another meeting and shifted to stand up. When she squeezed his arm and stood with him, her piercing eyes left no doubt of her concern. "Professor, please be careful!"

* * *

It was almost eight when they said goodbye and Jason sprinted back up the corridor to the landside hub of Tampa International. Delta was in "Airside E" and that meant a long run. On the way, he found Brad's cell number and called to let him know he was at the airport and on his way. *Christ, what a night*, he thought. *What's next?*

On the way down the E corridor he found himself looking over his shoulder, now thinking about people who might be following him. He forced himself to stop. He was being paranoid. Visions of hit men danced in his head.

The Delta Crown Room is a strange place to meet someone for dinner, Jason thought. *But then, dinner probably wasn't what Brad had in mind.*

It was almost ten past eight when Jason found the Crown Room next to Gate 67. Brad was pacing as he waited to escort him in as his guest.

"Sorry I'm late," panted Jason, holding out his hand, "getting through security is a bear," he lied.

"That's alright, we still have plenty of time. Let's get you signed in. I have a small room reserved and I'm having some food sent in."

They walked to the conference room Brad had reserved. Jason sat down on the clean side—there were papers spread everywhere, it was obvious that Brad had been hard at work.

"It's your dime," Jason said as he got settled, "and I mean that. I had to buy a ticket to get in here."

"Understand," Brad smiled, "sorry about that."

"It'll be on my next expense report. So what's with the intrigue?" asked Jason.

An attendant knocking on the door interrupted them with a plate of assorted sandwiches and a variety of soft drinks. They slid some of Brad's papers aside to make room.

"Thank you," Brad said as he gave the girl a tip and waited for her to leave, locking the door behind her.

"Doc, when we first met during your research funding tour, I was impressed by the work you were planning. I knew it was a long shot, but thought you might be successful and we may need to coordinate with other research activities. On the other hand, if you didn't succeed, we would learn a lot about what *doesn't* work, which is sometimes just as valuable. We really felt, as smart as you are, the outcome would be more the latter than the former.

"Of course, your funding must be accounted for and I make the standard reports to my management back at DOE. At today's session I called back during our break and just got off the phone with my boss again. He's more excited than I am. The work you guys have accomplished is outstanding and could prove to be a way out of the energy dilemma this country—and in fact the entire world—is now facing."

"I appreciate your enthusiasm," Jason said. "We've achieved some real milestones lately that look promising. So why the urgency and secrecy?"

"In a word, *timing*," said Brad. "It's more complicated than that, but the essence is timing."

"Go on."

"Okay, basically, the results you showed us today indicate we are much closer to a clean energy solution than anyone may have thought. There are many considerations."

"Which are?"

"Well, first off, keeping these results secret for the time being. It might not be prudent to publicize your work. Our first concern is the conference you're going to next week, what you'll be presenting and to whom. We know that conference has an international audience."

"I was planning to report on the results we presented today, but in much more detail, of course, since that will be a technical audience."

"Exactly my...*our* concern, and why I wanted to have this meeting. Has your presentation been announced?"

"Yes, it just has the standard title of 'CERC Research Update,' since we present at these things quite often."

"Good, how about the slides? I assume you send them out in advance?"

"I usually send them out a week before the meeting to give the organizers time to put them into a package for the attendees." Jason could see Brad grimace. "But with the board meeting today, I got behind on the technical package and intend to zip it in an email tomorrow. I've already given the organizers a heads-up that I'd be late."

"Good, that means I can breathe again," Brad said, exhaling his relief. "We'd like you to hold off on that. Just present something that indicates progress, but without the specifics you showed to us today. A more generic presentation."

"So let me get this straight," Jason replied, trying, but not succeeding, to avoid sounding confrontational. "You're asking me to withhold results that could ultimately free us from our dependence on foreign oil and the pollution that is poisoning this planet? For how long, and who is *we?*"

"Jason," Brad said, motioning to the scattering of papers on the table, "timeframe—I can't say for sure yet. I've been on the phone since I left the campus, working through this. And *we* goes well beyond my superiors, beyond the DOE in fact. It includes the State Department. I almost wish I hadn't reported your results today, but I had no choice. So now there's a spotlight on CERC, and you in particular. This is *big*, Jason."

"How big, really, Brad?"

"Just a minute."

Brad reached into his pocket to pull out his cell phone, selected a number from the directory, and hit send.

"Bob, Brad here."

...

"Fine, thanks, I have Professor Davidson here and I've been discussing our conversations from earlier this afternoon."

...

"Right, I hate to do this, could you have the secretary call me on my cell phone? The professor needs some convincing."

...

"Thanks," and Brad flipped the case shut.

"The secretary?" Jason asked.

"Let's hold on for a minute."

Brad's cell chirped alive. "Brad Spencer here."

...

"Yes, sir, I appreciate your help."

...

"Thank you, his name is Professor Jason Davidson," Brad said. "We're in a private room. I'm going to put this on speaker so the three of us can talk." Brad pushed the "speaker" button on his cell and placed it on the table between them.

"This is Jason Davidson," Jason said, not knowing who was supposed to be on the other end the call.

"Professor Davidson, this is Secretary of State Walter Jennings. Do you recognize my voice?"

Jason went blank for what seemed like a minute, but it was just a few seconds. He'd heard the secretary of state speak several times. There was no doubt in his mind who he was talking to.

"Yes, sir, I do."

"Good, then I'll get straight to the point. Mr. Spencer has been reporting the results of your work. Today he was able to report significant progress, which set off a variety of alarms. The international ramifications of your results could have profound impact on the security of our country, and I'm speaking with you in the strictest of confidence. Do you understand?"

"Yes, sir."

"Do you currently have an active security clearance?"

"No, sir, I don't."

"We'll begin taking care of that tomorrow. For now, we need to be having this discussion based on mutual trust. Do I have that trust from you, Professor?"

"You do, sir."

"Very well. Professor, the situation is this: should word of your group's advances get into the wrong hands, it could have unintended consequences. Specifically, it could disrupt the flow of oil to this country or at a minimum disrupt the price we pay for that oil. Should OPEC—and specifically Saudi Arabia—feel threatened by the advances your team has made, they might decide to withhold oil from us, and I don't need to tell you the ramifications of that action. On the other hand, they could decide to significantly raise the price if they feel the ultimate value of their reserves is threatened."

"I understand, Mr. Jennings."

"President Wells' concern is in regards to the time lapse between when we make an announcement of such breakthroughs and the time they become available on a scale that will allow rapid commercial deployment. Essentially, we are afraid of over-hanging the market."

"So the president of the United States is now involved in this?" Jason said, hardly believing what he was hearing.

"He just received a briefing, Professor."

Jason looked at Brad in amazement. Spencer looked back, shaking his head, indicating he had no idea it had gotten to the president.

"Look, there are people from all over the world coming to this conference, planning to hear what I have to say. As I've told Mr. Spencer, I will not be sending my slides until tomorrow, so I can keep the sensitive information out of the presentation."

"Professor, we understand the position you're in. But I need to tell you the president would prefer that you cancel your appearance. Something could get mentioned, even if not part of your formal presentation. He feels *very* strongly about this."

"I understand, Mr. Secretary, you can tell the president I appreciate his concerns and will take them into account. I'll be discrete."

After the call was ended, Jason could see that Brad was anything but happy with the results.

"I don't think 'discrete' was what the secretary of state and the president had in mind," Brad said, visibly upset. "Has it occurred to you that my career depends on how my boss and the secretary perceive my value? Not to mention the president of the United States! How many times do you think I'll have visibility at this level?"

"Sorry, Brad, but the government has been trying to slow down progress on electric vehicle technology for years."

"How so?" Brad asked, indignantly.

"Fasten your seatbelt, I'll give you the short version. Back in the 1990s, a small company called ECD perfected nickel metal hydride, or NiMH, battery technology and filed a large number of patents to protect their interests."

"So what, that's free enterprise," Brad jumped in.

"Absolutely, and there was nothing wrong with that, but this is where it gets interesting. Around 2000, General Motors formed a joint venture with ECD, creating a company that eventually became COBASYS, and seeded it with the technology and patents that ECD had created. GM had a controlling interest in the state-of-the-art battery technology that provides electrical power to all hybrids today."

"Sorry, still nothing wrong with GM wanting to invest in battery technology for the future production of electric cars."

"Agreed, Brad," Jason responded, "assuming they were interested in building electric cars. Instead, when they decided they didn't want any part of electric cars three years later, they sold their controlling interest to a company who wouldn't compete and would sit on the patents," Jason hesitated for emphasis. "And that company was National Oil."

"So you mean that National now controls the latest battery technology?"

"Exactly, and now COBASYS uses its patents to prevent any company from developing 'large-format' NiMH batteries, the kind that are required for electric vehicles, and all manufacturers are forced to license COBASYS technology for their hybrids that use a smaller format battery. And I needn't tell you that the oil and automotive industries control the most powerful lobbies and political action committees. When they say 'jump,' the administration asks 'how high?' and 'in what direction?'"

"So essentially, COBASYS is prohibiting the production of pure electric vehicles. How do *you* intend to get around this?"

"Remember from my presentation today, we're using a newer lithium-based battery technology that COBASYS doesn't control."

"Doc, you're playing with fire."

Chapter 12.
First Strike

The remainder of Jason's week was reasonably normal, as normal as possible given that CERC's research was now on the radar screen of the president of the United States.

It started with a visit from the Defense Security Service. They'd received a call from Secretary Jennings' office to begin the Top Secret security clearance process. They promised to accelerate his application, which meant immediately interviewing some of the references he'd identified, speeding up the standard background checks. Jason spent most of the morning filling out forms requesting information going back many years. He was necessarily vague on his use of marijuana during his college years; he *had* inhaled. He would have the results of his security application before he left for his conference in California. Somehow, Jason felt he'd pass. He had people in high places pulling strings and he had received a thorough scrubbing by NASA four years earlier.

On Tuesday afternoon he finished the slides he was going to email to the conference coordinators. True to his word, he cleansed them of the specifics Brad had been concerned about. He thought about asking Brad for a review then rejected the idea. In the government's present state of mind, and with the president himself objecting, they would censor everything. The watered-down presentation he put together was the minimum expected by the conference committee. Canceling his presentation was unthinkable. He and Rafi had been planning their presentation for months, people were coming from all over the world, and he'd promised Jill they would take Friday off to spend a long weekend on the coast prior to his presentation on Monday. Jill had already made arrangements with the school to take Friday and Monday as vacation days. There were too many reasons not to cancel—screw the politicians.

Getting to Santa Barbara would be interesting. There were only a handful of very large airports that served as hubs: Atlanta-Hartsfield, Newark, Chicago-O'Hare, and of course, LAX. In the past, Jason would have flown into Burbank just north of L.A. since it was a smaller airport. The rental car hassle was much less constraining, and it would be easier to drive north from there. Unfortunately, with the high fuel prices and "terror tax" the airlines liked to call attention to, the majors had cut back on direct flights to Burbank. This meant at least another hour in traffic to navigate their way north, and an additional forty-five minutes dealing with the rental car agency. The other option was a small commuter plane for the short hop from L.A. to Santa Barbara. Jill wasn't fond of flying anyway, and there would be no way to get her on a small plane. So they'd fly to L.A. and rent a car for the weekend, ending up in Santa Barbara on Sunday night.

Jason had lived in California for nearly ten years during his startup days, working with several companies in Silicon Valley and traveling extensively up and down the coast. Jill was an east coast girl who'd never been to California. She was looking forward to this trip.

The weather forecast for LA and surrounding area was looking good all the way up to Carmel. Silicon Valley and northern California were in for some of their usual drizzle and damp fog. But the pair would not be going that far north.

LAX was just as Jason had remembered, crowded and chaotic. A gateway airport to Australia and the Far East, international travelers elbowed their way through the mix of people at various choke points. If he didn't know better, it appeared the airlines were doing just fine given the traffic at LAX, but in truth, he knew many of the majors were in trouble.

Jill was a great traveler. They would be gone for five days and she was able to squeeze all of her clothes into a single carry-on, one of those wheely-deals. Jason had traveled extensively his entire career and would always take just one carry-on for his clothes, regardless of duration. He wasn't about to check baggage.

Their flight arrived at LAX at four in the afternoon with the rental car dance taking another painful hour. That put them on the freeway headed north in rush-hour traffic. The advantage of traveling with just carry-on luggage was more than just the assurance your luggage would be with you when you arrived at your destination. It also meant you could rent a sporty convertible and have room to put the top down. *This was going to be a special trip*, Jason thought. So he surprised Jill and had rented a silver Mercedes SL 500, the new hardtop convertible she'd been drooling over. When the shuttle bus stopped in front of their numbered slot, she couldn't help squealing and giving Jason a quick kiss. *Nice work, cowboy*, he mused.

The drive north on the 405 was as grueling as Jason had remembered. With lots of stop-and-go traffic in the cloud of fumes L.A. was famous for, they hadn't the slightest desire to put the top down. Jill had never seen traffic like it. In some places the freeway was six lanes wide in both directions yet it still crawled and occasionally came to a complete stop. In the past, Jason would have tried his luck on "surface streets" but that was a long time ago. Getting off at the wrong exit in L.A. could be dangerous. *Better to stay on the freeway and suck it up.*

The 405 led them to the 101, the Ventura Freeway, which would take them all the way to Santa Barbara where they had planned a romantic night. From there they would continue north the 240 miles to Big Sur and the Monterey Peninsula for the rest of their weekend, returning to Santa Barbara for the conference on Monday.

By seven they'd reached the coastal town of Ventura and decided it was time for a leisurely dinner. This would also let the traffic die down for the remainder of the drive. Their destination that night was Montecito, a small town just east of Santa Barbara.

By 8:30 PM they were on the road again, making good time to the west. At nine-thirty they pulled into the Montecito Hotel with its spectacular setting just off the beach.

"Let's take a walk on the beach," Jason said after they'd checked in and begun to unpack.

"Sounds great. Are these shorts appropriate?" Jill asked, pulling a pair from her bag.

"Well, you've certainly got the legs for them. But for *your* sake, you might want to change into long slacks and a sweater or jacket. This isn't Florida, kiddo. It's going to be cold down by the beach at this hour."

"You letch," Jill winked, waving her shorts in his direction, "I always thought California had a warm climate."

"You've been watching too much *Baywatch*," Jason smiled, "that's *southern* California, the middle part of the state is much cooler, certainly at night."

The two of them crossed under the highway at a pedestrian tunnel leading to the beach. Under the full moon, they could see and hear the surf pounding against the rocks. Jill seemed glad she'd taken Jason's advice. Living on Florida's Gulf Coast, she'd become used to balmy nights and wearing shorts year-round. She'd also become used to the gentle surf from the more protected gulf. This was quite different. The Pacific stretched to the west for over three thousand miles, with nothing to interfere with the waves until they crashed on the rocks below. The moon cast a soft light on the whitecaps many yards out to sea.

They walked hand-in-hand for about thirty minutes and then retraced their steps. Quietly, they took in the sights, sounds, and smells of the raw ocean, and absorbed the pleasure of just being together. When they returned to their room, they should have been tired, but the romantic evening led to a burst of sexual energy. They made love more than once, finally falling asleep exhausted in each other's arms.

* * *

They awoke at nine, dressing quickly so they could be on the road north to Monterey. It was a beautiful morning and Jason had the top down when Jill finally emerged, beaming from the night before, ready for the next leg of the trip. Their first stop was old Santa Barbara.

"How about some breakfast?" Jason asked as he re-familiarized himself with the town. "I know a great spot and I'm starved from all the walking last night."

156

"Sounds good," Jill agreed. "But you did a lot more than walk last night!"

"Yeah, that was one *hell* of a walk," he smiled as they entered the restaurant on State Street.

After breakfast, and before getting back on 101, Jason swung past the University of California, Santa Barbara campus where he'd be presenting on Monday. He hadn't been there for a while and wanted to reacquaint himself with the area, something that would reduce his stress level for Monday morning. After a quick drive through campus, Jason located the auditorium where he would be presenting—and the closest parking lot. With his scouting mission completed, he pointed the powerful Mercedes north again. Jill was glowing and Jason couldn't recall when he'd seen her so happy. Their relationship was filled with the typical stresses of two active working people. This trip was just the R & R they needed.

Carmel Valley Ranch was their next stop. A resort ten minutes east of Carmel, this would be their home for the next few days providing a base from which they could tour Monterey, Carmel, and Big Sur. The Monterey peninsula was shrouded in early evening fog that obscured its spectacular green beauty, extended down to the water's edge.

By Sunday afternoon, they'd seen most of what you could see in the Monterey area in two days. There was the town of Monterey with its famous Cannery and incredible aquarium. They took the Seventeen Mile Drive that passed the Pebble Beach Golf Course and emptied out near the beach in Carmel. They spent almost a full day walking the streets of Carmel off the backbone of Ocean Avenue that led to the white sand beach on the Pacific Ocean. Jill couldn't get enough of the Carmel boutiques. Jason had enough after the first few and waited patiently outside of each, talking with the other guys in the same position, while enjoying the warm sunny weather as Jill rummaged for souvenirs.

After returning to the ranch and repacking the car, Jason put the top down. Jill had her seat reclined so she could stretch out and absorb the afternoon sun that remained.

"Having fun?" he asked, knowing the answer in advance.

"This has to be one of the most beautiful places on earth," Jill replied.

"Take it from someone who's traveled most of the earth, it is."

They were just about to head out of the lot back onto Carmel Valley Road when Jill pulled Jason closer to her. She kissed him longer and deeper than usual. "I love you, Jason, this has been a wonderful weekend."

"I love you too, Jill." Although they'd said these words before, Jason felt something unique as he stared into those beautiful eyes.

The ride back to Santa Barbara was quiet and uneventful. Jason took time from his thoughts to see that Jill was deep into her own. He knew this trip would turn out to be an important step in their relationship. As they pulled back into the Montecito Hotel, Jason's cell phone rang.

"Hey, Rafi, how close are you?"

"Not very, Doc," Rafi replied. "My flight was delayed and I'm just now heading out on the 405. How are the rooms at the hotel?"

"Very nice. Have you had dinner yet?"

"Just the generic airline stuff. But don't wait for me, I'll stop somewhere along the way and grab a bite."

"Hey, what's that I hear in the background?" Jason asked. "Is that Bob Marley?"

"It is. I just bought a new peripheral for my iPod. It broadcasts my iPod over any FM radio, so I don't need to burn CDs anymore."

"Rafi, you *are* amazing, you'll have to show me. I can't be falling behind on technology. Drive safe."

"Will do, Doc."

Jason and Jill had dinner at the hotel. That evening they again fell fast asleep in each other's arms, spent from another night of passion.

* * *

The 6:30 AM wake-up call came all too soon. *This is going to be a long day*, Jason thought. He had scheduled a few one-on-one meetings with people who wanted to bleed him for information. Now he would need to be careful with what he disclosed. After a full day, they would have to make the trek back to LAX for their flight to Tampa at 9:00 PM. Jason got tired just thinking of it.

Over breakfast, he reached for Jill's hand in a way that was both different yet natural. Over the last few days they had been as close as lovers could be, but their touch now revealed something beyond that.

"Stay with me today, would you?" he asked.

"Of course, where else would I go?" smiled Jill.

"You know what I mean. I know most of this stuff will be boring for you, and stressful for me, but having you with me, even just in sight, will help."

Jason had told Jill a little about his conversation with Brad. None of the details, but he was going to probably disappoint some of his audience, and she understood that was adding to his stress.

"Sure, I want to keep you in sight as well. Don't you think we should check out and get going?"

Jason glanced at his watch and realized they'd spent too much time over breakfast. He needed to get to the campus and make sure the A/V guys had his presentation, and that the computer they were going to use was functioning properly. "Let's go."

The line at the hotel's checkout counter was longer than they would have liked. They could see Rafi up ahead, already checking out with one of the agents. It was Monday morning, and typically Mondays were busy for hotels that catered to a mostly business clientele. Jason was getting anxious and Jill sensed it. "Hey, give me the keys," she said, "I can get the last of our things loaded and bring the car around while you do this."

"Good idea," Jason replied, tossing her the keys. "Don't leave without me. I know how much you like that car!"

"Don't worry, I couldn't even afford the insurance," Jill smiled and took off with her things and Jason's jacket to get everything stowed.

Jason's cell phone rang as he was approaching the counter. He saw it was Bob Daniels, and thought he better take the call in case there was something cooking at the lab or something about the conference he needed to know.

"Morning, Bob," Jason said.

"Hi, Doc. Listen," Daniels sounded excited, "there's something you need to know."

"You mean they've canceled the conference?" Jason joked.

"No, listen, someone broke into our server last night."

"What do you mean broke in?"

"I mean *hacked* it." Daniels sounded more stressed than Jason had ever remembered. "Somebody hacked our *main server!*"

"When did it happen?" Jason asked, stepping out of line since he couldn't deal with Bob's news and handle checkout at the same time.

"The IT guys have some traps set that email them if someone tries to get into our systems without proper authorization. It's standard security."

"Sure," said Jason.

"They called me at about four this morning and I came right down."

"How bad is it, did they destroy anything, drop in a virus or anything like that? Tell me we have backups."

"Of course we have backups, but that's not the issue. Listen, when I got here I had them dump the UNIX logs to try and find out what happened. It turns out they didn't do anything destructive at all. They only took copies of some files. We can tell by the commands they used in the logs. I've started an IP trace."

"Well, that's a relief, I'd hate to start rebuilding that server from the backups."

"Doc, whoever these people were, they knew what they wanted. That server contains all of our email databases, presentations, and schedules. That's the stuff they went after, and specifically, your itinerary and presentations. I wanted to get to you as early as I could, hopefully before you left your hotel. I've got the IT guys starting an IP back-trace, but that could take days before we find out where this came from. I don't know what's going on, but you need to be careful. You might be in some serious trouble, pal."

"Thanks, buddy, I'm just checking out. I don't think…"

He was interrupted by a loud roar, perhaps a large firecracker or a car backfiring? Things got worse. Two shafts of red-orange light piercing through the windows of the hotel's office made the dull fluorescent-lit room erupt in violent gold and yellow flashes. The entire building began to shake.

Earthquake, thought Jason, and that's what some people began yelling. They were common out here. But that didn't explain the ball of flames that illuminated the office. Jason then thought an airplane must have crashed into the building or parking lot, his mind raced in pure panic mode. There were screams from two women standing near the glass exit door. Pandemonium broke out as everyone rushed to the windows, an absurd thing to do if there was danger just outside, but Jason joined them.

Then he saw it. It was a car, rolling slowly, pulled by gravity down the sloping parking lot. The car was completely enveloped in flames, tires burned off, rolling as if in slow motion, bouncing on bare wheels and what remained of the molten tires. *My God! That car just exploded!* For a brief second he had forgotten he was driving a rental.

Holy Jesus! That's my car, he realized. The ladies were still screaming, and he now knew why. He could see a burning body inside and his gut wrenched. It was Jill! The smell of burning rubber and sight of her in flames made him vomit. He tried to speak but his voice had left him. His breathing stopped, his muscles contracted. He threw up again. There were a handful of men in the parking lot trying to get close enough to attempt a rescue. But it was no use, the heat was too intense. His life, his love, was dead, hopefully killed instantly by the explosion. Jason lost it completely, screaming in agony.

The flaming, rolling pyre came to rest against a concrete platform that supported the hotel's large sign. More people had made their way out of the lobby and were looking at the horrific scene. Women were crying, turning their heads, unable to watch, yet unable to resist taking quick glances. Others were frozen in horror.

Jason crumbled as if the fire had melted him. Rafi, who had run out with the others, looked at him with wide eyes. Jason was on his knees, tears running down his face, fully absorbing what had transpired. Rafi tried to comfort him but he was beyond it. Sirens sounded in the distance, getting louder as they got closer. There was nothing anyone could do.

* * *

The rest of Monday was a blur. Rafi called the conference chair to explain what had happened; there would be no CERC presentation. The conference organizers were shocked by the news and provided their condolences to Jason through Rafi. An announcement would be made at the opening session.

By 10:00 AM the fire department had extinguished the blaze, the heat so intense it had melted the asphalt parking lot under the burning car. They cordoned off the area, not letting anyone past to glimpse the grisly sight. They tried to restrain him, but it was clear he needed to see Jill. If anyone had the right it was Jason.

His thoughts were complete chaos. The charred remains of the woman he loved were so grotesque that he prayed the explosion had killed her instantly. His mind raced between who to call in Jill's family—a family he'd never met—plus police reports, a funeral, where the body would be taken, and most of all, why or how this happened? All questions, no answers.

Rafi offered to stay and help in whatever way he could. Jason appreciated that, but knew this was something he had to do himself. He had to handle each step, otherwise there would be something missing for the rest of his life—he was in shock. The two men hugged, Jason still in tears.

The hotel offered him accommodations for the next few days and Jason gratefully accepted. On Tuesday morning he started making phone calls. He spoke with Bob Daniels, the man who he'd been talking to when the explosion occurred. Bob, who had heard the details from Rafi, indicated the entire team in Tampa was in shock and offered to do anything they could. Bob would talk to the school administrators to clear Jason for the next few days. The IP trace was continuing and with Jill's death, the police were now involved.

Jason went online with his laptop from his room and found a phone number for Jill's sister, Jane, in one of the *People Page* directories. She was married to a doctor in Cleveland and fortunately, Jason had remembered his last name. Jill had been the estranged rebel of the family, moving to Florida for college and staying, so Jason had never met any of her relatives up north. Now he would have to tell a woman he had never met that her sister was dead. Trying not to go into too much detail, Jason did his best to explain. He found himself crying on the phone with a complete stranger.

Fortunately, Jane was a strong woman, which took some of the burden off of him. This became apparent once the two of them got stabilized. Jane agreed to call all of the people on Jill's side. Jason would handle getting the body returned to Cleveland and insisted on paying for all of the funeral arrangements. He wanted to meet Jane to tell her what a wonderful sister she had, but figured she already knew.

Then there were the police reports. No one knew how the explosion had happened. Everyone agreed it was unusual for a vehicle of that quality to spontaneously explode, but strange things happen. They had to keep open the possibility of foul play, repeatedly asking Jason if he had any enemies who would want to harm either of them. He could only think of Bob's call and wonder if there was some sinister conspiracy tied to Sandra Bilson's warnings or his meeting with Brad. Things were moving fast, and he really didn't have enough information to coherently implicate anyone or any organization. Events seemed to be warning him of impending disaster, but he still couldn't believe that anyone would want him killed. Could his own naiveté have resulted in Jill's death? The thought chilled him.

CNN carried a small piece about the explosion on Monday night, after which the rental car company sent him a loaner at no expense. They were concerned about liability and it could take days for the police to determine if there was foul-play. The airline graciously offered to reschedule Jason's return trip. He would be ready to return on the same flight Wednesday evening.

* * *

It was time to go home. The rental car needed gas to get back to LAX and Jason found himself in a long line at a service station. Gas prices in Florida had worked their way up over six dollars a gallon, but here in California he could see they were paying $11.79 for regular. Based on the long line, there was a shortage even at that price. The irony struck him. He'd come here to discuss the work of his group, which could ultimately free the country from a whole set of energy-related problems. The never-ending Middle East war continued to escalate, and people out here were waiting in line to pay almost twelve dollars for a gallon of gasoline. California would just be the beginning, portending shortages across the rest of the nation.

The long drive back gave him time to think about the most horrendous week of his life. It had started on a positive note with a report that should have left his investors smiling. Instead there were the two clandestine meetings with Bilson and Spencer. In the last, he had been told the president of the United States wanted to cancel his presentation. Then, hackers broke into his server back in the lab, and finally, a catastrophic explosion that took the love of his life.

It was completely dark on the 101 and rain began to fall as he headed south. Only the lights of intermittent northbound truckers interrupted the deep depression descending over him. His thoughts went back to his meetings with Bilson and Spencer. The government had had its way, there was no presentation. And what about Bilson's concern over the impact their breakthrough would have on the oil industry or OPEC? *Life as I know it may be over,* he realized.

Chapter 13.
CIA Headquarters, Langley, VA

The CIA has approximately twenty thousand employees, making it the largest intelligence gathering and support arm in the world; the exact number is classified. "The Company," as the CIA is sometimes called internally, is organized into four distinct divisions: Operations, Science and Technology, Intelligence, and Administration.

Don Wilcox was a mid-level agent in the Intelligence Division running several ops around the world, keeping tabs on and infiltrating international crime syndicates. He managed agent ops in the Middle East, Africa, and South America. He was thirty-eight years old, divorced with a ten-year-old daughter, and engaged to a pretty and successful lawyer. Once thought to be on a fast track within the Agency, Wilcox' star was no longer rising at the same rate. He was not sure why, but thought it might have something to do with his divorce. Peggy, his ex, was well liked in CIA social circles, and was also well connected to the wives of certain higher-ups. It was also generally agreed that the Agency frowned upon divorces. Angry ex-spouses were a distinct liability. They had vendettas to fulfill, making them easy prey for anyone wanting information.

Despite that, Wilcox was a dedicated agent. The Company had been his life for almost fifteen years. He had a good position and took pride in work that kept America safe. His dedication drove him to put in hours well above and beyond a healthy workday. *Perhaps the underlying reason for the divorce*, he reasoned. Fortunately, his fiancée, Sandra, had an intense career herself and could relate to long hours at the office.

If running agents wasn't enough, it was good cover for the work that really mattered. He was assigned to head a secret CIA unit charged with inside investigations, effectively an Internal Affairs division, reporting directly to the Agency director, William Reynolds. With an organization the size of the CIA, bad apples in the bunch were a statistical certainty. However, the CIA couldn't acknowledge the organization. Its very existence was classified. Running an Internal Affairs unit was the most secret part of Don Wilcox' already too secret life.

Wilcox packed his three cell phones as he prepared to leave his Dolly Madison apartment at 6:30 AM for the short commute to his office at CIA headquarters in Langley.

Three cell phones were a professional necessity for Wilcox. He carried his standard issue phone for his intelligence job, another one for his Internal Affairs work, and a private one for his personal use. Each was an identical Samsung GSM unit so he only needed to be familiar with one set of operating procedures. To keep them straight he used different color faceplates and different ring tones. He used a green skin for his intelligence work, red for IA matters, and white for his personal use.

Working for the CIA, he had to assume his company cell phone could be traced at any time, although they would never admit it. When he had accepted his IA assignment with the director, he was given his second phone, confirming his suspicions, enough so to purchase a third, private phone. He paid cash for his third phone from a company that only used prepaid SIM cards, and he always paid cash for the minutes. Prepaid SIMs meant no monthly bill and thus no need for his address. The idea of no paper trail was comforting. He could check the phone any time he wanted to see how many minutes remained and then walk into any of several stores and purchase additional minutes. For safety, he always carried an extra SIM with plenty of time on it.

The day he purchased his personal Samsung, he bought another one for Sandra. She hated the inconvenience of carrying two phones, and thought he was being paranoid. Sandra's phone was the only one he called with his personal unit so as not to leave his number on any other phone. Sandra was the only person who knew Don's personal number. The only other calls he received were wrong numbers and he would answer only if Sandra's name appeared on the Caller ID. If another number appeared, he would let the call go to his voicemail, where he purposely left the default generic greeting to make sure no additional information was provided.

Don looked forward to his workdays and had done so since his personal life had gone into the toilet. The Dolly Madison Apartments were nice, as apartments go, but he owned, and was still paying for, a nice four-bedroom home just outside McLean, Virginia, that he could no longer use. He made a good salary, but in addition to paying alimony and child-support, he had to support himself. Gone was his BMW 3-series, replaced by a Chrysler LeBaron, and frozen dinners had replaced Peggy's good cooking.

Settling into his office, Wilcox had long ago dispensed with newspapers, preferring to get his news over the Internet—it was more current, and free. His favorite news site was CNN.com and this morning it carried a story about a car explosion in Santa Barbara. He clicked on the headline that took him to the full article.

A university professor by the name of Jason Davidson was in Santa Barbara for an energy conference. On Monday morning, his car exploded while he was in the hotel office checking out. His companion, one Jill Roberts, was killed. Authorities announced it had been an accident but they were still investigating. The article included color pictures of the flaming car, a man kneeling down in the foreground, and the gruesome image of a person in the driver's seat completely engulfed in flames. *Grisly*, thought Wilcox. *These names are familiar*. He picked up his private cell phone and pushed the speed-dial button for Sandra.

"Good morning, Don," Sandra answered.

"Morning, Sandy, are you at the office yet?"

"No, just sitting at the kitchen table, reading the newspaper."

"Well, break into the twenty-first century," Wilcox teased. "Go to CNN.com, there's an article you need to see."

Sandra took her phone into the den and brought up the site. "Okay, I'm there."

"See the article on the car that exploded in California? Click on that link and see if you know any of those people."

Sandra did as asked. "Oh my God! Don, that's Professor Davidson and his girlfriend, Jill!"

"I thought so. Didn't we meet them when they were in D.C. for a conference a few months ago?"

"We did," Sandy said through tears, "they're such a nice couple and she was just lovely. Does it say how this happened? I just saw the professor last week!"

"They say it was an accident, but haven't released details of their investigation."

"Don, this is crazy. I was with my client from National Oil last week and sat in on the professor's board meeting where he announced some dramatic new results."

"How significant?"

"Well, 'earth shattering' wouldn't be too strong. I met him that evening at the airport to warn him the oil industry wasn't going to welcome his discoveries, especially since they preclude using existing industry infrastructure. My God, you don't think..."

"They said it was an accident, but of course they may not want to publicize any suspicions yet. Plus it happened pretty soon after your meeting. If you're thinking this was some kind of oil industry 'hit,' it would probably take them longer to act. Tell you what, I'll do some checking and get back to you later."

"Thanks, Don. This is terrible! I need to call the professor, give him our condolences, and see how he's doing. Bye."

One of the benefits of working at the CIA was access to the information on various internal systems. The problem was, there were at least twelve of those systems. Fortunately, about two years ago someone in the IT department had come up with a Google-like search engine that would take search criteria and process it against all twelve systems. For curiosity's sake, Wilcox entered "CERC" into the search engine to see if it would return anything. To his surprise, three hits emerged:

Jan 20, 2010: CERC Clean Energy Research Center – Need to Know, Economics

July 1, 2011: CERC Clean Energy Research Center – Need to Know, Energy

September 5, 2012: CERC Clean Energy Research
Center – Need to Know, Strategic

Although he couldn't access the details, he could see there were hits going all the way back to the inception of the group, and these came from three different monitoring systems. Since each was labeled "Need to Know," a special password was required to see the details, and since he wasn't on the "Need to Know" list, he didn't have it. On the other hand, he could probably get it from the director with some logical justification.

He'd call Sandra later to give her an update. In the meantime, he had to get back to work, and that meant processing his email. The car explosion story had been a distraction.

The first item in his email queue was from "INTERN," which was the director's email address when he was operating in IA mode. From the timestamp on the message, Wilcox could tell it had been sent Sunday evening. *It's good to know even the old man works on weekends*, he thought with a smile. The encrypted message was requesting a meeting at 9:30 AM to discuss an IA matter, the death of an agent in Venezuela. Don already had an appointment at nine-thirty, but he would juggle that one in favor of the director. He issued an "accept" to the message, which placed it on both his calendar and the director's.

By quarter after nine, Don was on his way out of the building, heading for Café Tatti, a small Italian eatery that served as one of the director's standard meeting places. Tatti provided a small private room just a short walk from the back door. Such meetings were most always inconvenient and for that reason most contact was made using secure cell phones. However, when IA documents needed to be passed, Café Tatti was the director's first choice.

Wilcox entered the back door, said "hi" to the owner, Gio-vani, and walked through the kitchen into the private room a few minutes past nine-thirty. The director was waiting with a pot of hot coffee.

"Morning, Don. Coffee?"

"Good morning, sir," Wilcox said as he took a seat. "Coffee sounds good. What have you got?"

"Do you know an agent by the name of Bert Walters?"

"No, sir, he's not one of mine. Actually," Wilcox said after some hesitation, "I've heard the name and we may have been introduced at a conference several months ago. Is he in some kind of trouble?"

"You could say that. He's dead."

"Was it in the line of duty?"

"Well, it doesn't appear that way. Agent Walters' group was running an op out of Caracas. The local police found him in the Plaza Altamira early yesterday morning, slumped over a park bench, dead of a heroin overdose."

"Sounds like he got mixed up with the locals."

"It does *sound* like that, but there are a number of things troubling me. First, we had one other death in the Agency under similar circumstances. Second, it also was a local crime, or at least made to look as such. Third, I knew Bert and drugs don't make sense."

"How so, sir?"

"I recruited Bert Walters into the Agency five years ago, I knew his father from my days in the army. Bert Walters wasn't a drug addict—he was an athlete in college and a good one. I went to his wedding two years ago, wife's name is Martha. There appears to be a pattern here, and I'd like you to check it out."

"Have you talked to his wife?"

"Not yet, I'll do that after you've had a chance to talk with her. I'd like to find out what she can add to the story, and then I'll call with my condolences. Here's a copy of Walters' file with everything you need."

The director placed a thick manila envelope on the table with a seal that read: "Bert Walters, Deceased."

So that's how an agent's life gets summarized, Don couldn't help thinking, *'Don Wilcox, Deceased.'* "I'll get on it right away and see if I can meet with his widow this afternoon. Any kids?"

"One on the way."

"Oh no." After a long pause, Wilcox asked, "Sir, I have another matter I'm working on, could I ask a favor?"

"Go for it."

"An acquaintance of Sandra's and mine was involved in a car explosion in California on Monday. He escaped injury, but his girlfriend was killed."

"Sorry to hear that, but how can the CIA help?"

"This guy's a professor in Tampa and runs some kind of clean energy group called CERC. The explosion sounds suspicious and I thought I would check to see if 'the Company' ever had any interest in his group. I had three hits from three different systems dating back several years, but all of them came back as Need to Know."

"And you're looking for the password."

"Yes," Wilcox admitted.

"Well, I can't go that far yet, but I can look for you to see if there's anything relevant, and then we can make a determination if you have Need to Know."

"That would be helpful," Wilcox said.

"I'll see if I can have something for you by this afternoon when you call with an update from your meeting with Walters' wife. Now why don't you get out of here, through the back. I'll wait twenty minutes and leave through the front."

"Very good, and thank you, sir."

"Give my condolences to Martha and let her know I'll be calling."

Chapter 14.
Recovery

It was a long flight from L.A. back to Tampa. Jason was feeling a loneliness that he knew would be with him for a long time. He'd been so busy in Santa Barbara with the police and making arrangements for Jill's funeral that he hadn't had time to think. The flight was fairly empty, which gave him both the time and space to start the grieving process. The thought of never again seeing the person he loved was overwhelming. Flying back with the empty seat next to him brought home the finality.

Thursday morning rolled around too quickly, but Jason knew the best thing for him was get back into his routine. He could hear Jill telling him that. He was just hoping he could get through the day with some sense of productivity.

He walked into the lab early, hoping to beat everyone there, assuming everyone on campus had heard about his ordeal. No such luck as several of his engineers were hard at work. All activity stopped when he walked in the door. At first the atmosphere was subdued, the professor nodding to the troops as he walked through the bullpen. There was a stiffness throughout the room that was uncomfortable for everyone. Finally, Julie, one of the junior engineers, stood up and said, "Professor, are you alright? We're so sorry about what happened."

"I will be, Julie. It's going to take some time, but as some of you probably know, after losing a loved one, part of you will never get over it. Thank you for your concern."

By then, all the engineers had gathered around and Jason shook hands with each. The last person in the line was Bob Daniels who'd emerged from his office when he heard the commotion. That handshake ended in an embrace of the two men and more than one tear was shed.

Through choking voice and watery eyes, Jason addressed the group: "Thank you all for your concern. God bless you. I know those of you who had met Jill will miss her. I'd ask that if there is one thing you want to do, it's to continue on with the work you've been doing. We've made great strides on our project and Jill would want us to continue that pace. Thank you again." He and Bob retired to Jason's office.

"How've things been around here?" Jason asked.

"We're making good progress on our IP trace. As you know, it can be a long process. Rafi's working on it himself. The guy's an Internet wizard and wants to personally track this down to see if it might be related to what happened out there."

"It was good to have him with me, he was a big help during the first few hours. I know he wants to keep helping, he feels connected. Let me know what you find out..."

They were interrupted by Jason's cell phone.

Chapter 15.
The Club

On Wilcox' first call to the Walters' residence their phone rang several times without answer. He let it ring hoping to leave a message, but it just kept ringing. He assumed they had an answering machine so either it was full or Mrs. Walters had turned it off—either of those a good indication of depression. He let it ring some more. Finally, someone picked up, but didn't say anything. He could hear breathing.

"Mrs. Walters?" he probed.

"Yes, who is this?" Martha Walters said after a noticeable delay through muffled tears.

"My name is Don Wilcox, Mrs. Walters. I'm with the CIA and knew your husband," Wilcox fibbed. Technically, he knew *of* Bert and felt this might help open the door—quite literally—to talking with this grieving widow.

"I'm sorry, I don't recognize your name," she said, regaining her composure.

"I've just finished a meeting with our director, William Reynolds, and he asked me to give you a call. Have you met the director?" Wilcox asked, knowing the answer but also knowing it was always good to start with a question a person could answer yes to.

"I have. He recruited Bert into the Agency and was at our wedding. I'm not sure I feel up to any discussions right now. What do you want, Mr. Wilcox?"

"Mrs. Walters, I've been asked to review the circumstances surrounding your husband's death. I know you're feeling a lot of pain and you have our deepest sympathy regarding the loss of Bert. However, it would be valuable to talk with you as soon as possible to make sure we don't lose any information. Could we meet in person? This would only take an hour at most."

"Very good, Mr. Wilcox, how about at 11:00 AM at our house—I mean my house?" she said, choking up again.

"That would be fine, I'll see you shortly."

* * *

Driving to the Walters' home was painful for Wilcox in several ways. Visiting widows of recently slain agents was always depressing. He had been through this before and on occasion found himself struggling to ask the questions that needed asking, unsure of what to do in the face of emotional outbursts. The additional pain from this visit was that the Walters' lived just a few blocks from Wilcox' old home, an upper middle class neighborhood of two-story four-bedroom brick homes on half-acre lots. The visit would bring back memories of happier times, when he and Peggy had just moved in and all had seemed right with the world.

He arrived a few minutes early and waited in the car until exactly eleven o'clock. *She may have needed all the time to get ready,* he thought as he stepped from his car. Standing on the porch, he could see the storm door was open and just the screen door was latched. He knocked lightly on the aluminum doorframe and the obviously pregnant Mrs. Bert Walters appeared from around the corner, almost waddling to meet him.

"Good morning, Mrs. Walters," Wilcox said through the screen, "I'm Don Wilcox from the Agency and spoke with you earlier." He had taken his ID out of his wallet in advance and held it up in plain view against the screen as she approached.

She studied it for what seemed a longer time than necessary. "Please come in, Mr. Wilcox," Martha said as she held the door. "I'm sorry if it sounded like I was giving you a hard time on the phone. I've been under a lot of stress and find it difficult to talk about what happened, although I know it will be good for me. My mother will be staying with me for a while, which should help."

"Believe me, Mrs. Walters, you have nothing to apologize for. Your husband's death was a tragedy and it will take us all time to get past it. My goal is to help find out what happened and perhaps that information can put some of this behind you."

"Please call me, Martha."

"Thank you, Martha, and I'm Don, my father is Mr. Wilcox."

That got her to smile as she moved gingerly toward the kitchen with Wilcox in tow.

"Can we sit in the kitchen to do this? I have some coffee on and I just feel more comfortable in here."

"Absolutely," Wilcox said as they sat down across from each other at a small spotless kitchen table where he could imagine happy times in the past. Her eyes looked tired, it was obvious she hadn't slept much in the last few days.

"Where would you like me to start?" she asked. "I'm not sure I can shed any more light on what happened. As I found out early in our marriage, CIA agents don't talk a lot about their activities, and Bert was no exception. When he was in town, he kept a fairly regular schedule, and was usually home for dinner. I learned not to ask questions he couldn't—or wouldn't answer."

"First, let me give you my card," said Wilcox as he handed over his official CIA business card. "I know you're working with the appropriate administrative people at the Agency, but if you ever think you need some additional help, please call me at either the office number or on my cell. I'd like to help in any way I can."

And with that, the tears came. Wilcox felt out of place at times like this. Here was a person in obvious need of emotional support and neither of them felt comfortable making the first move. Wilcox stood with his arms out and she just naturally stepped into them. He was unprepared for the weight of her and her unborn child, in addition to the emotional weight she carried, causing him to stagger slightly.

"Oh, Mr. Wilcox, I'm so sorry," she sobbed with her head on his shoulder and her arms around him, thankful for the physical support.

"Martha," Wilcox said through watery eyes of his own, "this is as hard as life gets. Before I leave today I'm going to tell you to be strong, but right now, you need to grieve. I wish there was something I could tell you that would make it easier, but I know there isn't."

For several long minutes the two of them embraced. The crying had stopped and the silence was broken only by the sound of the coffee pot on the counter, the gurgling signaling it was done.

"Well," Martha said with the beginnings of a smile, "I'm glad I got that over with. Thank you."

"No thanks necessary," Wilcox said as they both sat down.

"Now, as I was saying," Martha began with renewed composure, dabbing at her eyes with a paper napkin, "Bert was very quiet about his work, so I don't know what I can add to what you already know."

"Perhaps there was something unsaid that would help; a look, unusual behavior, anything that might seem out of character. We train our agents well, but believe me we are still human and we carry our emotional baggage around like everyone else."

"Actually, there was something, and you just made me think of it. It started out as restless evenings. Bert was always a sound sleeper, but he suddenly started to wake up in the middle of the night. When he'd get out of bed, I'd sometimes wake up and find him here in the kitchen having a glass of milk and watching the news with the sound turned way down, trying not to wake me. At first I thought it might just be the stress of becoming a parent for the first time. It can have that effect, you know. Do you have any children?"

"I have a daughter, Amanda, who's just ten years old, and I know exactly what you mean," he said, resisting the temptation to mention his sad story of divorce, and hoping she wouldn't ask any more questions. If he wasn't careful, this could end up as a case of the emotionally blind leading the blind. "So, how did you resolve this?"

"Actually, we didn't. After a few evenings of his waking up early, I started asking Bert if there was something going on at work or something else that I could help him through. Initially he said it was really nothing, but the more I pressed, I could see something was really bothering him. I was hoping it wasn't me or the baby. So then I backed off because I knew if it had something to do with work, he wouldn't be able to tell me, and that would frustrate him even more."

"So did these episodes finally stop?"

"In a sense, but they turned into something else. Instead of waking up, he began having nightmares—and talking in his sleep, something he'd never done before."

"Do you remember what he said? Was anything intelligible? I've been accused of talking in my sleep and my wife said it was mostly nonsense. Sometimes, she said I'd just be speaking numbers!"

"It had something to do with someone pressuring him to go somewhere, or to join something, something that he didn't want to do. On several occasions, he mentioned a 'club' that someone wanted him to either go to or join and he wanted to join but just couldn't for some reason. Does this make any sense to you? Does it help?"

"Let's just say it doesn't hurt. There was something clearly bothering Bert, but I doubt it had anything to do with you or starting a family. I think you're right to believe it had something to do with work. Did he ever mention any names when he talked about this 'club'?"

"No, he never mentioned any person by name, but when he spoke about this club, it was always in the context of the CIA. Does the CIA have a health club or other such clubs that he may have been considering joining?"

"We do have a health club, but joining the CIA health club shouldn't be something that would cause stress. In fact, it's supposed to relieve stress." They both smiled. "Look, I've taken enough of your time today. I need to take into account what you've told me and see if I can tie that in with any other information I have."

"Good, thank you very much for coming over, even though I was difficult."

"It was my pleasure, Martha. I hope I can take what you've told me and make something out of it. I may have more questions down the road. Okay if I call you?"

"Of course, Don, if there's anything I can do to help, please let me know. I think it would help me deal with this."

Wilcox got back into his car, feeling like he'd made a new friend. He wasn't sure what he was going to be able to construct from the "club" business; nothing crossed his mind. On the drive back to his office, he pulled out his red phone and called the director.

"Hi, Don."

"Hello, sir, I've just left the Walters' home where I spent some time with Martha Walters. Can you talk?"

"Yes, and I have an update for you, but first tell me what you learned from Martha."

"As you know, sir, Bert was a Company man all the way and did very little talking about work. I didn't see or hear anything regarding his personal life that would cause him to go off the rails. He had a beautiful wife and was starting a family, he had everything to live for from a personal perspective."

"That sounds like him," the director said. "Ironic isn't it that in a situation like this, the type of people we hire into the Company and the training we give them makes it hard to find out what happened."

"It is, sir. There is one piece of information I came away with that might help."

"What was that?"

"Apparently, for the last several weeks, Bert wasn't sleeping well. His insomnia would wake Martha up and she'd find him watching television at 4:00 AM. Then it progressed to talking in his sleep and he was having recurring nightmares about joining some club."

"Did she say what kind of club?"

"No, but she said it was always in the context of the Company. She even asked if maybe he was worried about joining a Company health club," Wilcox smiled. "So that's really the only lead I have."

"Well, if this has anything to do with a club, it certainly wasn't a healthy one. There is one tie point that we may want to investigate."

"Sir?"

"As I think I mentioned, two weeks ago we had an agent killed in Singapore. He was in a bad part of the city, a place he shouldn't have been and was shot in a mugging, or what looked like one. There was a witness who saw the whole thing and came to his aid while he was lying on the street. All the agent could say was something about a 'club.' So here we now have two agents in the wrong place at the wrong time talking about joining a club. If two occurrences make a pattern, we may have something to go on."

"Agreed, I'll run with that. You said you had something for me, did you find out anything about those CERC references I told you about?"

"Yes, Don, let's shift gears for a moment. I ran the same query you did and of course came up with the same results. I was able to use the password and look at the details, and it appears the Company has been monitoring the work of this CERC organization for a long time. There is also a reference to the National Oil Company when they became an investor some time back. I find it interesting that an oil company would be funding work potentially harmful to their business in the long term."

"Yes, sir. You know, Sandy is consulting for National and I asked her that very question. She said National was interested in getting advanced knowledge of energy alternatives with the hope of adapting their infrastructure in some way to get a jump on the competition when alternative energy solutions become economical."

"Well, I guess that makes sense."

"At least it did. According to Sandy, at the last board meeting she attended, this Professor Davidson, whose car exploded in California, reported on some serious breakthroughs that would eliminate the need for *any* oil company infrastructure—don't ask me how. I wouldn't expect news like that to go down well with her client, or the rest of the oil industry for that matter."

"Interesting," Reynolds said. "There are some other troubling things I discovered that I should tell you. The first has to do with the CERC entries in the three systems in which you found them. They were anonymous."

"But aren't all entries in all of our systems tagged with the author's name?"

"Yes, each of these systems automatically logs the author of each entry along with timestamps and other tracing information. We do have the timestamps for these entries, but the *author* field in the database for each is blank. I've checked with IT and there's only one way this could happen. And that's if someone who knows how these systems are constructed—or figured it out— was able to break in and erase these fields."

"Okay, but wouldn't they leave an audit trail or tracks our IT guys could find?"

"I was hoping the same thing, but whoever did this was smart enough not to leave a trail. My other concern has to do with the safety of your professor. When I discovered the missing information in our databases, I called my counterpart at the FBI, Director Jackson. He shared with me that the professor's rental car explosion was not an accident. They found plastic explosive residue, something called PETN on what remained of the under-carriage of the car. He says it was a very professional job. That bomb was more than likely meant for him."

"I need to warn Sandy so she can contact Davidson."

"Don, better than that, I'd like to alter your mission a bit. In my reading of the CERC information we have on file, the profes-sor's work has acquired a national security label. Even though we don't know who's making these entries, that CERC group is on to something *big*. I'd like you to take on the professor and his team as a new project, prioritizing Davidson's safety. I'm also concerned we don't put Sandra in any kind of jeopardy."

"Very well, sir, I'll see if Sandy can set up a meeting. Can we issue the professor a CCW for his own protection?"

"I think that would make sense. Be careful, Don, and I don't need to remind you this is highly confidential. I think you need to inform Davidson the explosion was no accident, but the FBI doesn't want that knowledge in the general public as it could compromise their investigation."

"I understand, sir, and I'll keep you informed."

"Please do, there might be something big here and you may need additional resources, call me immediately if you do."

"Will do."

With that, Wilcox put away his red phone, and reached into his pocket for the white one.

"Hi, Don, how's it going?" answered Sandra.

"Have you had a chance to call Davidson?"

"Not yet, I thought I'd wait a while and see if you had any-thing to add."

"Good, and I do. Where are you? Are you alone?"

"At lunch, at that small restaurant on the first floor of my building. I'm alone."

"Okay, first off, that explosion wasn't an accident. The FBI found traces of plastic explosive under the car, but they want people to think it was an accident while they investigate."

"How did you find this out? All the news sources I've seen say it was an accident!"

"I'm working with the director himself on this one. He's taken a personal interest. He has access to all the right people. Basically, we believe Davidson was the real target of the explosion. The other thing I found out is that the CIA's been monitoring CERC since its inception. Also, the director has reassigned me to Davidson's case. I need to meet with him in person, ASAP. Can you set this up?"

"I can try, but where would you want to meet him?"

"It's been a while since we've had a getaway, let's take Friday off and go down to Clearwater Beach and stay at that little inn we like for the weekend. What about meeting him at Bill's Café on the beach for dinner Saturday night? Think you could get away?"

"I have to say, I owe myself some vacation time. We need to let him know he's in danger. I was going to call him this afternoon, but I'll do it right now."

Chapter 16.
Warning

"This is Jason," he said, not recognizing the calling number.

"Professor Davidson, this is Sandra Bilson," she said cautiously, not sure what kind of response she'd get. After all, she was calling a man who had just been through hell and probably hadn't emerged yet.

"Yes, Ms. Bilson."

"I'm sorry if this isn't a good time, Professor, but I just had to call, and please call me Sandy."

"Okay, Sandy, I've been getting a lot of calls today."

"Professor, I'm calling from a pay phone. We need to talk, but I don't trust your phone."

"What's wrong with my phone?"

She ignored him. "Can you call me back from a pay phone on my private cell number? I wrote it in pencil on the back of the business card I gave you at your meeting." *Don's not going to like this.*

"I have your card in my wallet. Is this subterfuge really nec..."

"Professor," she cut him off, "please just call me back, and after you do, destroy my business card." She hung up.

Jesus Christ, here we go again. Jason excused himself with Daniels and made his way to the pay phone out near the quad after stopping by his car to retrieve a handful of quarters he was looking for a way to get rid of. He couldn't recall when he had last used a pay phone. It seemed antiquated as he dialed the number Bilson had written down.

She picked up immediately. "Professor, sorry about the cloak-and-dagger, but you'll see why it's important. First, I just had to pass on my condolences, especially after our meeting at the airport. I can't believe this has happened. My fiancé, Don Wilcox, just called me with the news. I remember meeting Jill when you were in town for a conference. Don sends his condolences as well. She was such a lovely person." She started to cry.

"Thank you, Sandra, and thank your fiancé for me."

"I will, Jason," Sandra said sniffling, followed by what seemed a long pause. "Are you alright? Is there anything I can do?"

"Sandra, I'm as well as can be expected under the circumstances. At least I'm physically alright, I could have been in that car with Jill—in fact I *should* have been in that car with Jill. If only there was someway it could have been me instead of her," Jason said, beginning to choke up.

He's fighting it, Sandra winced. After an appropriate pause to let Jason compose himself, and to hold back her own emotions, she said, "Professor, I don't remember if I told you or not, but Don's a CIA agent here in Washington."

"Yes, I'd heard that."

"He saw the Santa Barbara story on the Internet, and he's taken an interest in the case."

"Sounds like there's more to the explosion than the cops are letting on," Jason said.

"Professor, Don has it on good authority that your rental car explosion was caused by a bomb, not an accident. He's also uncovered some other information he'd like to make you aware of, but he wants to do this in person, your phone may be monitored."

"Sandra, you're scaring me, and I don't need to be more scared than I am already."

"I'm sorry, but we're truly concerned for your life. Could you meet us Saturday night for dinner at a place called Bill's Café on the beach in Clearwater? I don't think that's too far from you. Don would like to share what he's learned."

"Sandra, I'm no pyro-technician, but I *thought* that car explosion was too violent for an accidental ignition, and I told the FBI that when they finally stopped treating me like a suspect. I know my way around Clearwater quite well. Bill's is only twenty minutes from the campus, and I've eaten there before. I don't think I can refuse. What time Saturday?"

"We'll meet you for dinner at seven-thirty. Don and I are staying down for the weekend. That's one of our favorite spots."

"Very good, I'll see you and Don there."

"Thank you, Professor, please be careful, and remember to destroy my business card."

"You mean it won't self-destruct?"

Chapter 17.
Presidential Review

After working late, Zeng rose early, glad to be sleeping in his own bed. His schedule had become more frenetic since accepting the oil assignment from President Wu, especially since his return from Riyadh. But his morning ritual hadn't changed. He was tempted to skip his Qigong workout, thinking it would be better use of his time to prep for his meeting. He wisely reconsidered. He felt strongly that early morning physical exercise was both healthful and invigorating and he wasn't getting any younger. Nonetheless, he was preoccupied with his upcoming morning, turning it over and over in his mind.

Xiumei awoke early to prepare her husband's congee. Like most men, Ju didn't share all the details of his work. However, like most wives, Xiumei seemed to sense something important was imminent and wanted to support her husband. He'd had meetings with President Wu before, but his body language said there must be something special about this one.

"Thank you, Xiumei," Ju said as he finished his breakfast.

"You were up late last night, I can see it in your eyes," Xiumei said. "Your car is in the driveway, should I ask the driver to wait?"

"Thank you, but no. I will get my valise and be on my way."

Xiumei met him at the door with his newspaper neatly re-folded from breakfast. He walked outside, stepping into the lush interior of the black limousine.

"Good morning, Mr. Minister," said his chauffer.

"Good morning, Chi," he replied. "Take me to the Great Hall this morning, I have a meeting with the president."

"Very well, sir," saluted the driver as he shut Zeng's door.

* * *

President Wu had been in his office in the Great Hall since 6:30 AM, early even by his standards. His staff hated it, but he knew they would not show it. They were fortunate to serve him and someday would tell their grandchildren about their great president. Wu's days had been starting earlier and ending later as governing such a large country grew in complexity.

"Heng, do we have Mr. Zeng on our schedule for today?" asked the president.

Thien Heng was President Wu's secretary and administrative assistant. The president had several assistants, some of whom handled more strategic matters. Heng was a secretary in the American sense, acting as Wu's receptionist, call screener and coordinator of his schedule. She was fiercely dedicated.

"Yes, Mr. President, Minister Zeng will be here at seven-thirty. Should I bring him to your office or arrange for a conference room?" she asked, somewhat rhetorically. It was always good to let him make last minute changes and sometimes to remind him such changes were possible.

"My office will be fine. Tea would be appropriate if you would."

"Certainly, sir."

* * *

Chi wheeled the car into Tiananmen Square stopping in front of the Great Hall. Ever since the 1989 protest march in the square, few could enter without seeing images of tanks shooting unarmed students, an event fixed forever in the minds of all Chinese. Zeng was one who remembered those days vividly. He stepped out in reverent observance and walked up the stairs, affixing a badge to his suit pocket that would get him through a very rigorous security checkpoint.

Meeting President Wu in his office made this day very special. Zeng hoped that someone of importance would see his arrival, although it was a bit early—perhaps on his departure then. He found his way to the secretary's desk. She was waiting for him and greeted him by name.

"Good morning, Mr. Zeng," said Heng standing and offering a polite bow.

"Good morning, Thien Heng," he had glanced at her name plate on the desk, hoping she hadn't noticed. Everyone knew that secretaries were powerful people who could make or break careers by setting appointments with their bosses—or not. "I'm a bit early."

"President Wu was just asking about you, please follow me."

As they entered Wu's office, he was standing at a credenza where Heng had arranged tea and other refreshments. Wu was looking out over the entirety of Tiananmen Square. *The master of all he surveys*, Zeng thought.

"Mr. President, here is Minister Zeng," she said.

"Thank you, Heng," replied Wu, as Heng disappeared from the room as silent as vapor.

"Good morning, President Wu," said Zeng, bowing in respect.

"A lot has happened since we last met, Mr. Zeng, and that was not so long ago. You have been very busy. Interesting work I trust."

"Mr. President, this has been the most intense and exciting period of my career in public office. I would like to brief you on my visit to Riyadh and my meetings with Prince Faareh. They were as important as we thought they would be, but went in a direction not entirely anticipated."

"Please proceed, Ju. However, before you start, was the prince the correct audience, or do we also need to open discussions with the king directly?"

"No, sir, Abdul provided good intelligence in that regard. Everyone in Saudi Arabia knows the prince is the decision-maker and next in line for the throne. The king will follow his lead."

"Very good."

"Abdul first introduced me to the prince at the palace office. As you and I reviewed on our secure call, I spent just fifteen minutes with the prince while I explained in summary the nature of our interest in a partnership. He grasped the importance immediately and asked if Abdul and I would meet him at his home for dinner. That evening, Abdul and his driver picked me up at the hotel and we drove to the prince's residence, actually, another palace. This was the most beautiful home I have ever seen. The portico was two stories tall and as long as the house, the entryway..."

"Mr. Zeng," Wu interrupted, "I can tell you were excited by the honor of dining with the prince and seeing his residence. I've been there twice myself, and found it just as fascinating as you are describing," the president smiled, nodding to Zeng that he should get to the heart of the meeting.

"I'm sorry." Zeng went back to his notes. "Over dinner, I presented our proposal. A thirty-five billion dollar development followed by a commitment for three million barrels per day up to twelve million barrels per day at prices from 30 to 120 dollars per barrel."

"Did the prince grasp it quickly?"

"Mr. President," Zeng replied, "Prince Faareh not only grasped the concept, he started taking it over!"

"What do you mean?"

"It's clear to me that Prince Faareh spends a lot of time thinking about the role oil will play in the future of his country. It's also clear that oil is their only current asset on which their entire economy and the royal family's political future depends, and this will be the case for the foreseeable future. I can see how this drives his current thinking and his interest in our proposal."

"How so?"

"When I first presented our ideas, I started by discussing our proposed joint development. Before I could begin to describe the other components, he had latched onto the thirty-five billion dollar number, implying it was not enough for a fifteen-year partnership. I then added the usage components of the plan, which he grasped just as quickly."

"Was he agreeable to the floor and ceiling numbers you presented?"

"I believe he was agreeable in *principle*, although he may want to come back with some alternatives, once he has had time to think about them. The prince is a skilled negotiator and will not give us his complete opinion at first, without additional negotiation. His attention was focused on the currency issue."

"Ju, Prince Faareh is a very smart man, which, of course, is why he will be the next king. We should not be too concerned if this negotiation takes several weeks to complete. I expect your perceptions are correct. What was his problem with currency? They sell their oil in U.S. dollars today."

"Exactly what I asked him, Mr. President, since I did not know where he was going with his concern either. That is where the meeting got *very* interesting.

"He had two concerns about the ceiling we proposed. First, he believes the price of oil will go well above \$120 per barrel. Although he cannot predict when, he thinks it will be soon. His reason for believing this is basically the same as our reason for wanting to secure our supply. He understands that oil has peaked on a worldwide basis, which is going to drive prices up dramatically. Today there is no country with excess capacity that can open their spigots to quench the thirst of countries like China and the United States. So we may get some push-back on the ceiling as he negotiates a higher number.

"His second concern about the ceiling has to do with pricing it in dollars. The prince maintains much of the rise in the price of oil is due to the weakening dollar relative to other currencies, which has forced OPEC to raise prices. If Saudi Arabia bought goods and services only from the U.S., then it would not be a problem. But most of their imports come from us, Japan, and our other Asian competitors, which means they receive less in trade when the dollar declines. Such weakening of the dollar would cause what he termed an 'artificial ceiling' since it would be reached as a result of the weak dollar, rather than the actual value of oil."

"That's very astute of him. This means he is considering pricing oil in another currency, and that could only be the euro."

197

"Correct, sir."

"I must also assume that he is aware of the consequences of such an action on the world's economies that currently depend on the U.S. dollar. Not the least of which is the United States itself. They are a peaceful nation, but as we have learned, they will fight when their security is at risk."

"Quite aware, sir, which led our discussion back to the thirty-five billion dollar development investment."

"I assume then he wants more than that, did he say how much?"

"No, Mr. President, the amount is not the issue. He doesn't want dollars at all. In fact, he doesn't want money! He wants a commitment from you that we will defend his country if and when the United States or others realize Saudi Arabia is the last source of oil on the planet. He knows if we come to an agreement along the lines we are discussing, causing them to switch their pricing from dollars to euros, the United States may well take military action."

"Indeed they might, Ju, and probably will. So Saudi Arabia is looking for protection as payment for our portion of the development expenses. What the prince doesn't realize is that we would have no choice but to defend our source, so from our perspective we are getting the development phase for free."

"Mr. President, I have had several sleepless nights since returning from Riyadh. The thought of going to war with the United States and the possible escalation to a nuclear confrontation is something I do not wish to consider."

"Ju, welcome to senior management. I cannot count the number of sleepless nights I have had since taking this office," the president said. "As we discussed, wars have been started over oil in the past. Every major economy in the world needs energy and those countries with the greatest demand are the same ones with the resources to wage war. As the world runs out of oil—barring the development of some alternative—war is inevitable. The winner will control the remaining oil, which, as we know, means controlling Saudi Arabia, a fact the Americans surely grasp as well."

"The prince feels the proposal we have presented, as modified by him, will protect the future value of their oil and their country for at least the next fifteen years. The issue that seems to trouble him most is the possibility of a new fossil fuel alternative that would undermine the value of their reserves," Zeng said.

"In one respect, Ju, the Saudis share our situation. They have tremendous national wealth, but their per-capita income is very low, which leads to a dangerous domestic political situation. The major difference is that the Saudis have no marketable skills and no other industry to turn to outside of oil, which is why they fear an emerging oil alternative. We, on the other hand, have many skills that will ensure our destiny as a world power, primarily because of our manufacturing capability, skilled population, and low wages. Like Saudi Arabia, this situation cannot endure and wages here will be rising as our population sees us being more successful. If we plan appropriately, we can time these events to maintain dominant market share of all manufacturing before our labor costs begin to equal those of our neighbors. So unlike the Saudis, our future would be just as bright with alternatives to fossil fuels."

After pausing to reflect, the president asked, "Ju, what are the next steps? Were any discussed?"

"The prince would like to refine our proposal and offer a counter. We can expect that he will raise the suggested ceiling. He will ask that we commit to payment in euros, and demand we defend their country against any American or Western coalition attack in return for the development of new oil fields. He said he would have his version to us next week."

"Did he have anything else to add?"

"Yes," said Zeng, "when we were discussing fossil fuel alternatives, I stated our intelligence did not see anything viable being developed. His response was intriguing. Apparently they have intelligence indicating there is one American university that has made significant breakthroughs, and he has sent me a copy of that report."

"Now *that* is worrying. I wonder where they are getting their information?"

Chapter 18.
Internet Back-Trace

The Internet was developed in the 1960s by the Defense Advanced Research Projects Agency, DARPA, an agency of the United States Federal Government as a way to interconnect government agencies with those universities and contractors involved in government research and development. The huge network has many characteristics for which its designers were proud, but even they could not have had an idea of its ultimate value as the Internet quickly expanded beyond the function of government research.

The entire operation is highly distributed. This architecture allows multiple nodes to be taken out of service without disrupting end-to-end connectivity. Each node is semi-autonomous, and in the event a neighboring node is no longer available, it will dynamically find alternate paths around that node.

Unlike the public telephone network that has a star topology, the Internet has no such hierarchy owing to its requirement that loss of a single node, or set of nodes, cannot impact message delivery. Tracing a telephone call is relatively straightforward. The telephone company owning the switch to which the destination telephone is connected has a physical line appearance connected to that phone. A call terminating at that destination telephone can then be traced to an incoming line or trunk. If the trace leads to a line, the search is over. If the trace leads to a trunk, the originator is connected to a different switch, where the trace continues until it leads to the source.

Tracing an Internet connection is much more difficult. It has no physical association since the perpetrator can be connected through a wireless hub in a public location. Furthermore, skilled Internet criminals can manufacture Internet addresses—IP addresses—that are essentially untraceable. A smart Internet hacker can manually route connections through other nodes on the network to make it appear like a connection is created from some machine that has nothing to do with the original transmission.

Tracking a connection backward from a destination IP address to an originating IP address takes an Internet expert with at least the same skill level as the expert who perpetrated the crime. Fortunately, Rafi was just such a person.

The team had been working on the trace all week. Daniels had set up the War Room with an eight-port network hub, several desktop computers and a laptop loaded with a variety of software to monitor and trace Internet traffic. When Daniels returned to the room, Rafi was holding court at one of the desktops, using a projector to beam the image of his screen onto the flat-white painted wall so all could observe.

"Rafi, how's progress?" Daniels asked. It was past 6:00 PM and everyone would be thinking about dinner.

"We've been able to track the first couple of hops, but we can't say yet how many hops we'll need to evaluate before we get to an edge of the network."

The goal of any Internet back-trace is to track the connection through internal network nodes to the machine from which the request entered the network. That machine would typically be a computer with direct access to the Internet, or an ISP, either a telephone company offering DSL access, or a cable company offering cable modem services.

"Need any help dealing with node operators to get their support?" Daniels asked.

"No, thanks, Bob, so far my contacts are working just fine. If I need help though, I'll give you a shout."

"The cops feel there may be a relationship between the access of our site and Jill's murder. In fact, Jason told me he's having dinner tonight with Sandra Bilson's fiancé, Don Wilcox. Wilcox is a CIA agent who's been assigned to this case. Sounds like the feds think the car explosion was no accident."

"Wow, now the feds are involved. Didn't we meet Wilcox at a conference in D.C. last month? Is he based in D.C.?"

"We did. And he *is* based in D.C. Anything I can get you guys?"

"Actually, we could use some food. Any chance for a couple of pizzas? We have plenty of Coke in the fridge."

Young engineers were known to function for long hours on nothing more than soft drinks and a few slices of pepperoni pizza. Many development shops provided free soft drinks, especially those containing caffeine, and CERC was no different. At CERC, soft drinks were considered "programming fluid."

The tracing procedure was taking just as long as expected, and Rafi had already worked backward through eleven nodes. It was close to midnight Saturday and the junior engineers had all gone home. Just Rafi and Daniels remained working on the last couple of hops—at least they hoped these were the last. After searching through the routing tables of the last node, Rafi looked electrified.

"Okay, Bob, here's the next IP address: 61.123.46.29, and guess who owns that domain?" Rafi asked with a weird smile.

"At his point, I'm ready for anything," said Daniels.

"*National Oil!*"

"Holy shit!" Daniels shouted. "I knew they were going to be upset with our results, but this is crazy. Can you continue the trace behind their firewall? I'd love to know where inside the company it originated."

"Well, here it is: 192.168.28.31, which is a local address inside their network, so we don't have access. Looks like you need to ask them to trace that one. They probably won't be able to do anything until morning. Let's get out of here and call it a night."

"Okay, Rafi, I think we've gone as far as we can. Why don't you go ahead? I need to clean up some things on my desk I should have gotten to earlier—this thing has consumed my life for days. I'll lock up on my way out. I may even give National a call tonight."

"Sure, Professor, it's been a long weekend, see you tomorrow." With that, Rafi powered down his machines, strapped his iPod to his arm, and headed for the bike rack and his ride home.

Daniels went back to his desk to catch up, but couldn't put the trace out of his mind. Could someone at National Oil *really* be involved in this? He needed to get hold of Nathan Wood. Surely Nathan would be able to get someone up at this hour for something this important. *But is that wise? Could he have been involved?* After contemplating this for a few minutes, he realized Nathan was his only way in, and he'd have to take the chance. Rummaging through his computerized contact file, he came up with Nathan's home phone number. Nathan had offered its use in case of emergency, and this seemed like one. Daniels picked up the phone.

"Hello," Nathan grumbled on the other end of the line. It was now almost one on Sunday morning.

"Mr. Wood, this is Bob Daniels, at CERC."

"Bob...Bob who...? Wait a minute—sorry, I'm still not awake. Bob Daniels? Is there a problem?"

"Hell yes, there's a problem!" Daniels said, feeling stressed with the lateness of the hour. "We've been working all night to trace back an Internet hacker who accessed Jason's files last week, before his car blew up in California. I hate to tell you this, but the trace goes back to your company."

"Bob, wait a minute," Nathan said, still sounding dazed. "I guess I'm not fully awake. You're telling me that someone from National Oil is responsible for breaking into your systems? I hope you have clear evidence of that!"

Daniels could barely hear Wood's wife in the background, *"Naaaaat, what's going on...Naaaat, what time is it..."*

"You're damn right we do!" he exclaimed. "I have a complete trace, and that's why I wanted to alert you before the police get this and all hell breaks loose."

"Okay, Bob, I'm sorry, you've got my attention. How can I help?"

"We've traced the connection through National's firewall to a specific internal IP address that will ultimately lead to a machine and, possibly, the person responsible. I need help from your IT department to continue the trace behind your firewall."

"Bob, most of the technology you just talked about went right over my head. All I understand is that you need help from our IT guys. Our networking group is staffed around the clock. I'll call the night manager, Jim Bishop, and have him call you. Would that be alright?"

"Perfect, Mr. Wood. I'm sorry to bother you with this so late." Again Daniels heard in the background, *"Naaaat, do you know what time it is?"*

"Mildred, shut up! I need to handle this!" Wood hissed, trying to muffle the mouthpiece of the phone unsuccessfully. "Listen, Bob, if National is involved in this, we need to know immediately. I appreciate your efforts helping us contain it until we know all the details. You can expect a call from Bishop within twenty minutes."

"Thanks, Mr. Wood, and I'll keep you informed," Bob said, and hung up.

Ten minutes later, Daniels' cell phone rang.

"Professor Daniels, this is Jim Bishop, the nightshift IT manager at National Oil. Nathan Wood called and asked that I talk with you directly. Apparently you've traced a rogue IP origination to our facility?"

"Hi, Jim, thanks for calling so quickly. The situation here is that we had an Internet break-in last week, one that may be related to a possible murder. In any event, we've traced it to the address of one of your externally accessible machines. That address led us to one of your internal machines to which we have no visibility. I'd like to send you an email with the information we have and see if you can trace it within your network. We're working directly with Mr. Wood on this, and we've promised to keep it quiet until we have a chance to update him."

"I've been instructed to help in any way I can. We don't do this very often, so I'm not sure how long it will take. I'll call you as soon as we have something."

"Thanks, Jim, I've just sent the email with all the information you'll need. Please call me on my cell phone as soon as you have anything, no matter what time you find it. This is high priority for us—and now the police too."

Chapter 19.
Bill's Cafe

Clearwater Beach isn't a city, it's a barrier island to the west of the city of Clearwater, Florida in the warm, relatively calm waters of the Gulf of Mexico. It sits on an isolated sliver of beach running for miles north and south, almost entirely devoted to tourists and recreation. To residents, Clearwater Beach is more like its own *state*—at least its own state of mind.

Bill's Café opened in 1981 on Baymont Street just off the beach and had become a popular restaurant for tourists and locals alike. Jason had been going there for years, most recently with Jill a month ago. *Ironic that Sandra and Don would choose this place,* he thought.

There was no good way to get to the beach other than going through the city of Clearwater. Jason had left his campus apartment at 6:30 PM thinking he'd miss peak traffic. It looked like others had the same idea. Finally he reached the Memorial Causeway that would take him west across Clearwater Harbor to the strand of sand that was Clearwater Beach. Once across, he could see and hear the Gulf's gentle waves as they lapped the white sands of Florida's west coast. Just a few blocks north he found a parking spot directly in front of Bill's.

The place was jammed. The regulars sitting at the bar were mostly fishermen. Some were charter boat captains, others commercial fishermen. What they had in common was their weathered features and hands that looked like old leather gloves. The differences were just as striking. Charter boat captains dressed a lot better and had all their teeth, at least the ones that showed.

Jason let his eyes scan the crowd, straining to pick out Sandra through the cigarette haze. He was considering going back to his car for his cell phone when he spotted her standing at a corner of the bar. She appeared to be scanning the crowd for him. As he walked toward her trying to get her attention, they made eye contact. She smiled as he got closer.

"Jason, I was about to call you. I was worried there might have been some confusion on the restaurant," she said as he approached.

"Sorry, Sandra, beach traffic on Saturday night can be a nightmare," Jason said, as he found himself struggling to be heard over the din of the crowd. "It may be difficult to talk in here, perhaps we should find somewhere else."

"Don't worry. Don arranged for a small private booth in the back. I was just out here acting as scout. Are you alright? You look tired," Jason could see Sandra's eyes begin to water. He fought back a similar urge.

"It's good to see you again," he swallowed hard. "Perhaps we should start making our way back to Don. He's going to get nervous about his fiancée walking around in a bar like this. The workday is over and these guys are interested in hooking something other than fish."

"You're right, let's go," she smiled, as she took his hand and led him through the crowd.

They entered an enclosed booth far enough back to be reasonably private; but the noise level was still a factor. It would help cover their conversation, but they would also have to raise their voices to be heard.

"Professor Davidson," Wilcox said, standing as they arrived, "I'm Don Wilcox. We met briefly a while back in D.C. when you were there for a conference. You had two of your engineers with you." Jason could tell that Wilcox was uncomfortable and avoided mentioning that Jill had also been there.

"I remember, and please call me Jason. How are you?"

"Sandra and I are fine, and we both express our sympathy. This experience must be devastating!"

"It's been tough."

"Sandra mentioned on the phone that the FBI determined the explosion was caused by a bomb," Jason said, then shifting his attention to her. "Do you think National Oil is trying to kill me? You told me at the airport that I was in danger."

Sandra held a finger to her lips as she saw the waiter bringing their order. When he left and had gotten far enough away, she said, "There's more. Don doesn't have all the pieces yet, but there is more."

"Professor," Wilcox said, "I got interested in your case after I saw the news on Thursday morning."

"You mean I have a case? Come on."

"The CIA has been monitoring your work—actually the work of CERC—since its inception over four years ago."

"You're kidding, right? Isn't monitoring by the CIA a bit much?"

"Not if you're the U.S. government and your funding research that could lead to the political destabilization of the world."

210

"Well, that wasn't one of our objectives," Jason said with a wry smile at Sandra.

"Professor, please," Sandra said. "The work you reported at the last meeting could affect many people. Establishment of a clean energy economy would cause severe dislocations *everywhere.*"

"From what Sandra told me, your group has come up with results that could, in fact, destabilize many economies of the world, and that's where the CIA comes in."

"Go ahead."

"The first thing we need to get on the table is your security clearance. The director has rushed it through. I have it with me."

"The director of the CIA himself?"

Wilcox slid a manila envelope across the table toward Jason. "The same. He's interested in your case and has assigned it to me as top priority. That's why I asked Sandra to set up this meeting. Everything we talk about tonight is Top Secret, is that clear?"

"Clear enough."

"Okay. I've told you the CIA began monitoring CERC four years ago. Even more interesting is that the director has discovered the records within our internal systems are without attribution, something that could only happen if they had been broken into."

"I assume you have backups for those systems?" Jason asked.

"Well, yes and no," Wilcox replied, sounding embarrassed. "We have a sophisticated backup system designed to backup records based on frequency of change. With the vast amount of records we keep, the designers concluded that we should only provide daily backups for those records that change daily. Monthly backups are provided for records that changed in the last month, and so on. Otherwise we would be backing up records daily that might only change monthly or yearly. Backups are kept online for four years and then moved offsite."

"Sounds reasonable."

"It does, until you find out that the missing records we are looking for had not been updated in four years, which means to recover them we need to get them out of offsite storage."

"How long should that take?" asked Sandra, having heard this for the first time.

"Normally not long, but we have an additional complication. The four-year anniversary was two days ago, which means the records we are looking for are somewhere in transit to the backup site."

"Christ!" Jason said, shaking his head. "Whoever did it had to know a lot about your internal systems and procedures to pull it off."

"Exactly. Reynolds has started a full investigation. I'll let you know what we find after they're restored. Next, is your car explosion…"

"You mean my *rental* car," Jason interrupted. My car is just fine—at least for the moment," Jason joked to break the ice.

Wilcox continued, "The *rental* car explosion wasn't an accident, but the FBI wants the public to believe it was, allowing whoever planted the bomb to think they've gotten away with it."

"Which turns me into what…bait?" Jason asked incredulously.

"Professor?" Sandra cringed.

"Sure, if whoever planted the bomb thinks they got away with it, they'll try again. I just pray some FBI agent who's watching me will catch them before they succeed."

"We're now assuming that you're a hunted man," Wilcox admitted. "There are people who want you dead, and they will probably try again."

"So, how do you suggest I protect myself, by holding up my Top Secret security clearance?" Jason said sarcastically.

"We'll get to that, but let's get back to the car."

"There's more?"

"The FBI found traces of a substance called PETN, residue from plastic explosives. That tells us whoever did this was a professional. It gives us something to trace and that's what we're doing now." Wilcox pushed another manila envelope across to Jason. "In this envelope is a CCW. Know what that is?"

"No."

"A CCW is a permit to carry a concealed weapon. Many of the states have them. The one I just gave you is a *federal* CCW, honored in all fifty states. That packet includes information on special situations, like airlines and the protocol they use for people like you."

"That's great, but I don't have a weapon to conceal."

With that, Wilcox reached down on the floor and retrieved a small blue zippered travel bag, set it on the table and slid it towards Jason. "You do now. In there is a Glock 31 .357 automatic with two seventeen-round magazines—something civilians aren't allowed to buy. There's also a box of ammunition and a shoulder holster. Have you ever fired a gun before, Professor?"

"I qualified with the M-16 rifle and Colt 45 Automatic in basic training in the Air Force. Unfortunately that was a long time ago."

"At least you've handled an automatic before. This is much better technology. In the CCW envelope you'll find the name and address of a gun range our agents in Tampa use along with an

213

introduction for you. Tomorrow's Sunday, but they're open. Go down there, ask for Harry, introduce yourself, and get comfortable with that weapon. Your life could depend on it. I've already told Harry you're coming and he'll give you standard agent training plus any additional training you think you need—or he thinks you need."

"Well, I was planning on doing some yard work at my Sarasota home, but this sounds like higher priority," Jason said wryly. His life was rapidly changing. Maybe humor would help.

"It is. And now there's the matter of communication. I suspect your phones are being monitored, especially if the Company has been watching you." Wilcox glanced at Bilson as if to give her a cue.

"We have a phone for you to use when we need to communicate," Sandra said as she reached into her purse and handed him a white cell phone, like the one she and Don used.

"That's a clean phone," Wilcox said. "I paid cash for it and it runs on prepaid SIM cards. There's one SIM card installed and one spare. Each has three hundred minutes of airtime in addition to a digital certificate that's used for encrypting our conversations. Are you familiar with encryption technology?"

"I used to teach computer science, one of my majors."

"Good. You'll need to monitor the airtime minutes remaining, and buy additional minutes when you need them. Pay *cash*, that's important. There are two phone numbers programmed into this phone, one for my clean phone and one for Sandy's. We carry them all the time and this is how we communicate when we want to make sure it's private. Don't use this phone to call anyone else unless I tell you they also have a clean phone. We don't know which phones are being monitored by whom, and we can't take any chances, so these phones are for our use only. I recommend you leave the phone alert set to vibrate mode so no one will hear it ring. I also recommend you don't answer the phone if you're in an uncomfortable situation. In those cases, let the call go to voicemail. The cellular network we're using will store the message in encrypted form, so it will only be decrypted if you retrieve the message yourself, and only if you retrieve it with this phone. Any questions?"

"This is all very *James Bond-ish*," Jason said, "I know he didn't drive a Jeep. Where's my Aston Martin? You have one waiting outside don't you?" Jason was unable to hide his cynicism.

"I know this is going to be uncomfortable and we're working hard to resolve the unknowns. Someday you'll be able to go back to a more normal life, but for the time being, this is the best we can do."

Feeling somehow important, but mostly scared, Jason put both of his envelopes into the blue travel bag. They finished dinner without any more discussions about the CIA, secure cell phones, or weapon technology. He relished the change. Until that night there had been no time to relax, at least he hadn't allowed himself that luxury. He'd not done anything except think about Jill and replay over in his mind the steps he might have taken that would have kept her alive.

It was almost one o'clock when Jason looked at his watch and realized he was a third wheel. Sitting with Sandra and Don, he found himself doing most of the talking. They'd been good listeners, but it was time to let them have their weekend together. He suddenly felt embarrassed.

Before he left, they asked him to test his new cell phone by calling each of them and then they called him. Sandra left a test voicemail message and then Jason tried to retrieve it with his old cell phone. The system let him enter his PIN, but when it went to play the message, it was incoherent garbage. Then he used his new phone to retrieve his message, and the message was retrieved perfectly.

He put his new "toy" in the blue travel bag with the rest of his "gifts" and headed out to his Jeep. As he left, looking through the window, he could see Sandra and Don cuddled in their booth. He wondered how long they had tolerated him, thankful for every minute.

On a normal Friday night, Jason would have driven south to his home in Sarasota, about a thirty-minute drive, where he'd meet Jill and enjoy the weekend. But getting back to *normal* would take some time.

He needed to be in Tampa in the morning to make his appointment at the shooting range. It would feel odd to carry a gun, but based on what he'd just learned, he'd get used to it.

As he approached his Jeep with a newly-heightened sense of paranoia, he couldn't resist getting down on his hands and knees to look underneath. He hoped he wouldn't find some unusual box suspended there. He wasn't an explosives expert but it didn't hurt to look.

Without the top, the late-night ride in the Jeep was sobering. His old cell phone rang, it was Rafi.

"Hi, Doc, I thought I'd give you an update on the IP trace. Is this too late?"

"No, I'm just heading back to the apartment, what did you find?" The call was making him think which helped clear the cobwebs.

"You're not going to believe this, but then you might. The trace finally led to a machine at National Oil."

After a long pause, Jason said, "Amazing, I wonder who... I'll need to call Nathan. Do we know where inside their network the connection originated?"

"We don't, since we can't access anything behind their firewall. Professor Daniels was thinking about contacting National tonight to see if they could help, so you may want to call him first."

"Okay, I'll do that next. Thanks for all your help—and I mean for everything. See you Monday."

"I'm glad to help. Professor, as for Monday, I'd like to take a few days off to visit my mother in Washington. With what's happened, she's concerned about me and I haven't seen her in quite a while. Would that be okay?"

"Sure, you've earned it. See you later in the week."

After the call he was fully awake. *Why would National Oil break into our server?* Through Nat, National already had all the CERC information available to them. *Why would they be interested in my travel schedule?* Something didn't make sense, but he needed more time to think about it. First he needed to touch base with Daniels. Jason had him on a one-number speed dial.

"Hi, Doc," came the quick reply, sounding less tired than Jason would have guessed.

"Hi, Bob, Rafi just called to give me an update. I can't understand what National is doing breaking into our servers. I was going to call Nat, but Rafi said you may have done that. Are you still at the lab?"

"I'm just on my way home. I was going to call you but after looking at the time, I thought I'd wait until morning, so I'm glad you called. I did talk to Nat and he was more surprised than we are. He asked that we not say anything to anyone outside National until we can resolve where the attack came from. I said we'd honor his request, I hope that was alright?"

"That's fine, we owe him that. Sounds like Rafi has been burning the midnight oil. Still have your concerns about him?"

"He is amazing, and as far as I can tell he's completely dedicated. I guess I've been wrong about him."

"How far did you guys get with the trace?"

"We can't see behind their firewall from our lab, so Nat got me a contact in their IT department, a guy named Jim Bishop who called me right back. I sent him an email with the addresses we had, and he's going to work inside their network to track it down. He warned me they don't do this very often, and it could take a while. We should probably hear something by Monday."

"Thanks, Bob, sounds like you've done everything you could. I'm just pulling up to the apartment. Let me know as soon as you hear from your guy at National."

Chapter 20.
Second Strike

Bob Daniels needed a rest. He'd been putting in many more hours than normal with Jason gone and working on the Internet trace, in addition to his normal teaching and grading responsibilities.

Daniels wasn't a wealthy man, living on a full professor's salary plus some investments from the startup where he'd met Jason. Though he didn't walk away with anywhere near the equity Jason had, he felt good about his successes.

He drove a Chevy Malibu. His second "hobby vehicle" was an old 1970 Chevy pickup. Home was a small beach house not far from campus in a crowded neighborhood that was established in the '50s. His property value had increased dramatically when developers started buying up and tearing down some of his neighbors' houses to build million-dollar waterfront homes. When he took time to consider his career, he figured he had about as much as he was going to get, looking forward to teaching and his CERC research to carry him through retirement.

The one extravagance he allowed himself was a good-sized fishing boat he kept moored in the bay at an old commercial dock. Lucky to have found any space at all, he had rented during the recession when demand was light. It felt odd to park his boat between commercial fishing trawlers, but he'd hate to look for a new space now.

Daniels got little sleep when he returned from the lab early Sunday morning. Later in the afternoon he went down to the dock to work on his boat. He would have preferred to be out on the bay fishing, but the inside of the boat needed painting, just the kind of mindless work he wanted.

One advantage of tying up with commercial trawlers was getting to know the captains, many of whom had recommended a little café just down the street. For a professor noted for his intellectual abilities, grubbing with a bunch of old sailors provided a welcomed change. It was late and Daniels was hungry, ready for an order of the best fish and chips to be found anywhere near Tampa Bay.

He walked into the cafe and said hello to Shirley, the gal behind the counter. Her husband, Stan, busy working in the kitchen, waved hello. He saw two guys he recognized from his dock at the counter and sat between them. Neither of them knew he was a professor and he wasn't about to tell them. To them he was just "Bob" and he liked it that way. He picked up the menu scanning it out of habit, though he already knew what he was going to order. His cell phone rang.

"This is Bob Daniels," he said, not recognizing the number.

"Professor Daniels, Jim Bishop—at National Oil."

"Yes, Jim, sorry, you caught me off guard. I didn't expect to hear from you until tomorrow." Daniels stood and stepped away for privacy.

"I thought this was important enough that we worked through the night. The results look strange—in fact, strange enough that we've checked and rechecked them. Best we can tell, the connection you gave us was created from outside our firewall to the internal machine you mentioned, and then back outside on the path you gave us. Does this make sense?"

"We call that a *hairpin,* Jim. And it might make sense, except that I don't understand how it came in from outside your firewall."

"I'm embarrassed to say, but we had a hole in our firewall that allowed incoming traffic on a port leading to that machine, a machine that belongs to a secretary in our HR department. Our people routinely leave their machines running and this secretary was no exception. We first became suspicious because we had serious doubts she'd be either interested in, or even capable of, doing what you say happened."

"So how do you explain the hole in your firewall that allowed it? Why would she need an incoming connection to her machine?"

"Well, first, we've closed that hole, so it won't happen again. Second, we routinely recycle machines within the company, giving the engineers the newest and fastest machines and moving their old machines to administrative positions. We cycle the oldest machines out of the company and usually donate them to churches for the tax write-off. Our records show this is what happened. The machine in question belonged to an engineer who was working on a project that needed the hole in the firewall. It was an approved project at the time, and again, I'm embarrassed to say we didn't close it after the project was completed. Someone on the outside used a port scanning program, found the hole, and exploited it."

"Okay, Jim, looks like we need to continue searching. Can you send me the new external address so we can add it to the path? We'll continue the search from our end." *Jesus, somebody needs to give this guy a lecture on network security!*

"Professor, I've documented our findings and put them in an email along with the trace information we've added. I'm going to send that to you and copy Mr. Wood. I know he's anxious to get an update. Let me know if there's anything else we can do."

"I will Jim, and thanks for your help. I'm sure Nat will be relieved this didn't originate from within National, although it appears someone was trying to make it look like it did. I'm heading back to our lab to open your email and get to work. Could you do me one more favor? Copy my boss on the email you're about to send. His address is *Jason.Davidson@usf.edu*."

"Will do, Professor, good luck."

"Thanks, Jim, bye."

Daniels had lost his appetite, and was glad he hadn't ordered. In some ways he was hoping Bishop would have taken until Monday to get his results, giving him an opportunity for one night of sound sleep. That wasn't to be.

He set his menu back on edge between the chrome-topped sugar container and napkin holder, waved goodbye to a bewildered-looking Shirley and walked back to his truck.

"Hey, Bob," Shirley yelled after him, her head sticking through the open screen door. "Everything okay?"

If he heard her, he didn't acknowledge.

Once back in his truck he headed straight for the lab. On the way, he decided to call Rafi. He was capable of continuing the trace on his own, but Rafi was much more proficient and no one could say how many hops remained.

"Hey, Professor, what's up?"

"Just heard from National's networking guy. Looks like we have more work to do, can you meet me at the lab?"

"I'm leaving to visit my mom in D.C. tonight, but I could come in for a while and leave for the airport from there."

"That works, I'll take any help I can get."

The engineering building and its parking lots were quiet enough during the evenings, but on Sunday evenings they were desolate. Daniels wheeled the old pickup into the parking spot closest to the entrance, even though it was a spot reserved for visitors. The overzealous security guys who roamed the lots at all hours would probably write him up. His truck didn't have a university sticker on it and it looked out of place. Then he'd have to explain to someone why he was parked in a reserved spot. At this point, he didn't care.

Daniels swiped his security card through the magnetic lock and opened the door to the War Room. It was just as he and Rafi had left it, so he powered everything up as he went into the kitchen and got a Coke out of the fridge.

As soon as his laptop came back to life, he went in and retrieved his email. There was the note from Bishop with the newly expanded trace. He was amazed at how lax corporate America was with their Internet security and wondered what other problems National might have as a result of holes in their firewall. There were plenty of tools a company could use to defend itself from such intrusions, many of them free.

As Daniels was about to get started with the next leg of the trace, Rafi walked in wearing his backpack and motorcycle helmet. In addition to his old Nissan, Rafi had two additional modes of transportation, a bicycle and a motorcycle. He rode his bicycle around campus, and his motorcycle, one of those Japanese "crotch-rockets," was for long-distance trips, like going to the airport. He would take his flight to D.C. after helping with the trace.

"Hi, Professor, have you started yet?" Rafi asked as he set his backpack down, setting the helmet on top of it.

"I just got everything fired up and have the next address we need to work on. It looks like an internal Internet domain, so we'll need to go at least one more step back in the chain."

The Internet is recursive and you can find out everything about it using the Internet itself, you just needed to know where to look. In this case, the place to look was in the published domain address lists that told who owned which IP addresses. Since this address wasn't in any of those lists, Daniels concluded it must be from an internal network routing node.

"Let's see if I can resolve this to the preceding link," Rafi said, going into an almost trance-like state typical of professional geeks diving into the Internet. Such knowledge can't be taught; it can only be learned through experience, and Rafi had plenty of that. Fifteen minutes later, he came up for air.

"Here you go. This is the next address in the chain. Let's see if the domain resolves to anything external."

Daniels then took the address and dove back into the Internet directory used to translate IP addresses into domain names. This time there was a hit. It came up as "CIA."

"There must be something wrong, this domain resolves to the CIA—that can't be right."

"Let me run it through a different directory service and see if we get the same thing."

Rafi logged on to another service and entered the IP address they had discovered. The results were the same.

"Let me try one more thing," Daniels announced. "I'm going to ping a well-known CIA URL to see what numerical domain comes up, then we can compare it to the address we're working on."

After a pause, he said, "There it is Rafi, the first two numbers of the IP address match. What the hell is the CIA doing connecting through National Oil to our servers here? We need to call Jason, we're going to need to get the CIA involved in this to track it any further and he can ask Wilcox to help."

"Good idea, I've got my cell phone right here, let's call him." With that, Rafi reached down, unzipped his backpack, but instead of pulling out his cell phone, he was holding a small automatic pistol with a silencer.

"Professor, I'm afraid you're going faster than I thought you would."

"What do you mean?" Daniels asked, his back to Rafi, still staring at his laptop's screen.

Rafi took two steps backward.

Daniels, seeing Rafi's reflection, looked up from his screen, peering directly up the wrong end of a 9mm automatic. His jaw dropped to the desk, heart in full race. He stood to face the student/killer.

"Rafi, what the…" Daniels said, rising instinctively.

"Professor, I said you're moving too fast. The project is moving too fast and you traced the IP connection too fast. I need more time. Sorry."

Daniels, with a quizzical look on his face, took one step back. Panic seized him. His body seemed to realize what was going to happen before his mind could catch up.

"You can't do this! Not here!"

"Actually, Professor, this is the best place to kill you. My fingerprints are all over this lab, which is where they belong."

"So I was right about you all along," were Daniel's last words.

Rafi's silencer was a good one; there was no bang, not even a pop, just a light *zip* as the bullet entered Daniels' forehead. A small red dot appeared between his eyes. Daniels was dead before he hit the floor.

Rafi returned the automatic to his backpack, found the spent shell casing near Daniels' feet, put it in his pocket, and calmly headed for his motorcycle.

Chapter 21.
Discovery

Don Wilcox was back on his Monday schedule, leaving Dolly Madison at about 6:30 AM to beat the traffic on the beltway. It had been a great weekend, an invigorating one with Sandra. For the first time in a long time he felt alive, although nothing had really changed. He was still the divorced guy trying to spread what used to be a good income across what had become two households. But Sandra made all the difference in the world. There was light at the end of the tunnel his life had become. Even if that light wasn't financial freedom, it was emotional freedom and a future with a woman he truly loved and who loved him. He had always been frank with her about his finances, and Sandra was well aware the alimony and child support would continue to drain away their lifestyle.

Sandra had an above-average salary and when combined with Don's discretionary income, they could live in relative comfort in the costly D.C. area. But every month there would be financial outlays that would remind them of their tenuous situation. Still, Sandra loved him, baggage and all.

The beltway was crowded as usual, but the lingering thoughts of his weekend with Sandra seemed to shorten the trip. Wilcox wheeled the gray Chrysler past the security guard at the entrance to the CIA Langley facility, flashing his badge at the guard. He drove into the underground lot where he found a spot reasonably close to the elevator. He was early, but needed the extra time to prepare for his briefing with Director Reynolds. He would update him on his activities investigating the mysterious deaths of two CIA agents, and his new assignment, Professor Davidson.

Winnie was there early as well, always cheerful, always positive. "Good morning, Don, ready for some coffee? How was the beach?"

"Morning, Winnie. Clearwater was wonderful as always. Sandy and I had a great time. And *yes* on the coffee, please. I'm going to be having one of those days."

"So I noticed from your calendar. I see you have the director at eight—is there anything I can do to help?"

Normally, Don would ask Winnie to prepare much of his presentation materials. However, the meeting with Reynolds was going to be covering his IA work. Even Winnie couldn't be trusted with the "invisible" part of his life.

"Thanks, Winnie, but I just need to organize the notes I put together over the weekend."

* * *

Also refreshed by the weekend, Jason was on his way into the lab. Saturday night had been a catharsis of sorts and he felt a deep appreciation for Don's and Sandra's efforts to buoy him.

Even Sunday had been enjoyable, if only for the novelty it brought. Jason had never set foot in a commercial gun range. He hadn't fired a weapon of any kind since his Air Force days. The only weapons his military career required were an oscilloscope and other electronic test equipment for his job as an Electronic Warfare technician on the old B52s. The only real danger he faced in those days was electrocution from 120 volts AC or 28 volts DC.

Harry, the gun range owner, was just as helpful as Wilcox promised. He started with the basics, showing Jason where the safety was, explaining how the gun worked, loading magazines, pulling the slide back to load the first round into the chamber, and then firing the weapon. There were other customers and instructors there that morning, but Harry devoted his attention to Jason. It was apparent the CIA was a good customer. Wilcox had asked for special treatment, and Jason got it.

When it was time to fire his gun, Jason loaded a full seventeen rounds into a magazine, slapped it up the butt of the pistol, pulled the slide back to load the first round into the chamber, took careful aim, and promptly missed the silhouette completely. He could only laugh. Harry smiled, spotting the problem instantly. Jason was squeezing the handle so tight in anticipation of the recoil that his entire body was stiff, almost as if the gun was supporting him instead of the other way around. He needed to relax his shoulders, arms, wrists, and hands to let them absorb the kick. The second shot went right through the silhouette's head, and Jason felt relieved. He even insisted that was where he was aiming.

After a lot more practice and a cleaning session, he walked out of the range confident in the gun and his ability to use it.

Jason worked his way through traffic looking forward to a more normal week. For his own emotional well-being, he had to get his mind back on his work. He had decided to wear the gun. His CCW came with a card signed by Director Reynolds that he kept in his wallet. The well-worn sport coat with leather patches on the elbows would now remain on all day. *It's going to take some time getting used to "packing heat."*

As he got closer to the campus, Jason heard sirens. By the time he was turning into the entrance, it was clear that something serious had happened to cause Tampa police to augment campus security. *What the hell is going on now!*

The closer he got to his office the worse it became. When he pulled into the engineering parking lot, he was shocked to see long strands of plastic yellow "police line" tape cordoning off the entrance to his lab. One vehicle stood out behind the tape, an old pickup truck. Then it hit him—the truck behind the yellow tape was Bob's! Jason choked and started to get what had become a too-familiar sickening feeling.

A crowd had already formed. Yellow police tape made a great magnet, like flypaper for humans. Jason had to maneuver slowly through the parking lot that remained open to get to his reserved spot several hundred feet from the lab entrance. As he got out, he saw a line of uniformed police. *Not good*, he thought, as he headed for the lab entrance.

"Just a minute, sir," a young city officer said as he stepped in front of Jason's progress. "No one is allowed in. This is a crime scene."

"I can see that, Officer. I'm Professor Jason Davidson, head of this lab," Jason said as he pulled his ID from his wallet.

"I don't give a shit who you are, man. My instructions are that no one crosses this line. Please step back."

"Listen, son, I'm responsible for this lab and everyone who works in it. That old truck belongs to my assistant professor, and he may be inside. If there's a problem I may be able to help."

"Professor, there was a man murdered here; whoever he was, he won't be needing your help. Please step back or I'll have to arrest you."

"Listen, Officer… Who's in charge here?" Jason raised his voice, looking around.

"Professor Davidson," A familiar voice came from behind. "Hold on a minute."

It was Ralph Kite, head of campus security. He saw what was going to become a scuffle and thought he could mediate the situation before it got out of hand. Kite was a big man in his mid-fifties who had retired from the Tampa police force for a job he thought would be less stressful. This event would change his opinion.

"Ralph," Jason said, "can you tell me what's going on here?"

"Officer, I can vouch for the professor. I'll take full responsibility for escorting him."

"Alright, Mr. Kite, but you *will* be fully responsible. This is going into my report," snarled the cop.

"I'm sorry, Professor," Kite said, turning to Jason. "These young guys get a badge and suddenly think they're Marshal Dillon. He was just following orders. I think you may not want to go in, sir. It's Professor Daniels."

"What happened, Ralph?" Jason could feel his gut wrenching, his knees buckling, afraid he already knew the answer.

"He's dead, Professor—I'm sorry, I know how close you were."

"What? *Dead?*" Jason moaned. Kite grabbed his arm to lend support.

"He was shot, Professor, we think some time last night. We haven't narrowed down the time yet. The Medical Examiner will have that soon. The janitor discovered the body when he noticed all the lights on this morning. I know you want to go in, but you really may not want to see him like this."

"I have to, Ralph. I have to."

Bob was his best friend, and as repulsive as it would be, he was still drawn to see the body. He regained his composure and felt strength returning to his legs. He moved through the doorway with Ralph Kite close behind.

There was no warning that could have prepared him for the sight of his dead friend lying facedown in a pool of blood. The color in Daniel's face had been carried away with the blood on the floor, leaving a chalky gray look with glassy, distant eyes.

Kite asked the ME team to give them a few minutes. They all backed away as Jason came near, walking quietly, respectfully, as though his friend could still be disturbed. *One last look*, he thought. As he bent down, he saw the bullet wound between dead eyes. There was little comfort in knowing that his friend did not suffer.

He felt like crying, but nothing came. *How many tears does one man have*? he asked himself. Standing up, he looked over to the table in the War Room and saw the computers still running.

"May I take a look at those machines? I'd like to find out what Bob was working on," Jason said to no one in particular.

Kite looked at the lead ME technician who gave him a nod. "Go ahead, Professor, we've already taken pictures and dusted for prints. So far we haven't found any prints that don't belong," Kite said.

Jason sat down and took a deep breath. He moved the mouse on each of the machines, which brought them back to life. Nothing looked particularly interesting until he got to Bob's laptop. He saw that Bob was working on an IP trace when he was killed. Jason hit the "PrtScr" button to capture an image of the entire screen, brought up the standard Windows Paint program, and pasted the image into it. He then saved it on one of the network servers so he could review it from his office. He repeated the process for each of the other four machines.

"Can I use my office now?" Jason asked Kite.

Kite looked at the ME people in the room, and again got a nod. "Yes, Professor, but let us know if you want to go anywhere else in the lab. These folks will appreciate that."

"Certainly. I don't want to interfere with the investigation," Jason said numbly as he picked up his computer bag and made his way to his office.

Sitting at his desk, he stared blankly at the door for what must have been ten minutes until he realized he was doing that. Then he began his routine of taking his laptop out of its carrying bag, plugging it in, and powering up. He called the University Dean's office and spoke with his secretary. It had been decided the campus would be closed for the day, out of respect for Bob and to allow the investigation to proceed unimpeded.

Good, Jason thought. *I can review what's in the lab and have time to think.* If there was any lingering doubt that someone was after him and his work, there was none now. The first thing he did was bring up the screenshot of Bob's computer. *Bob told me the trace had terminated at National Oil—so why was he still working it?*

As he pondered that, his email window came up. About half of the messages were junk and chit-chat that could be quickly eliminated with the "delete" key. He made a second pass through what remained.

There it was! The email from Bishop at National indicated their machine had been used by someone from the outside, which exonerated them from being the originator of the attack, if not from being stupid enough to leave an opening in their firewall. A copy had also been sent to Nat Wood. He would be pissed. *I can see the fur flying in National's IT department.* Jason needed to make sense of the trace information. If Rafi had not gone to D.C., he would have gotten him down to the lab immediately. Now he'd have to plod through this stuff himself.

Shifting back to the screenshot of Bob's laptop, he could see his friend had continued the trace to one last machine. There were "pings" to www.cia.gov, where the first two numbers of the IP address were 198.91, which matched the first two numbers of the last address they were tracing. "Holy shit!" Jason mumbled.

Bob had traced the connection to the CIA, the last thing he did before he was killed. Jason pulled out his new white cell phone. It was time to get Wilcox involved.

* * *

"Hi, Janet," Wilcox said with a half-smile, "is Director Reynolds ready for me?"

"He is, Mr. Wilcox, why don't you go right in."

Wilcox headed through the large double doors as Janet held them open.

"Good morning, Don, have a seat," said Reynolds. "Janet, will you close the doors, please? Thank you."

"Good morning, sir."

"Let's get right to it, what have you found out about our two agents?"

"Sir, there appear to be some common threads. Both were killed at times and in places where they should not have been. Secondly, it appears both of them were being coerced into joining some kind of association they didn't want to join, and they'd both called it a *club*."

"And what about your friend, the professor, I know you're personally interested in that one. Anything new?"

"Unfortunately, yes. Just before I came in here, Davidson called to tell me his assistant professor, a Bob Daniels, was killed sometime Sunday. They found his body today in the CERC lab."

"Did you ever meet Daniels?"

"I met him when the CERC team was in town for a convention. This is going to hurt their efforts, it's got to slow them down."

"Sounds like someone is trying to do just that. Did you give the professor his CCW?"

"I did, and also gave him a Glock automatic and some time on the shooting range in Tampa. And there's one more thing," Wilcox continued. "Davidson told me Daniels was killed as he was trying to trace back an IP connection. Apparently it was a connection someone used to steal information from CERC's servers prior to the attempt on the professor's life. He told me Daniels had traced it back here—to the CIA and has sent me all the information Daniels had gathered. I've got the S&T guys working to find out where it originated."

"That's interesting," Reynolds said. "Get me an update as soon as you have something. By the way, I have some information from my research. Remember I told you that we've been monitoring CERC's activity since its inception under a professor by the name of Will Elliot? "

"Yes, sir."

"There've been some new developments. We know we had a mole there, but the records have gone missing. Someone broke into the database and erased everything about that engagement."

"When did this happen?" Wilcox asked incredulously. "Who could have done it?"

"The best we can tell, it happened two days ago. We currently have no clue who could have done it. But it must have been someone with incredible computer skills to figure out how to transparently erase this stuff. Whoever did it was able to do so without leaving a trace. Our guys are working on that."

"I'll be anxious to hear what they find."

"I'll let you know as soon as I get something. And you let me know how S&T does with your Internet trace."

Wilcox left Reynolds' office and headed back to his own. He was anxious to check his email to see if there were any results from S&T. Sure enough, there were. Those S&T guys were as good as he thought, even as good as *they* hyped themselves to be. He needed to call Jason with the results, and hit the speed-dial button on his white phone. Jason's name popped up on the screen as he heard ringing on the other end.

* * *

"Hi, Don."

"Jason, I've got an update for you, actually two."

"Remember I told you the CIA had been monitoring CERC activity from the beginning? Well, now *all* the records pertaining to that work were erased from our databases two days ago. Whoever removed the attributions has gone back in and done a more thorough job. We have to assume there's a connection to what's happening to CERC."

"Great. What about the IP Trace?"

"Yeah, fascinating. You know the trace led to a hairpin through National Oil's machine. We feel that someone was trying to implicate them, distract us from the real culprit. We used Professor Daniels' information and confirmed the trace led here to CIA headquarters. That led to another hairpin through one of our machines and back out."

"Whoever did this certainly had patience, so where does that take us?"

"One more step, actually. We found the ultimate source was at a Starbucks coffee house right outside your campus."

"Incredible! You mean whoever did this started a few blocks from the server they finally broke into? I suspect the next thing you're going to tell me is that whoever did this was on a wireless connection, and not traceable."

"You got it. We have the original IP address within Starbucks' domain, but it's a wireless address that was dynamically generated by their router, obviously a customer on a laptop. But of course, there's no way to tell which customer it was—the joys of wireless networking."

"Okay, Don, thanks, can you email me that last IP address?"

"Will do."

"What are your next steps?"

"I'm on my way to a meeting in a few minutes, and then shifting my attention back to your case. I told the director of this latest development and he's become personally interested in following it—which will make it even a higher priority for me. I'll be in touch."

"Thanks, Don, bye."

Jason turned his mind back to Bob's funeral. He had known Daniels for at least four years, but had never heard him talk about any relatives. Emma was going to do some checking, but it was starting to look like he was in charge.

His left pocket began to vibrate. Pulling out the white phone, he saw it was Sandra.

"Don told me about Bob Daniels. Are you alright?"

"Not really."

"I'm so terribly sorry. This confirms that your work is too dangerous to someone. Are you carrying the gun?"

"I am. It's a bit uncomfortable, but given what's been happening, I'll get used to it."

"What about the funeral, when and where will it be held?" Sandra asked.

"The wake will be tomorrow night in a little chapel down the street from the campus, and the funeral will be held Wednesday morning."

"I'd like to attend," she said. "I feel I knew Bob well enough. I've already talked with Nat and I'll be representing National as well."

"Thanks, Sandra. I'll send you an email with the address."

"I'll make arrangements to stay at the hotel where National always stays. Be safe and I'll see you tomorrow."

"Okay, call me when you get in," Jason said, trying to hold back the emotion as they hung up. But it was too much. The pressure had been building; he hadn't had a decent night's sleep in at least a week. Jason bent over in agony with his hands flying to his face.

Chapter 22.
The Wake

It suddenly struck Jason that he'd never arranged a funeral. *Odd,* he thought, *a man of my age never having run into this situation.* He left home when he was eighteen to join the service, growing as far away from his family emotionally as he did in proximity. When his parents died, his brothers made all the arrangements. Now it was his turn. He hoped it wouldn't be an experience he'd repeat often.

Jason looked for Daniels' relatives, but came up empty. He placed an obituary with a few of the local papers attaching his phone number in hopes someone would come forth. That was all he could do. He decided to go to Bob's house on the beach to see if he could locate an address book or directory that might lead to someone—anyone. The police had given him Bob's keys and other personal effects. There was no one else.

He had been in Bob's house many times—many good times—but felt odd putting the key in the door and opening a home that was missing its occupant. The foyer door led to a small living room where Bob hosted the guys for Saturday poker nights, like the one he had recently attended. Down the hall was the kitchen and to the left were two small bedrooms.

Like Jason, Bob was a bachelor and the house reflected it. Jason knew his own home missed a woman's touch, but Bob's seemed to miss it even more. The house wasn't messy—the beds were made and the kitchen counters clear—it just felt...*cold*. It was eerie to see everything in the house as Bob had left it, frozen in time waiting for an owner who would never return.

The large room in the back served as Bob's office, where he really lived. It held his desk, which was a large old table Bob had wangled out of the university when they upgraded the library. The table overwhelmed the room, easily the largest piece of furniture in the house, and held his PC, printer, and fax machine. Next to the table was a file cabinet.

This was the room Jason remembered best, where he and Bob would sit on weekend evenings and watch a baseball game or just shoot the shit after coming in from fishing.

Jason sat at the table and started looking for anything that might be a telephone directory. He opened the file cabinet and took out a few large manila folders that looked promising. He brought them over to the couch, which was his usual seat—Bob had always preferred the recliner.

For no good reason, he switched on the TV as he always did, and that was when it hit him. Bob would never again reenter this home, never sit in that chair, and never ask Jason if he wanted a beer.

Rifling through the folders, the search was going nowhere. He pulled one last folder, which turned out to be a complete history of the CERC organization. Daniels had been collecting everything he could find on the group with the hopes of one day writing a book chronicling the team's success. He had everything: from Will Elliot's letters to the university proposing the formation of the group to the police reports on Elliot's death. One of those reports was the interview of Rafi Haddad regarding the night in question. Daniels had scribbled some notes in the margin—mostly unintelligible—about the wine that Rafi had brought that evening.

Jason looked up. He wasn't sure how long he'd been there, probably an hour—it was getting dark. It was time to go and he replaced the folders back in the cabinet.

* * *

The next day dawned gloomy with a cold rain—at least as cold a rain as you could get in Tampa, Florida. The forecast was for more of the same. *How appropriate*, thought Jason.

Bob was popular with both faculty and students, and it was comforting to see that his wake was going to have a good turnout. Among the crowd was a familiar face, although not a regular member of the university. Sandra Bilson looked business-like in a black suit.

"Professor," she said, extending her arms.

"Sandra, thank you for coming," he responded.

"I'm so sorry," she said.

"Have you gone in to see him?"

"I have. I'll wait out here—you should have some time alone."

Jason had been dreading this moment all day. It couldn't be worse than seeing Bob lying in a pool of blood. He dreaded it nonetheless.

The viewing room was crowded with people he recognized from campus. They were clustered in small groups, talking quietly amongst themselves, periodically glancing at the casket with a combination of sadness and shock on their faces. He saw a number of flower arrangements, one large one from the university, many smaller bouquets from school groups and individuals, and another large one from National Oil and Sandra's firm. As he got closer he heard his name being whispered. They nodded and parted for him to come forward, in respect for the man they knew as Bob Daniels' best friend. Jason nodded back as he made his way to the casket.

Though cliché, Bob looked at peace, a contrast from what must have been the terrifying last few moments of his life. The funeral director had done a good job cosmetically patching the hole in his forehead and dressing him in the sport coat Jason had retrieved from Bob's closet, the one he wore whenever he had an important meeting. A touch of formality was the tie Jason had seen him wear only once. A fitting tribute to the guy who insisted the next time he'd wear a tie would be at his own funeral.

Jason made his way back toward the outer hallway, nodding, shaking hands, and listening to whispered condolences. Sandra was waiting for him there.

"I never thought I'd see you in a suit, Professor," she said, attempting a smile. Her levity was welcome.

"As Bob once said to me, 'The next time will be at my funeral,'" Jason said wryly.

"Oh, please don't say that, not even jokingly."

"Sorry, it just slipped. The flowers are a nice touch, thank Nat for me as well."

"He kicked in the largest portion and my business partner and I wanted to do something as well. I only met Bob a few times, but I was always impressed by his intelligence and humor. A very nice man."

"He was that, a real gentleman, and a good friend," Jason said.

"Listen," Sandra said to pick up the conversation, "I know you need to be here for a while. I'm going back to the hotel. I still have some work to do tonight, and I've got high-speed Internet in my room. Then perhaps we could have some dinner? I was thinking about the little restaurant in the hotel."

"That would be fine. How about eight o'clock in the restaurant?"

"Great, see you then."

Chapter 23.
Third Strike

It was Tuesday evening and Wilcox was on the Beltway for a scheduled follow-up with Martha Walters. He had more questions, and after their first meeting, he was comfortable asking for the second meeting.

There was too much traffic for him to use his cruise control, but not so much that he couldn't manually maintain his seventy-five mph speed. He had one mile remaining of the far left lane before a lane closure. A temporary bridge abutment had been erected to allow replacement of an older bridge across the highway. It was time to merge to the right.

Though aggressive, Wilcox was a good driver, and signaled his intent to merge. There was a large SUV to his immediate right, so he did the logical thing, slowing down to pull in behind. But as he did so, he looked in his rearview mirror and noticed a car tailgating him. And the SUV to his right was slowing as well. Wilcox tapped his brakes to alert the guy behind that he needed to slow down, but the driver wouldn't back off. Perhaps he didn't see the signs warning of the lane closure ahead.

Wilcox had less than a half-mile to get into the lane on his right and decided to hit the accelerator to pull past the SUV, but it accelerated with him. Oddly, the driver tailgating him also picked up speed.

It took just a moment for Wilcox to realize that he was in the middle of something he had trained for at the academy. This was a textbook "flying diamond," a technique taught to agents as a way to eliminate a target. Only this time, *he* was the target!

The drivers around him were clearly acting in concert. His only remaining defense was to try to ram the SUV to his right. At almost eighty miles an hour, he was closing quickly on the bridge abutment. Even without the driver behind him, his brakes could not possibly stop him in time.

With his training coming to the surface, he rammed the SUV. The attacker was prepared for this maneuver and the big vehicle managed to keep Wilcox pinned in the left lane. He had time for one more try and rammed the SUV harder, to no avail. Only then, knowing he wasn't going to make it, was he close enough to look into the eyes of the man to his right. For a brief second, Wilcox thought he recognized him.

Running on pure adrenalin, he slammed on the brakes. The tailgater avoided collision by swerving into the right lane in the hole behind the attacker and the car following him. Wilcox' mind suddenly flashed to Sandra and other pleasant visions of his past. He had been outsmarted. He was dead!

He managed to slow down to seventy, but at that speed, the car compressed by three feet upon hitting the concrete bridge abutment. Decelerating from seventy miles per hour to zero in three feet created a force of about one hundred times the force of gravity, ripping Don's body apart. The steering wheel nearly cut him in two.

By the time the dust settled, the attackers were long gone. All that remained was the hulk of a crushed Chrysler full of blood and body parts. Miraculously, there was no explosion, only smoke rising from the radiator that embedded itself into the concrete, the car coming to rest on its left side.

Witnesses found it hard to believe that the occupant had not died instantly. Somehow, Wilcox lived long enough to scrawl something on the inside of his window, written in his own blood.

Chapter 24.
Caught

Wednesday morning greeted Jason with the same appropriately dismal weather. After a quick glass of orange juice, he again dressed in his black suit. The funeral would begin with a ceremony in the parlor chapel at 8:00 AM followed by a short drive to the cemetery. He had planned the day to be as brief as possible. Most of those attending were engineers, some of whom had come in from out of town. They would appreciate concluding early.

He pulled up to the funeral home in his black BMW at about 7:30 AM to be there when everyone arrived. He had driven down to his home in Sarasota the night before to swap the Jeep for a car that would be more appropriate. The funeral director waved him in to park behind the hearse as the first car in the procession. *A position of honor,* Jason thought.

Jason stood outside in the rain holding an umbrella advertising the name of the funeral home. He felt more at ease with the wake over and the casket closed, chatting with those arriving to pay their respects.

Shortly before eight, Sandra pulled up in her rental. He escorted her to the chapel, doing his best to keep them both dry. Once inside, he walked her to a seat in the back. He returned to his post at the entrance until it was time for the service to start and then took his seat in the front row a few feet from the casket.

Jason couldn't remember Bob ever going to church, or even mentioning church, but he felt a service of some kind would be appropriate. The problem was finding a minister or priest on short notice. Fortunately, Father Donovan, the campus Catholic Chaplain, was available. Father kept it short, which is what Jason had requested in keeping with what Bob would have wanted.

It was still gray and cold when they walked out of the chapel to their cars, but at least the rain had stopped. Jason and five other professors served as pall bearers, gingerly carrying the heavy coffin down the steps, placing it on the rails extending from the waiting hearse. The funeral director pushed a button pulling the coffin inside as Jason escorted Sandra to his car.

The ride to the cemetery was a short fifteen minutes once everyone got going.

"Certainly convenient," Sandra noted, breaking the silence.

"Bob's work was his life and he'd want to be as close as possible," Jason replied.

The hearse pulled up to the gravesite and the pall bearers carried the casket to the stand over the open grave. After more words from the chaplain, everyone was asked to bid their final farewell so the casket could be lowered.

Jason waited for the others to leave and moved to the casket alone while Sandra waited in the periphery of his vision. "This is it, buddy," he said.

Sandra moved to his side and latched onto his arm as they slowly returned to his car. Jason looked back a few times to see the cemetery workers begin covering the man he had known with six feet of dirt.

They rode back to the church, again in silence. Sandra again decided to break it.

"Would you join me for breakfast?" she asked, thinking it would be a good for him.

"Sure, I didn't have much this morning. We can eat at the hotel again. You'll be able to leave from there."

* * *

As Sandra went to her room to pack, Jason went to the restaurant, leaving his suit jacket and tie in the car, hoping he wouldn't need either for a long time. The hostess recognized him and gave him his regular table in the corner by the window. He sat facing the door so he could watch for Sandra. She walked in a few minutes later.

"You look better now," she said as she slid onto the bench on the opposite side of the booth. "I bet you're anxious to get back to work."

"I haven't given it much thought for the last week and a half until you mentioned it," Jason said.

"Sorry."

"That's okay. I'm concerned for the safety of everyone on the team. I have to assume the car bomb in Santa Barbara and Bob's murder are related, and if they are, the entire team is at risk."

"It is scary, perhaps with your DOE funding, Brad Spencer could arrange for additional security. Your work has to be tremendously important for the government."

Before Jason could respond, Sandra's purse began to vibrate. She reached in, felt around, and came up with her white phone.

"Must be Don," she smiled. "I tried to get him last night but could only leave him a voicemail. Would you excuse me for a minute?"

"Sure, why don't I step out?"

"No, I didn't mean *that*," she said.

As she looked at the phone, her reaction turned to concern.

"Hello," she said tentatively to the unknown caller.

…

"I can, sir, I'm sitting with Professor Davidson, how can I help you?"

…

Jason looked confused. Sandra was on the white cell phone, but not with Wilcox. She looked as though she was going to be sick.

"Sir?"

…

"Oh my God! No! No! It can't *be!*" she screamed. Her eyes welled up with tears as she instinctively reached across the table and grabbed his arm, squeezing as though her life depended on it.

"Oh…no," she cried.

She looked directly into Jason's eyes. He hadn't seen such hurt since he'd seen himself in the mirror that morning. She couldn't speak. Jason swung around to her side of the table to provide support. After several minutes of loud sobbing, she struggled to talk.

"How did it happen? He was such a good driver!"

* * *

It was getting late in the morning. The restaurant had emptied and they found themselves alone. Jason, who'd been hearing just one side of the conversation, waved the waitress over, and asked her to clear the table and bring two refills of hot coffee.

"Sandra, what the hell happened?"

"Don's dead. It was a *horrible* accident," she said, her voice shaking. "I need to bring you up to speed; you probably have questions."

"I am confused."

"That was Director Reynolds, he has one of Don's phones too. He would like to call you later."

"Sure, but..."

"And I actually work for the CIA."

"Jesus Christ, you're CIA? I thought you were a lawyer?"

Sandra was now regaining her composure but seemed as fragile as a paper doll.

"I *am* a lawyer, as are many agents, and I do provide lobbying services for National as my cover. But my real job is to monitor oil companies as we get closer to what you call Peak Oil. I focus on National. We have other agents monitoring all the major producers." She was talking through tears again and took a few moments to right herself.

"We need you to continue what you were going to be doing with Don—help us find out who is behind these killings... and now see if Don's death is related."

"Do you have reason to believe it wasn't an accident?"

"The director said that Don made some marks on the inside of his car door window just before he died. He wrote them in his own blood! Reynolds believes he may have been trying to tell us something. He's sending me an email with a lot of attachments. One of them will be a photograph of the inside of that window. I should be able to download it in a few minutes."

"I guess this means you won't be flying back tonight. Let's go to the lab and you can hook up to our network to get that email. I'd like to see what Reynolds is sending."

Sandra's eyes now looked like those of a raccoon, with her tear-soaked eye makeup running down her cheeks. "Good idea. I'll go up to my room and freshen up, I'm a mess. I'll meet you at the lab in about forty-five minutes," she said, her eyes still watering.

"You shouldn't be driving. I'll wait for you here."

* * *

The campus had become a ghost town. The police had cordoned off all entrances. Jason went to the entrance nearest the lab and was waved in by a guard who recognized him.

"Why don't you use Bob's office?" Jason told Sandra. "You should see a network cable on the side of the desk."

After getting himself situated, he walked next door to see if Sandra needed any help.

"I've downloaded the email from Reynolds and I'm saving the attachments," she said. "Just got the one with the attachment of Don's writing. I'll forward it to you."

In a few moments, a brownish red image of Don's scrawl appeared on her screen.

Jason pictured Don scratching this on his window in blood, as his last communication on earth. There had to be something important here.

The two of them stared at the unusual image for several minutes.

"Why would he write a backward 'F'?" Jason said just thinking aloud. "Maybe he was trying to write something else–an 'A,' or an 'E' perhaps?"

"I don't know," Sandra said, beginning to cry again at her lover's last communication. "I know Forensics would tell us that in the case of a serious head trauma, the brain can do some strange things. I hope it does mean something, but I think they'd tell us it may not."

"Let's start with the working assumption that it does," Jason said. "So what would he mean by *FAR?*"

"It may have something to do with his investigation of an internal CIA problem Don was working on. I'm going to open these other attachments and see if I can find a correlation."

Back in his office, Jason pondered the image on his own screen. He started thinking about words that started with F.A.R., or acronyms that might be represented by those three letters.

"Sandra," Jason yelled, "did you say this was taken from the *inside* of the window?"

"That's what Reynolds said," she yelled back. "The car was lying on its left side so they didn't have access to the outside of the window."

"What if Don was thinking—impaired as he might have been—that he was writing it to be read from the other side of the window—from the outside? I'm just trying to find a way to turn that backward 'F' around."

"What do you mean?" Sandra said as she came back into his office.

"I want to look at it as if I was looking from the other side of the glass."

"How would you do that?"

"I'm going to flip it digitally to create the mirror image, which is the way it would appear from the outside."

Jason copied the image into PowerPoint, and used the rotate tool to flip the picture horizontally.

"There you have it. Now it says either A.A.F. or R.A.F. I'm going to assume the first letter is 'R' since it doesn't have the same peak as the next letter, which is clearly an 'A.' What do you think?"

"It would help explain the misshaped characters if he was trying to write them backwards—mirror image, rather."

"The only R.A.F. that comes to my mind immediately," Jason smiled, "is the British Royal Air Force, but it's not clear why they would be involved."

"Jason, the first thing I learned as an agent is to rule nothing out."

Jason's left pocket started to vibrate. He picked up.

"Professor Davidson, this is William Reynolds. Do you have time to talk? And are you in a place were you *can* talk?"

"I do and I am, sir. Sandra said you'd be calling, and she's in the room with me. We're at my lab working on the materials you sent her."

"That's why I called you. I've assigned Sandra to be your liaison," Reynolds said. "We believe the deaths of Jill Roberts and Daniels are related to an organization that doesn't want your group to succeed. It's not yet clear whether Don's death is also related; we have more investigating to do. Make no mistake—you're in danger. We want to protect you, and we could use your help in finding out who's behind this."

"Sure. If I need to reach you on this phone, I assume you're on the speed-dial list."

"I'm on speed-dial number *one*."

"Of course," Jason half-smiled. "Anything else?"

"Please, work with Sandra, she knows what she's doing. She's very bright."

"She is that, sir. Goodbye." Jason hung up.

"She is what?" Sandra asked, having heard only half the conversation.

"He said that you are a pain in the ass," Jason replied with a face that got a rise out of her.

"Okay, smart-ass," Sandra replied, her eyes still watering, "let's get back to work."

For the next forty-five minutes there wasn't a word spoken. As Sandra went to work printing the attachments that Reynolds had sent her, Jason pondered, *What could have happened?* Jill, Bob Daniels, and now Don Wilcox—dead! What was the meaning of that mysterious message? He tried various combinations of the letters, substituting an 'A' for what really looked like an 'R,' first as an acronym, then as initials, then as an anagram.

He had been at it for some time, when he finally yelled to the next office, "Sandra, I need to try an idea out on you."

"What?" she yelled back.

Jason caught himself and smiled. The exchange was feeling like the "discussions" he always had with Bob. They called them "yell-a-thons." Whenever one had an idea to try out, he yelled for the other in the next office. Oftentimes the other person was engrossed in something else, or it was too noisy to hear clearly. Then would come an exchange of yells, until one or the other took the short walk next door.

Sandra pulled herself away from her files and stuck her head in Jason's office.

"Hi, *Bob*," he said.

"Hi, *Doc*," she answered, playing along. "So this is how you guys got so much work done. Did you ever consider just picking up the phone?"

"Always easier to yell," Jason said with a smile. "Low-tech, less wasted motion."

"What have you got?"

"My mind has been cluttered with what's happened the last two weeks. With what Don left, I've been totally confused," he confessed. "I obviously didn't know Don as well as you, but he seemed to be a conscientious person, someone whose dying message would probably be important, even with head trauma.

"Suppose he was trying to write the mirror image of a name, instead of a word or acronym or initials. The name would then start with the characters 'RAF,' and when I put that together with some other facts, I come up with Rafi."

"Rafi Haddad? Your lead engineer?"

"Consider the corroborating facts. Rafi was in the vicinity of each of these deaths. He was with me and Jill in Santa Barbara. Though he didn't travel with us, he stayed at the same hotel and was there the night before. He was working with Bob on the IP trace and could have been here when he was murdered; and he was in D.C. supposedly visiting his mother on the day of Don's accident." Jason paused to review the timeline that was forming in his head. "You know, Bob never trusted Rafi from the time we restarted CERC."

"Why not?"

"He wouldn't elaborate. He called it 'gut feel,' but I know it bothered him for a long time. The other day when I was at his house looking for a way to contact any of his relatives, I saw some of the research he'd done on the early days of CERC. Turns out that Rafi was at Will Elliot's house when *he* died three years ago."

"Interesting. So you don't think Don's death was accidental?"

"We can't rule that out," Jason answered. "But Rafi's proximity to all these deaths is a strange coincidence."

"Doc, how will you be able to prove it? All you have is circumstantial evidence."

"I know, so I'll just have to confront him this afternoon when he returns. And I don't have to bother reading him his rights."

"But if you're wrong?"

"Then I'll be one real horse's ass!" Jason said. "Once I bring him into my office, I'd like you to join me as a witness to whatever happens."

"Okay. Buzz Bob's extension and that will be my signal to come in."

"Good idea. I'll alert security that Rafi's coming. We don't want to spook him before he gets here."

"We'll need to be careful," Sandra said. "If you're right, he could be carrying a weapon."

* * *

Rafi's flight arrived at Tampa International at 12:30 PM without incident. He needed to act natural, which meant going back to his lab, and behave shocked about what happed to poor Professor Daniels.

It was a short ride at that hour. As he got closer he suspected that not all had returned to order. This was confirmed when he went through the entrance gate on Fowler Avenue. Even after showing his ID, the police refused to admit him until security was called to authorize entry.

Driving to the lab it was obvious the campus was still closed. He parked his motorcycle, locked his helmet in one of his bike's hard-covered saddle bags, and strode into the lab.

"Hi, Professor," he called from the bullpen, "I got here as soon as I could. I saw it on CNN this morning."

Jason walked out into the bullpen to greet his engineer.

"Glad you're back," Jason said as he put his hand out to shake Rafi's. Then he motioned to the blood-stained floor. "Bob was killed right there in the War Room as he worked on that IP trace."

"This is tragic," Rafi shook his head. "If it weren't for my trip home, I may have been here with him, and we might have been able to fight the intruder off. On the other hand, I may have been killed too."

"Yeah, tragic," Jason said as he led Rafi toward his office. "Come in and I'll give you an update."

Rafi followed Jason into his office and took the chair opposite the professor's desk. Jason felt no good reason to defer what was impending. If he was right about Rafi, this could end right here. If he was wrong, he'd probably resign.

"So how was your mother?" Jason asked as he got settled.

"Just fine, Professor. Thank you for asking."

"You couldn't have had much time with her, though," Jason said as he buzzed Bob's office.

"Professor?"

"Oh, let me introduce Sandra Bilson. Sandra, this is Rafi Haddad, our lead engineer. Rafi, this is Sandra Bilson, a consultant for National Oil. She came down here to represent National's interests during the investigation."

"Yes, I think we met briefly, some time ago," she said.

Rafi shook hands with Sandra as she sat down in a chair at the side of Jason's desk.

"What I meant about your mother," Jason continued, "is that I don't think you had time to visit her at all. You were pretty busy in D.C., weren't you?"

"I'm sorry, Professor?" Rafi said. "I had enough time with her. We had a good visit."

"Good, I'd like to talk to her? Why don't you call her and let me say hello? I haven't spoken with her in a long time."

Sandra knew where this was going and began shifting in her seat. Her cell phone chirped. She looked down to read a text message.

"Whatever you say, Professor, but this is a bit embarrassing," Rafi said as he turned and leaned over his backpack that was on the floor.

Time went into slow motion.

As Rafi removed his right hand from the bag, Jason watched carefully to see what was in it. At first, he couldn't tell; it seemed as though his brain was scanning a thousand images a second in a process of elimination. It suddenly became clear. It wasn't a cell phone but something that looked more like—or probably was—a pistol. There was no time to delay. Jason reached for his Glock as Sandra dropped her phone while reaching for her pistol.

The three people in the room flinched at the same time as the bullet entered Rafi's right shoulder, exited from the back, and embedded itself in the whiteboard wall behind him. The force threw Rafi and his chair backward, causing him to lose his grip on the backpack. The object he had retrieved flew across the room landing with the sound of plastic on linoleum. Jason and Sandra shifted their eyes in that direction. Rafi's head had hit the floor. He was out cold.

"Jesus Christ!" Jason yelled, the smoke rising from his gun, still feeling the concussion in his chest. "Now I know why I'm not a CIA agent."

"What do you mean? That was a good shot."

"I was aiming for his head. And what was that in his bag?" Jason asked, looking at the floor. "Sounded like plastic when it hit the tile. Tell me it's not a squirt gun!"

"No, Doc, that's a polymer gun designed to be undetectable by security scanners. Those are only issued by intelligence services," Sandra replied. "And that's not Rafi Haddad."

"What the hell?" Jason asked, standing with his gun still drawn. "We shot the wrong guy? Sure as hell *looks* like Rafi!" He walked around the desk kicking the plastic gun to the far side of the room. "And what happened to 'just circumstantial evidence?' You were about to shoot too."

"That text message I got was from Reynolds," Sandra said. "They restored the missing database records. This guy's name is Rafindra Abu Abdullah Muhammad. He's with the CIA, or was, but he's actually a Saudi double agent. He was initially assigned to monitor CERC and Will Elliot."

Rafi was still unconscious and Jason stooped to look at his wound. "Doesn't look serious, I think he got a mild concussion when his head hit the floor. Give me a hand and let's get him back in the chair."

"I'll call the police," she said.

"Don't do that."

"Jason, we've got to report this right away."

"Not yet." Jason had a look in his eyes that Sandra hadn't seen before. It worried her. "Get me the roll of duct tape in my lower right-hand drawer."

Sandra did as asked and Jason taped Rafi's hands behind him and his ankles to the chair legs with several revolutions of the sticky gray tape.

"This stuff will go down as one of the best inventions since the wheel," Jason said, as Rafi began to come around.

"Jason, I'm an agent of the Federal Government. I've got to report this right away."

"Report what? You're not here."

"What do you mean?"

"I need twenty minutes alone with this guy. Get out of here before he comes to. I'll call you with the complete story when I'm ready to have you talk with Ralph Kite, head of our security. His office is just inside the main gate. My call will be the first you've heard of this."

"You're not…"

"Look, Agent Bilson, I'm just a private citizen here. I didn't have to read him his rights, and I don't know a damn thing about the Geneva Convention."

Sandra could see it was useless to argue and was heading out the door as Rafi was regaining consciousness. His strength was returning quickly as he struggled against the restraints.

"You might as well kill me, Doc. I'm not going to say a word."

"I'm afraid those virgins that you were told are waiting will have to wait a little longer. I have no intention of issuing you a fast-pass to martyrdom. I do intend to find out what you've been up to."

"We've been trained to take beatings, you couldn't hit me hard enough or often enough to make me talk."

"That's okay; I'm going to let twenty-eight volts DC do the work for me. I knew I'd find a use for that old generator in the storage room."

"Go ahead; the heavy clamps on the ends of those cables will leave some serious marks."

"You're right, that's why I'm going to use wet towels as conductors. You'll be surprised what you'll talk about when your heart starts to fibrillate. Don't go away, I'll be right back."

* * *

As Sandra left the campus, she located the main security office, just inside the gate as Jason had said. A block away she found a donut shop that would be a good place to wait for Jason's call.

She avoided the donuts and was on her second cup of coffee when her cell phone rang. Jason recited the entire story just as it happened—minus her involvement. Officially, she had never been there. She stopped by security and introduced herself and the situation to Kite who followed quickly in his own squad car to the CERC lab.

Kite led Sandra into the lab with gun drawn, taking in the entire area with one sweeping glance.

"Jesus, Professor, what's going on in here? Did you shoot Rafi?"

"A slight altercation, Ralph. Yes, I did—before he could shoot me. Agent Bilson here is from the CIA."

"We've met."

"Officer Kite," Sandra said. "We have reason to believe the person in that chair, formerly known as Rafi Haddad, is actually someone else.

"And," Jason said, holding out a cassette tape, "he confessed to the car bomb and the killings of Professor Daniels and Agent Wilcox. He also confessed to poisoning Will Elliot several years ago. I've got everything on tape."

Sandra continued, "We need to have him taken into custody and see to his injuries. Can you take care of that?"

"Yes, ma'am," Ralph said, speaking simultaneously into the radio attached to his collar. Almost instantly, three large city cops appeared.

"The professor and I will keep his gun, the backpack, and its contents," Sandra told Kite. "We'll keep the evidence secure in the safe behind the professor's desk."

"That will be fine. I don't mind giving the CIA jurisdiction. Professor, are you alright?"

"Except for being hearing-impaired, I think I'm fine," joked Jason.

While they were talking, the three officers removed the duct tape, gingerly helping Rafi to his feet. They bound his hands behind him with a plastic fastener. As they led him out of the office and up the stairs to a waiting squad car, Rafi looked over his shoulder and asked, "Hey, Doc, how about letting me take my iPod?"

"You might like music where you're going," Sandra interjected, "but that iPod isn't going anywhere."

Jason added, "Why in the hell did you need to break into our servers, you had all the information on our trip?"

"I needed your rental car confirmation to find out what kind of car you were driving. Too bad you weren't in it when it blew up. Isn't the information age wonderful?"

Jason charged at Rafi. It was the first time in his life he wanted to kill someone. Kite kept them separated.

"With the information on that tape, we're going to have Will Elliot's death reopened," Jason shouted, stabbing his finger in Rafi's chest.

"He was an infidel, as were the others, as are *you!* Death to all infidels!" Rafi's last shouts as he vanished into the car.

After everyone had gone, Sandra turned to Jason and asked, "How were *you* so sure it was Rafi? You hadn't seen the message from the director."

"Actually, I wasn't sure, it's just that everything pointed in his direction. When I saw what he pulled out of the backpack wasn't a cell phone, I started to draw. Good thing he was pulling a gun instead of a hairdryer or we'd have a lot of explaining to do. Here's the cassette tape. I think you'll find it interesting. In addition to the murders, he mentions a rogue group of CIA agents called 'The Club.'"

"We need to secure the evidence in this room. I'll have one of the officers help me," Sandra said. "Then I'm going to call Reynolds and have him send someone from our S&T team down here tomorrow morning to help take that laptop apart. Rafi's probably just an operative, we need to find out who's calling the shots."

Chapter 25.
Naval Exercises

Missile Frigate *Jiaxing* was returning to its home port of Jianggezhuang when Commander Bian Guang received an urgent coded message to meet with the tanker *Feng Chang*, refuel, and head back out to sea. Destination: the Persian Gulf.

The message indicated no reason for the change, but like good officers everywhere, Commander Bian followed orders immediately, no questions asked. The questions would come from a crew out to sea for over six months looking forward to some time in home port. Bian's admiral was just issuing orders from above and would sit behind the same desk and sleep in the same bed regardless of how long deployments lasted. Bian would answer his crew as best he could. Like most commanders of large ships, the bond to his crew was stronger than the bond to his superiors.

Once turned around, Bian knew more messages would follow. He didn't have long to wait. The next order was to meet with a ship from the Royal Saudi Naval Forces (RSNF) for joint exercises in the Gulf. He was to be joined there by a sister frigate, the *Lianyungang*.

Of greater interest to Bian was what his messages didn't say. They didn't tell him what kind of maneuvers were planned, or what their purpose was, just that he would get those orders as he approached the Gulf. This probably meant his superiors were themselves unsure and were using the time to reach the Gulf to formalize details. Highly unusual in Bian's experience, but something he would not question.

* * *

Zeng's car pulled to a quick halt in front of the Great Hall. He couldn't remember the last time he was summoned to see the president on such short notice. He suspected it had something to do with the call just completed from Secretary Jennings. He tried to look calm as he walked quickly up the stone stairs, clutching the valise he'd hurriedly packed.

The line at the security checkpoint was longer than normal, and Zeng wondered if there was any correlation with his abrupt summons. He continued on to the president's office.

"Good morning, Mr. Zeng," said Thien Heng.

"Good morning, Heng," he bowed. "I'm sorry it took so long to get here. I hope I have enough materials with me to answer any questions he may have."

"Relax, Mr. Zeng. President Wu is more interested in seeing you than your materials," she smiled. "Please wait here while I announce your arrival."

Zeng paced back and forth, trying to cool off. He was sweating from the quick walk through the Great Hall carrying his heavy, over-stuffed valise.

"President Wu will see you now, Mr. Zeng," Heng said as she held open one of the two double doors leading to the president's office.

The president wasn't alone. Seated next to him at his small conference table was Xiong Jin, the minister of defense. Zeng knew then it was going to be an uncomfortable meeting. He and his Defense counterpart were sometimes seen as competitors. The president, for his part, seemed to enjoy that competition as it led to the best policies. Both men stood as Zeng entered.

"Please be seated, Mr. Zeng," the president said, motioning to a chair on the other side of the small table. "Heng was about to serve tea. Would you care for some?"

"Please."

"Minister Xiong and I have been discussing something important and felt we should consult you. We need to make some decisions quickly, and as you know, quick decisions require the review and opinions of those I trust."

"I am at your service, Mr. President," Zeng said.

"We have decided to schedule symbolic joint military exercises with Saudi Arabia, and I would like your advice."

"Very good, sir." Actually this wasn't very good. In fact, it wasn't good at all. But he couldn't intimate that, much less say it. Clearly, a lot had been going on in his absence, and Xiong was smiling in an odd way the president couldn't see. Even though he and Xiong were peers, it seemed the president always went for military advice first, a trait that had worried Zeng for some time.

"We want this exercise to be held in an open and non-threatening way to our other friends, both in the region and globally, which means we need to communicate carefully with each of them through your contacts."

"Actually, sir, we have already communicated with the Americans," Zeng said as forcefully as he felt he could.

"Really? And how did that happen?" the president said, turning his head and looking at Xiong, who looked quizzically back. As far as Xiong knew, only he and the president had been in on the decision.

"The Americans noticed that the *Jiaxing* and the *Lianyungang* changed course, heading for the Persian Gulf. I had a call from Secretary Jennings just before I was summoned here. The Americans already have concerns. I could tell from his voice that he was disappointed at not being informed, although, being a good diplomat, he didn't actually say that."

"And how did they notice?" the president asked, still looking at Xiong.

"Satellites, sir. The Americans can see the position of every surface ship in the world right down to the smallest lifeboat. They monitor changes in position in real-time," Zeng replied, glancing at Xiong.

"I suspect we should have gotten you involved in this discussion earlier, Mr. Zeng."

There! thought Zeng. *Perhaps that would wipe the smile off Xiong's face.* "I believe I was able to assuage Secretary Jennings' concerns, at least for the time being. I do need to call him back once we decide a course of action," Zeng was proud to report. *Another case of 'ready, fire, aim' on the part of the overly ambitious Mr. Xiong. One day this will get him into a position he can't get himself out of. Perhaps the president would do as he said and include Zeng earlier next time.*

"I have always appreciated your ability to think quickly and act appropriately," the president smiled. "Let's discuss the way forward. Do you think the Americans will inform their allies, if they have not done so already?"

"I don't think..." Xiong jumped in.

"We already know you don't think, Mr. Xiong, I was addressing Minister Zeng." A moment of silence ensued, Zeng letting the rebuke hang like foul air for a moment.

"I feel sure they won't, sir, as long as we inform them of our intentions quickly," Zeng finally replied.

"Good, Mr. Zeng. And now, with your input, let's discuss our strategy, and how best to communicate it." *Finally*, Zeng thought, *the president has learned his lesson*. "Mr. Xiong," the president continued, "would you explain our current situation."

"We have entered into an agreement with the Saudi Navy to hold joint exercises in the Persian Gulf," replied Xiong. "As you—and now the Americans—know, two of our missile frigates are headed in that direction. We think this is an entirely appropriate exercise, as the Americans hold such exercises with other countries regularly. Wouldn't you agree, Mr. Zeng?"

"The Americans do hold such exercises with their partners around the world, but this is not the same at all," Zeng said. "We are an emerging superpower, and have not held such maneuvers before. By itself this is one big difference and likely to attract attention. The other difference is that we are holding these exercises with Saudi Arabia, a country known to hold the last sizeable oil reserves. A partnership between China and Saudi Arabia will do a lot more than just raise eyebrows."

"Well, we have to…" started Xiong.

"Yes, Xiong, we do have to begin sometime, but we should have done so *after* appropriate diplomatic communications, not before. But since we cannot undo what has been done, we must go forward. What else is there to know?" Zeng asked.

"You should also know these exercises are really just positioning for a joint defense of Saudi oil reserves that will *not* be an exercise," Xiong said with a malicious grin.

"And what do you think the Americans will do when they find out this is more than an exercise? They already have a significant taskforce in the Gulf."

"Exactly, Mr. Zeng. This will move us closer to parity with their forces," Xiong said, looking furtively at the president, in hopes he would step in. It had become clear to the three men that Xiong was no match for Zeng.

"Yes, Mr. Zeng, it goes back to one of our previous discussions," Wu said, coming to Xiong's rescue. "Before the Americans invaded Iraq, it was understood they would not act militarily until they had exhausted all diplomatic channels, and they would never draw first blood. There have been those, including myself, who believed they tended to wait too long to react in the past. But with their invasion of Iraq, they have changed their approach. The very fact that they have significant forces already in the Gulf means they could take over the Saudi oil fields at will. I doubt at the time of the Iraq invasion the Americans really understood the long-term ramifications of their actions and how radically different they are being perceived by the rest of the world."

"But, Mr. President," pleaded Zeng, "does this mean we have given up on diplomatic channels even before they have been attempted?" He gathered his courage, then asked, "Is that why I was excluded from your earlier discussions?"

"No, Mr. Zeng," Wu replied. "We will not give up on diplomatic discussions with the Americans. However, because of their change in behavior, we will be prepared in the event those discussions do not bear fruit and the Americans again decide to act unilaterally."

"Very well, sir. How would you like me to structure my response to Secretary Jennings?"

"My thoughts," Wu said after some internal deliberation, "are to first apologize for not informing him in advance, claiming, rightfully so, that as an emerging superpower, China will need some training in the diplomatic discourse with other super-powers. However, we must not yet discuss the more serious nature of our activities with Saudi Arabia until we have completed the first step, our soon-to-be-public naval exercises. If you detect any abnormal concern from the Americans, we can hold more diplomatic discussions that should buy us time to get our remaining forces in place."

"Very well, sir," Zeng found himself agreeing with his president, unable to express the barrage of concerns flooding his mind. "I recommend that we do not change the course of any additional surface ships until we have had an extended dialog with the Americans."

"A good suggestion, Mr. Zeng," the president smiled. "We will restrict any additional movements to our submarines, which will not be visible to U.S. satellites."

"Sir, our two frigates and all of our submarines are not enough to deflect an American offensive," Zeng interjected. "Ultimately we will need to vector additional surface warships, and that will provoke the United States to action."

"Mr. Zeng, what will provoke the Americans is finding out Saudi Arabia has decided to start pricing oil in euros. After your meeting in Riyadh I had extensive discussions with Prince Faareh lobbying to hold off on that action. The prince believes, and perhaps rightfully so, that a number of changes need to take place simultaneously, including the exposure of their new relationship with us and the euro pricing announcement. The latter will destroy the American economy and probably result in the consequences we spoke of.

"Apparently, the proposal you put forth at your meeting has had a significant impact on the prince's thinking. He likes the idea of a guaranteed income as an insurance policy against alternative energy developments. But as you noted, he is wary of the ceiling and will only agree if that ceiling is priced in euros, which means he needs to separate oil from the dollar."

Great. My worst fear has come to pass, Zeng thought. *Prince Faareh has taken my proposal, made it his own, and is now putting it into action.*

Chapter 26.
iPod

"Professor Davidson, this is Dwayne Larson," Sandra said as she walked into the lab kitchen where she found Jason making coffee. "Dwayne is from our Science and Technology Division and will be working with you to analyze Rafi's laptop. Dwayne, this is Professor Jason Davidson."

"How do you do, Professor," Dwayne said as he extended his hand.

"How many people from the team are here with you today?"

"Jason," Sandra interrupted, "Dwayne *is* the team."

"Oh…impressive."

"I have access to a lot more people back in Virginia if we need them," Dwayne said, "but I should be able to take care of everything here myself."

"I like a man with confidence. Let's go back to my office and outline what we're going to do," Jason said as he led the way. "I'm sure you've done these investigations before. I'm interested in your methodology."

"Let's talk through the steps. Can I use your whiteboard?" Dwayne asked as Jason sat down behind his desk.

"Sure, just avoid the bullet hole."

Dwayne grabbed a marker and began drawing a block diagram. "The first thing we do is create a backup image of the entire machine, including the BIOS. That way, if there are any 'poison pills' that might destroy things as we're working, we can restore the machine to its current state. Then I install some standard antivirus software we'll use to scan the disk drives for any worms. But before running the scan, we place the computer in Safe Mode to make sure it has nothing running at startup that might interfere. Once we've scanned the machine and cleaned any viruses we can get to work looking for suspicious files and emails. We have some of our own tools I carry on my laptop that may help."

"Good," Jason said after putting on a pair of latex gloves. "You sound like an electronic Sherlock Holmes. Here's Rafi's laptop and iPod. I've set up a workstation for you in the bullpen."

Sandra went back to Daniels' old office to continue plowing through the hundreds of pages that represented Wilcox' caseload. She'd already consumed two reams of paper just by printing what she saw as the essentials. *At this rate, she could be a serious threat to the rain forest*, Jason thought.

For Jason, this was the time to get his CERC team restarted. Since his trip to California, all work had come to a halt. Bob Daniels had been distracted by the IP trace and then his murder had completely closed the lab. Jason had always worked to a schedule. During the early research it was difficult to establish a schedule with measurable milestones. Research was like that. But with all the technology in place, a firm schedule was now possible. The biggest challenge was the high-volume manufacture of the optical rectenna circuits. They were currently being handcrafted.

Dwayne was hard at work in his cube dissecting Rafi's laptop. Jason was impressed by his work ethic and knew, like most engineers his age, he was driven more by technical challenge than by salary. Jason was sure there would be something incriminating on that machine.

Forty-five minutes later there was a knock at his door. It was "the Geek."

"Sir, I've been through this machine, including the BIOS, and can't find anything abnormal, nothing I would consider suspicious," Dwayne said. "And in my job I've seen some pretty weird stuff."

"What about his email? Did Rafi use an email client to keep his messages on that machine, or did he access them using the browser from the university's server?"

"He used Outlook Express. It comes free with Windows and downloaded his email periodically from your server. That way he never ran out of space and his emails weren't sitting on the server visible to others," Dwayne explained. "I've looked through his 'Inbox,' 'Sent Items,' and 'Deleted Items' and haven't seen anything out of the ordinary. I think his machine is clean."

"What about his iPod, anything unusual there?"

"Looks like standard music downloads. He has quite a bit of music stored, mostly in MP3 format."

"Have you looked at what's on the iPod's disk?"

"Not sure what you mean, Professor. I assume it's just music."

"I'd like to see if Rafi had anything other than music on it. Bring it in, we can hook it up to my machine."

Dwayne went back to his cubicle and returned with Rafi's iPod and USB cable.

"Professor, this is a new one to me. Can you tell me again what you're looking for?"

"An iPod is just a small handheld computer specifically designed to play music that's stored on its internal hard drive. What's unique about this device, in addition to the software that controls it, is the high capacity drive it uses.

"When you hook an iPod to your computer to download music from iTunes, you're really just connecting a removable disk drive to your computer, at least that's how your computer sees it. But you can also store other files on it, in addition to music. Let's hook it up and take a look."

Jason slipped on his latex gloves and took the iPod and USB synchronization cable from Dwayne. He connected the special connector on one end of the cable to the iPod and the USB connector to one of the ports on his computer. He started the standard Windows File Explorer and took a look at all the devices and folders on Rafi's system.

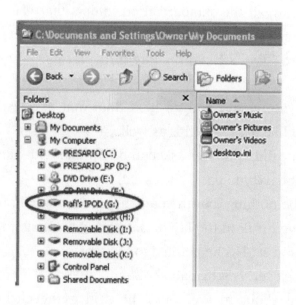

Rafi's iPod showed up as the G-drive on Jason's machine, and he used a notation tool to circle that drive. He clicked on the G-drive to look at the folders it contained.

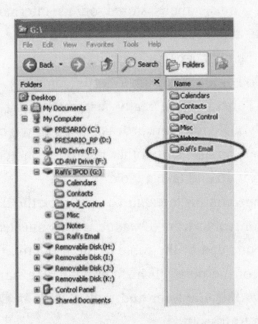

They saw all the standard iPod folders that iTunes used to synchronize the two machines. But there was one addition, a folder called "Rafi's Email." "Pay dirt!" Jason said as he encircled it.

"Dwayne, would you go next door and ask Ms. Bilson to join us? I'd like her to see this as well."

Dwayne did as he was asked and returned with Sandra.

"What have you got?" she asked.

"Maybe nothing, but then again, maybe something. In addition to using his iPod to play music, Rafi was using it to store his email," Jason said as he pointed to the screen.

"Very clever. Is it readable?" Sandra asked.

"We're about to find out," he said as he clicked on the folder."

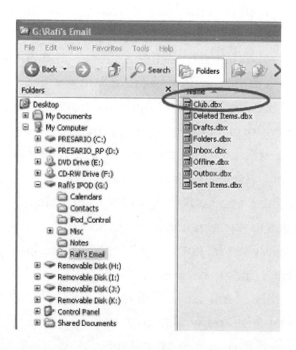

"These *dbx* files are database files Outlook Express uses to store email," Jason explained. "And these are all the standard email folders with the addition of one folder Rafi has created called 'Club.dbx.'" He circled it. "And looking at the timestamps, we can see they were updated the day he was caught; so Rafi got some email recently."

"Doc, as I was going through Don's work papers, I found he was doing an internal investigation into the mysterious deaths of two of our agents. Both agents had talked about some kind of club just before they died. Can we see what's in those folders? Rafi confessed he was involved in this 'club' business too."

Jason brought up Outlook Express on his computer and attached it to the G-drive, which was really Rafi's iPod. He was able to open the folders until he got to the one called "Club." It displayed digital nonsense, what an encrypted file looks like when it can't be decrypted into plain text.

"Looks like all the email in the 'Club,' 'Sent Items,' and 'Deleted Items' folders has been encrypted," said Jason. "That would explain why we didn't see anything strange in the folders on his laptop. He was using the iPod as his disk drive.

"If the items in the 'Club' folder were sent to Rafi in a digitally encrypted form, then we can assume his laptop holds both the senders' certificates and his own. The same would be true for his 'Sent' and 'Deleted' folders. Let's take the iPod out to Dwayne's cubicle and hook it up to Rafi's machine."

It took Jason just a moment to connect the iPod to Rafi's laptop. This time, when he got to the "Club" folder, he could clearly read the subject lines in each item. "Voila!"

"Jason, this is too clever," Sandra said. "No wonder Rafi wanted to keep his iPod with him."

"He carried it with him all the time. And we thought it was his love of music," Jason laughed. "It didn't matter if someone gained access to his computer. All of his sensitive information was being kept on the iPod, encrypted and decrypted by the certificates on his laptop. So someone would need both machines to understand what he was involved in. He did his best to make sure that didn't happen—until today."

Jason scrolled down the list of subject headers until one caught his eye: "Professor Davidson." "Jesus *this* looks interesting," he said as he clicked on the item. The message was instantly decrypted into plain text. It was dated three days before he left for Santa Barbara.

Subject: Professor Davidson
From: Prince

Your professor is to be eliminated
ASAP using a method of your
choosing. Your authorization is in
the attached email. Report when
mission has been accomplished.

"'Prince'?" Sandra asked loudly, looking over Jason's shoulder. "I assume this 'Prince' is not the Artist formerly known as...," she said sarcastically. "Can you open the attachment?"

With one click it appeared.

Subject: Davidson
From: VIP

Your reward of 20,000 euros will
be available in Sparbuch
73469013492. Password will be
sent when mission successfully
accomplished.

VIP

"My God! There's the order for your murder," Sandra said.

"Disappointing that I'm only worth twenty thousand euros. At least it's someone who considers themselves a 'Very Important Person.'"

"So, how do we find out who 'Prince' and 'VIP' really are?"

"Let's review what we know," Jason responded with re-newed determination after seeing his name on the hit list. "We have the public keys for both Prince and VIP. Any email that can be read using those public keys was actually sent and signed by those individuals. Also, neither of them know we have Rafi, and we need to keep it that way."

"I can take care of that," Sandra said. But if Rafi was com-municating with them periodically, when they lose contact they'll know something is wrong."

"Good point," Jason replied. "Let's look through his 'Sent Items' folder to see if we can find a pattern."

It didn't take long. Every two days between the hours of 12:00 PM and 1:00 PM Eastern time, Rafi would send a signed and encrypted message to Prince with just two letters in the sub-ject field: "OK." It would be easy for Dwayne to send the same message from Rafi's laptop every two days to buy time.

"Jason, I need to call the director and give him an update," Sandra said. "I also need to review the emails in Rafi's 'club' folder to see if there's a tie-in with the internal investigation that Don was working on."

This gave Jason time to begin calling each member of the CERC team individually. He reemphasized the importance of their work, reassuring them of the heightened security on cam-pus. And the team would be back in normal operation, assuming wall-to-wall security could be perceived as normal, when they returned the following Monday. About halfway through his calls Sandra returned with her cell phone.

"I have the director on the phone."

"Let's put him on speaker. See if Dwayne can join us; he may have some details that will be helpful."

Sandra brought Dwayne into the meeting and shut the door. The three of them huddled around the small cell phone that sat in the middle of Jason's desk.

"Good afternoon, folks," the director said. "Sandra gave me an update earlier. I wanted to see if there have been any new developments."

"Director," Sandra said, "it looks like we need to keep Rafi's laptop here for analysis, is that alright?"

"Perfect, just make sure we retain custody of all the evidence."

"The other thing we need to do is identify who 'Prince' and 'VIP' really are. To do this, the professor has a plan to use the public keys located on Rafi's laptop."

"Professor, I'm not an encryption expert, but don't we need the certificates that go with those public keys in order to the owners?"

"We do, but I suspect it will be harder than that since they wouldn't have used their real names when they obtained the certificates. The way I'd like to proceed is by going through the government archives of signed emails to see if the public keys we have will unsign any of those documents. Any documents that meet these criteria must have been signed with the corresponding private key, and based on the contents of those documents we may be able to determine the authors' real names. I assume we—you—do keep such archives?"

"Of course, since 9/11 we monitor an enormous amount of email sent in and out of this country, the archives have millions of messages in them. It would take an army of people years to find any matches."

"Only if we did it manually," Jason replied. "It should take less than a day if we use one of your Cray supercomputers and a program that I'd like Dwayne to write. Can I speak to Dwayne's supervisor?"

"Professor, as of this moment, Dwayne reports to you for the duration of this investigation. Dwayne, is that understood?"

Dwayne Larson was a mid-level analyst and programmer for the four years he'd been with the Agency. Listening to his director, his eyes were as big as quarters. The thought of getting his hands on a Cray supercomputer was orgasmic.

"Understood, sir," Dwayne replied with bulging eyes, nodding as if the director could see him.

Jason added, "What we need from you, Director, is a sample of those archives so Dwayne can write the software on one of our UNIX machines. Once we have that working, he can transfer the program to the Cray and begin processing the entire set of emails."

"Very well," Reynolds said. "I'll have Dwayne put in touch directly with the people who control the archives and give them instructions he's to have anything he needs. Now I need to ask him to leave the room. We have other matters to discuss. Thank you, Dwayne."

Dwayne left the office beaming. This was the opportunity of a lifetime. Sandra shut the door behind him.

"Alright, we have just the professor and myself at this end," Sandra announced.

"I look forward to hearing of your progress in finding the people responsible for these recent attacks on your organization," Reynolds said. "But I need to turn our attention to another matter that's developing today. Secretary of State Walter Jennings has joined me in my office and would like to bring us up to speed. Professor, I understand that you have met—or at least spoken with—the secretary in the past."

"I have, good afternoon, Secretary Jennings."

"Good afternoon, Professor and Agent Bilson. I need to preface my remarks by saying everything we discuss today is of the utmost secrecy and is not to be discussed with anyone else. We're talking *national security* here!"

"Understood, sir," Jason acknowledged, looking at Sandra with a "What now?" expression.

"Understood," echoed Sandra, shrugging her shoulders.

"As you may have seen on the news, the Chinese are starting a series of military exercises in the Persian Gulf."

"Sir, don't we and other nations hold such exercises routinely and sometimes jointly?" asked Sandra.

"We do, but in this case, we have additional information from Director Reynolds that these exercises are being held in conjunction with the Saudis. From satellite imagery the director provided, we can see that while the appearance to the public is just two ships heading into the Gulf, the Chinese are actually staging a large percentage of their Blue Water Navy for a quick response."

"Sir, I'm *way* out of my depth here. What would they be responding to?" Jason asked.

"*Our* potential response. We have reason to believe the Chinese are in the process of forging relationships that will assure them of an oil supply for the future. They are aware, as are you, that the world's oil supply can no longer expand to meet global demand. We believe they've developed, or are developing, relationships with those countries predicted to have the last remaining oil, which includes Saudi Arabia."

"But," Jason asked, "aren't we the people the Saudis turn to for protection? We haven't made any moves to control their oil output—have we?"

"Correct," Jennings agreed. "But there are two things working against us. First, the Saudis have never really liked us. They've certainly liked our money, but they have been, and still are, deathly afraid of the effects Western culture may have on their society. Remember, the wealth of that country is mostly controlled by only about six thousand members of the royal family, and they want to keep it that way. The last thing they want is a citizenry that thinks for itself."

"That would make one hell of a family picnic," Jason couldn't help thinking aloud.

"The other issue has to do with our standing as a member of what's now a global society. Over the first 230 years of our history, America has been the country viewed as the last to take military action, but when we take it, we win. Our actions in Iraq are seen by others to be those of an aggressor in light of the fact that our stated reason for invading that country was to prevent the use of WMDs that were never discovered. This one event has changed the world's perception of us as a country not only possessing the military might to dominate, but one willing to do so without *proven* provocation. We believe the Chinese are operating under those assumptions. If we put ourselves in their position, the only logical way to react to the geopolitical environment caused by the world's oil supply not keeping up with demand, coupled with our perceived behavior in Iraq, is for *them* to make the first move—because they now have reason to believe *we* will. We can only assume what we're seeing on the director's satellite images are the beginning of just such a move."

"Christ, that's scary," said Jason, "how can I help?"

"Professor, you can't help at this minute, but you can be *prepared* to help. We obtained the satellite pictures this morning, and since that time, I've been on the phone with my Chinese counterpart, one Mr. Zeng Ju. While Mr. Zeng claims their maneuvers are strictly exercises, I can tell he knows that we know there is probably more to it than that. In my last call to him, it became clear that China wants an assured source of energy. They view oil as the most critical form of that energy; but they, like us, would prefer to avoid the confrontation that would surely develop if we were both forced to secure our oil supply from Saudi Arabia."

"I assume this is where I come in?"

"Professor, this situation hinges on our development of alternatives to oil. I mentioned the work of your group, and Mr. Zeng said he'd also been following that progress, indicating he had access to inside information. Based on what I've learned today, we may now conclude the source of that inside information was the member of your team we have under arrest—a Mr. Haddad, I believe."

"So, Mr. Jennings," Jason continued after a pause, "I gather China would be interested in helping us bring our clean energy solution to market. The problem is that our president has not seen fit to fund alternative fuel research beyond a token amount, which has significantly delayed the ability to roll it out."

"Yes, Professor, unfortunately that's true. But with today's developments, I'm sure we can change the atmosphere here in Washington. That's what I meant by being prepared to help—that is, if I'm able to persuade President Wells to take the initiative."

"Very well, but I need to alert you to the reality that we still have much work to do. In addition to money, this will require a lot of people and considerable time."

"I've already had that discussion with Mr. Zeng. He appreciates that we would need a phased approach to our agreement. I think you'll find our friends in China to be very pragmatic. They understand oil can't be the world's source of energy much longer, even if they controlled all of it. They're quite interested in considering a longer term renewable approach while we work together to utilize the existing oil reserves in an equitable way.

"They don't want a confrontation any more than we do. I see this partnership as a way to avert what would surely be a crisis of a magnitude we've never seen before. Something that would make the current Iraq war look like *recess*. So, again, I'm asking you to be ready to help. That means being prepared to travel to Beijing on short notice with a party from the State Department if we can get this agreement out of the starting blocks."

"I'm prepared to go as soon as you tell me you're ready."

"Thank you Professor, I will communicate with you through the director as I understand he has a secure channel to you at all times. I meet with President Wells tomorrow and will keep you informed."

"Good luck with the president."

* * *

The three of them had gone back to their tasks. Around 6:00 PM, Jason could see Dwayne pacing outside, going back and forth between Jason's door and his cubicle. He was back again and Jason waved him in. The kid looked relieved.

"Okay, Dwayne, what have you got?"

"Professor, I've set up the UNIX account you gave me and Director Reynolds had the archive guys send me a thousand emails so I could get the program written. I've tested it and would like to review the design."

"Go ahead, and let's keep in mind this program you're developing is not intended to be a product. It just needs to run a couple of times at most. It's more important that we get results quickly, so any shortcuts you can find will be great."

"Basically, I have a set of public keys we're trying to match to emails that are kept in the archive. In the production run I'll have about twenty-five public keys and several million emails. The way I've written the program is to apply each key to each of the emails until one of them opens it. If none of them open it, I go to the next email. If one of the keys does open an email, I save the clear-text version in a separate file along with any information from the certificate. We'll then need to go in manually to read those that were saved in the file to see if they lead us to the owners of the keys opening them. I've run a test against the sample emails and I was able to open one of them because I was given the matching key for testing. I think I'm ready to run against the full archive on the Cray back in D.C."

"If you have access and an ID on the Cray, go ahead and transfer the certificates and your source code to that machine, recompile, and let it run. Let me know immediately what you get."

"Thank you, sir, I will, and thanks for giving me this assignment. This is the most important job I've had in my four years with the Agency. I've never had a chance to use our Cray and—"

"Okay, Dwayne, go get 'em!" Jason interrupted as he rushed out.

Dwayne didn't see Sandra smile. "The kid lives for this stuff," she said.

Chapter 27.
The White House

President Warren Wells' life had become a living hell. It didn't help that his vice president, Gerald Herzog, was in his office again, blathering on about some inane project that had no bearing on anything important. At least the lull gave Wells a chance to reflect on what was really bothering him...

The war in Iraq, inherited from his predecessor, wasn't going well and everyone knew it. But he had to maintain appearances. He'd been elected by a significant margin because he was of the same party as his predecessor. Voters feared changing horses in mid-stream. The trend in Iraq, according to intelligence from the field, wasn't showing improvement. In fact, the war was going down a rat hole. Iraq had deteriorated into a three-way civil war—and that was on a good day—with Baghdad becoming a training ground for terrorists.

The invasion had been easy, just a few weeks of high-precision bombing followed by a large surge on the ground to take control of Baghdad and a few other major cities.

Winning the peace was proving more difficult. Unfortunately, success was defined not just in military terms, but in leaving behind a stable Iraqi democracy. The insurgents were much more resilient than predicted and in hindsight, Wells wished his predecessor had followed the ground assault with much stiffer police action before a handful of insurgents swelled to thousands. *Success in Iraq should have been a three-act play,* he thought, *invasion, stabilization, and transition. Unfortunately, we had only scripted the first act.*

Considering recent headlines, America was having serious doubts over the reasons for invading in the first place. And what were those reasons? Wells himself struggled to remember. It was years ago.

The best intelligence in the world reported that Saddam Hussein had WMDs, and was providing safe haven for terrorists and training them in their usage. At least that was what the previous administration wanted to believe since it gave them cause to invade. Throwing nuclear weapons—the "Boogeyman" card—into the mix ensured wide support from the electorate. The clincher was having the secretary of state, the most credible and respected member of the cabinet, deliver that message to the United Nations, punctuating his points with a vial of white powder. *I wonder if that really was anthrax? Probably not, too dangerous. Perhaps powdered sugar…or baking soda.*

The best intelligence in the world proved unintelligent. The CIA director was thrown under the bus and forced to resign—someone had to take the fall. As compensation, he was given the Presidential Medal of Freedom Award…nice touch.

With no WMDs, the argument for invasion had to change. The reason shifted to the elimination of an obscenely mad and sadistic dictator, and creating a footprint for democracy in the Middle East. To some, these human-rights arguments morally justified America's actions. To other nations we appeared the aggressor. A fringe theory held that the real reason for the invasion was Sadam's threat to the president's father, himself a former president.

America had become the world's policeman, not satisfied with nation-building, but nation-building in its own image. Overlooked was that a true democracy must happen from the inside, not forced from the outside. Iraq needed to find their own versions of John Hancock, Thomas Jefferson, Benjamin Franklin, and the other Builders of the Republic: statesmen and patriots with strategy, vision and ideals. A tough act to follow, much less duplicate.

And what of America's borders? Having stirred up a hornets' nest of terror in Iraq, nothing had been done to keep the hornets out of the country. A number of tunnels were discovered between Mexico and Texas capable of transporting not only undocumented workers but terrorists intent on more than just picking tomatoes.

Then there was oil. Oil had been and still was the motivator and major catalyst in U.S. foreign policy. Iraq was tied with Iran for second place in proven oil reserves. Having a madman in control of such resources was unthinkable!

Wells' popularity was waning. The polls showed it. He could feel it. People were unhappy with the war; thousands of lives lost, and nearly a trillion dollars—and counting—down the tubes, a staggering sum even for those in government used to staggering sums.

Wells was feeling like the Little Dutch Boy. *But this Dutch Boy is running out of fingers,* he thought. The idea of a one-term presidency wasn't something that often entered his mind, but when it did, he thought it may actually be a blessing. But he was a good soldier, and for the good of the party he would run again. There was the issue of his legacy.

He dreaded the V.P.'s ninety-minute slot on his schedule. But Gerald Herzog had engineered his election and Wells would suffer through the weekly meetings. *Herzog's greatest value*, he thought, *is that of an insurance policy*. Having an inept and universally disliked vice president lessened the likelihood of impeachment. Wells' enemies would never push Herzog to the top.

* * *

Gerald Herzog was a smart man, at least smart enough to become governor of Oklahoma, which was where he figured his political ambitions would end. He began his career selling cars, and then running his father's oil company when his dad retired.

Gerald Sr., "the Old Man," had met Prince Faareh when the latter was a young man sent to the U.S. to learn the oil business from the customer's perspective. Faareh was smart, and some of the personal wealth burning a hole in his pocket found its way as an investment in Herzog Oil.

When Gerald Jr. got Herzog Oil into financial trouble, he picked up the phone and called the prince, looking for cash to tide him over. But the prince had a bigger idea and folded Herzog Oil into Middle East Oil, a company he had started. The buyout gave Gerald 10 percent of the combined company. Faareh had smart people running his company and Gerald's percentage became a huge windfall. To protect his interests, the prince suggested Gerald run for governor of Oklahoma.

Gerald did well at the state level, and after two terms, Faareh decided protection at the national level would be more valuable. But it wasn't clear that Gerald could translate his political successes to national prominence.

Warren Wells, then the governor of Colorado, had also been in the oil business. His pedigree and stage presence caught Faareh's eye. The prince's plan came together quickly: funnel money and influence through Gerald to get Wells elected. In return, Wells would have Gerald as his vice president, a position that allowed much more time to do the prince's work.

* * *

Wells' main consolation was that his personal investments in oil had proven wise. Regardless of the outcome of his presidency, he could retire quite comfortably. His trance was broken when his secretary buzzed him on the intercom. Disturbed from his thoughts, he heard Herzog wrapping up.

"...so I'd like to move on a bill addressing these issues..."

"Good idea, Gerald, why don't you do that. Excuse me for just a moment. Yes, Janice," Wells said, trying to look disappointed at the interruption.

"Secretary Jennings is here for his one o'clock. Will you see him now? He's a few minutes early."

"Absolutely, thank you." *Anything to get Herzog out of my office*, he thought.

Wells offered to have Gerald stay, knowing he wouldn't. Jennings passed him on his way in and was pleasant enough. But like the other cabinet members he considered the vice president a *wuss*.

Jennings had been to the Oval Office many times over the last two years, usually with a large group. He preferred one-on-one meetings. They eliminated all the role-playing that occurred whenever multiple cabinet members vied for the president's attention.

"Good afternoon, Mr. President," Jennings said as he entered through the curved door with hand extended. "Thank you for taking me early."

"Good afternoon, Walter," Wells said, taking his hand and looking forward to doing something substantial with the rest of his day. "I appreciate starting a little early as well." Translation: *Glad to get rid of Gerald.* "Have a seat."

"Sir, I'd like to brief you on what we see happening in China and how that may impact our relationship with Saudi Arabia."

"Good, Walter, I saw your note about the Chinese ships in this morning's PDB and found it intriguing. What can you tell me?"

"It's still a developing situation, sir, and I should warn you that what I tell you may need to be updated as soon as this evening. As I say, it's very fluid."

"Did we have any communications with the Chinese recently that would have alerted us to this action?"

"No, sir, we hadn't, and that caused me to call their foreign minister, Zeng Ju, to see if he could shed some light.

"He tells me that China and the Saudis are about to engage in a joint naval exercise that will strengthen communications between them; that it's nothing we should be alarmed about. He apologized again for not calling me in advance. He assured me these are just routine exercises—not unlike those we hold with some of our partners—and asked me not to alarm our allies. China will be making an announcement later in the day."

"Walter, our routine naval exercises *are* routine because they've happened a number of times before. I have trouble considering a Chinese deployment with Saudi Arabia routine, simply because it's the first such exercise to occur. Certainly, the first with Saudi Arabia. If you filter out the rhetoric, where do you think they're really headed? Is it just a routine exercise, or is it a precursor to something larger? We know they've already formed a relationship with Iran, trading nuclear technology for oil. They could be trying the same thing with the Saudis."

"Sir, on the surface it appears as Zeng said. Of course, if there were more, he wouldn't necessarily share it. What we don't know is what's under the surface, and by that I mean their submarines. If there were more to the story, those subs would be heading for the gulf as well, and we don't have as much visibility as we do with surface ships. It will take time to get tracking data on their subs."

"Okay, let's do that, but what should we do in the meantime? I assume we should honor their request and not alarm our allies. If, however, their announcement is not forthcoming, then we should go ahead and alert our partners since China will have broken a trust. And at some point, we'll need to stop accepting Mr. Zeng's apologies."

"Agreed, sir," Jennings said. "And to your first point, I think we need to have a working assumption that they're looking at more than a routine exercise, and we need to act accordingly. We should assume this is part of a larger initiative with the Saudis, something that includes oil and obviously doesn't include us.

"We need to come to the realization that China is now the second superpower, if not in military might, certainly in economic power. And it will be military might in the near future. Given their dependence on oil to fuel their growth, we should assume they'll be out making deals."

"Walter, if that's the case, we and our newest superpower may be headed toward a conflict over oil and those who have it, specifically Saudi Arabia. Do you see such a conflict any time soon? Should we assume one?"

296

"If we *assume* a conflict we'll need to act on that assumption and I'm not sure we have the resources. A war with China will surely take more than the war in Iraq and will carry a *real* nuclear WMD threat."

"We may not have the luxury of choosing to fight our wars serially. China surely understands that Iraq puts us in a weakened position militarily. They will want to exploit that. If they do, we'll have no choice but to engage them."

Both men knew that "engaging" China would be equivalent to World War III.

"Mr. President, both of our countries need to avoid such a conflict at all costs. The only way to circumvent a war over oil will be to drastically reduce energy demand by serious conservation and/or the development of alternative fuel sources."

"I know we've had the 'alternative' discussion before, and you're a proponent of that approach. But isn't a viable alternative to petroleum still many years off?"

"It's still a *few* years off, but has gotten closer with recent developments in renewable alternatives. We don't actually need the solution in hand today to deflect a conflict with China. We need to show them a roadmap to a fossil fuel alternative and how it would benefit them, lessen their dependence on oil, and provide a cleaner environment for all of us. If the roadmap is realistic, and it must be to achieve buy-in, they can plan for their future use of oil and begin phasing out that demand as they increase their use of alternatives, as can we. We need to open communication channels immediately to head off any relationship they may be forming with the Saudis while there's still time—*if* there's still time."

"Assuming we have a viable alternative at hand," the president replied. "Even though it may be a few years away, wouldn't announcing such a technology severely undermine the value of our own oil reserves and our entire oil industry? This was my concern with that professor at USF."

"Yes, sir, it would within a few years, but realistically, that's something we'll have to face ultimately. The end of economic oil will happen sooner than later. We need to prepare alternatives— and none of them can be brought on-line instantly."

Jennings' cell phone began to vibrate. He usually turned it completely off in meetings, especially those with the president. He left it on today in anticipation of more communications from Zeng. He glanced at his phone and saw that it was Director Reynolds.

"It's our CIA director, sir. He knew we were in this meeting and may have some intelligence on the Chinese movements. May I take it?"

"Please do."

"Hello, William, I'm with the president, what have you got for me? Any updates on China or the Saudis?"

...

"Professor Davidson? William, does this have anything to do with China?"

...

Wells was wondering what had happened to his meeting.

"Mr. President," Jennings said, seeing the consternation in Wells' eyes. He muted the phone. "I apologize for the interruption, but Reynolds has some information involving the vice president. He says it could influence our China policy. May I put him on speakerphone?"

"Well, if you think it's important enough to interrupt, perhaps it is."

"Go ahead, William, you're on speaker with the president."

"Mr. President, I have Professor Jason Davidson with me who will help explain what we've discovered.

"Hello, Professor, this is President Wells, what can you tell us?"

"Mr. President," Jason said in a voice not used to speaking to heads of state, "as Mr. Reynolds told you earlier, my group has made significant progress toward the establishment of a renewable energy infrastructure."

"Walter, is this one of the breakthroughs you were speaking of earlier?" asked Wells to the man in his office.

"Yes, sir, it is, and Professor Davidson was to give the presentation at the energy conference we spoke of—until the attempt on his life."

"Yes, I remember. Professor, please continue."

"We've had a number of incidents surrounding our progress. The first was a car bomb placed in my rental car that killed a friend of mine, the second was the murder of my assistant professor in our lab a few days ago, and the third was the possible murder of CIA agent Wilcox—probably all related.

"I've been working with the CIA to trace a chain of emails we discovered when we caught a member of our own team who turned out to be a renegade CIA agent. In fact, he was a double agent, something that Mr. Reynolds or Mr. Jennings can elaborate on later."

The president looked across the table at Jennings, who was nodding. "I've got it, Professor, please continue."

"After this man's capture, we confiscated his laptop and found an encrypted emails. The first, sent from someone called 'Prince,' contained the instructions for my murder. The second, sent from a person calling himself 'VIP,' gave the authorization order."

"Using the encryption keys we obtained from the laptop, and matching the public keys against our government archives of encrypted emails, we were able to match the public key of 'VIP' to three documents in the archive. By match, I mean that we were able to open them into a decrypted, readable form. The three documents we opened all appear to belong to Vice President Herzog. They were just internal memos, but they confirm the same person who sent them was the originator of the message to take my life."

Complete silence descended on the Oval Office. The president looked at Jennings, who appeared just as shocked as he was.

* * *

Wells and Jennings sat quietly for a moment, gathering their thoughts. This wasn't the meeting Wells had anticipated. Matters had suddenly taken a dark shift into corruption at high levels. *What the hell is this*, he thought, *and what will it do to my administration?*

"Walter, I need to get the vice president in here," Wells finally said.

"Do you want me to leave?"

"Actually, no. I'd like you to hear what he has to say. I hate to think this, but I may need a witness."

"Very well, sir."

"Janice," the president said as he hit the button on the intercom, trying to sound as normal as possible. "Can you get the vice president on the line for me? He should be in his office this afternoon."

In just a few moments, with the president and his secretary of state still in silent thought, Wells' phone rang. He hit the "speakerphone" button.

"Gerald?"

"Yes, Mr. President."

"You're on speakerphone. I have Jennings with me and we've just had a call from Director Reynolds who has been investigating some highly illegal activities surrounding a team of clean energy researchers, including two murders, and possibly three. The information we just received indicated you may be involved. Tell me these people have made a mistake."

There was a long pause before the vice president answered.

"Mr. President, these are serious allegations and should not be discussed over the phone. Could I meet with you in your office?"

"Of course." The two men hung up.

"I don't know about you, Walter," Wells said after a few moments deliberation, "but I didn't hear a denial."

"I'm sure there's some kind of explanation."

"I certainly hope so."

The two men again retreated into their private thoughts as they awaited Herzog's arrival. It was beginning to take too long; the vice president's office wasn't that far away. *Perhaps he's been detained*, thought Wells. *What the hell is going on?* He reached for his phone...

The sound of a gunshot cannot easily be confused with any other sound. Some say it sounds like a firecracker, others a car backfiring. But when you hear a gunshot in the White House, it is so incongruous it causes time to stop. Everyone in the building heard the ominous crack of a firearm.

A swarm of Secret Service agents barged into the Oval Office and ordered Wells and Jennings to get down behind the desk. They encircled it, forming a human shield.

The two men stayed on the floor as searches took place. But those were quickly terminated once the Secret Service ascertained the shooting was a single event. The president overheard conversations between agents and understood that his vice president had shot himself.

"Okay, guys, I need to see Gerald," Wells said. "Help us up."

Two agents did just that, and accompanied Wells and Jennings out of the Oval Office. Outside, confused secretaries and other staffers milled around in the hallway. They stopped upon seeing the president.

"We're alright," Wells said loudly, raising his hand above the heads of the agents encircling him, hoping to reassure everyone. He could see some of the shock begin to shed from the faces he passed.

His calm would prove short-lived. The scene in Herzog's office was grisly. Though Wells had a good idea what to expect when he entered, he was shocked anyway. "Jesus Christ!" is all he could say, shaking his head.

Herzog lay facedown on his desk with open blank eyes, a smoking .38-caliber revolver still gripped in his hand. Blood and pieces of brain tissue were everywhere—on the walls, on the furniture, even on the ceiling. An expanding pool of blood spread across the desk, covering papers, dripping on the floor.

A White House doctor had been called in and was checking the body, careful not to disturb anything that might be important to a forthcoming investigation. As he made an official declaration of death, he avoided touching a typewritten memo on the desk, stained with blood spatter mixed with pieces of brain tissue.

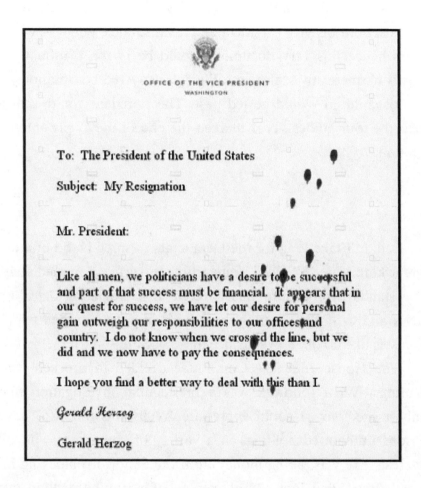

The stench of the gun smoke hung in the room. Even an echo seemed to linger. In the confusion, no one bothered to look at what lay on Herzog's desk. No one except Jennings.

"Mr. President, I think you should see this," Jennings said quietly, gesturing to that corner of the desk.

It took a moment for the letter's contents to sink in; it took less time for the ramifications to hit Wells. For a brief moment he considered pocketing the letter. *If I had only seen it first*, he thought, more shaken by the bloody memo than the bloody body. He didn't need to say anything and Jennings didn't need to ask; the answer to the question hanging over them was clear: Wells had lost both his vice president and his insurance policy. Twenty years hence this very document would be in the National Archives hermetically-sealed in a Plexiglas-covered box millions of school children would be led past. The president could almost hear the tour guides say it marked the end of the Wells administration.

* * *

It didn't take long for the Democrats to smell blood of a different kind. The "I" word, impeachment, surfaced immediately. The standard procedure was covered in excruciating detail on CNN and C-SPAN, riveting the American people to their television sets like no other event since the O.J. Simpson trial.

The House Judiciary Committee decided to proceed with hearings. What followed was a presidential investigation that only a proctologist could appreciate. Wells was found to have serious unreported holdings in a variety of companies with oil interests. He was taking money from the Saudis for blocking research into fossil fuel alternatives and for turning a blind eye when illegal activity slowed alternative energy development. There was enough ammunition for the Judiciary Committee to recommend impeachment to the full House. Adding insult to injury, that body—where Wells held a large majority—voted for impeachment, throwing the case over to the Senate for trial.

No sitting U.S. president has ever been impeached, and Wells would not be the first. His defense was to rely on his character, or at least his reputation, to wiggle off the hook. *After all, if the antics of President Clinton were not enough to impeach, I should be able to get a pass.* By the time the investigation had reached the full House, however, he knew there was no chance. A flood of thoughts rushed through his mind. Perhaps he wasn't as charming as Clinton, or as intelligent, or as good a communicator. Perhaps he should have tried denying everything as Clinton had done. But it was too late, the only alternative was to take the Nixon path and resign.

* * *

Jason Davidson was one of those Americans glued to his television set.

The president's resignation speech was succinct. What he did was illegal but it was the vice president who set up the system and negotiated with the Saudis. It was the vice president who communicated instructions. But ignorance of the details was no excuse and Herzog wasn't around to punish. Wells had violated the trust of the people.

After watching the resignation speech Jason forced himself from his recliner and went to the kitchen to make a sandwich. He could hardly believe what he just saw. Even though he knew resignation was the only option, witnessing the president's statement seemed surreal. He was opening a jar of mayonnaise when his white phone started to vibrate.

"Yes, Director, this is Davidson."

"Professor, I trust you've been watching the events unfolding in Washington."

"I have, sir."

"Good. Secretary Jennings is here, and he's asked if you would take a call from him."

"Certainly."

"Good evening, Professor."

"Hello, sir," Jason said, "how can I help you?"

"Professor, I have only a few minutes. Do you remember when I asked if you would be prepared to travel to Beijing?"

"Yes, sir, I do, and I'm still ready."

"Good. As you'll soon find out, I'm about to be sworn in as the president of the United States."

There was a pause as Jason grasped what he just heard. "Sir, I was probably absent from civics class the day my teacher discussed presidential succession, but I thought that it was: vice president, speaker of the house, president pro-tem of the Senate, and *then* secretary of state."

"Professor, I'd say your civics teacher did a good job. In this instance, however, our vice president was not exactly up to accepting—I saw the body. The speaker of the house has declined the position, as has our president pro-tem of the Senate, Senator Brewster, who just celebrated his eighty-fifth birthday. Both these men have proven themselves smarter than me, because I've accepted."

Before Jason could offer his congratulations, Jennings continued, "I remember our previous discussion a few days ago and your views on China's needs for energy. I've also been holding discussions with their foreign minister. Mr. Zeng believes we may have an opportunity to avert what could become a serious conflict between our two countries. I'd like to ask you to join me in a meeting with Mr. Zeng and President Wu in Beijing."

"Certainly, sir. How much time do we have to prepare?"

"I'll be arriving at Tampa International at 2:00 PM tomorrow. Can you be ready? We'll have plenty of time on the plane where I can provide more details about my discussions with Minister Zeng and we can plan our strategy. Bring all the materials you think you may need. Director Reynolds has suggested that Agent Bilson accompany us for continuity and security."

"I'll be there—and congratulations."

Chapter 28.
Air Force One

The limo arranged by the State Department picked Jason up at his apartment. He gave the driver directions to Sandra's hotel on the way to Tampa International. She emerged from the hotel followed by a bellman pushing a cart of luggage.

"Traveling light, I see."

"It's a girl thing," she said as she entered the limo. "Actually, since we don't know how long we will be gone, I decided to check out. You ready for this trip?"

"Ready as I'll ever be," Jason replied.

As they neared the terminal, Sandra called a number Director Reynolds had given her. A Secret Service agent directed them to wait with their bags at the departure curb.

Shortly, a black Chevy Suburban pulled up. Two agents stepped out, asked for their identification, and loaded their bags in the rear of the long vehicle while they stepped into the cavernous back seat. The driver followed a maze of access roads to a restricted area. The distinctive blue and white Air Force One was easy to recognize parked in a distant corner of the airfield hundreds of yards from the nearest plane.

Director Reynolds was standing in the doorway at the head of the stairs.

"Sandra, it's good to see you," he greeted.

"Sir," Sandra replied as they got to the top of the stairs. "I'd like to introduce Professor Davidson."

"Professor, we're glad you could make this trip."

"Thank you, sir," Jason said, shaking hands and peering through the door past the director. "Nice ride."

Reynolds took the two guests past the galley and the conference room to the guest seating area. They chose two seats toward the front.

"We have a long flight to Beijing," Reynolds said. "As we reach altitude I'll come back for you. President Jennings would like to brief us on the meeting."

The plane began taxiing as soon as they were settled. After bypassing all the other planes in line for takeoff, Air Force One rotated skyward. In a few minutes they were on their way to a cruising altitude of forty-three thousand feet.

* * *

"Are you two ready?" Reynolds asked as he made his way back to the guest seating area. "The president would like to meet now."

He escorted them through a labyrinth of corridors leading to the presidential suite. Jennings welcomed them, shaking hands with both. "Agent Bilson, thank you very much for your service to the country, you've helped give us a chance for a peaceful resolution to what's becoming a grave situation. Professor Davidson, Director Reynolds and others have been briefing me on your work."

"Thank you, sir," Jason said, a bit overwhelmed by meeting the man he had seen being sworn in a few hours earlier.

"Please sit down," Jennings said, "we have a long flight to Beijing. Let me bring you up to speed."

Jason flipped open his laptop to take notes.

Jennings continued, "Since we last spoke, we have had further notice from our submarine intelligence that in addition to the two frigates and a support ship, two of China's largest submarines are also headed to the Gulf.

"This triggered a call with Minister Zeng. After an hour of stressful negotiation, he and President Wu agreed to begin discussions on energy developments, including oil and alternative fuels. They believe they may have an opportunity opening negotiations with a new administration. And that's why we're headed to Beijing."

"Do we know what direction these discussions will take?" Jason asked.

"We have no formal agenda, but they'll be negotiating from a position of strength—our massive trade imbalance. China currently holds about five hundred billion in U.S. dollar credits, roughly half of that in U.S. Treasuries—our debt. This number currently grows at about ten billion dollars a month. We believe they're going to start unloading some of those dollars on more oil sources, and possibly buying U.S. oil companies."

"Would we allow them to do that?" Sandra asked.

"We wouldn't have to. But if we don't allow them to spend their dollars on what they and almost every other country wants, the dollar will weaken significantly. This could cause other economies to reduce their dollar holdings."

The room grew quiet as the ramifications of Jennings comments were absorbed.

"Their debt poses another problem for us," Jennings continued. "In the past, we funded our wars internally, which explains the sacrifices and rationing our people endured during the Second World War and why that generation was called the 'greatest.' Ever wonder why we don't feel the economic pain of the Iraq War? It's because we're funding the war with debt, held primarily by China. It will be our children and grandchildren who will be paying for Iraq."

"Great," Jason said, "our children who are fighting this war will have to pay for it when they return—if they return."

"Unfortunately."

"So you think China could stop investing in our treasuries?" Sandra asked.

"Possibly. Or worse, they could sell-off the debt they already hold causing the dollar to fall which could trigger a wholesale selling of dollars globally."

Again, no one spoke for several moments. Jason broke the silence, "There are times when it's good just to be a professor of electrical engineering."

"Not so fast, Professor, this is where you come in," Jennings went on. "The situation can be mitigated with non-fossil fuels. We need a viable alternative that can relieve demand pressure on the world's oil, and we need it soon. This will also increase their confidence in our future and thus our debt. Based on my understanding from Mr. Reynolds and the folks at DOE, the work of your team may be a light at the end of a very dark tunnel." Jennings paused for emphasis. "How are your sales skills?"

"Sir, I've raised capital for a number of startups, sold the products of those startups and ultimately sold the startups themselves. But I've never done business in China."

"Looks like you're about to. Both Minister Zeng and President Wu speak excellent English, so communications shouldn't be a problem."

"Then we need to discuss the issue of timing. We don't want to be in the position of promising something within a timeframe in which we can't deliver. The technology we rely on will take several years to reach volume production."

"Yes, and we want to be perfectly candid about that. These guys are smart businessmen and will understand the timeframes involved. We don't need a solution *today*. There's enough oil to meet both China's current needs and ours. Their concern is the future. If we can show them a strategy that weans us all off oil, provides a clean environment in a reasonable timeframe, and includes them in the business arrangements, that's what they'll want to hear.

"I suggest you use our flight to sharpen your sales pitch. We have a world to save. No pressure," Jennings chuckled as he slapped Jason on the back.

Chapter 29.
Beijing Summit

Beijing Capital International Airport would have been the ideal place to land. Instead, the president's delegation landed at Nanyuan, a military airport in the southern suburbs of Beijing where government security could be guaranteed on short notice. As they made their approach, Jason could see the military C141 Starlifter that had carried the president's car, other components of his motorcade, and the advance security team, tucked away in a remote corner of the tarmac. Before Air Force One had come to a complete stop, the president's limo and several of the black Suburbans he had seen in Tampa pulled up alongside. *How many black Suburbans does the government own anyway?*

It was 5:00 AM local time and the team would be heading first to the five-star Kempinski Hotel, not far from the Great Hall.

Jennings was the first to deplane and was met by U.S. Ambassador to China, Mr. F. George Abraham. The president introduced Jason and Sandra. They were escorted to the second Suburban in the caravan, each like the one in front of it, loaded with guys who spoke into their sleeves.

The convoy of black Suburbans proceeded down the busy streets of Beijing at breakneck speeds, weaving dangerously through the heavy traffic. Sandra explained to Jason that this was for security purposes. Anyone attempting to follow them would be obvious, triggering defensive actions.

Walking into the lobby of the Kempinski, Jason could see how it had earned its five-star rating. The president's team had a complete floor reserved. While the Secret Service had swept the entire hotel, their private floor had been combed for any possible foreign material or devices. There was only time to freshen-up.

At 7:30 AM Jason heard a knock at his door. Secret Service agents were telling everyone the caravan was ready for the short ride to Red Square and the Great Hall. As he stepped into the hallway, Sandra was doing the same. She appeared better rested.

The surreal nature of the trip hit Jason when the caravan pulled in front of the Great Hall of the People. His first impressions were overwhelmed by the architecture, traffic, language, and sheer number of people.

They mounted the steps with Jennings in the lead. "I believe that's Minister Zeng at the top of the stairs," he said over his shoulder.

"Good morning, Mr. President," Zeng said, as he recognized Jennings from his pictures. "Congratulations on your new office."

"Thank you for arranging this meeting. We are pleased to be here," Jennings replied, turning to introduce the rest of the team.

"Minister Zeng," Sandra said. "I'm scheduled to meet with your security staff and our advance team. Could you tell me where I can find them?"

"Certainly. My assistant, Mr. Chen, will take you."

"Good morning, Professor," Zeng said as Sandra and Chen disappeared up the stairs. "I hope you remember me from the energy conference in Geneva almost two years ago. I approached you after your presentation."

"Yes, sir," Jason replied, "I remember your interest." He didn't really remember him.

Zeng led them to a large conference room appointed entirely in red. *How appropriate*, Jason thought. Zeng then excused himself from the room, probably to let President Wu know his guests had arrived. It gave Jason time to power-up his laptop, connect it to the projector, confirm he could get a focused image on the screen, and dig the laser pointer out of his leather bag.

A side door opened and Sandra entered, taking a seat next to Jason, who was sitting next to Jennings. "All set," she whispered, though they were the only ones in the room. "Our guys have established the security protocol with Wu's team and have synchronized radio frequencies. I'm picking up everything in my earpiece."

"Great, a high-tech spook," Jason whispered back.

Zeng returned shortly, holding the door open for a very distinguished gentleman in his early sixties wearing a well-tailored dark suit and a red tie, carrying a notepad. At first he looked taller than he was. But when Jason stood he could see the man was just over five feet in height and had thick, jet-black hair swept straight back. *If this isn't the president, he's missed his calling.*

* * *

Zeng wasted no time. "Our American guests, I'd like to introduce the president of the Chinese Communist Party, Mr. Wu Jianzhong."

The Americans stood in unison and a chorus of "Good morning, Mr. President," rang out with heads going up and down in what Jason thought looked like "bobble-head" bows.

315

President Wu took the seat directly across from Jennings with an ominous red telephone sitting directly in front of him.

"President Wu," Jennings said, wasting no time, "we thank you for your invitation. One we hope will lead to a deeper understanding between us and our peoples."

"Mr. President," Wu responded, "let me congratulate you on your new position. My briefings with Minister Zeng indicate there is promise for improved relations between our countries, as we are improving relations with other partners, both old and new."

And there it was, on the table. Wu was alluding to the new relationship with the Saudis, which was Jennings' opening.

"Yes, Mr. President," Jennings said, "and one of your new partners is one of our old partners, Saudi Arabia, which is where we would like to begin our discussion."

"Certainly President Jennings, but let me remind you we have temporarily put our discussions with Saudi Arabia on hold to have this meeting. This was due to the intercession of Minister Zeng on your behalf. The only reason we are here is to understand why we should not proceed with the Saudis. The clock is running."

Jason was beginning to hope he'd have an opportunity to speak before World War III broke out.

Jennings responded, "We share your interest in expediting this discussion and for that reason, I will turn our portion over to Professor Davidson." No time for niceties.

The moment Jason both relished and feared had arrived. He'd been in many high-level, high-stress sales situations before. But the worst thing that could happen then was that a prospect might not be ready to buy. Walking away without an order was bad, walking away without a world a bit worse. He jumped in.

"President Wu, Minister Zeng," he opened, bowing to each individually. "I appreciate the opportunity to lead a discussion about alternative energy futures and the progress of my team at the University of South Florida. I want to start by addressing you not as a professor, but as a citizen of the world. A citizen with concerns that I believe are shared by the citizens of both of our countries."

"Well and good, Professor," said Wu, "but we need to hear specifics."

"Mr. President, you will get specifics, but I first need to provide the rationale for them."

He again had their attention.

"The world is running out of oil, and it will run out of oil before we actually use it all."

"I assume, Professor, you're talking about the concept of Peak Oil."

"Correct, and I'm sure Minister Zeng can provide you with more details. The world is moving toward a time when the energy required to produce a barrel of usable oil will exceed the energy in that barrel of oil. And this time will occur sooner than most people realize."

"And your point?"

"Establishing a renewable energy strategy is not an option. And deferring the establishment of that strategy will put us in jeopardy of not having enough time to establish one."

"So, is this the concern of your 'global citizen'?"

"No, most people have never heard of the concept of Peak Oil. Instead, they worry about terrorism; wars triggered by terrorism, like the current Iraq war; global warming; climate change; pollution; and energy shortages. They see our countries spending billions of dollars and thousands of lives combating these fears without progress. They don't understand that these issues are not really problems, but symptoms of one common problem, our continued dependence on oil—which does have a solution."

"So tell us of your solution," Wu said, rather indignantly.

"We can free ourselves from these fears by replacing our current fossil fuel-based economies with Electric Economies."

"But Professor," it was Zeng's turn to jump in, "the new thoughts for alternative energy are based on establishment of a Hydrogen Economy with transportation provided by fuel cell vehicles."

Wu's attention sharpened. He had been reading about the Hydrogen Economy as well.

Jennings stiffened, his face grew pale. Jason was losing his audience; he was not telling them what they had expected to hear.

Jason pressed on. "Sir, the proponents for the Hydrogen Economy are actually proponents for never leaving fossil fuels. Look who these people are, they are automobile companies and oil companies, all touting their work with hydrogen."

"But you have also been establishing breakthroughs with hydrogen."

"Yes, but our work with hydrogen is as a storage medium for electricity. We don't address distribution of hydrogen. Let me explain. The only effective way to distribute hydrogen is in liquid form. As you know, liquid hydrogen is minus 423 degrees Fahrenheit. The proponents of the Hydrogen Economy in our country all agree that we are decades away from having the infrastructure in place to support such an economy. America is a very impatient country. Saying that we will need to wait twenty years for something is equivalent to saying it will never happen, and that's just what the proponents want. They are providing research reports and demonstrations, knowing full well that what they are proposing will never reach fruition."

"Yes, but what about fuel cell vehicles, so-called FCVs? That is where all the transportation research is going."

"With apologies to the automobile companies, there is no such thing as a fuel cell vehicle. There are electric vehicles powered by batteries. A battery is a device that converts a chemical reaction to electrical potential. In the case of a fuel cell, that reaction is between hydrogen and oxygen. Therefore, a fuel cell is just a battery—nothing more, nothing less."

"So why the Electric Economy?" Zeng asked.

"First, electricity is a universal form of energy. It can be used to power our factories, heat and cool our homes, cook our food, and power our ground transportation. It is the only form of energy with this flexibility.

"Next, electrical energy is a common denominator among all types of energy. All forms of energy can be used to produce electricity. Some, like solar and wind, can generate electricity directly. Others, like nuclear and natural gas, create heat to turn the steam turbines of electric generators. Again, electricity is the only form of energy with this characteristic.

"Last, and perhaps most important, we already have a distribution system in place in the form of the electric power grid, and this is true in your country as well. The ubiquity of the grid means that we can tap into it anywhere to withdraw energy, and likewise, we can tap into it anywhere to insert additional energy."

"How do you propose generating electricity without fossil fuels? That is where a lot of coal and natural gas are used today," Wu pointed out.

"Today, America uses four trillion kilowatt-hours of electrical energy each year. Our calculations show that using just today's solar energy technology it would take five thousand square miles of solar panels to generate all the electricity we use. To put that into perspective, our state of Arizona is 115,000 square miles in area, so using just 5 percent of that space would produce all the electrical energy our country needs. A similar calculation could be done for China."

"Yes, but how much additional electricity would be required to power electric vehicles?" Wu was playing devil's advocate.

"Using our national transportation statistics, if all of our automobiles and light trucks were now electric vehicles, and assuming an efficiency of five miles per KWH, it would take an additional 10 percent of electrical energy. That electricity could be generated with five hundred square miles of solar panels."

"What would it cost and how long would it take to deploy that many solar panels?" Wu asked, now sounding at least interested.

"Using just today's technology at today's prices, covering that area would cost about three hundred billion dollars. The system would be phased in over a five-year period. Of course, over that period, additional research would bring costs down substantially. It's fair to say that the panels deployed at the end of five years would look very different than those deployed initially. That's the power of science and engineering when applied to new technology—essentially Moore's Law applied to the Electric Economy."

"Mr. President," Zeng said, "that works out to sixty billion dollars a year. At sixty dollars a barrel, we currently spend about 150 billion dollars a year on oil, almost three times as much."

"That's right," Jason responded, looking at Jennings. "And in our case, we spend twice that amount every year on the Iraq War. With this technology, after five years, our only ongoing costs will be maintenance of the system."

"Beyond the economic payback," Sandra couldn't help adding, "there are additional benefits. Think about waking up in a world five years from now with no dependence on foreign oil. Think about how that world would be: terrorists without influence; no reason to associate with countries that establish or support terrorism; individual foreign policies based on the marketing of clean energy technologies and devoid of the influence of oil. Our climate would have time to cleanse itself. There would be no oil tanker spills to foul our oceans, no tanker trucks carrying dangerous fuels on our highways, and no trainloads of propane blowing up in the center of our countries. And the profits from exporting this technology to other countries would pay for solving problems unrelated to energy, like AIDS."

"You've painted a grand dream for us, Professor," Wu said, "but what technologies will be used? How will they work? Let's start with the solar panels. It's time for specifics."

"As I said, we will start by deploying today's solar panel technology. Today's panels are constructed from silicon that can convert electricity from sunlight at between 10 and 12 percent efficiency. Our research shows that we can convert sunlight into electricity three times more efficiently by using a technology called optical rectennas, which deal with sunlight as an electromagnetic wave as opposed to photons. If we had this technology today, we would need less than two hundred square miles instead of five hundred to generate the energy needed for electric vehicles. But we can start with today's technology and phase in rectennas. They both generate direct current that can be merged into a single electrical source."

"Yes, Professor," Zeng said, his engineering background showing, "but all of the equipment in our homes runs on alternating current."

"As does ours, Mr. Zeng. Our system takes the direct current and processes it through a device called an inverter that converts the direct current to alternating current, 240 volts, 60 hertz in our case. Inverters for China would be matched to your requirements of 220 volts, 50 hertz—meaning that all existing household equipment could be used without modification."

"But what about excess? Storing electricity for times when the sun isn't shining is a big problem."

"It is. The excess electricity that we generate is used to convert household water into hydrogen through a process called electrolysis. This hydrogen is stored in tanks containing lithium metal hydride, at a density that is 30 percent greater than that of liquid hydrogen and much safer. This was our second technology breakthrough. Once the hydrogen tank is full, excess electricity is sold back to the power companies using a device called a 'Net Meter,' a power meter capable of running backward when we are generating more electricity than we are using, crediting the home owner. In the evening, power will come from the hydrogen stored in the tank, processed by a fuel cell."

"Impressive," Wu said. "Zeng, do we have this 'Net-metering' technology?"

"But Professor," Zeng said, caught up in the technology and ignoring his president's question, "you still haven't discussed transportation."

"As I alluded to earlier, transportation will be provided by electric vehicles using three-phase AC induction motors with matching three-phase AC inverters. The power source for these vehicles will be batteries—initially lithium-ion, then lithium-polymer. They will store one hundred killowatt-hours of energy, enough to drive over four hundred miles on a single charge when plugged into a standard socket. Since fuel cells are just batteries, at some point they may be a better solution than lithium-based batteries, we need to let that competition occur. In either case, the architecture of our vehicles won't change."

"But what will it cost to operate electric vehicles?" Wu asked.

"Electric vehicles are generally much less expensive to maintain. There is no transmission, no radiator, and no exhaust system. Drivers do not need to change oil or transmission fluid. As for fuel costs, electric vehicles get five miles per kilowatt-hour of energy. Homeowners who are generating their own electricity will pay nothing. Those who are buying their electricity typically pay five to ten cents per kilowatt-hour in the evening, when their cars would be charging, so their costs would be between one a two cents per mile."

"Very impressive, Mr. Davidson. Your thoughts, Mr. Zeng?"

"I think it holds promise. The questions are how soon, how much will it cost, and how long can we wait?"

"Mr. Zeng," Wu offered before Jason could respond, "We had a similar problem with our telephone systems, a choice between the old fully-wired infrastructure and wireless cellular technology, the next generation. We have a successful history of skipping technology generations. Perhaps we should consider doing that again. While we still need oil for the immediate future, we could be planning for what the professor calls an Electric Economy. It could be a mistake to invest entirely in today's infrastructure that would not support tomorrow's needs.

"That still leaves us with two questions, Professor. How long will it take to prepare this new technology, and what kind of business model are you looking for?"

"President Wu, the timeframe and business relationship questions are related, and I will address both shortly. But first, we should discuss our short-term needs for oil as we evolve into a renewable energy economy.

"Since the 1960s the OPEC cartel has controlled the price of oil keeping it at a level that maximizes their profits and discourages development of alternate sources—a delicate balance. Each of us has been negotiating with OPEC individually, striking agreements that best suit our individual needs. This is what I believe is happening with your proposed agreement with the Saudis. Instead, we need to form an organization of consuming nations that will counter the weight of the producers. We could call this organization OPAC, for the 'Organization of Petroleum *Alternative* Countries,' with China and America as founding members. This organization would allow us to buy time keeping oil prices under control while we get our alternative energy replacement into high-volume manufacture, a project that would also be a joint effort of OPAC."

President Wu and his foreign minister sat upright in their chairs. They were finally getting to the business arrangements.

"And now for timeframe," Jason continued. "As I said, the architecture for an Electric Economy relies on the two new technologies I discussed, hydrogen storage and efficient solar energy conversion. The devices we need are currently very labor-intensive to produce in quantity. I propose we partner to manufacture them via a license that would allow China to leverage its large, highly-skilled and cost-effective workforce, while we in the U.S. work on automation. Working together we should be able to begin deploying demonstration sites almost immediately and be in full production in two years."

"And what would happen to China when automation is ready?" Wu asked, thinking about his country's future.

"President Wu, something has become clear to me over the last several days and much clearer just today. Our two countries have synergistic capabilities. Instead of repelling each other through competition, we need to embrace each other through partnership recognizing each others' strengths. We propose that once automation is created for production of these technologies in volume, we would license it back to you as well."

"But, Professor," Wu said, playing devil's advocate again, "aren't you afraid of the reaction you will get at home over the loss of jobs?"

"Mr. President, America cannot lose jobs it never had, and in this case, we'd be outsourcing this work to China from the beginning. And President Jennings," Jason said as he turned to face his new president, "this means America needs to expand on its role of innovation, relying on our partners for manufacture at labor rates we cannot match. Even with automation, change on such a massive scale will produce millions of jobs for both countries. Our country needs the equivalent of an 'Innovation Revolution,' similar to the creation of NASA and the race to the moon stimulated by President Kennedy in the sixties. This means a much-improved education system to craft the minds that will keep the wheels of innovation turning. We can get our trade deficits under control through license revenue as we lead the world to a new technology revolution. The Electric Economy may become the next Internet in terms of business opportunities."

"Interesting," President Wu said to no one in particular. Then, looking directly at Jennings, he said, "Mr. President, if we were to proceed, what organization or company would we be working with?"

That was a big "if." The expression on Jennings' face went from elation to panic. The day had gone much better than he had hoped. But the team hadn't discussed their strategy for closing; he hadn't believed they would make such progress. It was that time, but Jennings couldn't take the next step. He shot a quick look to Jason.

Without hesitation, Jason took two business cards out of his shirt pocket and handed one to each of the world leaders.

> **Hydro-Gen Corporation**
> **Tampa Florida**
> **813-555-2411**
>
> **Jason Davidson, PhD**
> **Founder and CEO**
> jdavidson@hydro-gen.com

"Gentlemen," Jason said, "I have formed a new company, Hydro-Gen, to provide those very services. This company will hold the necessary patents for what will be an integrated Hydrogen Generation System."

Sandra had been watching the twists and turns of the discussion in amazement. She was witnessing another side to the professor, another facet.

Wu slid his copy of Jason's card over to Zeng. The Americans weren't sure how to interpret that.

Wu sat quietly for a moment, seeming to contemplate everything that had transpired. He shifted his gaze to Jennings.

"President Jennings," Wu said with some deliberation, "you realize that terrorists will try to stop your progress."

"Only too well."

Silence. No one spoke as Wu was either taking notes or doodling on his pad—Jason's mastery of Chinese could not detect the difference.

Jennings broke the silence. "President Wu, it seems this meeting…"

Wu held up his index finger, apparently the universal sign for "give me a minute."

He slid his notepad of scribbles over to Zeng who took a moment to read what his president had written. Zeng picked up the red phone, spoke a moment in Chinese, and replaced the handset.

Jennings tried again. "Mr. President…"

Again the finger. More silence. Wu went back to his notepad.

The red phone rang with a strange tone completely foreign to the Americans. Zeng picked it up, spoke more Chinese, and passed it to Wu.

"Prince Faareh, this is President Wu. I have received your counter-offer. I am afraid we have no deal."

Chapter 30.
Going Home

The flight home from Beijing on Air Force One would be much less stressful than the flight going. They were all tired. Their one-day meeting had turned into one *very* long day for everyone.

The beautiful rooms reserved for them at the Kempinski hotel went virtually unused. The team went back just to retrieve their luggage and change into more comfortable clothes.

Once on board the presidential jet, Jason and Sandra made their way to the same seats they had on the way out, hoping to finally get some sleep. It wasn't to be, at least not then. Jennings' steward arrived after takeoff to tell them the president wanted to convene a short gathering in his quarters to review their meeting. *A good idea*, Jason thought, *if we weren't so damn tired.*

As they wound their way forward, the entire crew was much more laid back. Entering the president's conference room they discovered he and Reynolds sitting at his conference table with a bottle of Krug champagne between them.

"Come in, you two," Jennings said, waving them in, "I'd like to review our meeting today while it's fresh in our minds." *Great*, thought Jason, *the guy's still in high-gear.* "But first," the president continued as he poured four glasses of champagne and stood up, "we should drink a toast to a very successful trip. An historic meeting between two great nations. I asked the head steward if they had anything suitable for a toast, and he came up with this little beauty." Jennings patted the bottle gingerly.

Champagne gave Jason a headache, but for this occasion he'd deal with it. Following the president's lead, they each stood and raised their glasses.

"To world peace, a bountiful, clean energy future, and the prosperity and security of the United States of America."

Excellent goals, Jason thought, *but there's still a lot of work to do.* There was the sound of a four-way clinking of hand-etched presidential glassware followed by the downing of the expensive French wine.

"Jason," the president said, "I want to thank you for your contribution. I never dreamed we would get Wu's full commitment. And without those business cards, we may never have had the opportunity to close the deal. Is that company something you'd really like to pursue?"

"Mr. President, Hydro-Gen is for real. I formed it six months ago as a registered Delaware Corporation."

The small conference room went quiet enough to hear only the hum of the four engines carrying them back to Tampa.

"I've been waiting to announce my company and today became the day. The last several weeks have been spent putting together patent applications for the integration of all the technologies I presented. I'll be submitting them tomorrow. I intend to partner with the Chinese and package the technologies and systems as we discussed. I'll see that the patent holders of the individual technologies get their share. All I ask is that you expedite my applications through the Patent Office; it sometimes takes years to secure patents and these can't wait."

"I'd say I have no choice," Jennings concluded, "but what about your career at the University, and the CERC group?"

"Sir, academia is a great place to do research, but not to do business. The research work required to roll out clean energy technology is mostly completed, it's time to raise some serious capital and get into production, which is the mission of my new company. There's clearly a market."

"Sounds exciting, and that market could be worth millions, but won't you miss your students?"

"Actually, it should be worth *billions*." Taking a moment to reflect, Jason continued, "The University knows my background. I've been a technology mercenary going where opportunity has taken me. The opportunity will now be in energy and that's where I'm going. Following the money will also be in the best interest of the country.

"As for the students I'm working with today, those with an entrepreneurial leaning will become my first employees. The others will continue on in academia, and hopefully successful careers."

"Interesting thoughts, Professor. As for me, if I want to keep my job, I'll be running for election next year and need to prepare my platform. Here's a question for you—if we were to make a concerted effort to completely eliminate our dependence on imported oil, how long do you think that would take?"

"We currently import about 60 percent of our oil. Fortunately, a third of that is from Canada and Mexico, countries that I hope are still our friends. And we use 67 percent of our oil for transportation. The most direct route to eliminating our dependence on just OPEC imports would be to begin moving to electric vehicles."

"But how long would that take?"

"Well, you did say a *concerted* effort, and under those circumstances I believe we could to it in four to five years."

"How 'concerted' would that be?"

"A national policy mandating that 20 percent of new cars sold in this country are electric vehicles in year one, 40 percent in year two, and 100 percent in year five."

"But how would we solve the range problem for long trips? Even if we can travel four hundred miles on a charge, how could we take longer trips?"

"Easy, anyone taking a trip longer than four hundred miles is probably going to be using the Interstate highway system. The government would need to deploy rapid charging stations at intervals along those routes; the existing rest areas are spaced appropriately. All other, normal charging could be done at homes or businesses."

"Excellent. So back to my platform, this trip has inspired me to consider just three 'planks:' Security, Energy, and Education. They give me an acronym that will be easy to remember, SEE."

"Mr. President," Sandra smiled, "perhaps you should be in marketing."

"Let me try my pitch on you three: 'Security' comes first. We need to secure our borders to prevent another attack that would disrupt our lives and businesses. The Iraq War has made us a magnet for terrorists. We cannot withdraw our troops until we have a strategy in place to repel invaders who will surely follow.

"'Energy' means self-sufficiency from renewable sources. This will calm the world's fears, create a new industry for America, remove our dependence on Arab oil, and eliminate one very large reason for future wars. Eliminating the world's dependence on unstable Middle East countries will effectively quarantine them. They will either become good global citizens or remain in ever-declining isolation to the point of insignificance.

"And lastly, 'Education' reforms are required to innovate our way to this new energy future, and beyond.

"We have an opportunity—actually a responsibility—to return this country to greatness, saving trillions on a war that can't be won militarily, saving trillions on the dollars we currently send to Arab countries for their oil, and *generating* trillions of dollars for the clean energy technology that will be exported to every country in the world.

"If we consider terrorism an ideological conflict, the elimination of our need for imported oil will allow us to change the rules by which we play the game into one based on intellect, a game in which we have no equal. In addition to eliminating current threats, it will eliminate future threats posed by unstable Middle Eastern countries wishing to develop nuclear capabilities. Severing our dependence on their oil will allow us to deal with such situations… appropriately."

A moment of silent contemplation followed. The three guests looked at each other around the table, each understanding the gravity of what the president meant by "appropriately."

"Sounds like a winner," Jason said, with nods all around. "This country has been plagued by politicians for a long time. It's time we had a statesman with a real strategy."

"My platform needs to be a winner or I won't be president," Jennings said after some reflection.

"Sir?" questioned Reynolds, obviously caught off guard.

"I intend to run a very different campaign. The details of the 'SEE' policy that I'm going to put forth—and I will email you folks with a draft for your feedback—will be controversial. Some points within this policy will require new laws and others may even require constitutional amendments. I'll be presenting my platform to the American people shortly. With six months remaining I'll give Congress until one week before the election to get the necessary legislation lined up. This will be a referendum on the tools we need to move our country forward. If the legislation is not in place by the election I will withdraw my name."

"Now *that*," said Jason "will be a different kind of campaign. Your platform will be an ultimatum."

"Let's just say it will be a condition of my running for office. Perhaps I should call it my 'manifesto.'"

After a few minutes of contemplation, Director Reynolds broke the silence, "I think you'll have at least four votes."

"William, that's a start," Jennings smiled. "Professor, I'd like to enlist your help with the details of my Electric Economy plan when we return. Would that be possible?"

"Of course, sir," Jason replied.

"I know your current plans don't include teaching, but do you *ever* see yourself returning to academia?" Jennings asked.

"Sir, when clean energy technology plays itself out as a business, I'll be back to the University researching whatever's next, assuming I'm still alive."

"Speaking of being alive, Professor," Reynolds chimed in, "we need to keep you that way. I'm still concerned about the security of you and your team. An agreement with China doesn't eliminate all the dangers. As you've said, it will take a while to get a solution in place, and there will be some very unhappy people in the mean time."

Sandra interjected, "Director, you raise a good point. These past few days have given me the opportunity to think about my career. I believe it's time for me to move into the private sector. Jason's new company is going to need legal and security support that I can provide. We've been talking about this on the plane ride. And God knows he can't shoot straight!"

Only the two of them understood the inside joke. They laughed about it as they returned to their seats.

Settling in for the remaining trip, Sandra asked, "Jason, this has been quite a trip. If you could talk to anyone right now, who would it be?"

"Easy—Bob Daniels. I hope he knows how important his work was," the sadness coming back. "I actually talk to him all the time; he just doesn't answer."

"I'm sure you miss him," Sandra said, caught off guard by the response, and Jason's reaction. "But I mean someone who's still here."

"Well, in that case it would have to be you."

"I'm flattered. But you can talk to me anytime—and I hope you will. I was thinking about someone you've never talked to before but would like to meet."

"At one point I would have said the president of the United States, but now I can take him off the list. I guess I'm drawing a blank."

"What about Carol Hendrick?"

Jason's eyes glassed over and a visible chill went down his back.

"Are you alright?" she asked.

"How do you know that name?"

"Bob told me."

"That sonofabitch! That was a name we held sacred. Carol was our inspiration. She's still one of mine. When did he tell you?" Jason smiled, shaking his head.

"I cornered him at the end of that board meeting I attended. I heard him mention 'Carol' to you and was curious. It sounded like an inside story, and those things can be important."

"That sonofabitch," Jason repeated. "You know, he had a thing for you."

"How do you think I got her name?" she smiled. "I did some research and talked with her yesterday. She lives with her parents in Ocala and has gone back to school. I told her what she meant to you and Bob. She'd like to meet you."

"You mean she's okay and lives just an hour away. Jesus Christ, that's amazing! *She's* amazing. I need to see her. Take the ride with me?"

"Sure, I'd like to meet her too."

They spoke little after that, falling fast asleep. And they slept all the way to Tampa International when the jolt of wheels on concrete awakened them with a start.

"Morning, sunshine," Sandra said.

"Good morning," Jason said, clearing his head and checking his watch. "The limo should be waiting for us. It's just 3:00 AM here; let's get you settled at the hotel."

"Good idea—I hope I can get a room at this hour."

The black Suburban swung by the Air Force One stairway as they were stepping off. The driver picked their luggage up off the tarmac placing it in back as they stepped into the rear passenger compartment.

"Driver," Sandra said, "can you drop me at the Waterside Hotel first?"

Before the driver had a chance to acknowledge, Jason said, "Actually, driver, just take us to my apartment. We're not sure she can get a room at this hour, and we can't have this young lady sleeping on the street. Is that alright?" he asked her.

"I certainly don't want to spend the night as a bag lady."

The limo dropped them off in Jason's driveway. He fumbled with his keys to open the front door, "Are you sure this is alright? I really was concerned about you getting stuck at that hotel. I could still take you."

"It's fine, Jason. I appreciate having a place to stay tonight."

He showed Sandra to the one guest bedroom that doubled as his office. It had a single-size bed with access to the bathroom shared with the master bedroom.

"If it's alright with you," Jason said, "I'd like to jump in the shower while you get settled. I'm pretty quick, and that way you can take as much time as you like—or at least until the hot water runs out."

"Sure," she said, "I'll get unpacked. If you're like most guys, you'll be done by then. Good night, Jason."

"Good night, see you in the morning. Then we can figure out what day it is." They both laughed as they disappeared into their separate rooms.

While carefully unpacking her things in the sparsely furnished guest room, Sandra couldn't help contemplate what the future might hold for her personal and professional life that had been turned upside down.

By contrast, the man on the other side of the wall threw his bags in the corner of his bedroom. Jason would unpack the next day. It felt good to be home. The shower was nowhere near as nice as the one at the Kempinski, but he knew exactly where to set the mixing valve to get the right temperature. For several minutes he stood under the steaming torrent, forehead against the cold tile, feeling the stresses of the last few days—the last few weeks—run down the drain. Thoughts of Jill, thoughts of Sandra. Thoughts of loss confused with thoughts of hope.

Epilogue

A week after returning from Beijing, Director Reynolds, Jason, and Sandra each received the following email:

To: Director Reynolds, Agent Bilson, Professor Davidson
From: President Walter Jennings
Subject: My 'Manifesto'

Folks: Thank you for joining me on our trip to Beijing and your contributions. As I mentioned on the way home, I have given serious thought to my "SEE" policy that you helped inspire. Before I go public I'm requesting feedback from a number of people including yourselves. I welcome your comments.

President Jennings

The SEE Policy:

1. SECURITY

1.1.   Iraq: Withdraw our troops as we begin to eliminate our dependence on Middle East oil. Iraqis are going to kill each other whether we are there or not. The war on terror is an ideological war and can be won intellectually without firing a shot. Let an Iraqi leader emerge. The leader we put in place has a distinct advantage. If he can leverage that into control, then control is his. Otherwise someone else will fill the void.

1.2.   Border Security: Erect a physical AND technological wall. Technology to include Ground Penetrating Radar and GPS. Unlike the Berlin Wall that was meant to keep good people in, our wall will be meant to keep bad people out.

1.3.   Profiling: Establish a profile of terrorists who would be dangerous to our country. Deport profiled individuals and bar any from entry or re-entry.

1.4.   New World Order: Based on civilized behavior. Invite—even help—the uncivilized to participate when they can demonstrate civilized behavior.

1.5.   Planet Security: Prioritize our space program to focus on protecting us from comet and asteroid collisions that could eliminate the human race. Exploration of other planets can follow.

2. ENERGY – The Electric Economy

2.1. Electric Vehicles: First, lithium battery propelled, and then fuel cell—let battery technologies compete. Enlist the help of GM, Ford, and Toyota to build electric cars with technology licenses from Tesla Motors and other pioneers. Establish a national Zero Emission Vehicle mandate requiring 20 percent of all new cars and light trucks to be battery powered the first year with 100% of these vehicles to be battery powered by the fifth year. All such vehicles need to be able to travel at least forty miles before using fossil fuels. Example: Chevy Volt.

2.2. Nationalize the Electric Power Grid: The power grid is already critically important and would benefit from national 'balancing.' Using the grid to distribute energy for transportation will put all of our energy distribution "eggs" in that basket. Need to nationalize for standardization and security. Just as we have the National Highway System—and for many of the same reasons—we need a National Electrical System.

2.3. Deploy Electric Vehicle Rapid Charging stations along major Interstate routes. Initially government owned-operated, then auctioned to private companies when critical mass has been achieved.

2.4. Deploy solar energy collection system within our southwest "solar furnace" to feed the grid and generate 100 percent of our peak demand electricity. Keep and upgrade existing nuclear facilities for generation of off-peak power. Phase out or upgrade fossil fuel-fired generation plants.

2.5.   Partner with China to manufacture and export our energy technology.

3. EDUCATION

3.1.   Eliminate the teachers unions (NEA, AFT) for grades K-12. Our educational system needs to be a meritocracy. Employment and promotion as an educator should be based on ability like most other endeavors in a capitalistic society.

3.2.   Fund the Innovation Revolution. Refocus students on science and technology curriculums. Reward and keep good educators with appropriate salaries, competitive with corporate pay.